"I am embroiled in a [barcode] **at the**

"If I share with you what I know," Matilda went on, "you will find yourself embroiled along with me."

She'd expressed a wish to study their chess game, but now she was taking pieces off the board, lining them up in order of rank. Her white pawns, Duncan's black pawns. Her bishop, knight, rook, and queen, her king.

"Matilda," Duncan said, getting to his feet, "please calm yourself. You have made a minor slip by letting Stephen see your prayer book. He will carry your identity to his grave if need be, as will I. I'd rather not. I'd rather see you free of the burdens you carry, else I shall never have an opportunity to properly court you."

She went still, Duncan's king in her hand. "Did I hear you aright, Mr. Wentworth?"

"My name is Duncan. Your hearing is excellent."

She set the king down slowly, next to the white queen. "You seek to court me?"

"I most assuredly do."

Based on the lady's expression, this disclosure astonished her almost as much as it surprised Duncan.

HIGH ACCLAIM
FOR GRACE BURROWES

"Sexy heroes, strong heroines, intelligent plots, enchanting love stories.... Grace Burrowes's romances have them all."
–Mary Balogh, *New York Times* **bestselling author**

"Grace Burrowes writes from the heart—with warmth, humor, and a generous dash of sensuality, her stories are unputdownable! If you're not reading Grace Burrowes you're missing the very best in today's Regency Romance!"
–Elizabeth Hoyt, *New York Times* **bestselling author**

MY ONE AND ONLY DUKE

"Skillfully crafted and exquisitely written, Burrowes's latest is pure gold; a brilliant launch to a promising series."
—*Library Journal,* **starred review**

"A delicious read. Best of the Month pick."
—Apple Books

A ROGUE OF HER OWN

"With flawless prose, delicious wit, and an unerring ability to bring complex characters to life, Burrowes revisits the engaging Windhams and delivers another winner; pure reading gold."
–*Library Journal***, starred review**

NO OTHER DUKE WILL DO

"Those who prefer their historical romances to sound and feel historical will savor *No Other Duke Will Do*."
–NPR

TOO SCOT TO HANDLE

"A well-plotted, beautifully written story made all the more satisfying by its delightful secondary characters."
–*Library Journal*, starred review

"Delightful plotlines, heartfelt emotions, humor and realistic, honest characters, have turned her Windham series spinoffs into a fan favorite...a gem of a read."
–*RT Book Reviews*, Top Pick

THE TROUBLE WITH DUKES

"The hero of *The Trouble with Dukes* reminds me of Mary Balogh's charming men, and the heroine brings to mind Sarah MacLean's intelligent, fiery women...This is a wonderfully funny, moving romance, not to be missed!"
–Eloisa James, *New York Times* bestselling author

"*The Trouble with Dukes* has everything Grace Burrowes's many fans have come to adore: a swoonworthy hero, a strong heroine, humor, and passion. Her characters not only know their own hearts, but share them with fearless joy. Grace Burrowes is a romance treasure."
–Tessa Dare, *New York Times* bestselling author

WHEN A
DUCHESS
SAYS
I DO

GRACE BURROWES

FOREVER

NEW YORK   BOSTON

Copyright © 2019 by Grace Burrowes

Excerpt from *Forever and a Duke* copyright © 2019 by Grace Burrowes

Cover illustration and design by Elizabeth Turner Stokes. Cover copyright © 2019 by Hachette Book Group, Inc.

Forever

Hachette Book Group

1290 Avenue of the Americas, New York, NY 10104

read-forever.com

twitter.com/readforeverpub

First Edition: April 2019

Forever is an imprint of Grand Central Publishing. The Forever name and logo are trademarks of Hachette Book Group, Inc.

The publisher is not responsible for websites (or their content) that are not owned by the publisher.

The Hachette Speakers Bureau provides a wide range of authors for speaking events. To find out more, go to www.hachettespeakersbureau.com or call (866) 376-6591.

ISBNs: 978-1-5387-2898-7 (mass market), 978-1-5387-2897-0 (ebook)

Printed in the United States of America

OPM

10 9 8 7 6 5 4 3 2 1

To those who speak up

Acknowledgments

I knew as I started the Rogues to Riches series that Quinn Wentworth would be my first hero, but I was surprised when quiet, scholarly Duncan Wentworth stepped forward for second book honors. Hidden depths, my friends...fascinating, well-hidden depths. Duncan turned out to be every bit as fierce as Quinn, and in his way, even more determined to overcome early hardships.

I thank my editor, Leah Hultenschmidt, for inspiring me to take on the challenge of writing the Wentworth stories, and the whole lovely team at Grand Central Forever for getting this book into your hands. Mostly, though, I thank you, my readers, who make it possible for me to do what I love and have tons of fun doing it. Now, onward to Duncan and Matilda's happily ever after!

WHEN A
DUCHESS
SAYS
I DO

Chapter One

The rabbit's heaving sides testified to a battle lost, a soul surrendering to death.

Duncan Wentworth remained amid the trees, studying the creature where it lay at the edge of the clearing, a strip of thin leather noosed around a furry back foot. The little beast had been caught on a game run between Brightwell's home wood and the river, where sunny banks were still green with the last of the fall grass.

The rabbit twitched at a disturbance from the direction of the village, though the snare made flight impossible. Even struggling against captivity might result in a permanent injury, so delicate were the creature's bones.

A stout, bareheaded fellow in rough garb emerged into the clearing.

"Now aren't you a fine, fat coney," the man muttered. "Just the right size to fill up a goodwife's stewpot."

A poacher, the bane of every English landowner, and not a poacher on the verge of starvation.

"I told Jeffrey the bunnies love their clover, didn't I?" he went on. "Too bad for you, little varmint." He knelt by the rabbit, a serious length of knife gleaming in his hand. "Say your prayers, stupid beast, for you've had your last meal. Off to market with you, or my name's not Herman Treacher."

Duncan stepped into the clearing. "A moment, if you please, Mr. Treacher."

Treacher heaved to his feet, the knife held before his ample gut. "You're on private property, sir, and sneaking up on an armed man is never smart."

He was faster than he looked, and he clearly knew to watch Duncan's hands. A career thug, then, rather than a countryman supplementing his means through crime.

Duncan took up a lean against the nearest sapling, an oak struggling to find sunlight amid the mature specimens. The rabbit had been too desperate for nourishment to sense a trap. Tomorrow, a hound or a fox might put an end to such an unwary creature.

Nevertheless, these were Duncan's woods. He'd sought their tranquility as an antidote to months of posturing among London's good society. That Treacher would foil Duncan's plan was the last straw on the back of a camel noted for surliness on a good day.

"As it happens," Duncan said, "we're both on private property, though only one of us is trespassing."

Treacher tossed the knife from hand to hand, a rudimentary distraction Duncan knew better than to watch.

"I'm the one holding the weapon, guv. I'd say that makes you the uninvited guest at the party. Run along, and I'll be about my business."

Not bloody likely. Poaching in a forest was a capital

offense. If Treacher had any sense, he'd dispatch the witness before finishing off the rabbit.

Alas for Treacher, that scheme did not fit with Duncan's plans.

The rabbit growled, a sound Duncan hadn't heard since his youth. Treacher was startled into focusing on his prey for the single instant necessary for Duncan to kick the knife free and tackle the blighter.

Duncan lacked his opponent's brawn, but he'd spent years brawling as only a minister's wayward charge could brawl. He had Treacher facedown in the clearing, a beefy arm hiked halfway up his back, when a sharp point prodded Duncan between his shoulder blades.

"Let him up, your worship, and I might allow you to live. Insist on more foolishness, and yon coney won't be the only one going to his reward today."

Well, of course. The senior officer had arrived, and Duncan's failure to anticipate that development meant he deserved the bother of defending his rabbit against two criminals.

He'd been too ready to use his fists, too ready to take out his frustrations on any willing fool. Without easing the pressure on Treacher's arm, Duncan glanced over his shoulder. Assailant number two was smaller and in possession of an equally shiny, sharp knife. The larger knife lay two feet to Duncan's left—convenient, because he was left-handed—and could easily be collected as Duncan got to his feet.

The rabbit remained caught, a careless animal, but possessed of enough self-respect to growl at a bad fate. So too, would Duncan give these imbeciles a better fight than they were expecting.

"Get him off me, Jeffy. Bastard's about to break me arm."

Not break, dislocate. The challenge was to achieve that

aim, grab the knife, rise, turn, and deal with Jeffrey all without stepping on the rabbit. First, Duncan would affect the posture of a man defeated and in fear for his life. Second, he'd—

"Drop the knife." This voice was feminine, annoyed, and a surprise.

"Says who?" Jeffrey asked.

"A woman holding a gun," Duncan replied. "And from the look in her eyes, I'd say she knows what to do with it. Madam, good day. Duncan Wentworth at your service, though I apologize for the lack of a proper introduction. A pleasure to make your acquaintance."

She had dark eyes, probably brown when viewed from bowing-over-her-hand distance. Her hair was the rich hue of mink in summer, her figure on the gaunt side of trim, and she was of barely medium height. She put Duncan in mind of the rabbit—small, spare, ready to bolt.

The lady was not pretty—her looks were too dramatic for that. Defined brows, a determined chin, cheekbones made a tad too prominent by her thinness. She was attractive, though. Holding that gun with an air of impatient disgust, she was undeniably attractive.

"Dammit, Herm," Jeffrey said, stepping from behind Duncan. "You've gone and snagged the bleedin' property owner. You said he was a London gent what never wastes his time in the shires."

"Drop the knife," the woman said, her tone that of a governess on her last nerve. "Now."

"I'd do as the lady says." Duncan rose and collected the weapon Treacher had lost in the undergrowth. "Then you'd be well advised to run like the demons of hell are in pursuit." He tested the blade against the pad of his thumb. "Just a suggestion."

Jeffrey dropped the knife, even showing enough sense to cast it a few feet away, rather than attempt any dramatics.

Treacher struggled to his feet, cradling his right arm. "Let's leg it, Jeffy. This was all your idea—nobody else would think to poach in a haunted woods, you said. Now me arm's half busted, and we haven't got no rabbit, and the swell is making threats."

The lady sidled around the clearing, putting herself between the rabbit and the men. The barrel of her gun—a nasty coaching pistol that could easily have brought down a horse—remained marvelously steady in her grip.

"*Au revoir,* gentlemen," Duncan said, stepping to the lady's side. He was ready to let this pair go for now, but he was not ready to see the woman dart back into the woods along with the rabbit and the poachers.

Treacher cast one longing glance at the snared rabbit and lumbered off into the trees, Jeffrey following silently.

The woman dropped to her knees beside the rabbit. "We have to let it go. I need the knife, provided it's sharp." She sounded frantic to free the rabbit, though her hand smoothing its fur was gentle. "Do something, please."

"Have a care," Duncan replied. "If you inspire the beast to struggling, it can break its own leg, or, worse, mangle that back foot. What's needed is calm."

A set of pliers would have come in handy, but the home farm was a good half mile off, and carrying the rabbit, snare and all, such a distance would never serve.

Duncan considered the situation and the woman. She was not a girl, fresh from the schoolroom. He'd spent years in schoolrooms, as both pupil and teacher, and she hadn't the look of one whose life had been indentured to book learning. Her cloak was velvet and well made, though the hem was dusty and one button was missing near her waist.

She wore no gloves and her hands were clean, though what manner of lady carried a loaded gun when strolling through a peaceful wood?

"The snare is secured by a stake driven into the ground," Duncan said. "I'll attempt to lift the stake free so we have some purchase to unknot the leather from the rabbit's foot. All must be done slowly and without agitation to the captive."

"You've done this before."

"Many times." Though not recently, more's the pity. When he'd freed the snare from its stake, Duncan produced his own knife—much smaller than the poachers' weapons—and used the tip to work at the knotted leather.

The rabbit bore this all with stoic calm, or perhaps the lady's soft caresses soothed its little heart. Her scent distracted Duncan—meadow grass with a hint of pine smoke, not a fragrance he'd find in a Mayfair ballroom, but pleasant.

Sturdy and fresh rather than feminine.

"That's it," he said, when the knife point had loosened the noose about the rabbit's foot. "Another moment, and—"

The ruddy little wretch used powerful hind legs to shove itself away from the noose before Duncan could get his knife out of rabbit range. The point of the blade scored the flesh of his wrist, ripping through the cuff of his shirt and creating a bloody mess.

The rabbit darted across the clearing, paused long enough to whump a foot against the earth, then disappeared into the bracken.

"Warning his mates," Duncan said, tugging one-handed at his cravat. "Some thanks for a heroic rescue."

"Let me." The woman batted his hand aside. She withdrew the pin from Duncan's linen and soon had his neckcloth off. "Was your knife clean?"

"Yes. Though if your concern is infection, I should probably pour the contents of my flask over the wound before you bind it."

His flask was in the inner right-hand pocket of his coat, which meant her assistance was necessary to produce it, lest Duncan get blood all over his London tailoring. He didn't give a damn for fashion, but wasting money was, in his estimation, among the deadliest sins. Wasting time surpassed even that offense.

The lady knew what she was about with an injury, and applied a quantity of brandy to the wound. Duncan's vision dimmed and his ears roared, though the sensation of her hand on his shoulder, and her quiet "Steady on," penetrated the fire raging along the wound.

"Considering that you've arguably saved my life," Duncan said, as she wrapped his cravat about his wrist, "might you spare me your name?"

She used his cravat pin to secure the bandage tightly enough to suppress further bleeding without causing discomfort. His blood stained the white linen, though the stain wasn't spreading. A flesh wound, thank God. If Duncan had lost his life to an ungrateful rabbit, his cousins in Mayfair would have laughed at his graveside.

"You should thoroughly clean that wound," the lady said. "Strong spirits are helpful, but honey is more effective. Promise me you won't neglect it."

"The wound will be healed before I can neglect it." Wentworths were tough. They healed well and quickly, on the outside. "You're in my woods, alone, where all manner of ruffians apparently lurk. Might I escort you to your destination?"

She collected her pistol and the shorter knife, passing the longer one to Duncan. "That won't be necessary. Tell your gamekeepers what you came across this morning. Those were professional poachers, not a pair of farm lads trying to add a little meat to their mama's stores."

Just like that, she was prepared to leave him in the middle of the woods.

"My thanks, then, for your timely intervention, but I truly must have a name for so brave a rescuer."

"No, you must not. You are the owner of Brightwell?"

"I have that honor." Or that challenge. Cousin Quinn's sense of humor was complicated and given to irony.

Duncan's ownership of Brightwell looked to be a further annoyance to her, as if she'd found not one but two sets of poachers in her woods. She shoved her pistol into a pocket of her cloak, shook out her hems, and—incongruously, for a woman possessed of both a knife and a gun—bobbed a curtsy.

"I'll bid you good day. Please see a physician for that wound."

Duncan would do no such thing. The damned scratch had bled copiously, which always boded well for a swift recovery, and physicians cost money.

"Before you abandon a wounded man alone in the wilds of Berkshire," Duncan said, "won't you tell me if I've found the ghost in my gatehouse?"

* * *

A lady's education was a sore hindrance when she needed to curse. Duncan Wentworth was the soul of courtesy, though, so even if Matilda had known some vile oaths, she might not have used them in his presence.

Might not. Life had become unpredictable, and Matilda's reactions and choices unpredictable as well.

"Both your gatehouse and your woods are haunted?" The compulsion to flee had her heart beating like the snared rabbit's, but she'd seen the speed with which Mr. Wentworth could move. One moment, he'd been a gentleman at his leisure, lounging against a tree. The next instant, Treacher's knife had flown through the air, and Treacher had been facedown in the bracken.

"I cannot speak for the spirits inhabiting my home wood." Mr. Wentworth picked up his battered felt hat and slapped it against his thigh. "If I were a clever poacher, I'd put about word that Brightwell's forest was haunted, and then add credence to the rumor by carrying a lit torch down the game trails on a moonless night. Some truant boy tippling his papa's brandy would recite a tale of ghosts to his friends in the schoolyard, and lo, my woods are haunted."

He'd more or less divined Matilda's scheme. "And your gatehouse, Mr. Wentworth?"

He ripped the leather noose from the stake, stuffed the cord in his pocket, and threw the stake in the direction of the river. A wet plop followed, though the river was a good twenty yards on.

"My gatehouse is uninhabited, like the rest of my out-buildings. I came up the drive last night after moonrise, and what should I see but smoke drifting from the chimney. No lamps lit, the windows shuttered, but clearly, somebody in residence."

He noticed smoke by moonlight. *I really must learn to curse.* "Perhaps Jeffrey and Mr. Treacher availed themselves of your hospitality."

Mr. Wentworth put Matilda in mind of the leather that had snared the rabbit. Lean, supple, and strong, though his strength would be hard to discern beneath fine tailoring and society manners. He noticed his surroundings, and thus Matilda nearly hated him.

"Perhaps *you* will avail yourself of my hospitality," he said. "I am new to the area and would acquaint myself with a neighbor whose timely appearance spared me a good deal of bother."

I am not your neighbor. "It was of no moment, Mr. Wentworth." *I frequently take the air in woods I don't own and wave a pistol at ruffians.* "I really must be going. Good day."

She gathered her skirts and would have moved off toward the river, but Mr. Wentworth's hand on her arm stayed her.

"I must insist, madam. Midday has arrived, and I neglected to break my fast. My cook will be wroth with me if I similarly disregard my luncheon. You did me a great service, and the least I can do is offer you some sustenance."

His invitation balanced a vague plea with a vaguer threat. Matilda did not believe the plea for one moment, no matter the sincerity in his blue eyes.

She didn't dare ignore the threat, however, not when he could have her arrested for breaking and entering. With that air of gravitas, he'd easily convince the magistrate that Matilda had been intent on poaching.

Then too, his threat came with an offer of free food.

By tonight, she'd be ten miles away, though she had hoped to winter at Brightwell. The property had belonged to an aging duke who'd died without sons. She and Papa had visited the duke years ago, making Brightwell a regular stop on their summer travels. His Grace would part with a painting in exchange for a manuscript or figurine, and Papa would come away richer for having imposed on ducal hospitality for a fortnight.

In the past week, Brightwell's gatehouse had been

a sanctuary, though, of course, Matilda was trespassing. Another activity for which a lady's education hadn't prepared her.

While Matilda sorted through options and mentally bemoaned a lack of criminal skills, Mr. Wentworth pretended to admire the autumn foliage. He was tall, brown-haired, and looked of a piece with the trees shedding the last remnants of their summer finery. Matilda put him at "indisputably mature." Well north of thirty, still south of forty. He would age well and slowly, and most women would consider him handsome.

Matilda considered him a serious problem.

"The house is in that direction," he said, gesturing away from the river. "The day is cold enough to justify a toddy, though I'm also in the mood for beef and barley soup. My tastes are not refined, which doubtless drives Cook to despair."

Oh, ye winged seraphs. A hot, spicy, restorative dose of spirits, a steaming bowl of beef stew...Matilda's feet started moving without her giving them permission to do so. She hadn't had fresh bread in weeks, hadn't had butter since losing her post at the inn.

"I cannot stay long, Mr. Wentworth."

"All the ladies say that, which is a polite way to remind me that I'm poor company. I set a humble table, my conversation is dull, and my favorite society is that of long-dead philosophers. You may limit yourself to two bites of ham and a single spoonful of compote, then be on your way, if you're still awake. Ladies have been known to catch up on their slumber when assigned to be my dinner companion."

He was making a jest of himself, though Matilda found no humor in his remarks. Desperation did this—stole humor, rest, pleasure, all the blessings in life. Then came autumn, when pilfering by moonlight from neglected gardens was no longer possible and orchards were stripped of their fruit. Every ounce of Matilda's energy was often spent piling up deadfall to burn at night.

Her plan—take a job in service, save money, and eventually take passage from England—had turned out to be no plan at all.

"I have bored you already," Mr. Wentworth said. "I'd discuss the weather, but that strikes me as belaboring the obvious when in the out-of-doors."

"Tell me what brings you here from London."

"How can you tell I've come from London?"

Oh…piffle. "You arrived last night from somewhere. Your attire—but for your hat—is exquisite. One assumes your clothing came from London even if you did not."

She had all but admitted that she recognized Bond Street tailoring—woefully foolish of her.

"I originally hail from Yorkshire," he said. "Several years ago I moved to London to be with family, and until last month I considered London my home."

They emerged from the trees into the park that stretched from Brightwell's back terraces. The formal gardens were a wreck, separated by overgrown hedges and punctuated with toppled statuary and cracked urns. For several mornings past, Matilda had found peace behind these hedges.

"A metaphor of some sort," Mr. Wentworth said, surveying his gardens.

Despite the sunshine, the scene was melancholy. Dead leaves carpeted overgrown beds, lichens encroached on the walls, and the scent of wood smoke hung in the air. Winter approached with the relentlessness of a funeral cortege.

"Some would say these gardens are romantic," Matilda replied. A lady's attempt at conversation.

"Some would be idiots. The cost alone...but one doesn't discuss finances. I promised you a meal. This way."

He set a brisk pace down the gravel walk, no pretense of matching his steps to Matilda's or offering an unneeded arm for her to lean on. She had no grasp of foul language. Mr. Wentworth, she concluded, had little gift for social dissembling.

A fine quality in a man. She'd learned too late to appreciate it.

He led her to a door that opened onto a wide stairway landing. A flight of steps descended into what Matilda knew to be the kitchens, cellars, and pantries; another flight led up to the floor that housed many of the public rooms—parlors, library, music room, gallery.

Between the sun beaming through the tall windows, and the heat wafting up from the kitchens, the space was blessedly, wonderfully warm.

"May I take your cloak?" Mr. Wentworth asked.

Matilda did not want to part with her cloak. Her dress was decent enough—she'd traded away her Paris finery within a week of leaving home—but with every item of clothing she removed, she became easier to describe. A purple velvet cloak was simple to identify. Pair that with a gray wool dress, plain cuffs, half boots with frayed and knotted laces, and she became a specific woman, with specific people looking for her.

Mr. Wentworth's steady gaze suggested he knew all of that, and lying would be pointless. Matilda unfastened the frogs of her cloak.

"One does wonder how Brightwell came to be yours," she said. "The house has good bones, and the locals recall it as a lovely property."

"The locals who claim more than their threescore and ten

years, perhaps. The estate was imposed on me. The dining room is this way."

An evasive answer, which cheered Matilda. A man with secrets was less of a threat to a woman with secrets. She followed Mr. Wentworth down a corridor free of dust and cobwebs, and equally devoid of art, furniture, or flowers.

"The previous caretaker all but looted the place," Mr. Wentworth said, ushering her into a small parlor. "The excuse of record is that assets were liquidated to pay expenses, but what expenses does an empty house incur? Fortunately, the thieves hadn't grown bold enough to help themselves to larger items of furniture, and they were too ignorant to steal the best of the art."

What would Mr. Wentworth think of a woman who'd helped herself to apples, eggs, beans, and other overlooked produce?

That question was rendered irrelevant by the scent of fresh bread, beef stew, and cloved ham. Hunger had made Matilda's senses sharper and turned Mr. Wentworth's "humble table" into a feast.

"Ladies first," he said, pouring water from an ewer by the hearth into a porcelain basin on a side table. Linen cloths had been arranged in a quarter-fan beside the basin, and for the first time in weeks, Matilda prepared to wash her hands in warm water.

"I ought by rights to send you to a guest room for this ritual," Mr. Wentworth said, "but my staff wasn't expecting company."

While Matilda washed her hands and surreptitiously patted a warm, damp cloth against her cheeks and brow— bliss without limit—Mr. Wentworth went to the door and addressed somebody who remained in the corridor.

Matilda's host washed his hands, as a footman set a

second place, bowed, and withdrew. Mr. Wentworth had no sooner seated her than a maid bustled in carrying a quilted shawl lined with flannel.

He took the garment from the maid and draped it around Matilda's shoulders. Somebody had hung the shawl near a hearth, for the flannel was warm.

She hadn't eaten for three days. She hadn't rested well for weeks. She hadn't been truly comfortable in an eternity, and the sheer delight of a warmed shawl nearly had her in tears.

"Let's start with the soup, shall we?" Mr. Wentworth said, ladling Matilda a generous portion. He set the bowl before her, and for a moment, she wallowed in the sensation of steam wafting up to her chin. The scent was hearty, the taste...oh, the taste. Salty—salt was necessary for life— rich, aromatic, with a hint of some spice. Tarragon, perhaps, though pepper was well represented too.

Matilda consumed her food slowly because she'd learned what came of gorging after a fast. Mr. Wentworth ate prodigious portions, though his manners were fastidious. The meal should have been awkward—a lady did not dine in a gentleman's exclusive company, much less with a gentleman to whom she hadn't been introduced.

A lady also did not have to debate whether to shiver all night or waste another day's energy collecting wood. She never viewed winter as a mortal enemy, never stared at some farmwife's laundry while considering whether to commit larceny. Ladies were lucky creatures.

"Another roll?" Mr. Wentworth asked, holding up a basket.

"No, thank you."

When Mr. Wentworth went to the sideboard for a second helping of ham, Matilda secreted a pair of buttered rolls in her dress pocket. If she'd been told that each roll consumed meant spending a month in the underworld, she could not have given them up.

She managed to purloin a thick slice of ham to go with the rolls, but forced herself to stop at that. Of the pear compote, she took only three bites—sweets were dangerous on a deprived stomach—but she had two cups of hot China black tea, perhaps the most fortifying aspect of the whole meal.

She was contemplating a third cup when Mr. Wentworth rose and brought a plate of tea cakes to the table.

"I have a sweet tooth," he said, as if confessing a penchant for excessive wagering. "If you are similarly afflicted, take all you like now. The rest will not go to waste."

He moved around the end of the table, pausing by the door. Did his wrist pain him? He'd certainly eaten with dispatch, and had not relied on a footman to serve them. Many gentry maintained only a minimal staff, though Mr. Wentworth struck Matilda as something other than—more than?—gentry.

He'd not asked her any more personal questions, which was fortunate. All Matilda had to offer him was a widow-in-difficulties story that he'd recognize as a hastily concocted fiction. He resumed his seat at the head of the table and poured himself another cup of tea. "I trust you enjoyed the meal?"

"Very much. Your cook is to be commended." And if this was his idea of humble fare, then what menu would he put forth for a dinner party?

"And you are warm enough?"

What was he up to? "I am quite comfortable, and I thank you for your hospitality, Mr. Wentworth, though I must be on my way. The meal—despite the irregular circumstances—was much appreciated."

And please God, would he seek the company of his dead

philosophers rather than escort her from the property? Her belongings, meager though they were, were at the gatehouse, and she could not leave the area without retrieving them.

She tried for a gracious smile, though doubtless, desperation shone from her eyes.

Mr. Wentworth ran a finger around the rim of his wineglass. "The door to this dining parlor is locked, madam. No servant will intrude. You have the privacy of the confessional, more or less, and I suggest you use it to your advantage. My first footman has retrieved a haversack from the gatehouse containing a few effects such as a lady fallen on difficult times might possess. My best guess is that you intended to steal the poached rabbit from the snare, but I ruined your plans."

Oh.... *Perdition.* The key was in the lock—Mr. Wentworth hadn't locked her in so much as he'd locked his staff out. The impropriety of that gesture was equaled only by the perceptiveness that had inspired it.

Matilda could dash his wine into his eyes—a tavern maid had taught her that trick—and bolt, but her cloak was somewhere in the house, as were her belongings. Decamping without them would be mortal folly.

She could fall to weeping and spin a tale, though Mr. Wentworth did not strike her as susceptible to tears.

She could offer her rehearsed story and leaven it with a bit of truth. A pickpocket had explained to her that a little honesty made the mendacity more convincing. The child could not have been more than eight years old, but had had good health to show for his light fingers and lying.

"I thought I could kill the rabbit before the poachers returned," Matilda said. "I couldn't do it. I stood in the trees for a good quarter hour, arguing with myself. Then you showed up in the shadows at the edge of the clearing."

The small recitation left a lump in her throat, not because holding a gun on armed men had been upsetting—she'd very nearly gloried in those moments, and *that* was upsetting—but because the rabbit had gone free.

She'd been spared the terrible decision to kill the rabbit, and the little creature had gone free.

Mr. Wentworth poured her a third, hot, lovely cup of tea. "A tender heart can be an endless burden. Do go on."

Chapter Two

Duncan's wrist throbbed, and such was the inconvenience of his injury that even lifting a teapot worsened the pain. More fool he, for using a sharp blade in the vicinity of a desperate creature—two desperate creatures. The lady had eaten with the measured focus of the newly starving, and her hands had trembled through her first and second cups of tea.

"I might be able to shoot game roaming freely," she said, "but to see that poor beast ensnared . . . and that was my fault, you see."

"You set the snare?"

She dropped a small lump of sugar into her tea, the first he'd seen her sweeten her drink. "I disturbed the rabbit on my rambles and drove it into the snare."

Her afflictions included a conscience in addition to a tender heart, and yet, she'd stuffed a gun into the pocket of her cape and buttered rolls in the pockets of her dress. The part of Duncan that had delighted in the novelty and variety of the Continental capitals took notice of that.

She was interesting, an anomalous element in an otherwise dreary landscape of responsibility and drudgery. Damn Cousin Quinn for his dubious generosity anyway.

"Shall I ring for more tea?" Duncan asked.

"No, thank you. I must be going."

"Madam, you must be staying. My footman's mother's knees are aching, incontrovertible proof that our first snow of the year will soon arrive. The temperature dropped even during the two hours I spent inspecting my home wood."

Two hours devoted to avoiding the home farm, the gardens, the dairy, the laundry, the tenants, the vicar, *the vicar's nosy wife* ...

"Then the sooner I'm on my way, the better." She cradled the teacup in her hands, as if she'd take the warmth rather than the sustenance with her.

"That I cannot allow. You are a guest in my home and, I suspect, a damsel in distress. Permit me to impersonate a knight errant and set right what I can."

Every sensible knight knew that damsels in distress merited aid so that they might take their problems, drama, and difficulties elsewhere. Duncan did not want this woman to leave, though, which was very bad of him.

She was an antidote to boredom, a distraction from the weight of resentment. When Quinn's next letter arrived asking for a progress report, Duncan could reply that his home wood had become a hotbed of violence and intrigue, with armed felons and intrepid maidens lurking behind every tree.

Though of course, that would bring dear Quinn charging up the drive, for the Wentworth family would not allow Duncan to hoard drama for his own entertainment.

Then too, the lady might not be a maiden, though that didn't signify.

"I am loath to impose," she said, hunching over her teacup. "You have been most generous already."

She did not set aside her last cup of tea, rise, and curtsy, and Duncan knew why. That locked door, the blazing fire in the hearth, the evidence of a hearty midday meal, made this cozy dining parlor a haven from the cruelty of a harsh world. She longed for sanctuary, which yearning he would exploit shamelessly to ensure she didn't take a precipitous leave of him.

"I have merely provided a meal from stores that are more than ample. You, on the other hand, provided timely intervention at a delicate moment. I am in your debt, and Wentworths always repay their obligations."

Duncan had been about five seconds away from disabling the first poacher and disarming his mate, but a moral creature would need a morally sound reason to accept aid.

"I would have done the same for anybody," she said. "It's nothing."

Duncan had been careful not to touch his guest, other than to drape the quilted shawl about her shoulders. He hadn't offered his arm as they'd paraded through his ruin of a garden, hadn't bowed over the lady's hand, hadn't helped her to remove her cloak.

Now, he patted her wrist, which was alarmingly boney. "My life, while insignificant in the greater scheme, is not *nothing*. I could at this very moment be lying in that clearing, a knife in my ribs, blood pooling beneath me. My fate might have been a painful expiration from loss of blood, or the more protracted agony of succumbing to the elements. My assailants would never have been held accountable, and then I'd have had no choice but to truly haunt that forest."

Her hands cradling the teacup were too thin, the veins a blue tracery beneath pale skin. Her smile, though, was a study in warmth. Her whole face became illuminated, her gaze softened, her mouth curved to reveal straight white teeth. Her smile conveyed shared delight and a tantalizing hint of mischief.

"You have a dramatic imagination, Mr. Wentworth."

Stephen Wentworth, Duncan's sole pupil for many years, claimed Duncan had no imagination whatsoever.

Stephen was apparently wrong for once. "I will use that imagination to conjure lurid tales of the horrors facing a woman alone in this benighted shire. Foul weather and vexatious felons are the least among them. Am I to stop at the posting inn on the London road next month to learn that a strange lady was found frozen in some cow byre, the very woman who today saved my life?"

Duncan was not afflicted with a tender heart—not anymore—but he had a thriving horror of waste. That he should rattle around in a house with fourteen bedrooms while this woman sought warmth among the livestock was an affront to common sense.

And be damned to propriety. He was a preacher's nephew—that couldn't be helped—but also a Wentworth.

She set aside her tea, which had to be tepid by now. "Sheep byres are warmer. The ceilings are lower, the beasts less skittish, and they leave tufts of wool..."

She fell silent. In the north those tufts of wool were called hentilagets. Poor children gathered them up from the hedges and brambles, to be spun into yarn and knitted into stockings. Duncan could well recall the coarse, greasy feel of the wool, the tenacity of the thorns, and the delight he'd taken in the coin earned.

Though Uncle had decreed that the money had to go

into the poor box, and Duncan had lost his enthusiasm for gathering wool from ovine sources.

"Let me help you," he said. "Better still, why don't you help me?"

Ah, that piqued her attention. She regarded him with the wary uncertainty of a woman whose opinion of men had acquired some tarnish, or possibly a thorough coating of rust.

"In what capacity could you need aid?"

"I am a scholar of modest intellect, and in recent years, I've traveled much on the Continent. I'd like to transcribe my notes for eventual publication." Though, thanks to dear Cousin Quinn—may he choke on his strawberry leaf coronet—Duncan had no time to work on his transcriptions.

"You need an amanuensis? A secretary?"

"Badly. My penmanship is abominable. If you have a lady's hand, then you are the perfect resource to aid me." An imaginative fabrication, once again proving that Cousin Stephen was an idiot.

She set a tea cake draped with lemon icing on her plate. "What would my wages be?"

Duncan named a modest figure, not low enough to be insulting, not high enough to raise her guard any higher than she'd already raised it.

"Plus room and board, of course," he said. "We will share our mealtimes, that we might discuss the work without intruding on the rest of the day."

She took a bite of her lemon cake, closing her eyes as if the nectar of the gods graced her palate. Duncan helped himself to a raspberry cake when he realized he was watching to see if she'd smile at him again.

"I will take supper with you," she said. "Breakfast will be a tray in my room, lunch will likely be a tray in your library. You do have a library?"

"Largely devoid of books, but yes." Books were fungible, like small tables, lamps, carpets, and silver. "Do you speak French?"

"I do. I haven't used it in some time."

How careful she was. "Other languages?"

"Enough Italian to stumble through a libretto, thanks to a solid foundation in Latin. Functional German. Good conversational Russian, though my command of the written language is wanting."

He had the sense she'd not disclosed the whole of her skills, but she'd said enough. She was either well traveled or well educated, possibly both.

A diplomat's daughter?

"You are ideally suited to assist me. I'll have my housekeeper, Mrs. Newbury, give you a tour of the premises, such as they are, and show you to a guest room. We can commence work tomorrow after breakfast."

Duncan braced himself for effusions of gratitude, though really, what did it matter to him if one more hearth was lit or one more mouth fed? Restoring Brightwell on the terms Quinn had set out was an impossible challenge, and a few coppers in either direction were of little moment. Doubtless Duncan's new amanuensis would soon decamp for parts unknown in any event.

The lady finished with her lemon cake and drank the last of her tea. "I can find my way to the kitchens, Mr. Wentworth. I'll doubtless locate the housekeeper somewhere in the same vicinity. Was there anything else you wanted to say?"

How extraordinary. *She*, who likely hadn't had a decent meal in weeks, was dismissing *him*.

"I have two questions, and you will answer them honestly or my offer of employment will be rescinded."

She put another lemon cake on her plate. "Ask."

"Are you married?"

"I am not." *Thank God.* The words hung in the air, a world of relief unspoken. She'd run from her own family, then, or from the king's justice.

"What is your name?" Duncan asked.

She rose, and the tea cake was no longer on her plate. In her pocket, then, and Duncan hadn't seen her purloin the sweet.

"You may call me...Miss Maddie."

"As in Madeline?"

"Miss Maddie will do."

Duncan got to his feet as well, because a gentleman did, and because he wanted to beat her to the door. "I can't write out a bank draft to Miss Maddie."

"Then pay me in cash." She twisted the key, slipped through the door, and was off down the corridor.

Duncan stood outside the parlor long enough to make sure Miss Maddie took the steps to the kitchens, then he returned to the table, collected the remaining tea cakes, and prepared to locate some of the notes he'd taken while touring the Continent.

They were on the premises somewhere—had he instructed the staff to put them in the estate office?—and he had until tomorrow morning to find them.

* * *

The staff was either well trained or desperately attached to their wages, because thirty minutes after stuffing herself at the lunch table, Matilda sank into the first hot bath she'd had in far too long. She even washed her hair, because God knew when such an opportunity might befall her again.

Mrs. Newbury, a statuesque woman of African descent, had declared that touring the premises could wait until Mr.

Wentworth's guest was properly settled. She'd left Matilda a brown velvet dress with an old-fashioned high waist. What the garment lacked in stylishness it made up for in sheer comfort and warmth.

A tap on the door interrupted Matilda's inspection of her guest room. "Come in."

"Beg pardon for intruding, ma'am," the maid said. "I'm to see if you need anything, and set them buckets out in the corridor for the footmen." Her speech carried a hint of the Dales: *set 'em bookets out in t'corridor*.

"You're not interrupting anything," Matilda said. "You're from Yorkshire, aren't you?"

The girl, a sturdy blonde, scooped two buckets from the tub. "Aye, ma'am. Mrs. Newbury says them as are from the north are good workers. Mr. Wentworth were raised in Yorkshire." She carried the water out and returned with a pair of empty buckets.

"Mr. Wentworth has only recently acquired Brightwell?"

"Aye. Had it from his cousin, who had it from the old duke. Place went to rack and ruin, Mrs. Newbury says, but Mr. Wentworth will set it to rights, see if he don't. The tenant farms are right enow. Mr. Manners's ma's knees say we're in for snow."

She brought in two more empty buckets, filled them, and placed them in the corridor as well.

"Do you know when the laundry will be finished with my dress?" Matilda asked.

"We do laundry on Monday, like a proper household. Mrs. Newbury is in the attics now finding you some more outfits. We've dresses up there to clothe half of London. I'll send along a tea tray, shall I?"

She pushed the wheeled tub toward the door, going slowly enough that the remaining water wouldn't slosh.

"Don't put yourself to any bother," Matilda said.

"Tea's no bother. Himself rings for trays at all hours, and now, when a proper body ought to be inside before a roaring fire, where is he? Mucking about in the garden. The Quality is daft, though you didn't hear that from me."

"What is your name?" The question was hard to ask, because Matilda had learned that parting with a name was an act of trust.

"Molly Danvers, ma'am. I'm the upstairs maid, now that we have a guest, and you mustn't think anything of me. I'm a chatterbox."

The girl was friendly, as contented staff could be in the homes of gentry.

"A tea tray in another hour or so would be appreciated." Small, frequent meals were easier on a recovering belly than feasts. That wisdom had come from the laundresses at the tavern where Matilda had tried to work. She'd been let go for falling asleep on the job one too many times.

The other women at the inn had done what they could for her. One had gifted her with a pair of wool stockings, a few had pressed hard-earned pennies into her hand, but they'd all known that turning an inept maid out with winter coming on was tantamount to a death sentence.

And still, Matilda had not turned her steps in the direction of home.

She closed the door behind Danvers and went to the window. Down in the garden, a man in a floppy felt hat used a long-handled scythe to hack away at the overgrown shrubbery. With each sweep of his blade, more of the unkempt hedge fell to the cold ground. Mr. Wentworth worked with the unhurried, efficient rhythm of a countryman, and gradually fashioned a border where rioting bushes had been.

"That is not the physique of a scholar," Matilda murmured,

for he wore no coat. Soldiers had that lean, tough build. Coachmen had the same ability to ignore the elements, even as isolated flakes of snow drifted down from a pewter sky.

The swing of Mr. Wentworth's scythe was entrancing, like the cadenced narrative of a skilled storyteller. Why had he offered her sanctuary? She was a damsel at death's door, and he'd conjured a pretext for adding her to his household.

If the past months had taught Matilda anything, it was that good luck always came at a price, while bad luck was free. Beggars could be choosers, though, and despite every instinct telling her to take her buttered rolls and her pilfered tea cake and run, she'd stay at least the night.

In the morning, after a sound sleep in a warm bed, she'd find the fortitude to leave this place and never come back.

* * *

"So you've banished Duncan to the shires?" Stephen Wentworth asked.

Quinn gave no sign he'd heard the question, but then, Quinn was holding the baby, a fat little cherub by the name of Artemis Ann Wentworth. Wee Artie had two older sisters to lead her astray, though Stephen intended to shoulder a doting uncle's portion of that effort as well.

"I haven't banished anybody anywhere," Quinn replied. "Take the baby."

Stephen found two stone of grinning, drooling, Wentworth female deposited upon his lap.

"Greetings, niece. Be kind to me now, and in fifteen years, I'll teach you how to tipple brandy."

"You'll do no such thing," Quinn growled, prowling off across the playroom. "How long can it take one duchess to change her dress?"

"You're my only begotten brother," Stephen replied, bouncing the baby on his good knee. Actually, both of his knees were good. The problem that consigned him to a wheeled chair for much of the day was lower, halfway between his left knee and ankle. "Jane is giving you time to deliver your homily about the perils of young manhood."

"Which sound advice you regularly ignore. Will you visit Duncan on this trip?"

The instant Stephen paused in his bouncing, the baby waved her arms. Typical Wentworth, always instigating.

"I haven't been invited to Brightwell, probably because Duncan got a bellyful of my company on the Continent and has only had six months to recover from years of travel. What is Duncan doing out in Berkshire, anyway?" Stephen lifted the baby overhead—not so high, when a man was seated—and the little beast grinned uproariously.

"Drop that baby," Quinn said, extracting a rubber ball from the toy chest, "and I won't get a chance to kill you because Jane and the aunties will see to the job before the child has ceased squalling. The nursery maids will feed your carcass to the dogs, and Ned will carve your headstone."

"How I treasure the comfort of familial affection," Stephen replied, cradling the baby against his chest. "From what I recall, you set the tenant properties at Brightwell to rights and broke the entail so you could sell the place."

Outside, the weather was threatening nastiness. Fools with two sound legs might consider the first snowfall beautiful, while Stephen hated snow. He'd made the journey from Paris back to London in part because traveling after winter set in was tantamount to torture. Unlike Duncan, Stephen hadn't remained in Merry Olde once the Season had ended. He'd popped in at his own estate for one excruciatingly boring week, then taken himself back to the safety of the

Continent, where Jane's matchmaking wasn't a threat to a young man's sanity.

"I did break the entail at Brightwell," Quinn said, tossing the ball against the wall with one hand and catching it with the other. "Duncan showed no interest in commerce, and Jane thought he needed to be where he had some interaction with people other than family and servants."

Jane was a dear woman who thrived on a challenge—witness, she'd married the head of the Wentworth family—but she didn't know Duncan as Stephen knew him.

"She means well," Stephen said, turning the baby upside down—slowly—then righting her. "But Duncan's version of good society is Socrates or Marcus Lugubrious. I dragged our cousin to coffee shops all over the Continent, sat him down in the middle of lively arguments about everything from American government to abolition, to the analgesic properties of intoxicants, and do you know what he did?"

The baby wiggled in Stephen's lap, stretching out her arms toward her papa. Quinn lobbed the ball into the toy chest, retrieved his daughter, and headed for the door.

"Let's repair to the library before I break another sconce."

As children, neither Quinn nor Stephen had had toys. Anything they'd acquired that might have diverted them—a tattered deck of cards, an old hat—had quickly been destroyed by a father fonder of gin than he'd been of his own children.

"Was the sconce lit when you broke it, Quinn?"

"One of them was." Quinn opened the library door and preceded Stephen inside. "If you dragged Duncan to a coffee shop, he probably sat in a corner—close enough to a lamp to have a little light, far enough from the fire to avoid anybody's notice—and read some damned book, while you made fourteen new best friends and beggared yourself buying them all drinks."

Not exactly. Stephen had learned that young Englishmen intent on making a good impression earned only contempt and a sore head with that tactic.

"Duncan truly doesn't enjoy the comradery of his fellows." This baffled Stephen, who found the company of other people one of few comforts in the midst of chronic pain.

"He didn't enjoy the company of *your* fellows," Quinn said. "Young men intent on wenching and inebriation."

A man in a wheeled chair was not seen as a man, but rather as an outsized child, his gender relevant only in so far as the fellow must be decently dressed. Stephen had come to this conclusion before his sixteenth birthday and had been forcing himself to walk periodically ever since.

The only person to support him in that endeavor had been Duncan, and Duncan hadn't needed any mortifying explanations either.

"Quinn, I'm no longer eighteen. I am of an age to marry, in line to inherit your title until such time as you present me with a nephew, and yet, you insist on thinking of me as a university boy consumed by lust. Is it possible—let's call this a wild theory—that your view of Duncan is similarly misguided?"

Quinn put the baby to his shoulder and rubbed the child's tiny back. The duke's hand was nearly large enough to cover that back, and yet his touch could not have been more gentle.

"It's possible I do not see any of my family clearly. Jane instructs me on that point regularly, but I knew Duncan as a lad. He was the older cousin who tried to help, but hadn't the means. I am beholden to him."

For a Wentworth, a personal debt was a more sacred

obligation than any tax owed to the king or tithe owed to the church.

"You owe him, so you disown him?"

For years, Duncan had fought for Stephen, though his firearm of choice had been reason and his longbow nocked with relentless determination. Because of Duncan, Quinn had installed a lift in the family's London town house. Because of Duncan, Stephen had been given the freedom of the saddle, a medication Stephen still relied on in frequent large doses.

To advocate for Duncan, however ineffectively, felt good.

"We are not disowning him, Stephen. In all of your wanderings, did Duncan ever show a friendly interest in a woman?"

Oh, for God's sake. "He never showed a friendly interest in another *person*, Quinn, though he's inexplicably tolerant of children and dumb beasts. People are specimens to him, an experiment in progress, a chess puzzle. His near acquaintances are the classical philosophers, his greatest recreation is to sit of an evening with a glass of brandy and stare into a modest fire as it burns down to coals. You torment him when you force him into the society of squires and goodwives."

"Jane disagrees with you," Quinn said, kissing the baby's fuzzy head. "Jane says he's lonely, and that we'll soon lose him to endless travel if he's not given an opportunity to form some meaningful associations."

Jane was a preacher's daughter and had a way with a sermon. "You disagree with Jane."

The look Quinn shot Stephen was exasperated and wonderfully honest. That glance was sent from one adult brother to another, allies in the ongoing investigation of the Great Feminine Mystery.

"I have suggested to my duchess that Duncan's version of happiness does not comport with her theory."

"Which suggestion Jane batted aside like a new maid going after cobwebs, but there's our Duncan, in godforsaken Berkshire, surrounded by the racing crowd, the hunt set, and the farmers' daughters who'd love to marry into a ducal family."

The baby got a fist wrapped in Quinn's hair. No gray there yet, but then Quinn was only in his mid-thirties. If anything, he seemed younger now than he had ten years ago.

While Duncan had always seemed grown-up. Not lonely, exactly, but inured to life.

"I compromised with my duchess," Quinn said. "Duncan has one year to make the estate profitable, after which I will take over management of the property for him. If at the end of one year, he has not brought Brightwell up to scratch, then management of the property remains in his hands, though I will hold a life estate."

Quinn was big, dark, unfashionably prone to muscle, and easy to mistake for a bullyboy in fine tailoring. He'd used that perception to his advantage when establishing his bank, and yet, he was also shrewd in a way Stephen had never had to be

"And because of that life estate," Stephen said, "Duncan cannot easily sell the property. Either he learns to manage Brightwell in the next year, or he learns to manage it over the next decade—if he wants to escape back to his travels. Is this kind, Quinn? Even schoolboys eventually win free of having to study topics they abhor."

Quinn settled onto the sofa with the child in his lap. "Duncan has more than enough brains to bring Brightwell 'round. All he wants is motivation to accomplish the task. What does the future hold for him otherwise? Another five years touring the Continent with some spoiled lordling?"

"Many men have a worthwhile career as tutors," Stephen said, a career he'd consider but for his damned leg.

"Those men are not our cousins. Jane wants Duncan settled. If he gets Brightwell sorted out in the next year, then he can lark about wherever he pleases."

"I'd best pay a call on him," Stephen said. "I know a bit about managing a property, which affliction we must also lay at dear Jane's feet."

She'd prevailed on Quinn to give Stephen a modest estate when Stephen had turned twenty-one, because, in Jane's estimation, a young man needed his own quarters. This was Jane's euphemism for ensuring Stephen's dubious friends and paramours did not disturb the ducal household.

"You own the best property of the lot," Quinn said. "Also the smallest acreage. Althea and Constance wanted more distance from London and needed a challenge."

Althea and Constance, Stephen's older sisters, wanted dowering, in other words, and productive land was the sweetest asset a doting brother could add to the marriage settlements.

Both sisters remained unmarried, despite having dowries overflowing with sweetness.

"I do thank you for your generosity," Stephen said, though was it generous to exile a fellow upon his majority? "The Continent is endlessly fascinating, but one wearies of wandering." For a time, then one wearied of staying put. "I'll trot off to Berkshire in the morning."

"You'll mount a sneak attack?"

Duncan had lived with the ducal branch of the family for years—when there had been money, but no title—and yet, in some ways, Duncan was still apparently a stranger to Stephen's siblings.

"I could send him a note, Quinn, but if he was in the

middle of a good book, he'd shrug, set the note aside, and neglect to inform his housekeeper. Did you know he sought to publish a travelogue of our itinerary?"

"Everybody is publishing travelogues."

And Quinn, who had not learned to read until late adolescence, had no time for literature that merely entertained and broadened the mind. He could glean more about a person from examining their ledger book than any priest had ever learned in a confessional, but Quinn had probably never read a complete work of fiction.

"Do you read anything other than the bank reports, Quinn?"

"I read to the children." He nuzzled the baby's nape. "I like poetry. Some poetry."

That made sense. "Poetry doesn't take thousands of words to tell a story."

"Exactly. Poetry gets straight to the point and does in twenty lines what Duncan's philosophers couldn't sort out as well in an entire book."

"So have you memorized a poem to spring on Jane?"

Quinn rose again, the child cradled against his chest. "Speaking of Jane, she must have decided to wedge in a nap along with changing her dress. Before you leave for your missionary work in Berkshire, stay a few days and let Jane cosset you. The girls and I could use the reinforcements."

He quit the room on that admission, the baby waving a damp fist at Stephen over her papa's shoulder.

Duncan might not be lonely, but Stephen certainly was. He left a volume of Wordsworth's poetry so "The Daffodils" was open on the low table before the hearth—Quinn's preferred end of the sofa—and sent a footman to inform the stables that he'd ride for Berkshire in the morning.

Chapter Three

"I thought we discussed the undesirability of your death from exposure to the elements." Duncan stopped short of the desk at which Miss Maddie of the Abundant Caution sat swathed in two shawls, a third shawl draped over her lap. "This will not do, madam."

He'd sent her a note to meet him in the library after she'd broken her fast, and then he'd been waylaid by his game-keeper. Mr. Hefner had taken fifteen minutes to convey that before the snow had started he'd found snares set along three different game trails by the river.

Miss Maddie remained seated, an indication that she was indeed a lady. A servant, a runaway governess, or a house-keeper who'd stolen a few too many spoons would have popped to her feet.

"You said to meet you in the library, Mr. Wentworth. This is the library."

"This is an ice cave with a few books in it," Duncan said. "Come with me."

She did not so much as gather up her shawls. "Where are we going?"

"To the darkest dungeon in the dankest cave in the magical land every schoolchild knows to be secreted beneath the farms of Berkshire."

Her gaze went to the two-story windows, which helped make the library impossible to heat. She regarded the falling snow with the sort of bleakness Duncan might have expected from Stephen, for whom a snowfall was tantamount to house arrest. At least twelve inches had come down during the night, and more was slowly accumulating. Nobody would travel in this weather.

Nobody with any sense. "You sought to leave this morning," Duncan said, the realization oddly disappointing. Was his company truly so unappealing that she'd rather fend for herself on the open road than transcribe his journals?

"One doesn't like to be a burden, Mr. Wentworth." She was still too skinny, still pale, but her eyes had acquired a battle light, albeit one with the wick turned low.

For now. Stephen had had the same frustrated air when Duncan had taken him on as a pupil, and great conflagrations had blossomed from that dull spark—thank God and Wentworth stubbornness.

"Did no one ever tell you that pride is a sin, Miss Maddie?"

"Did no one ever tell you that sermonizing is the province of clergy, Mr. Wentworth?"

"As it happens, I studied for the church and actually held a curate's post. If you would be so good as to join me in the estate office, I will humbly attempt to contain my joy at your continued company. The estate office is kept so warm that you will not even be able to see your breath."

"Where is the rabbit?" she asked, rising. "I ask myself, if the creature has only its fur coat for protection, and can thrive despite weeks of bitter weather, where does it shelter?"

The question had philosophical underpinnings that Duncan ignored. "He burrows into the ground and dreams of sunshine and clover." Or possibly the company of warm, friendly lady bunnies. One didn't say that in polite company, but nature was nothing if not preoccupied with procreation.

Unlike Duncan.

"Your housekeeper found me some clothes," Miss Maddie said. "I will consider them a loan."

"You may have them, madam. My wardrobe boasts as many dresses as I need for the present."

She gave him an exasperated look when he was trying, with his usual lack of success, to be humorous.

"I am not a criminal, Mr. Wentworth, though I have taken dropped apples from orchards and scraps from the middens of a busy inn. I would rather admit to those petty wrongs than be a charity case."

He held the door for her, and she swept through, clearly unaware that even with so small a detail, she revealed herself to be a woman born to privilege.

One who envied solitary rabbits their dark winter burrows.

"I wonder if the rabbit nibbling from my garden considers itself to be committing any wrong at all," Duncan said, opening the concealed panel that led to the footmen's stairs. "The estate office is on the next floor up. The higher vantage point allows me to gaze despairingly upon my acres. Did you sleep well?"

She rounded the landing and paused, her hand on the owl carved into the newel post. "I slept so well, I woke up more exhausted than when I went to bed."

Duncan knew that kind of sleep, the kind that flattened a man already lying in a ditch of bone-deep fatigue.

"Then I must not deluge you with my brilliant prose until tomorrow," he said, resuming their progress up the steps.

She followed more slowly, suggesting that even climbing a staircase taxed her. "A mere cascade will do for today, thank you. Why do your acres cause you to despair?"

They didn't, not yet. They drove Duncan to resentment worthy of an adolescent scholar forced to repeat a dull exercise for the third time. The despair would come in a year or so, when Quinn announced that Duncan's sentence was to become permanent.

Duncan opened the door to the estate office, a blast of warmth pouring into the corridor. "Welcome to my dungeon."

Miss Maddie stopped short a few steps past the doorway. "I hadn't realized Berkshire was prone to tornados." She moved into the room turning in a slow circle as Duncan closed the door. "Will a short man singing to himself soon appear and offer to bring order here if I'll surrender my firstborn after marrying the prince?"

She referred to a children's tale, one featuring a troll or some other objectionable fellow with a long name. The children of the poor were not generally read fairy tales. Books were expensive, and really, what would be the point? Most poor children were born knowing princes and good fairies never saved the day.

Duncan had eventually learned that lesson too.

"This is the organized version," he said, gesturing to piles of paper and ledger books stacked haphazardly on every level surface. The chairs alone were free of the estate's administrative wreckage. The cats left alimentary evidence of their displeasure if Duncan infringed on their territory to that extent.

Miss Maddie pushed back the curtains from the window above the desk. "Where do we begin?"

Beyond the glass, Brightwell had become a setting for a Norse tale of giants and magic bears. All was blanketed in fanciful curves and drifts of white, a deceptively soft tableau that might have been the death of Miss Maddie Pay-Me-In-Cash.

The sun cut through the overcast in slices of gold that turned the falling snow into a thousand diamonds dancing down onto a bed of blinding white.

I have missed England. The thought was preposterous and unwelcome, but Miss Maddie was also gazing out on the wintry scene with banked yearning in her eyes.

Who or what did she miss? Who or what did she regret? "We'll soon be chilled to the bone if you insist on having the draperies open, madam."

She took a seat near the blazing hearth. "I don't chill so easily, and reading is best done with a quantity of light. You never answered my question."

"Says she who dodges interrogations as nimbly as a hare."

She twitched up her shawls, covering herself from the ears down. "Are we to engage in productive enterprise, Mr. Wentworth, or waste the morning in pointless contention?"

"Pointless contention can be another name for philosophical debate."

Well, damn. Somebody had taught her the tutor's most effective weapon with unruly scholars—the disappointed silence. Perhaps she had been a governess after all. Duncan pulled a bound folder from the shelves at waist height and untied the ribbon.

"Let's determine whether you can decipher my penmanship, for without that ability, the entire enterprise is doomed."

She accepted the papers he shoved at her, then reached toward her face, her hand dropping back to her lap.

"Use mine," Duncan said, extracting a pair of spectacles from his breast pocket.

She took them, held them up to the light, then used the hem of a shawl to polish the lenses. Perched on her nose, the spectacles imparted a prim air, which for reasons known only to snowbound imbeciles, made her oddly attractive.

"Prostitution in Paris," she recited, "is undertaken with none of the outraged hypocrisy that characterizes the English version. The French are pragmatic even in this, albeit joyfully pragmatic, or so the coquettes would have their clientele believe. The trade is plied—"

"Enough." Duncan retrieved his essay. "You can both decipher my handwriting and translate French at sight. Good to know."

Her expression was disgruntled. "You establish that from three lines of prose?"

"My handwriting is worthy of every pejorative in Dr. Johnson's lexicon. For the sake of continuity, you'd best start at the beginning of my travels. In a general sense, the itinerary begins near your shoulders and ends near your feet."

That description had a risqué interpretation, though the lady chose to ignore it.

She rose and walked around Duncan to the shelves nearer the window. "Then my first priority is to put the material in chronological order. I trust you were conscientious about dating your observations?"

"Yes." *Maybe. On occasion.*

The room smelled of leather—the best of the bound volumes had been moved here away from hordes of mice in the library—with a faint undernote of coal smoke. Miss Maddie, by contrast, exuded the fragrance of roses. Good old damasks, their perfume straightforward and assertive. Somebody had doubtless stored rose sachets·among the dresses in the attic, or perhaps the staff had put rose-scented soap in Miss Maddie's guest room.

"The task seems simple enough," she said, reaching for the first folder on the leftmost shelf. "I'll see you at dinner."

Dismissed again, which should be a relief. "If you need anything, the parlor across the corridor has a bell pull."

"I need solitude, Mr. Wentworth, and a good deal of time."

She needed a step ladder, a footstool, and about three months of good nutrition. Duncan bowed and gave her the solitude.

* * *

"Where the hell could she be?"

Lieutenant Colonel Lord Atticus Parker had slept, awoken, danced, and dined with that question drumming in his mind for the past four months.

"Somewhere safe, God willing," Thomas Wakefield replied. "Matilda has endured Moscow winters. A little snow won't bother her much."

And that was the problem. Matilda Wakefield had endured Russian winters, forced marches on the Peninsula as little more than a child, Viennese ballrooms, Paris intrigues.... She'd be entirely too unbothered by a life in hiding. She was a lady—a widowed duchess, no less—but she was also her father's daughter.

Wakefield poured another portion of port into both glasses. The snow had stopped, and a howling wind had come with nightfall, meaning roads would drift closed by morning.

"You haven't heard anything?" Parker asked.

Wakefield's jovial façade faltered. "Do you think if I

knew where my only child was that I'd be sitting on my backside swilling port and pretending an optimism I don't feel? Brigands abound, women are vulnerable, and from what we know, she took very little in the way of money or valuables with her."

Matilda had taken an unusually broad linguistic education, a fine appreciation for art, and an unfeminine penchant for chess, though damned little in the way of practical necessities. She had also taken the key to Parker's advancement in a military too happy to remain at peace.

Parker bore a certain fondness for the lady—he'd courted her, after all—and no fondness at all for her father. "I could go back to my superiors," he said. "Have them put out discreet word that she's missing. Every village and hamlet has a militia of some sort."

"And have her name on handbills all over the realm?" Wakefield replied. "Thank you, but no. You may not care to protect Matilda's reputation, but I certainly do."

More likely, Wakefield protected himself at Matilda's expense. "Her reputation won't do her much good if she's dying of a lung fever somewhere in East Anglia."

Wakefield rose, a lean man aging handsomely. He was an old hand at the diplomacy game, sometimes representing his government officially, sometimes unofficially. He dealt in the gentlemanly business of procuring art, which was in truth a matter of looting the treasures of European aristocratic families left destitute by war.

"She's not in East Anglia," Wakefield said. "She's not hiding out in any of the ports. She's not in Edinburgh. I doubt she's in Paris for I've too many friends there. I fear she's gone to Boston in truth."

This was the story they'd concocted. Matilda had seen much of Europe, but had supposedly developed a fascination with the New World. She was enjoying the hospitality of French friends who dwelled in Boston, and no date had been set for her return.

And thus no date had been set for her to wed her dashing lieutenant colonel, hero of the Battle of Colina Azul.

"I've sent inquiries to the American seaboard," Parker said, rising from the table. "Your daughter agreed to marry me, and her disappearance will soon grow awkward."

"My dear colonel," Wakefield replied in his most patient tones, "she might well be dead, and a little awkwardness is hardly the greatest of my concerns. Perhaps if you'd been a more doting fiancé, we might not be in this coil."

As long as the weather had been decent, Wakefield had maintained a sanguine confidence in Matilda's self-sufficiency, perhaps too sanguine. His testiness now was reassuring, suggesting that he had not, in fact, hidden away his only offspring.

"Matilda evidenced no desire to be doted upon." A relief, considering Parker hadn't the least notion how to dote on anybody save perhaps his horse. One could learn to waltz from a dancing master, but from whom, especially in the army, did one learn to dote on a female?

He hadn't regarded this shortcoming as a problem because Matilda was singularly lacking in dote-ableness.

"The self-possessed ladies," Wakefield said, "are precisely the ones most in need of cosseting. I speak not as a diplomat, but as a man once happily married. Shall we to the chessboard?"

Ever the statesman. "I promise, when we find Matilda, I will dote, cosset, and fawn endlessly, if she'll assure me she's done with her adventures."

Wakefield led the way down a paneled corridor to his study. The town house was a monument to understated good taste. Fine art was on display—a Chinese vase here, a Dutch landscape there—but without ostentatious staging. The domicile was quietly lovely, much like the lady who'd dwelled here.

"Shall you be black or white?" Wakefield asked, taking down a chess set from shelves behind his desk. "Guest's choice."

"Which would you choose?"

"Both have their charms."

Matilda had learned chess at an early age, presumably from her father, and she was a devoted student of the game. Parker himself had only occasionally won a match against his affianced bride, though her game was by turns measured and erratic.

That combination of impulse and logic did not bode well for his efforts to locate her, much less before her father found her. Nonetheless, Parker would persist. This was not a battle he could afford to lose, even if that meant drastic measures where his prospective father-in-law was concerned.

* * *

The snow began to melt, and Matilda knew the time had come to take her leave of Brightwell. In less than a week, she'd made little progress organizing the shipwreck that was Mr. Wentworth's estate office, another regret added to the many she already carried.

The difficulty lay in his journals, which were by turns keenly insightful, jocular, philosophical, and compassionate. He of the brisk pragmatism, resented acres, and half-empty house had created that most tempting of lures, good literature.

Though Mr. Wentworth's penmanship truly was atrocious.

This, oddly, made him less objectionable in Matilda's estimation.

"I intrude only to ensure you haven't perished beneath a mountain of books or been tripped by the feline demons haunting my realm."

Matilda peeled Mr. Wentworth's spectacles from her nose, for there he stood in the doorway, letting out all the warmth and looking unexpectedly dear. He lacked charm, he wasn't genial, he had little in the way of witty banter, but he'd shown her more honor and decency in a week than she'd encountered in the previous four months.

"Please close the door, sir." Had she been so engrossed in the wonders of Tuscany in summer that she'd not heard him knock?

He obliged but remained across the room. "That fellow you mentioned from the fairy tale must have dropped by, the one who brings order to chaos in exchange for a squalling infant."

Mr. Wentworth had missed supper the past two nights. From what Mrs. Newbury had said—and left unsaid—Matilda gathered that he was required to make up numbers at his neighbors' gatherings.

And therein lay one last problem she'd have to resolve before she took her leave of him. "Please have a seat, Mr. Wentworth. We must broach a delicate topic."

He took the chair behind the desk, a chilly perch because Matilda kept the draperies open. She needed the warmth and respite his hearth provided, but she needed to see freedom more.

"I'm not paying you enough," he said, rearranging pencils in a silver pen tray. "Very well, your wages are increased by half."

He shouldn't be paying her at all, especially in light of

how she planned to return his hospitality. "That will not be necessary."

"You are giving notice, then, mere days after taking on your task. I cannot blame you. If I can't read my own handwriting, then there's little hope—"

She rose and rearranged her shawls. "I am not giving notice." Nor would she ever give notice. She'd steal away under tonight's cold quarter moon when the rest of the household slept. "My concern at present lies elsewhere. You have been socializing with your neighbors."

Mr. Wentworth made a face like a boy served a plate of cold turnips when he'd expected pudding.

"According to some law held sacrosanct by rural hostesses," he said, "males and females must be matched, like bookends or Dutch trotters. We're to parade from the parlor to the dining room in pairs, converse in the same fashion at table, and waste our evenings in twosomes. God forbid the carpet should be rolled back for dancing after supper, and some unfortunate is forced to sit out a reel for lack of a partner. I suppose this explains why a gentleman always turns pages for a lady and, conversely, so the Commandment of Two remains unbroken."

He wasn't even peevish. He offered a bored aside, his chin braced on his hand, index finger extended along his cheek.

"What have you told the neighbors about me?"

"Do you know, Miss Maddie, that when I enter a room, you immediately position yourself between me and the door, or at least as close to the door as I am?"

A man who'd observed everything from the forced smiles of Parisian coquettes to the Roman bridges still in use in Vienna would notice that.

Matilda returned to her seat. "I sit for long periods poring over your essays. I pace to stave off restlessness. Your staff looks in on me from time to time, and they will doubtless mention in the market and to their families that you have a female guest. How will you explain me?"

Mr. Wentworth pinched the bridge of his nose—a nice nose. Neither too large nor retiring, but assertive enough for a man of his intellect. His chin and jawline were similarly just right—defined without shading into boldness. Gainsborough or Lawrence wouldn't have done him justice—they created portraits of fashion on human mannequins—but a Bernini sculpture would have been a fine medium for Mr. Wentworth's likeness.

Provided the sculpture was one of the artist's works portrayed with clothing.

"How will I explain you." Mr. Wentworth rose and went to the hearth, putting Matilda in mind of a scholar getting to his feet to demonstrate his rhetorical skills. "I am required to explain another human being? Is it not burden enough making sense of my own situation? You decline to explain yourself, therefore, the question vexes me. You appeared in my woods at a time when an ally was much needed, and I repay my debts. Is that sufficient explanation?"

Something was vexing him, though he hadn't raised his voice. He used the coal scoop to add fuel to the fire, and then rearranged coals on the grate to allow air to circulate.

"In the village," Matilda said, "somebody will mention that a lady has come to bide at Brightwell. The poachers, wherever they are, will grumble about a woman waving a gun at them on the Wentworth property. Sooner or later, over a glass of port or in the churchyard, somebody will inquire of you regarding your guest. What will you say?"

She needed to know this before she left Brightwell: What tale would he concoct about the woman he'd found in his woods, if he'd say anything at all?

He replaced the fire screen flush against the bricks and tapped the end of the poker against the hearthstones, shedding minute portions of ash and coal dust onto the stones. Next, he swept the leavings into the ash scoop, and dumped the lot into the dustbin.

How could such a tidy man have left his journals in such chaos?

"I don't know what to say about you; *ergo*, I'll say nothing." He dusted his hands and perched a hip against the desk. "I had supper last night with Squire Peabody, who is the magistrate for our district, and your situation did not arise at any point in our conversation. Nonetheless, you should know that I won't lie, Miss Maddie. Not on behalf of a woman who could well bring the constabulary down on my household for high crimes or infamous deeds."

Was any virtue rarer or more irksome than honesty? "The constables are not pursuing me. Does your penchant for telling the truth stem from your training for the church?"

One boot swung impatiently. "I prefer honesty because lies are a damned lot of bother and seldom solve more problems than they create. I will tell the rubbishing neighbors that you are a connection fallen on hard times, and I am indebted to you for past generosities. You have agreed to assist me in restoring Brightwell to its former glory, and as I am without a hostess, your presence is most appreciated."

Why must he have such a gift for euphemism? "Don't add that part," Matilda said, "about the hostess. Such a comment begs the question of when you'll be entertaining."

He rose from the desk. "Excellent point. No mention of needing a hostess, then, though if I did let on that you are here as the lady of the house, then the invitations might cease." He turned his regard on the ceiling—a plain expanse of plaster—as if importuning the Almighty to deliver him from such tribulations.

"If you don't want to socialize, then simply refuse the invitations."

He paced away from the desk, his prowling making the room feel smaller. As estate offices went, the dimensions were commodious, particularly with many of the books shelved and the papers organized into boxes stored in the cabinets. Mr. Wentworth circling the desk made Matilda want to stand closer to the door.

"But how does one refuse an invitation without arousing exactly the sort of questions you allude to, Miss Maddie? If I decline a dinner party, then at the Sunday service, I'll be asked if I'm under the weather. If I send regrets to my neighbor's musicale, some squire or other will ask if the plaguy books have fallen behind, which they have, by a decade or two."

"You dislike accounting?"

He tossed himself into the chair behind the desk. "I have a proper respect for accounting. What's wanted with Brightwell's finances is something on the order of legerdemain. Even my cousin, the brilliant man of means, hasn't found the time to bring this place to heel, suggesting that unless I learn to traffic in the dark arts, the task is impossible."

Matilda rose, poured him a brandy at the sideboard, and brought it to him. She'd done the same for Papa and the colonel more times than she could count. So far, she'd refrained from helping herself to Brightwell's spirits.

"My thanks," Mr. Wentworth said. "Feel free to join me, if you're inclined to ward off the chill. I have female cousins who can ward off chills at the pace of Scottish coachmen."

Matilda ought not. Ladies did not partake of strong spirits, though the aroma of apples and sweet spices, autumn sunshine in Acquitaine, and memories treasured by winter fires called to her. Who knew if she'd ever enjoy such a luxury again, much less in such good company?

"Come," Mr. Wentworth said, rising to put his full glass in her hand. "'He who aspires to be a hero must drink brandy.'"

"Samuel Johnson," Matilda replied, loving the familiar feel of the glass against her palm. "Dr. Johnson made no provision for what girls, women, or heroines should imbibe."

"Perhaps he didn't feel qualified to expound on the subject, or perhaps"—Mr. Wentworth could pour brandy and aim a curious gaze in Matilda's direction—"he knew that women can be heroines without the fortification of spirits."

He saluted with his glass and took a sip, so Matilda tasted hers as well.

The nose was exquisite: dignified, complex, and alluring. On the tongue, the brandy blossomed to keep the promises of sunshine on old wood, spices, and a hint of crème brûlée. She swallowed, and the fire in her belly started quietly, then gained strength until another sip became imperative.

"The drink meets with your approval," Mr. Wentworth said, "while my rejoinder, should I be asked about my houseguest, did not meet with your approval. Consider this, Miss Maddie: The Wentworths are an eccentric family.

"The current owner of Brightwell was born in direst poverty," he went on. "My cousin considered himself fortunate to wear footman's livery, and then had to abandon even that occupation. He is now titled, wealthy, and well matched, and he holds his title because of his fortune, not the other way around. If I say that you are a connection from former days fallen on hard times, then who is to gainsay me?"

She could believe Mr. Wentworth possessed aristocratic

blood when he posited his question with such assurance, though a title, wealth, and eccentricity nearby on his family tree was bad news for Matilda indeed.

"Your family situation compounds the problem," she said. "A sudden rise in fortunes is a natural source of curiosity and begs further questions. Why can't I simply be a competent amanuensis whom a fellow traveler recommended to help you organize your journals?"

Stay as close to the truth as possible, in other words.

Mr. Wentworth stared at his drink. In his lack of expression, in the absence of a rejoinder to Matilda's suggestion, she grasped that his travel journals were not something others knew of.

"You cannot be ashamed of having kept a diary of your journeys?" she said. "Your talent with a pen is far above the scribblings of the average peripatetic Englishman." She planned to leave him and his brandy, his warm fires, and soft shawls in a matter of hours. The least she could do was offer him a few honest compliments before she departed.

A tap on the door had Matilda nearly spilling her drink, while Mr. Wentworth made swift progress across the room.

"Beggin' your pardons, sir, ma'am." The chatty maid—Danvers—stood in the corridor, curtsying repeatedly. "Cook said as I ought to find you and let you know that Mrs. Newbury is fallen sick. Cook thinks we might need a doctor, and the nearest quack is five miles off, and with all this snow…"

"Mrs. Newbury is ill?" Mr. Wentworth asked.

"She's took to bed, sir, and Mrs. Newbury never takes to her bed."

"What are her symptoms?" Matilda asked, casually setting her drink on the desk. Heaven forbid the help should find her taking spirits with the master.

"Missus has the flu, Cook thinks. Fever and chills, sore throat, and aches. Doesn't want nothing to eat and won't let nobody near her."

"This will not do," Mr. Wentworth said. "The housekeeper is the household repository for medical knowledge. What has Mrs. Newbury asked for in the way of tisanes and plasters?"

The maid glanced down the corridor, then past Matilda's shoulder. "I'm sure Mrs. Newbury knows the tisanes and whatnot where she hails from, sir, but she isn't from around here. We ask at the vicarage if the apothecary can't help, or we make do."

Mr. Wentworth's gaze went to the shelves crammed with books and monographs. "Perhaps we have an herbal somewhere on the premises, a treatise that might shed light on what's to be done for her."

"I have yet to come across such a book," Matilda replied, "and I've handled every learned tome, treatise, and pamphlet in this room." She'd also seen influenza become lung fever and carry off healthy adults in less than a fortnight.

Mr. Wentworth pinched the bridge of his nose, the picture of a man preparing to shoulder one more burden he hadn't asked for. Danvers stood in the doorway looking pale and worried.

Mr. Wentworth would not ask Matilda for aid, or perhaps he *could not*, while the quarter moon would rise for the next several nights.

"Influenza calls for honey," Matilda said, "and lemons and whisky if you have them. Mint compresses, white willow bark tea by the gallon, and salted beef tea kept hot at all times."

She followed the maid through the door and left Mr. Wentworth alone in the warmth of the estate office.

Chapter Four

Duncan had stayed away from the estate office for two and a half days, even subjecting himself to the company of his neighbors lest he be tempted to assess the progress Miss Maddie was making.

Or to assess *her*.

She looked marginally better. Rested, tidier. Still haunted but not as gaunt. Still cautious, though her hands didn't shake.

The transformation in the office left Duncan shaken. Where books, papers, and other estate flotsam had covered every level surface before, she'd freed the furniture of detritus, organized the books, and done God knew what with the papers. The silver pen tray, wax jack, and standish gleamed; the air no longer bore the musty scent of unbeaten carpets; the sconce chimneys were free of soot.

A man could manage his estate from amid such order. Would a woman make such an effort in an office she intended to abandon?

Another tap sounded at the door. "Come in."

A footman entered bearing a tray laden with a tea service, suggesting the kitchen wanted to impress Miss Maddie, for Duncan certainly hadn't ordered any tea.

"Miss Maddie is looking in on Mrs. Newbury," Duncan said, and thank God for that, because medicine was one field of study Duncan had left Stephen to pursue on his own.

"And we're that glad she is," the man replied. More of a boy, but then redheads tended to look youthful, especially skinny, freckled redheads. "Mrs. Newbury is a good soul, and influenza is a perilous misery. Where would you like the tea, sir?"

The servants at Brightwell were unnervingly friendly. In London, as Lord Stephen Wentworth's tutor and relation, Duncan had made a place for himself between staff and family. The result had been adequate stores of both privacy and deference.

"The tray can go on the desk. Has Miss Maddie had the maids dusting in here?"

The scent of jasmine wafted up from the teapot. Duncan hadn't known his larders included any jasmine-scented brew.

"She did indeed, sir, and suggested we might start on the library next, because a lot of these books would be better displayed there. Will there be anything else?"

Biscuits had been arranged in a little circle on a porcelain plate bordered with pink flowers. "The library is damp. What few books remain under this roof will disintegrate within a year if we move them to the library."

"Miss Maddie says a few good fires in all the library hearths at once will dry the whole room out, particularly when the weather's so beastly cold and the shelves are empty of books. I could have the lads see to it, sir. Wouldn't be any problem. The maids could give the shelves a good going over with beeswax and lemon oil. That will help keep the damp and the bugs away."

The house could go up in flames, and the library would remain standing, a cavernous, moldy mausoleum housing the remains of aristocratic vanity and the skeletons of numerous insects.

Though the footman was trying to please his master, trying to take pride in the household.

"Your name is Miller?"

"Manners, sir, as in good manners."

They'd had that exchange before, probably more than once. Manners was the first footman, meaning two or three other young fellows took orders from him. The weather had everybody cooped up inside, and if any condition contributed to an increased incidence of mischief among scholars or domestics, it was boredom.

"Very well, have at the library to the extent you can without letting your other duties lapse. What else has Miss Maddie got up to?" Besides transforming Duncan's personal dungeon into a tidy, inviting office? Besides rescuing him from armed poachers? Besides turning his cramped scribblings into legible, coherent prose?

Duncan had no doubt that Miss Maddie had a plethora of other skills and abilities, a talent for unobtrusively taking her leave among them.

Manners peered into the dustbin, then rearranged the tools in the hearth stand. "She's quiet, sir. Even Danvers hasn't much to say regarding our guest. The lady is polite, she thanks us for the smallest consideration, she's lonely."

Duncan poured himself a cup of tea. "From what evidence do you reach that conclusion?"

"Mrs. Newbury said," the footman replied, refolding a wool blanket draped over the sofa. "Mrs. Newbury claims

Miss Maddie has the look of a woman without a home, and that's a lonely person to be."

A scold lurked in that observation, one intended for the conscience of any man thinking to neglect his new household and let lands and buildings pass into the keeping of an absentee landlord.

"Has the staff noticed anything else regarding our guest that I ought to be aware of?"

Manners appointed himself curator of the art on the walls and went about the room straightening frames. Even the pictures had been dusted, revealing sketches of flowers, birds, and young livestock.

"Miss Maddie is forgetful," Manners said. "Danvers finds things in odd locations, and says the old duke had a reputation for the same quirks when he got on in years."

"Such as?"

"A plate of biscuits in the drawer of the night table," Manners said. "Buttered toast wrapped in a table napkin and left on the top shelf of the wardrobe. Nothing is stolen, mind, but it's peculiar behavior."

The same behavior kept many a squirrel alive through England's bitter winters. "Forgetful, as you say, though Miss Maddie is preoccupied with establishing order among my papers, a daunting task. She is welcome here as long as she pleases, though I gather she'd rather we were discreet about her presence."

She'd been more forthright on that topic than almost any other, though did she raise the issue so that she might bide at Brightwell longer or that she might leave, safely and soon?

"We're not stupid, sir." Manners's ears turned red, but he didn't apologize for his rejoinder. "Nobody has been off the estate since the snow arrived, and I doubt the roads will be clear enough for us to attend services this Sunday."

"We'll have prayers in the family parlor."

Manners looked relieved, though this pronouncement meant Duncan would have to dust off a Book of Common Prayer and play preacher.

Another reason to resent dear Cousin Quinn's gift from here to Prague.

"Is anybody else showing signs of illness?" Duncan asked.

"No, sir. Mrs. Newbury isn't used to our winters. We told her the first winter would be the worst, but now she has the flu."

Meaning that even with Miss Maddie's care and skill, the housekeeper might not see a second winter. "Have we sent for the physician?"

Manners's gaze traveled the four corners of the room, a junior officer inspecting the barracks. "That's ten miles round trip in this weather, sir."

"Then the sooner somebody leaves, the sooner they'll return. We have daylight and sound horses."

Still Manners would not meet Duncan's gaze. "Probably a lot of flu hereabouts. Doctor Felton might not even be home."

"Send the best rider we have, or I'll go myself. It's not as if this household can't pay for the physician's services, and we do very much need our housekeeper." Then too, Miss Maddie might fall ill, an unfair recompense for her willingness to take on yet another of Duncan's burdens.

"I'll send MacIntosh, sir. He's from up north."

Whoever MacIntosh was. "Be about it, please." Duncan refrained from directing Manners to ensure that Miss Maddie partook of a tea tray.

And to ensure that she had at least two of her shawls.

And also a pair of decent reading glasses.

Miss Maddie would flee into the winter night if Duncan attempted that degree of fussing.

Manners gave the journals lining the shelves one last perusal, bowed, and withdrew.

Duncan started on the biscuits—buttery, sweet, with a hint of lemon, which implied Mrs. Newbury would have the honey and lemon toddies Miss Maddie had ordered. An hour later, he was still resisting the temptation to poke his nose belowstairs—no lord of the manor committed that folly without good cause. He instead perused the journal Miss Maddie had been reading

Provence in summer. One of his more fanciful maunderings. His fingers itched to take up a pen and edit the words on the page. Delete that extraneous phrase, substitute the Anglo-Saxon term for its Latinate cousin because the occasional two-syllable punch could lift a sentence from soothing erudition to effective communication.

But if Miss Maddie could do battle with influenza on behalf of a near stranger, then Duncan could trouble himself to review another year of Brightwell's ailing books. He set aside the journal, closed the curtains behind the desk, and opened the ledger book that he'd been ignoring since Miss Maddie's arrival.

* * *

Matilda knew better than to ask an ill person for permission to provide treatment. One gave orders in a sickroom, and most patients were comforted by that.

Over the course of the afternoon and evening, Mrs. Newbury's symptoms did not improve, nor did Matilda expect them to. Influenza was a fierce foe, and could retreat only to strike with renewed force.

At Matilda's direction, none of the staff came into the housekeeper's apartment, but rather, met Matilda at the door.

Willow bark tea was kept hot on the parlor stove in Mrs. Newbury's sitting room, and the scent of mint, also steeping on the stove, filled both chambers.

"You should leave me," Mrs. Newbury said, twitching at the quilt. "You will become sick, and you will die, and for no reason other than your English stubbornness."

"Nobody will die if I can help it," Matilda said, laying the back of her hand on the housekeeper's brow. "You are still warm, but not burning up. Shall I read to you?"

"The doctor will not come. You should be honest with me, Miss Maddie. If I'm to die, you should tell me." Such dignity and such ire lay in those quiet words.

"Who will look after Mr. Wentworth if you die? Who will send him the trays he doesn't order? Who will concoct menus that even he, in his endless distraction, will enjoy?"

Matilda had tried many gambits to engage Mrs. Newbury in conversation: Acquaint me with the staff here. What can you tell me of the Wentworth family history? Who are Brightwell's neighbors?

Mrs. Newbury had replied with terse answers: The staff was hardworking and loyal. The London Wentworths had owned the property less than five years, so who knew their history? The neighbors minded their own business.

Other questions could not be asked: Tell me of your family. How did you come to be in England? Is there anybody you'd like to send a letter to? To a woman forcibly removed from her homeland early in life, those questions were likely to bring on sad memories.

The topic of Mr. Wentworth, however, had Mrs. Newbury scooting up against the pillows. "That one. He works too much and too hard. Harder than a farmer with no sons. What family lets such a learned man clear ditches and trim hedges?"

Matilda imagined him, coat off, impervious to the

elements, his rhythm with a spade or blade steady and relentless.

"Is the estate in difficulties?"

Mrs. Newbury gestured for her cup, which held the bitter willow bark tea. "The Wentworths are scandalously wealthy. Nobody knows how the duke acquired his fortune, but they are awash in money. Have their own bank, if you can imagine such a thing. Mr. Wentworth—our Mr. Duncan Wentworth—is a cousin, and he joined the family in London to serve as a tutor to the crippled brother, Master Stephen. He's Lord Stephen, but he doesn't put on airs. They have all that money, and they send Mr. Wentworth here, a scholar, and expect him to fix what became a shambles of an estate years ago."

Her dark eyes held disdain for a family who'd set up one of their own to fail.

"Is Mr. Wentworth in disgrace?" Banishment was usually reserved for those in disfavor.

Mrs. Newbury sipped her tea. "When we are in disgrace is when we need our family most." She passed Matilda the cup, along with an inquiring glance.

Oh, no. No confessions. Not when Matilda had learned that the title Mr. Wentworth so casually disdained was that of a *duke*.

"Which ducal title has the honor of gracing the Wentworth escutcheon?"

The housekeeper lay back and closed her eyes. "The Duke of Walden. I'm told the previous duke was a lovely old man who grew senile at the very end. He sometimes wouldn't leave a room for weeks, and talked to people no longer among the living. His factors took advantage."

As factors were wont to do. "Mr. Wentworth has been traveling in recent years, hasn't he?"

"All over the Continent with Lord Stephen. Not like his lordship could go by himself, is it?"

Matilda had no intention of tarrying in a ducal household, even if that household was at present managed by a cousin. Nonetheless, a puzzle was emerging.

Why did Mr. Wentworth bide here, scything hedges, clearing ditches, and half freezing, when he was connected to wealth and had traveled the world? Why had he offered Matilda sanctuary and what would he expect in return? She was as helpless to ignore that conundrum as she was to walk past a chess game in progress without assessing the play.

"Send Danvers to sit with me," Mrs. Newbury said. "Or leave me alone. I'd rather you leave me alone."

"I'm off to the library to fetch a book, though I'll be back."

In Matilda's absence, the patient was more likely to fall asleep, and sleep was as effective a remedy for influenza as anything.

Matilda tucked in the covers, turned down the bedside lamp, and filled the water glass on the night table half full. Mrs. Newbury shifted to her side, facing the wall, and Matilda took her leave.

The staff respected Mrs. Newbury; they also liked her. If she died, she'd be mourned, and the same could not be said of everybody. That not-very-cheering thought led to others: Would Papa mourn Matilda's passing? Would he be relieved? Both? What about the colonel?

Should she take ship for America and put it about that Matilda Wakefield had died?

The widowed Matilda Talbot, rather, if she used the name she'd been traveling under recently.

Matilda could not afford to let those thoughts plod in their predictably melancholy circles, for melancholia, like influenza, could be contagious. She was building up the fire

in Mrs. Newbury's parlor stove when she realized the door
to the corridor had been left open several inches. No wonder
the sickroom was gradually cooling.

Mr. Wentworth stepped out of the gloom.

"If you have questions about me, Matilda, then you
should simply ask them, not interrogate my staff when they
are ill and unsuspecting."

Matilda. "How do you know my name?" What else did
he know, and what would he do with the information?

"I *did not* know your name. You disdained to answer
to Madeline, and Matilda was a guess based on probabil-
ities." He gestured toward the doorway. "Come with me.
The patient deserves her rest, and you and I have matters
to discuss."

If Matilda tried to bolt past him, run down the corridor,
and dodge out the kitchen door, he'd catch her in the first six
steps. And if she made it through the door, at night, alone,
in the cold, without so much as a cloak...?

Hopeless. She closed the parlor stove, rose, and dusted
her hands. "I don't want to leave her for long."

"You haven't taken more than five minutes away from
Mrs. Newbury's side since noon." He started for the kitchen,
his stride brisk. "The doctor refuses to come."

"You are angry." Mr. Wentworth's temper did not display
itself in a raised voice or even a sneer, but rather, in diction
more clipped than usual, in a marked economy of syllables.
How angry would he be when Matilda left without so much
as a thank-you?

Or would he be relieved?

He halted amid the cozy warmth of the kitchen. "I
am...my rage is without limit. I sent money with the
groom, lest the doctor think Brightwell's circumstances too
straitened to pay his fees. The issue is not money."

The issue was good old English hypocritical prejudice. "We'll manage without the quack," Matilda said. "English doctors are deplorably ignorant, in any case. The medical expertise on the Continent and even in Scotland is much more advanced."

Mr. Wentworth rubbed the back of his neck. "Stephen said as much, many times. You must be hungry."

A clock ticked on the mantel above the great hearth. The hour wasn't late by polite standards—barely ten o'clock— but the servants went to bed as soon after supper as their duties allowed, and thus the kitchen was deserted and lit only by embers in the hearth and a single sconce burning near the window.

Matilda put a hand on her belly. "I forgot to eat."

"Easy to forget, when ignoring the appetites has become a habit. I was too pre-occupied to do justice to the trays that appeared on my desk as if by magic."

He was opening and closing cupboards and drawers in a manner that would have scandalized Cook, had she known the master of the house was rummaging belowstairs unsupervised.

"What are you looking for?"

"Bread, of course." He set a loaf wrapped in linen on the counter. "The cheese will be in the window box. I'll fetch a bottle of cider from the butler's pantry, and we'll fend off starvation for the nonce."

Matilda found a quarter wheel of cheddar in chilly prox- imity to the window. She was slicing bread—thick enough to toast, not too thick to make sandwiches—when a small boy scooted into the kitchen from the hallway that led to the pantries.

"I was only resting for a moment, sir. The kitchen is ever- so-warm. I wasn't stealing nothing. I wouldn't steal when I already have everything I need, would I?"

The lad looked about eight years old to Matilda, though he could be older. The yeomanry did not enjoy regular nutrition, and their offspring were often stunted as a result. This young fellow was quivering between indignation and terror, and spared Matilda not even a glance.

Mr. Wentworth followed the child into the kitchen. "What's your name, boy?" He set a jug on the counter with an ominous *thunk*.

"J-Jinks, sir."

Mr. Wentworth put his hands on his hips. "Your *name*."

"Hiram Arthur Jingle, s-sir, but I wasn't—"

Mr. Wentworth waved a hand. "We'll need more bread than that, Miss Maddie. Jinks, wash your hands and be thorough with the soap or it will go badly for you."

The child shot to the copper sink and used an overturned bucket as a step stool. Water splashed while Matilda cut four more slices of bread.

"That's half the loaf, Mr. Wentworth. Cook will think an invading army has plundered her kitchen."

"That's a hungry boy, Miss Maddie. I'll see to the cheese."

Whoever the child was, he'd soon have a full belly. Hard to dislike a man who fed hungry children—and hungry women. Jinks set out plates and got down mugs while Mr. Wentworth supervised the cheese toast.

"This is college boy fare," Mr. Wentworth said, sliding a piece of bread dripping with melted cheese onto a plate. "Jinks, you will mind your manners. We've a lady at table with us."

Jinks was minding the cheese toast, his gaze fixed on the platter like a cat watching a mousehole. Matilda poured three servings of steaming mulled cider and brought them to the table, as the fragrance of cinnamon filled the kitchen.

"Miss Maddie." Mr. Wentworth held a chair.

She sat, though the moment was awkward. The boy was watching his employer, perhaps seeing for the first time how a gentleman held a chair for a lady.

Mr. Wentworth loomed over the boy. "Hands."

The child held up his hands, palms down.

"Other side."

The child obliged.

"We must acquaint you with a nail brush, Jinks. You can tell a lady by her hands. You can tell a lout by his even more easily. Sit."

Jinks scrambled into a chair, and the concussion of feet kicking at chair rungs followed.

Mr. Wentworth sliced each piece of toast across the middle, putting two triangles on Jinks's plate after he'd served Matilda.

"For what we are about to receive," Mr. Wentworth intoned, "we are grateful, even if Cook scolds us halfway to perdition in the morning. Jinks, bow your head. The toast will still be on your plate when the grace is concluded."

The child bowed his head.

"And should the Almighty see fit to bless our impromptu feast," Mr. Wentworth continued, "we hope that He will send an angel down the passage to have a look in on Mrs. Newbury, whose swift recovery would be the answer to many prayers. Amen."

The child darted a glance at Mr. Wentworth, but didn't touch the food until Matilda picked up a piece of her toast.

"Amen," she said, biting into a piece of heaven. The cheese was barely melted, the toast made from fresh bread warmed to perfection. "This is good."

How she had missed hot food. How she had missed sitting down to eat with others rather than cramming sustenance into her mouth as she dodged behind a hedge.

How she had missed spices, which turned mere cider into ambrosia.

Jinks slurped his drink and wiped his mouth on his sleeve, then went back to demolishing his toast.

Matilda expected Mr. Wentworth to scold the boy, or at least instruct him on the use of a table napkin, but Mr. Wentworth was consuming his own portion as if he sat down to supper with the boot boy regularly.

I studied for the church. Why hadn't he taken up that vocation—or had he?

Matilda ate in silence, trying to appreciate the food despite the impending interrogation from Mr. Wentworth. All too soon, the toast was gone, extra slices of bread and cheese had been wrapped in a napkin for Jinks, and the boy sent up the servants' stairs to his frigid quarters in the attic.

"Let's finish the cider, shall we?" Mr. Wentworth suggested when the food had been put away and the table swept free of crumbs. "Confession can be a thirsty undertaking."

"I have no sins to confess," Matilda said. "But I do wonder why, if you love children as much as I think you do, you are an itinerant bachelor who barely tolerates the company of his neighbors."

Mr. Wentworth divided the remaining cider between his mug and Matilda's. "You invite me to lead by example. Very well, but the tale is neither complicated nor pretty. Have a seat, and I'll find us a few biscuits."

* * *

"What the hell are we doing not five miles from where you nearly got me killed?" Herman Smith muttered.

Last week, they'd been Treachers. Sometimes they were Smiths. In Wales they tended to be Joneses. Up north,

Roberts, Taylor, or Brown would do. No matter the last name, Herman and Jeffrey always seemed to find themselves without funds, and in the path of winter and summer storms when only the meanest of accommodations were to be had.

"We are warm and comfortable," Jeffrey replied, swirling his pint. "Enjoying fine ale, flirting with the friendly tavern maids. Have another mug, Herm. Nobody's going anywhere until this snow melts."

Their money was going somewhere—straight into the pockets of mine greedy innkeeper. "Leave the women alone, Jeffy. They'll steal the coins you don't part with voluntarily."

Women were trouble. Herman's own mum had told him that, God rest her larcenous and often violent soul.

"This is snuggling weather," Jeffrey replied, lifting his tankard in the direction of a chubby maid with a saucy gaze. "Nothing wards off the chill like a wench."

The common room of the Drunken Duck was full of the usual storm refugees: a stranded coachload including a pair of inside dandies, a topside farm lad traveling into London to look for work now that the harvest was in, as well as the coachman, guard, and grooms. A foursome of young swells heading into the Midlands for foxhunting had kept the tavern maids hopping for the past two days, though the innkeeper had to be thrilled to have such custom at such a lowly hostelry.

"You might start a friendly game of whist with the young swells," Herman suggested. "They can afford to lose a bit of the ready. They've been at the cards for the past two nights."

"We don't get above ourselves," Jeffrey replied, quietly. "Bad enough you involved me in that little situation in the haunted woods. I'm not about to fleece four lordlings who've been fleecing each other for two straight days."

The haunted woods had not been Herman's fault. Any estate that had gone for years without the attentions of a proper gamekeeper was likely to be overrun with varmints, and snaring a few rabbits was purely in the way of public service.

Would that Brightwell was more than five scant miles away.

"What kind of woman pulls a gun on a pair of peaceable fellows like us?" Herman inquired of his empty tankard. "We never harmed nobody, and every rabbit meets with his eventual reward."

The skinny little woman with the gun was giving him nightmares. Bad enough the landowner had come stumbling by, but he hadn't been waving any firearms, hadn't raised a hue and cry over one wee rabbit.

"Forget the woman," Jeffrey replied, taking a sip of his ale and letting out a slow, froggy belch. "We got away, while she likely didn't fare as well."

"Whaddya mean?"

"She were underfed and twitchy. Her clothes were dusty and missing a few buttons. That was a woman with troubles. I'm guessing his worship added to her trouble after we so kindly left them their privacy."

"Maybe she added to his. She had the gun." Though now that Jeffrey remarked upon it, what was a woman *doing* with a loaded gun, alone, deep in the peaceful Berkshire countryside? No decent, sane female traipsed around a forest by herself.

Or brandished a weapon when she might have gone quietly about her business.

"On second thought, get the cards, Herm. It's late enough

the swells are the worse for drink. We'll start up a friendly game, you 'n' me, and them as wants to join in will be welcome."

"I thought you said—"

"Get the cards. If this snow doesn't soon melt, I'll be talking gibberish, and not because I've imbibed too much ale."

Herman got the cards.

Chapter Five

What to tell a woman who'd not surrendered even her full name?

Duncan raided the biscuit tin to the tune of a half dozen pieces of shortbread and brought them to the table. While Miss Maddie watched, he wrapped two pieces in her table napkin and passed them over.

"For later."

She held out the plate containing the remaining four pieces. "For now. You were kind to that boy."

"While I suspect life has not been kind to you." Duncan did not want her confidences, for secrets were a burden on all who kept them. He also did not want her secrets wrecking his attempts to set Brightwell to rights. The conundrum was irksome, while a late-night sweet shared with another was comforting.

"Life has been very good to me," Miss Maddie said,

nibbling the smallest piece. "I am in good health, I am at liberty, I have been well educated and seen much of the world, relative to many. What of yourself?"

Lead by example, one of the bishop's few admonitions that had been useful where Stephen was concerned.

"I was raised in straitened circumstances, though I was better off than most. My father took the king's shilling and promptly got shot for desertion. I have no memory of my mother. An uncle took me in. My aunt was a good woman who mitigated my uncle's harsh notions of discipline where she could."

That factual recitation brushed over nights spent locked out of the vicarage in bitter weather, meals set before a famished boy that he was not permitted to consume, blows to the head—those left no marks—without number, and knees so sore from kneeling to pray that Duncan still occasionally limped after overtaxing himself.

"Finish my cider," Miss Maddie said. "A little sweetness goes a long way."

Was she speaking metaphorically? Duncan poured the rest of her drink into his mug. "What else would you like to know?"

"You studied for the church?"

Studied was too genteel a word for the passion Duncan had brought to his training. "I did."

"Why?"

Always a thorny question. He stalled by dipping his shortbread into the hot, spicy cider. "I had seen the job of vicar done poorly. In my arrogance, I thought I'd have a better approach. I was wrong and never made it past my first curate's post. I enjoyed academics, enjoyed the company of my fellow students, enjoyed the notion that I might contribute something to a community eventually. When it came to being part of a congregation and supporting its leadership, I was not successful."

He'd been a raging failure.

"If I'd dipped my shortbread," Miss Maddie said, "it would have disintegrated all over the table and gone to waste."

Duncan dipped the shortbread again and held it out to her. She might not share her truths with him, but she could share a bite of humble goodness.

After an entirely too sober perusal of him, the shortbread, the shadows lurking in the corners of the kitchen, and perhaps her own conscience, Miss Maddie took the treat, nibbled off a small portion, and passed it back.

"Why did you leave the church?" she asked.

"I lacked a proper vocation." The bishop had said as much. *Examine your conscience, and you'll find that this might not be the path God has in mind for you.* "I had the skills necessary to instead become a schoolteacher, so I pursued that livelihood."

And had been a raging failure all over again, until Aunt—widowed, thank the timely intercession of the Almighty—had taken pity on him. Her generosity had arrived too late, or perhaps Duncan's pride had been the issue. He'd spent several years flogging himself with that question before becoming absorbed in Stephen's situation.

"Is any of this prosaic tale even true?" Miss Maddic asked. "I can understand a ducal family sending a younger son into the church, but allowing him to become a schoolteacher? They are an impoverished, overworked lot seldom held in any esteem."

Not by their so-called betters, but the esteem of the scholars was a more precious commodity. "The title came long after I'd left the church. I loved teaching. If I was patient and wily enough, I knew I could put some learning into the heads of the farmers' and tradesmen's children. That learning might make them a little safer, a little more successful than they'd be otherwise, a little harder to cheat and exploit. You are absolutely right, though: Teaching is one step above starvation in most villages."

That sad truth was the limit of what Duncan was willing to admit in an effort to win Miss Maddie's trust, and he'd managed not to lie outright.

Time for some turnabout. "So tell me, to the extent you can without violating confidences, how you come to be alone in the wilds of Berkshire at this time of year."

She gathered her shawls—two—and scooted on her seat, like a scholar preparing to recite. "I am widowed, and bad luck has me making my way home to Dorset."

Her air of self-possession suggested she might be widowed, and the bad luck was believable enough, which left Dorset for the falsehood.

"I haven't traveled much in Dorset recently," Duncan said. "I did spend some time there as a younger man. Whereabouts is your destination?"

"A small village on the coaching road south of Shaston."

Shaston did indeed enjoy a fair amount of coaching trade, something any map could have revealed to her.

"Such a pretty town, nestled in the shadows of such pretty hills. I suppose you've worshipped at St. Matthew's?"

More fussing about with the shawls. "Occasionally."

Duncan could accept her dissembling and let her go, for on the first fine day, she'd doubtless melt back into the woods where he'd found her.

Part of him would be relieved. He had an estate to set to rights, a house to restore, ledgers to sift through, and, time permitting, journals to edit. Sooner or later, some Wentworth or other would arrive—no need to send notice when ambushing family—and the whole business would become awkward and complicated.

Though how much more awkward and complicated to be a woman without means or defenses, alone in the English countryside? Compared to that situation, Duncan's concerns were trivialities.

He rose, rather than watch his guest squirm. "Miss Maddie, you are an inept liar. This is to your credit. The fifteenth-century church in Shaston is St. Peter's, and Shaston is one of few villages in Dorset to sit atop a high hill. You've never been there, and you don't seek to go there."

She bowed her head.

Duncan let the silence stretch. He'd learned to hold his tongue. Too late, at far too high a price, but he had acquired the skill.

"I am not wanted by the magistrates," she said, hunching her shoulders. "I haven't gained the notice of any thief takers."

But she clearly feared somebody. Duncan came around the table and took the seat next to her.

Wild creatures were said to have two impulses when faced with danger: one to flee, one to turn and fight. Some animals—rabbits, burros, cats—adopted a third choice. They became motionless, blending into their surroundings, barely breathing, hoping to become invisible to their foes.

Miss Maddie fit that description, remaining seated at the table, wrapped in her shawls and her silence. She doubtless longed to dodge off into the night, just as she longed to rail against Duncan's inquisition. He could feel that tension humming in her unspoken words and in her stillness.

He considered what puzzle pieces he had and connected them with logic and intuition, for the simple truth was, he did not want her to go. For her sake, he did not want her to be alone, battling the elements and God knew what foes with only a rusty pistol and a worn cape for protection.

And for his own sake, too, he longed for her to stay. Foolish of him, but he was no stranger to folly.

"If you are not fleeing the law per se," he said, "then you are either the victim of a crime or you have witnessed wrongdoing, and your safety is jeopardized as a result. Of the two, the latter is the more difficult posture, but in either case, you have nothing to fear from me."

He took her hand, tucked the table napkin containing the shortbread into her grasp, and closed her fingers about the sweets.

Her gaze put him in mind of the rabbit's, not the snared animal's blank acceptance of doom, but the bewildered gaze of a captive granted a reprieve.

"I will stay with Mrs. Newbury for the remainder of the evening," he said, lifting Miss Maddie's free hand in his own. "You will rest. We will speak further of your situation if, as, and when you decide the topic needs another airing."

He kissed her knuckles, set the warm cider at her elbow, and left her alone in the kitchen's cozy shadows.

* * *

In her toasty, curtained bed, Matilda had played chess games in her head as she'd tossed and turned. She'd twice risen to count her pieces of shortbread—four, because she'd taken all the remaining treats to her room. Before retiring, she'd also looked in on Mr. Wentworth and Mrs. Newbury.

The housekeeper had been sleeping peacefully—a very hopeful sign—and the master had been reading a French Psalter by the light of three candles.

What sort of woman was attracted to a tired man reading scripture in French late at night?

What sort of woman trusted that same man when he was so adept at catching her in her lies?

"I know the answers." Matilda could admit that to herself in the early-morning solitude of her pretty bedroom. "Any decent man will loom in my eyes as a hero, until, being decent and *English*, he writes to Papa and ruins everything."

She took a fortifying swallow of the tea Danvers had brought and rose, though no clever plan had occurred to her in the dark hours, no brilliant strategy for dealing with Mr. Wentworth. If she told him what had sent her onto the king's highway in the dead of night, he'd be implicated and guilty by association.

If she fled the safety of Brightwell she'd be dead by spring, and Atticus Parker would never even know her fate.

Her disappearance likely didn't trouble him much from a sentimental perspective, but his pride was doubtless smarting. Ye gods, what an idiot she'd been.

She set her tea tray on the sideboard in her sitting room, collected her shawls, and made her way through the frigid corridors to the little parlor where she'd first taken sustenance at Brightwell earlier in the week. The day was brilliant, as only a sunny day on a snow-covered landscape could be, and thus the stairway, while cold, was flooded with sunlight.

Matilda paused outside the dining parlor, heart thumping for no reason. Why should the prospect of an informal meal fill her with nearly as much trepidation as a night spent in the open countryside had?

"Good morning." Mr. Wentworth rose from his seat at the head of the table. He did not smile—did he ever smile?—but he did hasten to close the door behind Matilda and lead her to the place set at his left hand. The hearth held a wood fire that crackled merrily, counterpointing the dripping from the eaves beyond the window.

Had Mr. Wentworth ordered that place set for her for the past several days, only to be left to a solitary meal?

"I trust you slept well?" he asked, putting the teapot by her plate.

"As well as can be expected. How is Mrs. Newbury?"

He held Matilda's chair for her, a courtesy that had upset her the previous evening and upset her all over in the morning light.

"Mrs. Newbury passed a fairly peaceful night, though fevers plagued her in the small hours. She permitted me to read to her in French, suggesting a constitution of considerable fortitude. A maid is sitting with her now."

The scents of bacon and toast would likely always have the power to intoxicate Matilda, so substantial were they. A woman in hiding didn't cook bacon lest a passerby detect the scent. A woman in a hurry never bothered to build a fire merely to toast her stale bread.

"Would you care for some eggs?" Mr. Wentworth asked.

No footman guarded a laden sideboard, no maid bustled about replenishing the tea or the toast rack. The meal was set out on the table *à la française*, with warming trays keeping the omelet, bacon, and ham hot.

"Eggs would be lovely, but not too much. I need to save room for my buttered toast."

Mr. Wentworth served her a modest portion, then did the same for himself. He set the butter dish beside her teacup. "Where does this morning find you regarding my travelogues?"

Matilda buttered her toast, thoroughly but not gluttonously, and nattered on about Pompeii and Napoleon's plundering of ancient treasures, even though she knew every detail she shared, every comment she made, revealed a glimpse of her past.

A glimpse of *her*.

She'd come down to breakfast prepared to answer in some fashion the questions Mr. Wentworth had posed last night: Who are you? What or whom are you fleeing? He'd never voiced those specific queries, but he had invited her to answer them.

And he'd half answered them himself: *You are either the victim of a crime or you have witnessed wrongdoing, and your safety is jeopardized as a result.*

Matilda had chattered her way to an empty plate plus a second serving of eggs before she realized that Mr. Wentworth would not renew last night's interrogation. He'd said they'd speak again at the time of her choosing, and he'd meant what he'd said.

Exactly what he'd said.

He'd finished his tea and patted his lips with his table napkin before Matilda found the courage to attempt the topic.

"How did you know?"

He'd half risen, and settled slowly back into his seat. "How did I know that you were the victim of wrongdoing or the witness to it, rather than the perpetrator?"

She nodded, grateful for the closed door, even as the sound of the snowmelt trickling from the eaves plucked at her nerves. Cold alone was dangerous, but cold and wet was a deadly combination.

"Logic," Mr. Wentworth said. "In a sense, the witness to a crime has no good options. Confessing the knowledge turns the witness into the criminal's sworn foe. Ignoring the knowledge burdens the witness's conscience and makes the witness an accomplice. Nobody benefits from an involuntary relationship with a criminal. Shall I ring for another pot of tea?"

His tone was detached, and the morning sunshine revealed the man he'd become in middle age. A handsome face would shade toward distinguished, gray would dust his temples. He'd still be attractive, at least to a woman who valued gravitas, decency, and learning.

"No more tea, thank you," Matilda said. "I want you to know something."

He waited. Just that, while Matilda peered into the dregs of her cup and prayed she wasn't making a serious mistake— another serious mistake.

"I agreed to accept a certain man's matrimonial addresses. The man who sought my hand in marriage turned out to be less appealing than I'd thought him to be. I was preparing to cry off, but he's well connected, while I am...My position was delicate."

The colonel was a decorated war hero, a marquess's spare. He was a good catch, possibly even a good man, but Matilda could not marry him.

Mr. Wentworth gently pried Maddie's empty teacup from her grasp. "Did you sign any settlement papers?"

"No, I did not. The discussions hadn't progressed that far. Perhaps my father signed papers, but I was never presented with any agreements." She was a widow and should have signed any agreements on her own behalf. "Why?"

"Then, madam, you are truly no longer engaged if you don't wish to be. No suit for alienation of affections can arise from my offer of employment, and your former follower has no legal authority over you. No date was set, and you have simply cried off, as is a lady's right."

Matilda hadn't been sure what the legal ramifications were for a failed engagement in England, but she trusted Mr.

Wentworth's assessment. Atticus had never quite proposed. He'd assumed that permission to pay Matilda his addresses had been consent to marry.

"You relieve my mind," she said. "Though I still dare not return to my family."

"Then you must remain here at Brightwell as long as you please. I haven't time to see to my journals, while you have both time and the ability to make them more presentable. If you'll excuse me, my gamekeeper has decreed that I must be harangued about our management of pheasants. If I fail to appear for supper, you may conclude that I have died of stupefaction, for Mr. Hefner is a loquacious soul."

He bowed over her hand—such a warm grasp he had—and, once again, left Matilda alone.

She helped herself to a crispy slice of bacon, holding it to her nose before taking a bite. Something about her exchange with Mr. Wentworth didn't sit well. She'd not lied, but she'd not nearly explained the whole situation to him.

He knew that.

She was reaching for a second piece of bacon when insight struck. Mr. Wentworth also knew what it was to be the victim of or the witness to a crime. Logic might eventually have revealed to him why Matilda was in flight, but experience had allowed him to leap to that conclusion.

And then Matilda knew something else: His tale of studying for the church and finding a vocation in the classroom also wasn't a lie.

Neither was it the whole explanation of his situation, not nearly.

* * *

For two days, Duncan buried himself in physical labor when he couldn't escape the carping of his gamekeeper, his tenants, or his conscience. The staff left him more or less alone, but then, they had Miss Maddie to occupy them.

Duncan groomed his horse to a high shine, knowing the contrary beast would roll in the first available patch of mud—and the second.

He shoveled snow from the garden walkways, creating a circular path in case nobody in particular needed an idle outing in the frigid sunshine.

He shoved trunks around in the attic to better organize the enormous framed portraits stacked by the dozen, then assisted the footmen to haul the paintings down to the long gallery from whence they'd been taken. Some of the ancestors bore a resemblance to the present crop of Wentworths—height, brown hair, blue eyes—but none of them wore a priest's collar.

Neither did Duncan, though he sometimes woke in the night struggling to breathe, as if the noose of holy orders remained about his neck. That was Miss Maddie's fault, of course. A woman without protection, one victimized by circumstances, was salt in old wounds.

"What the hell are you doing?"

Stephen Wentworth stood in the doorway to the gallery, leaning on the jamb, a stout cane in his left hand. He made an elegant picture in his aristocratic attire, though Duncan knew the casual posture cost him.

"The expeditionary force has arrived. What took you so long?"

Stephen moved into the room at the slow, uneven pace that was the limit of his abilities on foot. "Damned English weather. Quinn and Jane send their love, Ned says hello, and, good lord, what a homely fellow the third duke was. Puts me in mind of you."

"He was a soldier, away from home for years at a time."

"A wanderer, like me," Stephen said, peering more closely at His Grace, "and like you. How are you getting on?"

Trust Stephen to exhibit not a scintilla of tact. "I'm furious."

His lordship smiled, leaving no doubt as to which Wentworth had inherited the family's entire complement of charm.

"The stable lads remarked as much to the gardener, who heard the same sentiment from the footmen, and they were in agreement with the gamekeeper. Our Mr. Wentworth is in a right taking o'er summat."

Duncan spared a moment to solve the puzzle, for Stephen had likely ridden up Brightwell's drive less than fifteen minutes ago.

"You came in through the kitchen because the front lane hasn't been shoveled. You overheard the boots—Jinks—or the maids, or both in conversation with an under-footman or scullery maid."

"The housekeeper is apparently on bedrest recovering from an illness, else I'm sure the staff would have been less inclined to gossip. What has you in a swither?"

For all his charm, Stephen had also inherited a Wentworth's portion of tenacity.

"This place." *And that woman.* "You're in time for dinner, and the fire in the family parlor is kept lit. Let's leave Their Graces for the nonce and you can interrogate me in private." Until Miss Maddie joined them, not that Stephen would exercise much discretion before a lady.

"Have you missed me?" Stephen asked, leading the way into the corridor. "I've missed you. Nobody to lecture me about the history of every village I pass through or every vintage I have sent up from the wine cellar. Nobody to cast a pall of gloom over every weather report. Your dour nature is soothingly predictable."

"While your company is a circle of purgatory not even the denizens of Newgate would choose over incarceration."

To appearances, Stephen was merry, irreverent, and thick-skinned. Closer acquaintance, which had taken Duncan years to achieve, revealed a brilliant young man plagued by bouts of melancholia and in constant physical pain.

"You have missed me," Stephen observed, as they processed down the hallway. "You might have sent a fellow a note: *Dear Lord Purgatory: In over my head with this estate management nonsense. Plato's wisdom unavailing. Make haste to my side. My love to your horse, Cousin Dunderpate.*"

"When I walk beside you, I am forced by the decorous pace you set to notice my surroundings," Duncan said. "That deal table, for example, is probably three hundred years old. Some wealthy merchant lusting for acceptance among the squires will pay good money for it."

Stephen thumped past the table in question. "We can make an inventory in order of ugliness. You should be glad Quinn and Jane didn't come with me. I had a devil of a time convincing them not to break out the traveling coach."

Duncan waited at the top of the steps while Stephen got his cane organized into his right hand so he could grasp the bannister with his left. If Stephen's physical progress through life was slower than that of other men, his mental progress outpaced a swift on the wing.

"Quinn and Jane would never travel this time of year with the baby," Duncan said. "I trust Artemis is in good health?" The question was carefully timed for when Stephen had to watch every step, the better to spare Duncan's dignity.

"Little bugger is fat and jolly. Jane has to instruct Quinn

on the need to maintain some dignity in the nursery, or our duke would spend all his time singing lullabies and reading fairy tales. Could this house be any colder, Duncan?"

"This is balmy compared to three days ago. How's the leg?" Another question timed to preserve the dignity of all concerned.

"It reaches the floor," Stephen said. "No better, no worse. I'll not be leaving you until the weather has cleared up. Snow and ice are the very devil, and mud is no improvement."

Even rain made Stephen's life more difficult. "You are welcome for as long as you care to remain. I honestly have no idea how to go on with the estate business, which Quinn ought to have realized before he devised my penance."

"I'll teach you what you need to know," Stephen said, rounding the landing. "Money comes in, money goes out. The object of the game is to bring more in than you send out."

"Thank you for that penetrating insight. Though how do you determine whether the sums reported by your stewards, tenants, farmers, and factors are accurate, and not the result of some creative accounting which they've had ten years to put in place?"

"You suspect fraud?"

"For God's sake, Stephen. Brightwell was a lamb to slaughter when the old duke's faculties failed. The house staff is trustworthy, but I can smell the speculation from my land steward. Everybody from the dairyman to the game-keeper to the swineherd is waiting to see whether I'm wise to their schemes."

Stephen started down the next flight. "You apparently are. What will you do about it?"

"Shovel snow, groom my horse, wrestle portraits." *Fret about Miss Maddie.*

"And your efforts to date have solved nothing."

"If I sack the swindlers working for me now, a new lot of swindlers will take their places. I need only make this place profitable for one year, and I'm free to go about my business."

The stairwell became colder as they descended, and because the sun was setting, the way also became darker.

"Quinn knew exactly what a fouled-up situation he was dumping into my lap," Duncan went on. "Why would he do this, Stephen? I'm nobody's fiscal conscience, nor do I want to be."

"Jane put him up to it," Stephen said. "She's *his* conscience. Next year, when you're too decrepit to spend the winter in Vienna, you'll be glad you set your household to rights. The place has good bones."

Miss Maddie had said as much. Miss Maddie, whom Duncan had been avoiding, and who was not from Dorset.

"I have hired an amanuensis," Duncan said as they approached the family parlor. "Somebody to edit my journals and see to my correspondence." Miss Maddie could assist with his correspondence, if he asked her to.

"Your handwriting defeats even my powers of divination," Stephen said. "Though a good secretary can learn almost anybody's penmanship. Where did you find such a paragon? Is he another disillusioned parson with a permanent squint?"

The door to the family parlor opened, and Miss Maddie stood before them in her two shawls.

"No," Duncan said. "You are as usual in error. Miss Maddie, may I make known to you my cousin, Lord Stephen Wentworth. I comfort myself with the knowledge that our connection is at some remove. Lord Stephen, Miss Maddie. Behave in her presence or I'll break your sound leg."

Stephen bowed with the support of his cane and came up flashing the smile that was still the subject of swoons in Paris.

"Miss Maddie, pleased to make your acquaintance. What did you ever, ever do to deserve a sentence of hard labor with Cousin Duncan?"

The lady curtsied. "I consider myself fortunate to have my post, my lord. Mr. Wentworth, shall I leave you and your guest privacy at dinner?"

She clearly wanted to. She wanted to bolt from the room and probably from the house. "Lord Stephen's feelings would be hurt if you declined to join us, and I would be subjected to a meal in tedious company. You must not think of leaving."

Maddie stepped back, admitting them into the warmth of the parlor. She made polite conversation about the weather and she laughed at Stephen's flirtations, but Duncan caught her glancing at the darkness gathering beyond the window.

She was thinking of leaving. She was always thinking of leaving, and he must not forget that, ever.

Which also made him furious.

Chapter Six

"Your cousin is friendly," Matilda said, shoving the treatise on Italian farming back between the wonders of Sicily and the challenges of a Venetian winter.

Mr. Wentworth tapped the blunt end of his pencil against the desk blotter. "A life largely confined to a wheeled chair has developed in Stephen the need to charm people to his side. You favor the verb 'to hare' as in to hare about."

The next essay Matilda came to was on Pompeii, which had struck Mr. Wentworth as sad, a graveyard desecrated by morbid curiosity rather than sanctified by respect for the tragedy that had formed it. Matilda agreed, but hadn't been able to name her emotions about the place until she'd read his treatise.

"You will edit out my excesses, I'm sure," she said. "To racket about, travel, career, journey, sojourn, make haste...the synonyms abound."

"You are down to one shawl today."

She pulled the shawl closer, as if that might prevent Mr. Wentworth from inspecting her.

In the week since Lord Stephen's arrival, Matilda had enjoyed relative peace. His lordship bantered with Mr. Wentworth at the dinner table, rather like a puppy teasing an old hound. The old hound tolerated the fussing and could occasionally be jollied into a tail thump or two, but the game was mostly played by the youthful contender.

Lord Stephen and Mr. Wentworth had ridden out to call on tenants when the snow had partly melted, and closeted themselves in Mr. Wentworth's sitting room with ledgers and an abacus on the drearier days. When Matilda happened to pass that doorway, which she did several times a day, the steady click of beads and soft murmur of voices assured her that work was in progress.

"This office is cozy," Matilda said. "My other shawl is draped over the back of your chair."

She was coming to think of this room as her domain, which was most unwise. She worked here, nothing more. Daily, she resolved to leave once the household was abed. Each night she found a reason to put off her departure. Clouds obscuring the moon, a cutting wind, a sky that threatened more snow…But the most tempting reason to stay was seated at the desk.

Mr. Wentworth leaned forward to free the shawl hanging on the chair, took a sniff of the bunched-up wool, and then wrapped it about himself.

"Damned window gives off a chill."

"You could sit closer to the fire." Matilda loved to sit by the fire, candles gathered near, while reading Mr. Wentworth's discourse on some exotic city. He had a knack for noticing details—how the ducks in Austria quacked versus the ducks in Hyde Park—that charmed her more than Lord Stephen's smiles and wordplay ever would.

"If I sat closer to the fire, I would be in your way, and if there's one aspect of domestic life that I cannot abide, it's a fussing female."

Matilda paged through the treatise that covered the scenic and tedious journey from Venice to Vienna. Mr. Wentworth had a tendency to leave correspondence between the pages of his treatises, as well as receipts, scrawled notes, and other mementos of his travels.

"I quite agree," she said. "A fussing female is far more irksome than a fussing male. The fussing male usually only fusses—noise, grumbling, harrumphing, and the like. The fussing female is often engaged in a task while she fusses. The compounded annoyance, of fussing and activity, can drive one to Bedlam."

Matilda had yet to find a love letter stashed between the leaves of Mr. Wentworth's journals. His would be short and to the point: *Please be advised that the author of this epistle holds the receiver thereof in high regard. W.*

"What have you there?" he asked, rising.

"The journey from Venice to Vienna, where Lord Stephen learned from the wagon master how to curse in German."

"It's more accurate to say Lord Stephen taught the wagon master to curse in English. I took some editorial license for the benefit of my English audience."

He truly did see these journals as one day being published, but apparently hadn't done anything to achieve that objective, which was a loss for the reading public.

"When I'm through with the south of France, I'll start your Italian essays." *If I'm still here.*

Mr. Wentworth peered over Matilda's shoulder. He was tall enough to do that, which should have made her nervous, though it did exactly the opposite. Matilda was less nervous when he was on hand and accomplished more on the days when he didn't ride out. Her food settled more easily when she took her meals with him, and she'd learned to distinguish his footfalls on the carpets and stairs from everybody else's.

"I'll put Vienna up here," he said, taking the treatise and reaching above her head. "The German capitals being of less interest than the Italian. Italy is cheaper, and to most traveling abroad, that matters."

"How goes the war with the ledger books?" she asked.

Matilda could sidle along the bookshelves and put distance between herself and Mr. Wentworth, and a week ago she might have. Now, she wanted to re-tie his cravat, for either he or his manservant had left the knot off center.

"Stephen has a head for figures," Mr. Wentworth said, gathering his shawl. "I am competent with numbers, but I don't enjoy them. More to the point, I know exactly what the finances will reveal. In the usual fashion, my steward has over-procured everything from fence posts to harness leather. Mr. Trostle sells the excess for cash to the small-holders, who know they're getting a better price than the sawmill or tanner will give them.

"The steward then claims the inventory has been used on the Brightwell estate," he went on, "which assertion is impossible to contradict. My dairyman sells a dozen weanlings and records only eighty percent of the revenue realized, and so on and so forth."

Schemes such as these were so prevalent as to be regarded by some as a perquisite of senior employment in a large English household. The lines of integrity were blurred by custom: Housekeepers were often entitled to the unburnt ends of wax candles, butlers to the empty wine bottles.

Housekeepers were thus tempted to change candles more frequently than necessary, while butlers opened more bottles of wine than were needed to accommodate a meal. The excess was consumed belowstairs rather than allowed to go to waste, and life went on.

If the land steward was that obvious about his graft, though, then Mr. Wentworth needed to put a petty king in check.

"Make an example," Matilda said. "Drop by the lumber-yard where the fence posts were purchased, ask the merchant for his version of the transaction. Do the same with the tanner, and then confront your steward before witnesses— Lord Stephen and a pair of footmen will do nicely. Your dairyman will give notice within a fortnight."

Matilda's hands were in motion before she'd given them leave, and they reached for Mr. Wentworth's cravat. He stilled, like a wild creature focusing on approaching footsteps. And yet, he tolerated her re-tying his neckcloth, even to the moment when she centered the plain gold pin anchoring the whole.

A man with eyes that blue should have a sapphire pin, even for everyday.

"You have no husband at present," Mr. Wentworth said, shifting to regard himself in the glass-fronted bookcase near the sideboard. "But you had a father or brother whom you regarded with some affection, or perhaps a husband gone to his reward. Nicely done."

"I like order." Matilda craved order, now especially. "I apologize for presuming, but you were off center."

He swirled her shawl from his shoulders and settled it over hers. The gesture was as graceful as a dancer's and much more alluring.

"That I am," he said, "off center. The condition is of long standing. You needn't trouble yourself over it."

He remained before her, his hands holding the hems of her shawl. If he tugged, she'd step closer, and she'd do so willingly.

"Onward to Vienna," he said, moving toward the door. "I'm thinking of hiring an under-steward."

"A trainee, before you sack the crook you have now. Shrewd. An assistant dairyman hired at the same time would attract less notice."

"Though paying double wages will take a toll." He paused by the door to look around the office, which was an altogether lighter, tidier place than it had been when Matilda had arrived. She'd also prevailed on the staff to equip the room with lavender sachets to discourage bugs, and had the carpets beaten halfway to...Dorset.

"You mentioned that Lord Stephen is friendly," Mr. Wentworth said. "I have instructed him that utmost discretion is necessary regarding your presence at Brightwell."

"Thank you." Matilda hadn't known how to raise that topic.

Mr. Wentworth's expression shifted, becoming even more severe than usual. "If Lord Stephen's friendliness ever approaches the point where you feel burdened or threatened, you will apply to me immediately."

Lord Stephen was a flirt, but as Mr. Wentworth had pointed out, his lordship was a flirt who could not give physical chase. He could reveal a woman's secrets in the churchyard, though, a thought that had kept Matilda awake at night.

"If his lordship should overstep, what would you do?"

"Break his arms, then put him in a coach for London with instructions never to return upon pain of death." *Arms* plural, and Mr. Wentworth was in earnest.

Matilda crossed the room and kissed his cheek. "Thank

you. That is the most charming expression of gentlemanly regard I have ever received."

He slipped out the door before she could make an even greater fool of herself.

* * *

The snow was melting, which Duncan took for a false dawn before winter blossomed into full nuisance-hood. Mud for Stephen was more than a nuisance, though his lordship loved to be on horseback.

"The sunshine feels good," Stephen said. "That doesn't change whether we're in Sardinia, Copenhagen, or god-forsaken Berkshire."

The morning was winter-bright and winter-cold, but, as Stephen had said, the sunshine was a benevolence on Duncan's exposed cheeks and brow. Like the kiss of a woman who did not bestow affection casually.

"Why don't you have your own sawmill?" Stephen asked. "You've trees enough."

"I suspect Brightwell still has its hedges, groves, and forests because stealing lumber cannot be done subtly. Had my steward taken down a hedgerow of elms, the theft would have been obvious to all, and the proceeds hard to disburse when lumber must season before being sold."

As a consequence, the home wood was large and overgrown, the hedgerows wide and equally unkempt, and the game abundant. No wonder poachers had been attracted to the property.

"You like that your manor house hides within a forest primeval," Stephen said. "If I visit again next year, I'll find vines choking the drive and ivy enshrouding your windows. I do wonder if I'll find Miss Maddie tucked away with you here as well."

"Ask her and I will toss you from one of those windows. She is not to be pestered by your curiosity or by your wandering hands, Stephen."

Though Maddie's hands on Duncan had felt . . . he searched for words, rummaging around in French and German before resorting to English: delightful, soothing, upsetting, presuming, *good*.

She had fussed with him as women tidy their menfolk, part admonition, part affection, like the tap of the sword on a knight's shoulder in the accolade ceremony. For those moments, holding still so she could straighten his cravat, Duncan's mind had been empty of thoughts. He'd been a purring tomcat, purely enjoying physical closeness to a comely female.

Enjoying being cared about personally, however mundane the expression of that caring.

"They will ask about your Miss Maddie," Stephen said. "The sisters, Quinn, and Jane. Even Bitty likes to know what's afoot with Cousin Duncan."

Bitty—Elizabeth—was Jane and Quinn's eldest, a busy little sprite of five. Duncan adored her, despite her tendency to climb on his person, investigate his pockets, and demand stories by the dozen.

"Stephen, you will respect my confidences where Miss Maddie is concerned or you will no longer be welcome in my house. Whether I am employing a female amanuensis, a French under-gardener, or three running footmen from darkest Peru is nobody's concern but my own."

Stephen's horse came to a halt and lifted its tail. "So she's a damsel in distress." Stephen rose in his stirrups and leaned forward while equine flatulence joined the morning breezes. "Duncan's damsel in distress. How can I possibly keep that miracle to myself?"

The horse resumed its plodding.

"You taught yourself to walk," Duncan said, "when every physician in London claimed the cause was hopeless. Surely you can manage to maintain silence on one very dull topic."

Stephen changed the subject to the various trees flourishing on Brightwell's acres, until Duncan drew his horse up in the sawmill's main yard. The place reeked of mud and the pungent tang of cut lumber. The morning air was punctuated with male voices singing to the rhythm of the saws about a frog marrying a mouse.

"Why did we travel all over the Continent," Stephen murmured, "when we could have instead enjoyed the many wonders of nearby Berkshire?"

They'd traveled for different reasons. To prove that Stephen's disability was an inconvenience, not a death sentence. To broaden their minds. To escape the increasing respectability of Quinn and Jane's household, and all the domesticating that went with it.

Also to put distance between Duncan and the past.

"Morning, gentlemen," a large, blond fellow said. "Tobias Pepper, at your service."

Duncan touched his hat and remained in the saddle. "Duncan Wentworth, late of Brightwell, and my cousin, Lord Stephen Wentworth."

"Plymouth!" Mr. Pepper shouted. "Take the horses for the fine gentlemen."

If somebody took the horses, then Stephen would have to dismount. He rode with his canes affixed to the saddle by means of a leather scabbard such as soldiers used for a rifle or sword. Even with a pair of canes, heavy muck was slow, uncertain going.

Stephen kicked his feet from the stirrups and slid down the horse's side, meaning Duncan was to do likewise.

"Always a pleasure to meet a new neighbor," Pepper said. "Heard you was come to Brightwell. Fine old property like that needs tending."

Pepper's observation held more curiosity than reproach. Would Pepper and Brightwell's steward transact more business? Would Brightwell open its own sawpit? What exactly prompted members of the ducal family to call upon the mill owner in person?

"You have a fine property too," Stephen said, doing his impression of the Eager Young Lord. "Have you considered installing a circular saw?"

If an invention had been patented, Stephen knew of it. If the military was designing a new weapon, Stephen often sent them critiques of the proposed features. Circular saws powered by steam were popular among the Dutch, and the Americans were using them too. The navy had a few, though such modern machinery had yet to find its way into the countryside.

"The circular saws make a damned lot of noise, your lordship," Pepper replied. "Pardon my language. My men are hard workers and we turn out good lumber."

"Your men can turn out a dozen boards a day, assuming they're working elm or ash," Stephen replied. "The circular saws can turn out two hundred boards a day, even working oak."

Duncan was about to send Stephen the "stop showing off" look, except Stephen wasn't merely displaying his head for facts and figures. He was putting Pepper on the defensive, a possible prerequisite to obtaining honest answers.

"If your worship is considering opening a sawpit and getting one of them fancy saws, isn't that a discussion to be had with Mr. Trostle?"

"My steward is otherwise occupied this morning," Duncan

said. "If you can spare us a few minutes in your office, I'd like to put some matters to you directly."

The singing stopped—a cat had devoured both the frog and the mouse, though first the couple had spoken their vows—and only the rhythmic whine of a saw continued.

"My office is around to the side," Pepper replied with the air of a boy who knows exactly how a trip to the woodshed will end.

The conversation confirmed what Duncan had suspected: Trostle was a thief, and not a very bright one. Pepper knew what had become of the fence posts he'd sold to Trostle at a fair price, because the yeomen who'd bought them from Trostle had bragged in the village pub of their bargain. Those same neighbors didn't dare alert Duncan to the scheme, or they'd be buying their lumber at Pepper's higher prices.

"And what you hear in the pub," Stephen said, climbing onto his horse twenty minutes later, "is bound to be more reliable than anything you hear in the churchyard."

"Or from the pulpit," Duncan muttered. "Trostle is also selling our honey, cheese, flowers, and kitchen produce." Mrs. Newbury had passed that much along in innuendos and asides. "The London distributors give him two receipts. One for my books, one for his own. She's seen them transacting business on market days."

Stephen sheathed his cane in its scabbard, and if anybody thought it peculiar that Stephen used the lady's mounting block, they knew better than to say so.

"How can you even consider allowing Trostle to remain in your employ?" Stephen asked. "He's relying on Mrs. Newbury to keep his secrets, implicating her by silence, and doubtless threatening her position with a few casual remarks. I hate Trostle and I've not even met him."

The singing from the sawpit resumed, this time a tale

about walking hand in hand out past the lea rig, where, according to the lyrics, activities other than ploughing or herding were on the couple's agenda.

"Trostle is likeable," Duncan said. "The best villains usually are."

"And you don't want to sack him? I'll sack him. Turn Miss Maddie loose on him and he'll be gone before noon."

Her again. She nestled in Duncan's thoughts like a friendly kitten, always finding the warmest, softest places to bide.

"Stephen, if you think to pry from me the secrets of her past, the exercise is pointless. I don't know her secrets and I don't wish to know them. She is under my protection, as any member of my household is, but that doesn't entitle me to invade her privacy."

Or her bedroom, though she'd invaded Duncan's dreams. In the deep quiet of the night, he felt her kiss on his cheek, softer than the winter sunshine, warmer and more welcome. Why had she done that? Why had she given him—a man she barely knew—such an unmistakable sign of approval and affection?

"Yours is the minority view among Wentworths," Stephen said. "To a Wentworth, privacy is like the pretty paper hiding a gift, there to be torn aside. Though if in five years of sharing coaches, inns, meals, and scenic views with you, I haven't found the key to tearing aside your infernal silence, then I can't expect to make much progress with Miss Maddie, can I?"

"Don't try, Stephen. A confidence should be offered, never compelled."

And that was what her kiss had been—a confidence. Duncan's mind should have been eased to have put the right term to the gesture, but like Stephen confronted with a prettily wrapped gift, Duncan's curiosity was only enflamed.

"Sometimes, a confidence is offered without the confider knowing it," Stephen replied. "We're in for more snow."

"And with Yuletide mere weeks away. What a shocking departure from the norm."

"We're in for more snow by this time tomorrow. Might I build a lift at Brightwell? The back stairs will have smaller landings if we implement the design I have in mind, but large landings don't serve much purpose. I can install some dumb waiters, too, the kind that bring items up from the kitchen by using a lift in a cupboard. You could do with some laundry chutes as well."

No, Duncan did not need laundry chutes, but anything that resulted in less use of stairways was of interest to Stephen.

"I suppose your modernizations will make the place easier to sell," Duncan groused. "Do your worst, but keep accurate records. Quinn will likely have Mrs. Hatfield go over my books before he admits I haven't made this place profitable."

"I'd sooner meet Wellington over pistols than have Mrs. Hatfield nosing about my ledgers. I know the bank needs a competent auditor, but that woman takes a missing penny as proof of felony motives."

Duncan liked Mrs. Hatfield, though he wondered where she'd come by her accounting skills. "I would rather miss a few pence than deny you the joy of your little projects. You are quarrelsome when bored, and I treasure my peace."

Stephen's little projects always became major, noisy, messy undertakings—also expensive—but they made him happy and made his life easier. If turning Stephen loose redesigning the back stairs made Quinn's challenge harder to meet, well, Duncan hadn't expected to succeed, and this morning's outing only made the prospect more daunting.

"You should sack Trostle," Stephen said, as the horses slogged through a particularly long set of mud puddles. "Sack him now."

Stephen was right, of course. "You offered that opinion previously."

"Think of it this way: If you allow him to continue his pilfering and petty tyranny over the staff, you are worse than he is, leaving a thief to run your estate and encourage more larceny. A competent fellow of spotless moral character is on hand to do the job, and he will attract others of similar integrity."

"Do you refer to yourself?"

Stephen turned his face to the sky, where clouds were trying to crowd out the sun to the west. "You aren't even jesting. I refer to *you*, Cousin Dunderpate. You don't lie, you don't pry, you don't engage in fisticuffs when you know you could lay the other fellow out flat with one punch. You probably don't even want to know that Miss Maddie's last name is Wakefield."

Stephen rode on, as if that revelation was on the order of a missing jar of jam having been found.

"Stephen, if you've been sneaking about, putting the servants up to sneaking about, or in any way—"

He held up a gloved hand. "How you wound my tender spirit. In the first place, I wouldn't admit to sneaking about, if one of my lurching gait could be said to sneak. In the second, I didn't have to. I was quibbling over a line of scripture, and Miss Maddie fetched her Book of Common Prayer, your library having none to offer. I happened to notice her name inscribed in the front, and a date of birth. She was christened at St. Andrew's, Holborn. She's twenty-eight, by the way. Nearly doddering, though not so venerable as you."

"This is what you meant, about confiding without meaning

to." Every child was given a Book of Common Prayer by a doting godparent, auntie, or vicar. Even Uncle Victor had given Duncan a copy, a fine, sizeable version suitable for a vicar's nephew.

"Precisely. If Miss Maddie didn't want me to know her last name—truly, truly did not want me to know—she would not have passed the book into my hands."

Not so. People slipped, they mis-stepped, they grew weary and careless. Sometimes.

"You will tell no one," Duncan said. "You will forget whatever you glimpsed or thought you saw. A prayer book is highly personal and likely one of few possessions she values."

Stephen turned his horse up the Brightwell driveway, another expanse of muck, ruts, and mud bordered by dirty melting snow.

"I've already forgotten that her last name is Wakefield, her mother's name was Delores Gunning, and her father's name is Thomas Wakefield."

Maddie had people. Duncan had assumed so, but knowing their names did not ease his worry. The worst betrayals came from the closest ties.

"Right," Duncan said. "Forget the lot of it, unless you also saw her middle name. That you may forget as soon as you tell me what it is."

Chapter Seven

A tactical retreat was called for, though Colonel Lord Atticus Parker had to give notice of the retreat to his quarry—his other quarry. Searching for Matilda while keeping a close eye on her father had become a complicated undertaking.

"You're off to the shires to foxhunt in this weather?" Wakefield asked.

Parker poured himself a cup of tea. Wakefield served an exquisitely aromatic China black that was cause on its own to pay a call.

"To a soldier, weather is immaterial, though boredom is a constant foe. Racketing about the Midlands in pursuit of vermin passes the time."

Wakefield used a delicate pair of silver tongs to drop a lump of sugar into his own cup. "Have you descended to crude innuendo where your former fiancée is concerned, Colonel?" Wakefield's tone was mild, his manner pleasant, as always.

"My *former* fiancée? Has Matilda corresponded with you, communicating news I should be aware of?"

Wakefield used the sugar tongs to set a tea cake on Parker's plate, though Parker didn't care for sweets.

"If her actions don't make her position on the matter of marriage to you apparent, then a full-page ad in the *Times* would be unavailing. Unless you'd have me believe the press gangs are now stealing the widows of German dukes, she left this household of her own volition."

No press gang would willingly tangle with Matilda Wakefield, known on the Continent as Matilda, Dowager Duchess of Bosendorf.

"Have you ruled out a foreign government taking an interest in her?" Parker asked. "She accompanied her husband to various pumpernickel courts, attended all manner of social events, and called upon diplomats and influential people without number. Perhaps her former in-laws have decided she was privy to too many state secrets. She also traveled with you from her girlhood on and saw much even before her marriage."

Almost all of which she recalled, if what she'd seen had been in print or handwriting. She had that sort of mind, but was less accurate with spoken words, thank heavens.

Wakefield took a leisurely sip of his tea and set down the cup and saucer with an equal lack of haste.

"Most children who've lost their mothers end up in their father's care," he said. "I could not trust servants to tend to a grieving girl in my absence, and Matilda seemed to enjoy the travel. As for her in-laws, German dukes are thick on the ground, though in point of fact, Duke Karl was Germano-Danish. I've made inquiries, and her former in-laws have no idea of her whereabouts."

He popped the tea cake into his mouth, the casual gesture

only adding to his elegant, relaxed demeanor. Wakefield was very, very good at what he did, and he'd been doing it for a very, very long time.

"His Grace of Bosendorf promised Matilda a home and family of her own," Parker replied. "She told me that she married him because she longed for a place to settle down and raise children." That rare admission from a woman who was usually so self-possessed had formed the basis for Parker's courtship of her.

"And Matilda—my Matilda—thought an officer in the British military would afford her a fixed address? Doesn't that strike you as odd, Colonel?"

"Yes." And yet, Matilda had spoken as earnestly about longing for a home as ever she'd spoken about anything. Had she spoken too earnestly? Deceptively?

Not that it mattered. "I'm in truth off to listen at keyholes rather than foxhunt," Parker said. "Galloping to hounds is good sport, but the fellows usually get to gossiping while they're riding in and enjoying their hunt breakfast."

"Then the serious drinking starts around the card table," Wakefield said. "Ah, the stupidity of youth."

The insult was almost undetectable amid the affability.

"The serious drinking can lead to seriously honest talk. If someone's mama has recently hired a new companion answering to Matilda's description, if someone has heard talk of a governess particularly adept at languages or chess, then I'm more likely to catch that bit of gossip among the lordlings at Melton than I am in your drawing room."

Wakefield refreshed his tea. "I must ask myself, though, why you persist in this quest, Colonel? You have no claim on Matilda, she's been gone for months, and my best efforts—your best efforts—to locate her have been fruitless.

I applaud your tenacity, but at some point, tenacity becomes a curious obsession."

Wakefield was clever, declaring the betrothal null and void, casting devotion as obsession, and doing all of this damage over tea and jam.

"You claim to have loved your wife," Parker said. "If I told you she was alive and well somewhere, but troubled, or unable to come to you despite yearning to do so, would you sit here sipping tea and reading Ovid?"

Wakefield peered at him over his teacup. "Outraged swain does not sit well upon you, Colonel. You might, in your way, love my daughter, but as the man who has known Matilda since her birth, I can assure you, she does not love you. I would also hazard that the regard you developed toward her during the months of one social Season in no way matches what a man and woman married for years can share. I must ask you to desist in your attempts to locate my daughter."

And there it was, the gauntlet Wakefield had declined to toss down since Matilda's disappearance.

"Have you heard from her, sir?" Parker asked.

Wakefield looked him straight in the eye. "I have not. Have you?"

Parker bit off half the tea cake. "Of course not."

"Then please take her departure and her silence for your congé."

A sensible man would, in the usual circumstances. "I've had another idea regarding her whereabouts."

"None of your ideas have had a happy result, Colonel. Again, I must insist that you no longer regard Matilda's whereabouts as any of your affair."

The damned tea cake had raspberry jam in the middle, and a seed lodged itself along Parker's gum.

"Your request does you no credit as a loving father,

Wakefield. What man wouldn't accept any and all aid in locating his missing daughter?"

Another unhurried sip of tea. "What man would continue to tolerate the meddling of the very person whom that daughter obviously seeks to avoid? Make yourself scarce, by all means, and then perhaps Matilda will deign to send me a few lines. As long as you so publicly call upon me, as long as your uniformed buffoons are watching for her at the ports and turnpikes, she can't contact me. You are doing more harm than good, to be blunt, though I have every sympathy for you."

Wakefield, as always, made sense. "You suppose she's somewhere in London, then, and able to keep watch on your doorstep?"

Wakefield sighed, the gentle long-suffering of a very patient man. "I have no idea where she is. I have corresponded with every friend, acquaintance, and business associate with whom I dare raise this matter. I have paid thief takers and runners and people you would not turn your back on in broad daylight. Matilda is intelligent enough to know exactly to whom I will turn. She's a widow with means and she's taken measures to remain hidden."

A convincing hint of exasperation laced Wakefield's words.

"We need to cast a wider net and go back further among your acquaintances," Parker said. "Your closest business associations now are with the great families in Kent, Surrey, and Sussex, but what about those relationships you formed when Matilda was younger and you traveled less on the Continent?"

Wakefield rubbed his forehead. "You expect me to recall transactions from more than fifteen years ago?"

Doubtless Wakefield had them all documented in journals

and ledgers, for his success among the British aristocracy depended on balancing unassuming friendship with a shrewd mercantile eye.

"I expect you to recall the houses where you bided for more than a week or so, the ones like Petworth, where visitors were a constant happy stream, and a young girl might have formed pleasant memories."

Wakefield rose. "For God's sake, Colonel, Matilda is not among Lord Egremont's horde at Petworth."

"You don't know that for a certainty, and you sold the earl valuable art on many occasions. The place is huge and she could easily hire on as a maid or under-housekeeper."

"With what references?" Wakefield asked, pacing before the hearth. "With what experience? From what agency? You have taken leave of your senses if you think Matilda has gone into service in the household of some duke or earl. Servants gossip like magpies, and a chambermaid who muttered in French or knew a Caravaggio from a Tintoretto would draw certain notice. Matilda's hands are those of a lady, her table manners, her speech—she would have little success passing for a servant."

This was true. Matilda was intelligent, but even a smart woman would have difficulty blending into the world of the English servant class when she'd spent few of her formative years in England. Her employers were unlikely to notice her differentness, but her fellow menials would.

"I don't intend to stop looking for her," Parker said, getting to his feet. "I understand your concern, and I promise I will be discreet, but I must ask you to provide me a list of those great houses and properties that would be known to Matilda or that she'd recall fondly."

Wakefield braced a hand on the mantel. "Ask me? With what authority does a failed suitor ask me do to anything?

Honestly, Colonel, I understand that defeat for a military man is a difficult pill to swallow, and I am of course worried for my daughter, but your searching for Matilda is likely the very reason she's still in hiding."

No, it was not. "We'll talk more of this when I return from Melton, though I'll send my direction that you might keep me apprised of any developments."

This apparently amused Wakefield. "You demand an accounting from me of what goes on here in London, while you ride off for a month of drunkenness and chasing maids. Yet you expect me to believe concern for Matilda rather than male pride drives your pre-occupation with her whereabouts. Safe journey, Colonel."

Parker respected Wakefield—one needn't like a man to respect him and he knew better than to trust him.

"I go only that I might expand my search for a woman I esteem greatly and whose welfare concerns me to the utmost. I wish you good day."

He withdrew his gloves from his pocket and was pulling them on when the painting over the mantel caught his eye.

"I've often wondered why you keep that landscape in such a prominent location when you have far more impressive art elsewhere in the house. Is that a Gainsborough?"

Wakefield moved away from the hearth, for the first time betraying a hint of impatience. "As a matter of fact, it's a Dupont, Thomas Gainsborough's nephew. He was a fair hand with a landscape, though not the equal of his uncle. Poor man didn't live long."

"The property is attractive." The painting depicted a manor house amid mature trees in their summer glory. A boy flew a kite on the lawn, a spaniel yapping at his heels. The house could have been any one of a hundred country homes, neither immense nor ostentatious, but lovely all the same.

"Who owns that house?" The *only* English landscape on display anywhere in the Wakefield dwelling deserved further study.

"A duke now deceased owned it. I'm fairly certain the property is in Middlesex or somewhere west of there. I bought the painting from the previous titleholder because he didn't care for the child in the foreground. The old man loved his hounds, though. He died some years ago and I have no idea who owns the place now."

For a moment, the unflappable Thomas Wakefield had been off center. His savoir faire had returned in the next instant, but mention of this painting—this painting that Matilda would have seen day in and day out—had disturbed Wakefield's equilibrium.

"I have little use for spaniels or house pets of any kind," Parker said, moving toward the door. He wasn't that keen on children, truth be told. "Do keep me informed."

He bowed and withdrew, and as he accepted his hat and greatcoat from the butler, he turned his thoughts to the long trip north to the Midlands. The journey would be made longer still by a detour to the wilds of Middlesex and Berkshire, but then, hunting a missing fiancée was much more pressing business than running some starving little fox to ground.

* * *

Matilda was engrossed in Mr. Wentworth's journey down the Italian coast from Nice to Rome. His companion in all of his travels was the same Lord Stephen now a guest at Brightwell. The youthful version of his lordship had been difficult, given to melancholia and rages, then to trying his hand at serial inebriations, all the while spending hours of every day in his Bath chair.

"You're reading of our famous travels," Lord Stephen said.

He leaned on a stout cane and the doorjamb. Matilda had noticed that he did this as a matter of habit: paused on the edge of every clearing, taking stock, probably charting the course with the fewest steps to whatever destination he'd chosen. She had learned the same caution for different reasons.

"I am translating those accounts written in French or Italian," she said, "and editing for clarity as I go. You had some adventures."

Lord Stephen had climbed the rigging of the Italian vessel in the middle of heavy seas, and all Mr. Wentworth had remarked on was "the lad's prodigious strength and courage."

Who could look upon such rash behavior with a calm eye and see only strength and courage?

"I was experimenting," Lord Stephen said, leaving the door open and settling in beside Matilda "Looking for ways to escape the pain."

"Pain?"

He whacked his boot with his cane. "Pain. Unrelenting, miserable, maddening pain. I've yet to figure out how to turn that suffering into attention from the ladies. Doesn't seem sporting when all the hale and hearty fellows can't compete with me on the same *footing*."

Matilda smiled, though she wasn't fooled. Lord Stephen's pain was real, and so too was his unwillingness to trade on anybody's sympathy.

"Where are we now?" Lord Stephen asked, peering at the journal in Matilda's hands. "Oh, sailing south to Rome. I nearly fell into the sea like Icarus; had a bit too much grog before going aloft."

"More experimenting?" He'd left the door open, as was polite, but the result was an eddy of cold air around Matilda's ankles.

He took the journal from her, closed it, and set it on the low table. "I want to have the damned leg cut off, you see, but I'm not brave enough to simply order it done. Somewhere on this earth must be a means of sending a man's mind elsewhere so that necessary adjustments can be made to his person without him being cognizant."

He spoke of brutal surgery in the same tones Papa had used when assessing Dutch Renaissance paintings.

"If you drink to the point of inebriation, or take opium or the nitrous gas, then you think you will be brave enough to part with your leg?"

"Not brave enough, asleep enough, though then there's infection to worry about. Let's have done with such cheery discourse and turn our talk to *your* adventures."

No, let's not. Matilda reopened the journal and pretended to read of the shipboard fare served to passengers on their way to Rome.

"You needn't fear that I'll pry," Lord Stephen said. "I've been forbidden to pry, and if there's one individual on the face of the earth whose admonitions I will at least consider, it's Duncan Wentworth. He never asks anything for himself. Have you noticed that?"

Mr. Wentworth had asked Matilda to stay. She'd begun to hope a little of that request had been for himself, not out of blasted chivalry.

Though the chivalry was precious too. "I have noticed that Mr. Wentworth, unlike some, is every inch a gentleman."

Lord Stephen patted her hand, the gesture less than reassuring. "He'll fillet me if I attempt to flirt with you in earnest, and that's fascinating. A crack has appeared in the unchanging façade my ever-stalwart cousin shows the world, and thus I must be concerned."

Matilda ran her finger down the page, mostly to touch Mr. Wentworth's crooked, slashing penmanship.

"One suspected your unannounced visit, rude though such behavior might appear, was in fact a gesture of concern, my lord."

"Wentworth concern is a fierce variety of the polite interest you might be acquainted with, so fierce that I must warn you, Miss Maddie: You trifle with Duncan at your peril. He has suffered much, and I won't allow you to heap more difficulties upon him."

Trifle with Duncan Wentworth? Matilda wanted to do more than trifle with the man, and that was cause for alarm. Under the warmth of her covers, in the darkest hours of the night, she had considered the complications resulting from an affair with Mr. Wentworth and lectured herself endlessly on the folly thereof.

"I am a temporary employee in Mr. Wentworth's home, Lord Stephen. Even if he would entertain familiarities from a woman on his staff, I doubt a lady in my circumstances would appeal to him."

Lord Stephen rested his walking stick across his knees. The cane wasn't a delicately carved ornament but in fact functional. Close examination revealed a mechanism near the handle that doubtless released a bayonet from the base. The handle was gold, meaning it would make a heavy cudgel for fighting in close quarters.

"A lady in your circumstances," he said, "which remain undisclosed, and yet those circumstances trouble me."

"Then I'd advise you to school yourself to patience. Mr. Wentworth gave you that cane, didn't he?"

Lord Stephen ran a long, pale finger down the dark shaft, the way some people would pet a favored hound.

"For my eighteenth birthday. He had it made in Berlin and it was waiting for us when we arrived. I like guns, but this cane is the only weapon I own personally. I am not by nature violent, and owe you an explanation for my protectiveness where Duncan is concerned. He doesn't take an interest in women."

Ah, well. There were men like that. They either preferred the company of other males or they simply weren't ruled by lust. Matilda had met many such men and generally liked them. Her late husband had been more interested in his automatons and music boxes than in chasing the maids, and thank heavens for that.

Until meeting Mr. Wentworth, Matilda's interest in men hadn't been much in evidence.

"Mr. Wentworth's business is his own, Lord Stephen. I wish you'd keep any gossip you're determined to share to yourself." A lie, of course. Matilda had a terrible curiosity about Duncan Wentworth. From his journals she'd learned that he was not a happy man, and yet he was a good man. Most unhappy men took the other road and found fault with others all along the way.

"Not gossip," Lord Stephen said. "One shudders at the insult. I offer an explanation, if you please." He used the tip of his walking stick to nudge at a bouquet of purple chrysanthemums on the table. "In five years of living with Duncan in close quarters, I lost count of the fair young ladies whom I either attempted to charm or had pleasant encounters with."

"This is not fit talk between near strangers, my lord."

"In all those years," he went on, "Duncan might have allowed himself three private dinners with very discreet, comely widows. The ladies invariably made the overtures, and they were invariably ladies of means and standing of whom he never spoke personally."

Exactly. Duncan Wentworth was a gentleman. A true, old-fashioned gentleman.

"Duncan's missing a foot, you see," Lord Stephen said, nudging the bowl again. "When it comes to the ladies. He had some falling-out with his vicar back in his curate days, something to do with a woman, or misbehaving with a woman. I was too young at the time to even know I had a cousin Duncan. It all went to hell somehow, and Duncan became a teacher."

"Youthful indiscretions, even *your* youthful indiscretions, don't interest me, my lord. Your willingness to malign Mr. Wentworth is of even less moment. If you don't mind, I have work to do."

"I do not malign him, you daft woman. If I love anybody— and I am fairly certain I do not—I love Duncan. He's short on charm, long on loyalty. Smarter than he's given credit for because he's also humbler than your average genius. I should know—I am a genius, in case you've overlooked the obvious. I'd be dead four times over but for Duncan. If you mean him any harm at all, whatever you're running from will seem like salvation compared to what I'll do to you."

This diatribe skirted the edges between an adolescent tantrum and an entirely believable threat. Lord Stephen shoved to his feet—he could be nimble, Matilda must not forget that—and he maneuvered around the end table.

"Is that all you wanted to say to me, my lord?"

He fluffed his cravat, which was perfectly centered, the lace falling just so. "If you need help, I can finance a journey anywhere you'd care to go, no questions, cash by this time next week. I've already sent for some funds to tend to a few projects I'm planning."

The offer was tempting, ye gods was it tempting, except Papa and the colonel were doubtless watching every port. Matilda remained seated, because in this instance, she was the lady, and Lord Stephen the presuming young fool.

"You will have to learn to give up your cousin Duncan sometime, my lord. He loves you too. I read that on every page of these journals, so you will have to be the one to let him go. I wish you good day."

A family resemblance emerged as Lord Stephen's countenance went blank. Mr. Wentworth frequently wore that unreadable expression, though often all it meant was that he was thinking. He was prodigiously given to thinking, and as much as Matilda loved reading his journals, she also longed to meet him across a chessboard.

More cause for alarm.

"I see why he's taken notice of you," Lord Stephen said. "You have the same ability he does to tell the whole tale from a few snippets of the text. Heed my words anyway, Miss Maddie, for everybody's sake."

The quiet crackle of the hearth fire was joined by a soft snick and a glint of steel. Then Lord Stephen was holding out a single purple bloom to Matilda.

A warning. The drama was charming, and the loyalty touching. She took the blossom, though the whole discussion had been unnerving as well.

Lord Stephen left, shutting the door behind him, and Matilda moved to a chair closer to the hearth. She was still twirling the little flower beneath her nose and staring at a description of Lord Stephen in the rigging when Mr. Wentworth's characteristic double knock sounded on the door.

* * *

"Miss Maddie, good day."

Duncan had dodged breakfast, claiming an appointment with a tenant. The meeting had gone well, inasmuch as everybody had made small talk, predicted snow, and consumed a portion of bitter ale appropriate to warding off the chill, or perhaps to purging the bowels.

Duncan had taken a few cautious sips rather than find out.

"Mr. Wentworth, good morning," Miss Maddie said, tucking a single purple blossom back into the bouquet on the parlor table. "I've been sailing with you from Nice to Rome. Lord Stephen is in the crow's nest, and the captain is swearing about crazy Englishmen."

Duncan ought to make up another excuse—looking for Stephen, perhaps, who dwelled perpetually aloft in one sense and frequently provided an occasion for profanity, today being no exception.

"You will think we left a trail of foul language across the Continent," he said, closing the door. "Might I join you?"

"Of course." She was safely ensconced in a reading chair, preserving Duncan from the folly of sitting beside her.

He took the corner of the sofa nearest the fire, also nearest to her. "I paid a call on the vicar on my way back from Mr. Jingle's tenant farm."

"Is he related to the Jinks on your staff?"

"The boy's uncle. My steward is dishonest." Well, wasn't that the most inept conversational transition ever to be dumped into a lady's lap?

"You have alluded to this previously. I gather many stewards are less than honorable, though most know to be discreet about it."

"I stopped by the vicarage to introduce myself to the shepherd of our local flock and to inquire of him whether a physician who refuses to attend the ill when summoned is deserving of a quiet spiritual rebuke." Another graceless conversational gambit, but then, Stephen's remarks had been unsettling. Had his lordship left the door open on purpose, or had he meant to threaten Miss Maddie in private?

"What did the vicar say?"

"He said, 'More tea, Mr. Wentworth?' and 'How are you getting on at Brightwell, Mr. Wentworth?' Mrs. Newbury's very life was imperiled, for all Dr. Felton knew, coin was available to compensate him, and he would not come because my housekeeper has skin as dark as some Italians."

Duncan was furious—still, though Mrs. Newbury had recovered—but he was also bewildered.

Miss Maddie set aside the journal. "Are you certain the physician based his decision on that factor?"

Rather than meet her gaze, he stared at his hands, a pair of good, strong hands that could have delivered a very succinct sermon to the idiot doctor.

"I want to beat the blighter to flinders, Matilda. I want to cast him into the bowels of a ship and force him to listen to the moans of the dying for weeks, while his own strength ebbs...." He curled his fingers into fists, then opened his hands, trying to let go of violent impulses. "We outlaw slavery here in England and pretend its evils don't touch our shores."

Miss Maddie regarded the bouquet, probably the last they'd have for months. She had gained some color, and her features were no longer as sharp. Duncan liked simply looking at her, though more than once, Stephen had caught him staring.

"I can draft you a letter," she said, "informing the doctor that because his healing vocation is untrustworthy, you will in future depend on the local herbwoman in case of sickness. She is reputed to be reliable and genuinely dedicated to the well-being of others. For serious illness, you will send to London for a consultation with His Grace's personal physician."

Duncan propped his chin on his hand, turning that plan over in his mind, looking for flaws, and finding none. "That is brilliant. That is worthy of Stephen in a rare mood, also quite sensible. Do we even have a local herbwoman?"

"Cook would know, but in my experience the healers in England are a safer bet than the physicians or surgeons."

"Splendid."

A happy silence took root, because Miss Maddie had solved one problem. Shame in rural communities was often more effective than a cudgel. Duncan had forgotten that.

"You mentioned your steward," she said, curling her feet under her and tucking her hems over her toes. She wore one shawl again, a heavy plain wool blanket of a garment, but only the one.

"Mr. Trostle is skimming transactions, mis-stating sums collected, and intimidating all who'd call him to account by either involving them in his schemes or implying that he'll make them sorry for crossing him."

"How long has he been in his present post?"

How long since Duncan had noticed a woman? Truly noticed that the curve of her cheek and the curve of her eyebrow—the same graceful arc—both begged to be traced by his fingers? He liked Miss Maddie's stillness, her focus on her task, her lack of airs.

He also liked her figure, though she kept that swathed in shawls for most of the day.

"I beg your pardon?" he asked.

"Mr. Trostle," she said. "Has he been on the estate long?"

"Four years or so. His Grace hired him through a factor. The duke well knows that matters are in disarray here, and he expects me to sort it all out. Stephen says I should sack Trostle, make a public example of him, though I'd like for an understudy to have a few weeks to gather information first."

"Sound. Advance your pawns before you draw enemy fire."

A chess analogy. How that suited her. "Do you play? Chess, that is."

A struggle ensued, if her expression was any indication. While her features remained composed, her eyes told another tale. A mention of chess—a humble old game usually enjoyed by totty old men—moved her nearly to grief.

"I have played, mostly against my father."

Did Duncan tell her that her father's name was no longer secret? Did he continue to hope that she'd share that information freely?

"I want you to know something," he said, rising to cross the room. "I overheard Stephen's threats earlier. He left the door open, as a gentleman should, and in his great passion to protect me from the schemes of one impecunious woman, he ensured any passing footman would hear his daft declarations as well. Stephen enjoys drama."

Miss Maddie untucked her feet and drew her skirts over them. A glimpse of plain black stockings ought not to affect Duncan, and yet, it had. Slender calves, slender feet. High arches…he wanted to get his hands on them, learn those contours with his palms and fingers and lips, and he wanted—even more—to play chess with his amanuensis.

Country life was driving him daft.

"Stephen is protective of you," Miss Maddie said. "I admire loyalty in anybody."

"Loyalty, though, can be misguided. Stephen mentioned that the church and I parted on bad terms." Stephen had made a muck of passing along information he himself didn't understand.

Miss Maddie toed on her slippers. "Shame on the church, then."

She sat halfway across the room, and yet, Duncan caught a whiff of roses. "You're sure I'm innocent of wrong-doing?"

"As certain as I am of anything. Had you kissed some-body's daughter, miscounted the money in the building fund, or committed another of the usual indiscretions, the bishop would have posted you to some congregation in Northumbria, where you'd have served out a few years' penance. The Church of England cannot afford to forgo the services of its indentured curates."

She was wonderfully logical. "I was guilty of a worse sin. I expected moral consistency from my superiors, and did not handle disappointment well." More than that, he might tell her someday.

He took down a chess set from the shelves beside the window, and Miss Maddie's gaze fixed on the wooden box in his hands.

"Shall we play, Miss Maddie?" *Shall we play at trust and affection and all manner of folly?* Duncan knew better than to even think that, but what had years of knowing better earned him except shelves of messy journals and a plundered estate?

"I would love to."

Chapter Eight

Thomas Wakefield's staff was charmingly eclectic, in the opinion of his Mayfair neighbors. His porter was Corsican, his butler German. One footman was Spanish, another Portuguese, though they looked remarkably alike to English eyes. The housekeeper, the chef, and his staff were French, the under-footmen included an Erse-speaking Highlander and a Russian. One of the grooms was Rom, while the coachman was an Englishman.

Between them all, they could eavesdrop on almost any conversation and bring back an accurate report. In the unlikely event the staff had to speak before one of Wakefield's guests, the language used was deliberately broken English.

In the servants' hall, their grasp of world affairs would have shamed most Cabinet ministers and did provide frequent enlightenment to their employer. Their card games were unintelligible to any save themselves.

"Has our intrepid colonel decamped for the Midlands?"

Wakefield asked his porter. Carlu was responsible for managing the network of post boys, urchins, hostlers, and other worthies who contributed to Wakefield's store of knowledge.

Despite the chill air, this discussion was taking place in the town house garden, where eavesdropping was nearly impossible, though safety in the form of surveillance from the house and the mews was guaranteed.

"If the colonel is traveling to Melton, he took an odd route," Carlu replied. "To go north, we'd expect a departure from Smithfield, taking the Great North Road up through Peterborough."

"Bollocks." For invective, few languages could compare with English. "He went west?"

"Out Oxford Road, sir." Carlu tugged his scarf up around his mouth. Doubtless the man was cold, but he was also hiding his words from prying eyes. "His coach followed with very little luggage strapped to the boot."

The worst of all possible reports. "He's going to Brightwell, damn him and his commanding officers. He might not know precisely where the place is on the map, but it's a ducal holding, and the locals take pride in that."

A neglected ducal holding where Matilda had formed some of her best memories, drat the luck. The painting over the mantel had been her sole suggestion when Wakefield had been appointing his London house. The one time a guest had admired the painting, Matilda had sent her Papa such a look of admonition he'd known that to sell that landscape would have been a betrayal in her eyes.

"Sir, I hesitate to be indelicate," Carlu said, stamping his feet, "or to suggest that all possibilities have not come under your most excellent consideration, but even an intrepid colonel, if traveling an imprudent distance from his equipage in this devil-begotten English weather, might suffer an accident."

Carlu's dark eyes held such hope, such a plea for the reasonable course. He was Corsican, after all, and reasonable to his very toes.

"What if Matilda loves him?" Wakefield asked. "The bloody bore managed to turn her head. Why else would she have agreed to marry a man who will drag her all over creation, though he can't play more than middling chess?" Matilda longed for a permanent home, the one simple comfort Wakefield hadn't been able to provide her until eighteen months ago.

She was a woman who could move easily in the best society of any European court, and yet, she was a stranger to her homeland.

"If she loves that arrogant excuse for a clodpole in scarlet," Carlu said, "then she will grieve for him, but what manner of lady in love leaves her fiancé's side without a word and stays away from him for months?"

A damned clever one. "No accidents, Carlu. I need the colonel to remain in obnoxious good health for the nonce." Wakefield needed as well to find Matilda before the clodpole—the colonel—did, and Brightwell was one place Wakefield had not thought to look.

"For the nonce," Carlu said. "That is English for until you come to your senses, perhaps? Or until the eternal suffering referred to as the English winter can arrange another fate for his colonelship?"

"Get into the house and tell Ambrose you're in need of a toddy. You've had Parker followed?"

A dark-eyed gaze worthy of a Renaissance angel turned upward to sullen clouds. "What have I done, what have I ever, ever done to merit such a lack of faith from one whom I esteem so greatly? Tell me, for I will not sleep, I will not eat, I will not partake of Ambrose's most excellent toddy, until I have learned of my transgression and set all to rights with my treasured employer. The wound in my heart that your doubt has riven exceeds the bitterness of Lucifer when cast from the glories—"

Wakefield pointed to the house. "My apologies for even hinting that I doubted your competence or your loyalty, but I am a father sorely worried for my daughter, as she is doubtless worried for me. Enjoy your toddy."

Carlu bowed, his expression fierce. "We'll find her before the colonel does, sir. Depend upon it."

A lazy flake of snow drifted down and landed on the rough wool of Carlu's scarf.

"From your lips to God's ears." Though the timing would be delicate, and if Wakefield bungled, he and Matilda could both end up dead or worse.

Carlu strode into the house, leaving Wakefield alone in the frigid garden. He was watched by loyal eyes at almost all times, as Matilda had been, and yet, she'd slipped away. The why of her departure was still unclear, though every explanation Wakefield came up with was bad for both him and his daughter.

The challenge was to fashion a solution that boded even worse for Colonel Parker.

* * *

Secrets were like elaborate millinery. They weighed more the longer they were borne about. Matilda's secrets were piling up like snow on a frozen lane. She knew not only the Brightwell property, but this very chess set. Her recollection of the house had been vague—children were not allowed to roam grand premises at will—but she would never forget the pieces on the board. She'd learned the game sitting across from the old duke, whose patience had been matched only by his appreciation for strategy.

Mr. Wentworth had given her the choice of color, as a polite host would, and Matilda chose white simply to start the game as quickly as possible.

Please let his chess be interesting.

Her prayer stemmed from two sources: First, she had a passionate longing for a good game. She was as starved for the complexities of the chessboard as she'd been for shelter, sustenance, and human kindness.

Second, she wanted a stretch of time to sit in the same room with Duncan Wentworth, in intimate congress of any variety. Intimate congress with his mind would do splendidly, for a well-played chess match stripped away all fig leaves and pretenses.

Which meant Matilda would have to lose, of course. For her own fig leaves and pretenses had become necessary to her survival. She had thought to start out with the Bishop's Game, then changed her mind in favor of the venerable Italian Game, a shade less aggressive. Mr. Wentworth made the predictable moves in response, suggesting he had some familiarity with traditional play.

An hour later—an hour during which Matilda had lost her slippers, forgotten her problems, and eschewed any notion that she must lose—she had Mr. Wentworth in check. The delight of that, the sheer, crowing pleasure of it, the sense of coming home to herself, was better than all the warmed shawls and fresh biscuits in England.

After a silence—delighted on her part, brooding from Mr. Wentworth's side of the board—he moved his king, one small square forward, the direction his king must not even consider going, and the game became...a *draw*.

Matilda stared at the board, then at her opponent—he was still brooding, doubtless waiting for her reaction—then at the board. How long had it been since she'd had an opponent this worthy? An opponent this enjoyable?

"I am astonished," she said. "I am wonderfully, delightfully astonished. I was completely distracted by your rook, which I was sure I'd capture twenty minutes ago. You and your timid bishops have hoodwinked me."

She hadn't smiled like this—pure glee, undiluted joy—for months.

"While your myrmidons were determined to waylay my queen. You have a ruthless streak, my dear. You keep it well hidden, but the chessboard reveals all. I have not enjoyed a match this much since Stephen dragged me to St. Petersburg in the depths of winter."

My dear. She beamed at the chessboard with the same sense of satisfaction and contentment she would have turned on her empty plate at the conclusion of a banquet.

"My father used to say that the Russian winter has created a race more indomitable than angels and wilier than devils." She should not have mentioned Papa, or Russia, and she most assuredly should not be smiling like a complete gudgeon because Mr. Wentworth had played her to a draw.

A draw. She hadn't been able to win or lose, hadn't been able to control the outcome of this game. What a surprise, what a relief.

"Would you care to play again?" Mr. Wentworth asked.

She could keep him in this parlor for days, while she forgot to eat, drink, or even move. "I'd like to study this game first, if you don't mind. Perhaps tomorrow?"

He rose and bowed. "I will look forward to that, Miss Wakefield."

The chessboard clamored for study, for a replay of various

moves, a review of the options Matilda had discarded. Mr. Wentworth had slipped through her defenses and seen through her strategy. When had she lost sight of his cunning, when had her vigilance...?

"Mr. Wentworth," she called over her shoulder as he reached the door. "A moment, please."

He returned to her side. "Ma'am."

Matilda could not summon a smile, she could not even regain the sense of warmth she'd enjoyed since joining Mr. Wentworth's household.

"You called me Miss Wakefield, and yet, I've never told you my surname."

He moved his king back into check. "I apologize. I did not mean to presume, but my upbringing emphasized proper address, and I..." He fell silent, staring at the board.

"You are unhappy with yourself for using my name."

"One doesn't like to intrude. Might we discuss this?" He held out a hand, and Matilda took it.

She ignored the pleasure of touching a man she esteemed greatly, ignored the even simpler joy of clasping hands with another human being. Mr. Wentworth had spoken her name, a name she'd not used since fleeing London and had told to no one.

He'd used her name, and that made Duncan Wentworth her enemy.

* * *

Stephen had the same capacity for utter absorption that Matilda Wakefield had, though with Stephen, the physical signs of concentration were harder to discern.

Matilda bit her lip.

She blinked, she frowned. She sighed and scowled.

The composure she habitually wore like one of her blasted shawls fell away when she played chess, leaving a brilliant mind and a lovely woman on display. Her fingertips were calloused, and a fading scar across the back of her left wrist looked like a healing burn. Duncan had been as fascinated with her hands as he had with her plundering rooks and charging knights.

"Stephen has a theory," Duncan said. "He has many theories, and this one might have merit. May I join you?"

He'd led her to the sofa. When she gestured to the place beside her, he took it. People seated side by side need not maintain eye contact, which made confession easier on all concerned.

"Lord Stephen offered me passage to anywhere I chose," Matilda replied, "provided I'm willing to wait until next week for his coin to arrive."

Thanks be to the Almighty for the sorry state of English roads. "You are tempted to leave. You've been here little more than a fortnight, and you are tempted to leave Brightwell."

Leave me.

"I don't want to," she said, "but my situation is complicated."

Duncan waited, reassured by both her reluctance to depart and her admission.

"If I tell you the whole," she said, "you are implicated in something that might be criminal, seriously criminal. If I tell you nothing, you will think I have no regard for you and am merely intent on abusing your hospitality until it suits me to abandon my post."

No frowns, sighs, or scowls gave Duncan any clue to the emotions weighting these words. This was an opening gambit Matilda had mentally rehearsed many times.

"Can you tell me anything?"

She toyed with the fringe of her shawl. "I want to, but my silence protects you."

"Does your silence protect others?"

"Yes."

Damn and blast those others for allowing a woman on her own to carry this burden. "You told me the law was not pursuing you."

"Not the magistrates and runners, not that variety of law."

"And no husband searches for you?" Duncan needed to be certain of this.

"No husband, but we've discussed my erstwhile fiancé. You have no wife, I take it?"

That Matilda would ask gratified him inordinately. "I did, briefly, long ago. She did not live to see her eighteenth birthday. Ours was a cordial union of near-strangers. I do not regret taking those vows, and I hope my late spouse is at peace." Informing Quinn of that brief marriage had been excruciating, though admitting the tale to Matilda was a relief.

"I was married once," she said, smoothing her shawl over her skirts. "That union was also brief, and while I don't regret my choice, my husband was...cordial is a good word. He was cordially distracted much of time, fascinated with clocks, music boxes, and automatons. I have always longed for a home of my own, and my present fiancé—let's call him Alphonse—took notice of that yearning. He would allude to *someday*, when he had a proper household, when the children came along, when his life was more settled, and with each casual comment, he was watching for a reaction from me. I did not realize he was courting my dreams until too late."

"You've traveled much."

"Yes, which to a man of your background must be obvious. Tell me of Lord Stephen's theory."

She'd traveled much and longed to settle, while Duncan was forced to bide at Brightwell and longed to wander—a puzzle for another day.

"Stephen says that if we wish to disclose a secret, we find ways to do that, even if we don't admit our wish to ourselves. I mentioned your name, for example, though I was determined to maintain a respectful silence on that topic."

Duncan wished to take Matilda's hand. She had allowed him to take her hand to escort her across the room, and she had bid him to join her on the sofa. She'd kissed him on the cheek, once upon a time.

"I hope I haven't disclosed any secrets to Lord Stephen."

Duncan twined his fingers with hers, lest she bolt away. "You permitted him to peruse your Book of Common Prayer, and therein, he saw your name, date of birth, your parents' names, and the parish where you were christened. He conveyed that information to me and to me alone."

Matilda pressed her forehead against Duncan's arm. "I cannot believe I was that foolish. I cannot fathom how...I must leave. I must burn that blasted book, and I must leave. I dare not wait for Lord Stephen's coin. I should decamp this very night."

No, she should not. "You carried your prayer book to prove your identity, if the need arose."

She drew back enough to regard him. "I also carried that prayer book in case somebody had to identify my remains."

Duncan considered that salvo, which was in itself a significant gesture of trust. "You are in a very great lot of trouble, Matilda Wakefield. You had better tell me the whole of it."

Her gaze fell on the chess set, and Duncan braced himself for a combination of lies and truth, all couched amid a truly perplexing set of puzzles.

Firstly: What other varieties of law could reach into the English countryside, if not magistrates and runners?

Secondly: Was Matilda protecting family, and, if so, from whom?

Thirdly: If, in fact, the wisest course was for Matilda to flee to a distant corner of the earth, would she allow Duncan to flee with her?

"I am embroiled in a situation that has consequences at the highest levels, Mr. Wentworth, though my involvement began unintentionally. If I share with you what I know, you cannot claim the same innocence and will find yourself embroiled along with me."

Stubborn woman. She'd fit right in among the Wentworths. "I enjoy nothing so much as a conundrum, which you apparently face. Embroil me, Miss Wakefield."

She rose and paced across the room. "You must not call me that. Not when Lord Stephen could barge in here, not when a servant could listen at the keyhole. For all anybody knows, I stole that prayer book or purchased it used. I am Matilda to you, or Miss Maddie, but never Miss Wakefield."

She'd expressed a wish to study their chess game, but now she was taking pieces off the board, lining them up in order of rank. Her white pawns, Duncan's black pawns. Her bishop, knight, rook, and queen, her king.

"Matilda," Duncan said, getting to his feet, despite the protest from his right knee. "Please calm yourself. You have made a minor slip by letting Stephen see your prayer book. He will carry your identity to his grave if need be, as will I. I'd rather not. I'd rather see you free of the burdens you carry, else I shall never have an opportunity to properly court you."

She went still, Duncan's king in her hand. "Did I hear you aright, Mr. Wentworth?"

"My name is Duncan. Your hearing is excellent."

She set the king down slowly, right next to the white queen. "You seek to court me?"

"I most assuredly do."

Based on the lady's expression, this disclosure astonished her almost as much as it surprised Duncan.

* * *

The coachman and grooms, borrowed from Parker's titled older brother, were unhappy to be poking around the countryside, and Parker was unhappy as well.

"She's below middling height, dark-haired, and pretty, though not stunning," Parker said.

The squint-eyed old fellow minding the tollbooth scratched under his cap. "Pretty, shortish, dark hair. That certainly narrows it down, guv, and you say she came this way sometime in the last four months?"

If Matilda had come that way at all. London sat at the confluence of many roads and could be escaped through dozens of turnpikes. Foot traffic often skirted the tollbooths, and Matilda was also a competent horsewoman.

"Or perhaps in the last two weeks."

The old man shot a glance at the coachman, the same glance Parker had seen passed among enlisted men: *Did you know yon gentleman is an idiot?*

Parker was traveling out of uniform, the better to blend in among the hunt crowd and the squires. "She would have been intent on reaching a ducal property to the west of here, one that changed hands in the past few years."

"A ducal property sits at the end of every cow path this close to London, sir, and they change hands every time some old buzzard goes to his reward."

The pikesman spoke patiently, which Parker supposed was more than he deserved. "This is my card. If you should happen across a female traveling either direction, one who appears to be a lady fallen on hard times, dark-haired, petite, please notify me. She might be speaking a language other than English, but you'll notice her comprehension of English is excellent."

Parker's card disappeared unread into a pocket, suggesting literacy was not required of his majesty's tollkeepers.

"Why might you be looking for the young miss, sir? Is she a fugitive from the bench?"

The old man was apparently impervious to the cold, while Parker's toes were turning to ice. "She's not a fugitive, and there's no reward..."

A coach horse stomped, the harness jingling in the frigid, gray air. Parker realized his error while the tollkeeper examined the bare trees lining both sides of the road.

"There's half a crown in it," Parker went on, "for the person who leads me to her. We are sweethearts, and her father has tried to come between us, but she's of age, and so, obviously, am I."

A clearly unimpressed perusal of Parker's person followed. "'For aught that I could ever read, could ever hear by tale or history, the course of true love never did run smooth.' I'll keep an eye out for your lady, guv. Best be on your way now. Snow's coming."

The tollkeeper raised the turnpike and waved to the coachman, who took up the reins. The groom clambered onto the back of the carriage, while Parker lingered, wondering what else he might have said, asked, or threatened to improve the odds of finding his intended.

"John Coachman," he called, "pull up at the next inn we pass that caters to the wealthy."

The coachman nodded, his hands full of a team eager to be down the road. Parker climbed into the coach, the footman closed the door, and the next instant, the team was trotting off to the west.

Parker's past dozen stops had been fruitless, and the next dozen likely would be as well, but at a fancy coaching inn, he would doubtless find a copy of Debrett's. With some study, he could create a list of dukes who'd died in the past ten years, and their holdings immediately to the west of London.

The list couldn't be that long, and through diligence and determination, Parker would flush dear Matilda from her covert before she stumbled into a dire fate on her own.

* * *

For years, Duncan had told himself he wasn't like the other Wentworths. His cousins were a noisy, bickering lot toward whom he felt a reluctant affection while maintaining a dignified distance. Long before becoming a duke, Quinn Wentworth had presided over that branch of the family like a papa lion. For the most part, he pretended an aloofness that fooled nobody. Let one of his siblings be threatened, and he roared into the affray. Where those Wentworths went, some sort of mayhem was always in progress. The cousins could be impulsive, unpredictable, bold, and self-centered. They had a morality all their own, and seldom apologized or looked back.

Duncan had spent most of his adulthood looking back, second-guessing himself, and apologizing to a woman long dead. As he crossed the parlor to join Matilda by the chess set, he was focused on the future for once, and glad of it.

"I suspect marriage to me would solve many of your problems," he said.

"While it would compound yours."

How much trouble could she be in, if no legal authority sought to find her? "On the contrary, Matilda, marriage would simplify my life considerably. For example, this house is a mystery to me. I've never lived in so grand an edifice and have no idea how one goes about managing such an establishment. Relations with the neighbors loom as equally daunting. Except for a short stint as a curate, my situation has never called for socializing in any regard. In the country, one must socialize."

"You haven't a cousin or sister who could be your hostess?"

Duncan sought much more than a hostess. "My lady cousins bide in the north like a pair of Valkyries. They fly down for the social Season and leave the ballrooms littered with fallen men—half the fellows smitten, half of them reeling from the worst setdowns of their pampered, arrogant lives—and half the shops in Mayfair reeling with orders."

Matilda finished lining up the chess pieces. "These would be Lord Stephen's sisters?"

She had the black king and the white queen paired, as they'd been on the chessboard before the game had concluded in a stalemate.

"And that brings us to another reason why I'd be well advised to marry." He took her hand, curling her fingers in his. "My ducal cousin chose for his duchess a woman of unassailably Christian inclinations. Jane would like to see me wed."

"I'm no saint," Matilda said, studying their joined hands. "On the Continent, in France especially, women are permitted much more freedom than they have in England. Even here, a widow has some latitude."

Color rose to suffuse her cheeks and even her ears. How un-saintly had Matilda been, and had she enjoyed those encounters? The unhappy curate from Duncan's past scolded him for having such impure thoughts. The man holding Matilda Wakefield's hand mentally told the curate to sod the hell off.

"My sense of French women," Duncan said, "is that nobody permits them anything. They do as they please and all of French society is happier for it."

Matilda smoothed a hand over Duncan's lapel, and the resulting sensation somehow managed to register behind his falls.

"I did like France," she said. "I liked a few fellows there too. French men aren't possessive, in the usual case, unless you marry them. Then they can be a bit ridiculous My husband was affectionate when he recalled he had a wife, but we were married less than a year. The English are ridiculous about controlling unwed females, and then English husbands seem to forget they have wives at all."

She did it again, brushed her hand over the wool of Duncan's jacket. Perhaps touching him pleased her the way touching her pleased him.

"If your current difficulties did not beset you," Duncan said, "would you allow me to court you?"

The fragrance of roses beset him, bringing to mind blooming gardens, honey-drunk bees, and cats curled contently on sun-warmed walkways.

She moved closer, not quite a lean. "I believe I would. I haven't thought in terms of courtship for some time. I saved my husband the bother of managing his servants, while he provided me a fixed address. With the colonel—with *Alphonse*—he didn't court me so much as he decided that I would suit him, or so I thought."

More small admissions. The late husband had had a large enough household that the servants required management, meaning he'd been wealthy or even titled. The dunderheaded suitor who'd let her slip away had been or was in the military. A colonel, meaning he was a well-connected dunderhead.

"He decided you'd suit," Duncan said. "What did you decide?"

"That I would suit him. I was wrong." She closed the distance remaining between them, mere inches, wrapping her arms around Duncan's waist and giving him her weight. He was thus half enfolded in her shawl with her, a warm place to be.

He embraced her, carefully, as he would have embraced someone frail from long deprivation. Matilda was not frail—slender, certainly, but she was gaining flesh, and she was in good health.

Duncan, however, was suffering from deprivation, from years of being a proper escort to his cousins, a proper dance partner to the wallflowers, a proper influence on Stephen. Propriety slid from his grasp and set free all manner of strange and wonderful yearnings.

Arousal—good old male desire—joined surprise and a difficult tenderness.

Matilda Wakefield could hurt him, even more deeply than he'd been hurt by the loss of his young wife. The harm would be unintentional, and by taking Matilda in his arms, Duncan was making a rash, Wentworth-style dare that he could either weather that pain or—he was a Wentworth—slay the dragons who pursued her.

"I won't suit you either," Matilda said, resting her cheek against Duncan's chest. "In my present circumstances, I can't suit anybody."

Lord God, she felt wonderfully female. Whoever that husband had been, whoever the amorous Frenchmen were, they'd given her an appreciation for a lover's embrace, because Matilda had bundled in close and fitted herself to Duncan's body curve by curve.

"I can't offer you anything," Matilda said. "Nothing lasting, nothing permanent."

Duncan's wife had vowed to love, honor, and obey him until death did them part. She'd survived mere months, and love had never come into it.

"Matilda, you needn't be concerned with suiting me. In this, at least, I must suit you, and you must suit yourself."

She peered up at him, all lovely brown eyes and feminine mystery. "I fear you are correct, Mr. Wentworth."

"Duncan."

Her smile was mischievous and a little sad. "Duncan." Then she kissed him.

Chapter Nine

Jane, Duchess of Walden, had taken to duchessing like a mare to spring grass, much to her own astonishment. Raised as a preacher's daughter, widowed early in her first marriage, and then wed to Quinn Wentworth out of necessity rather than romance, she'd never expected to end up with a title.

Or to fall top over tiara in love with her duke.

A title was a great responsibility. Jane had charities to oversee, entertainments to plan, and a duke to partner, and *such* a duke. Quinn Wentworth had scrapped and fought his way up from the slums to become one of London's wealthiest bankers, then with an equal lack of decorum found himself the bearer of a lofty title and married to Jane.

Quinn was settling in to his station, year by year, though he still liked to growl at and figuratively pounce upon the unsuspecting peer in the House of Lords from time to time. Jane was having a grand time *not* settling in to the role of duchess, but rather, comporting herself like a Wentworth.

She had no lapdog. She had a big, black, toothy Alsatian who answered to the name Wodin. He'd been a gift from the footmen and was much beloved belowstairs.

She held duchess teas, gathering with others of her ilk, kicking off her slippers, and comparing notes on the delicate art of being married to a duke. In Jane's opinion, Quinn was, of course, the best duke of the lot, having not been spoiled by the typical aristocratic upbringing. The other duchesses conceded that he was exceedingly handsome, and one had even allowed that Quinn "bore a resemblance to a younger version of my Percival."

The best part of being a duchess, however, was that Jane's opinions were never brushed aside as those of a mere woman, an impecunious widow, or a lowly minister's daughter. She bore the constant weight of public scrutiny, but by God, she was no longer a silent, invisible wretch dependent on her father for grudging charity.

"You have that look in your eye," Quinn said, taking off his glasses. He was past thirty and jaw-droppingly gorgeous in a tall, dark, and delicious way. His Grace was also regarding Jane with a particular look in *his* eye.

He was at the desk in their sitting room—the bedroom no longer had a desk—while Jane was on the sofa pretending to go through correspondence. Mostly, she was sharing a quiet hour with her husband before they'd attend a musicale. Quinn loved music and had developed skill at the keyboard in the past few years.

"What sort of look do you refer to?" Jane asked, shuffling her letters into a stack.

"The hatching-one-of-your-plots look. It's too soon for another baby, Jane. I must stand firm on that. Artemis should be at least a year old before another one is on the way."

"I agree." Artemis was a gloriously healthy little stoat,

meaning she put demands on Jane that quite honestly sapped a mother's energies.

"Althea and Constance have gone north for the winter," Quinn said, joining Jane on the sofa. "That leaves you free to fret over Stephen and Duncan. Which one are you worried about?"

Quinn had noticed that Jane was worried, while she had considered herself merely preoccupied.

"You don't think they're lovers, do you?" she asked. "If they had that sort of attachment my view of the situation would be very different."

Quinn stretched out on the sofa, resting his head against Jane's thigh. "You'd still fret. Duncan has never inclined toward men that I know of, but then, for the past five years he's been traveling more than he's been in England. With Stephen, I can't be sure. For all I know, he might fancy both women and men at the same time, as many as a bed can hold."

Not that Quinn would care, for which Jane loved him.

"Something's afoot, Quinn. Stephen is a conscientious correspondent and we haven't heard from him since he decamped for Brightwell."

Quinn stroked Jane's knee. "He's likely trying to help Duncan put the place to rights. Stephen's property runs like a top, and the boy's not stupid."

Stephen hadn't been a boy five years ago. "You gave Stephen a small estate in excellent repair. Pulling Brightwell back from ruin would be unknown terrain for him."

Jane's marriage was an ever-changing and fascinating terrain. Who would have thought that a man's idle touch on a lady's knee could have erotic repercussions, for example? Jane stroked Quinn's hair in retaliation, and for the sheer pleasure of petting her husband.

Quinn turned on his side, a more comfortable posture for a man of his height. "Stephen did send a request for funds to the bank. He ordered a substantial sum sent out to Brightwell."

"That makes no sense. Brightwell is not his to invest in. Would he be making Duncan a loan?"

"Duncan would not ask Stephen for a loan."

Wentworths understood money as only people raised without it could. Jane's upbringing hadn't been as difficult as Quinn's—hell's muck pit would have been inviting compared to Quinn's childhood—but she knew less of Duncan's youth.

"Would Duncan ask you for a loan?"

"No, nor would I offer one. He has funds. His wages were generous as Stephen's tutor, his expenses next to none. He has been investing wisely for nearly a decade, and his aunt left him a tidy property in Yorkshire that's brought in steady rental income. If need be, Duncan could retire to his Yorkshire acres and live a very comfortable, gentlemanly existence."

Jane gave Quinn's ear a stout pinch. "We can't let that happen. Yorkshire is much too far away. He'll bury himself in a mountain of Latin translations, send us an annual letter at Yuletide, and grow reclusive."

Quinn's hand glided lower, stroking Jane's calf. "Duncan thrives on travel. He'll not grow reclusive. I suspect he might hold on to the place out of sentiment. His wife is buried near the property."

"His *wife*? How could I be a member of this family for five years and not know Duncan is a widower? How like a Wentworth, to be so needlessly stoic about such terrible loss."

And how like Duncan, especially. Myriad moments flashed

in Jane's memory: Duncan patiently showing Bitty how to tie her boots, his tolerance with Althea and Constance's bickering, his loyalty to Stephen. A man bereft of immediate family valued the relations remaining to him.

"I didn't know Duncan had lost a wife when I first sent for him," Quinn said, giving Jane's calf an oddly pleasurable squeeze. "Stephen was in serious difficulties, and the tutors and governors I'd hired were making his situation worse. Duncan came south straightaway, but before he took a shilling of my money he acquainted me with some of his past, lest I hear it from anybody else. Are you undressing me, Your Grace?"

"Loosening your cravat. We'll need to change before we go out. Tell me the rest of Duncan's story."

Jane would also need to stop by the nursery. Artemis was old enough to take warmed gruel several times a day, but she also still needed her mama.

"I don't know the rest of his story," Quinn said. "He told me he'd left the church over theological differences with his pastor and bishop, and had taken a wife who did not survive long after giving birth. The child perished as well, and—"

"*Duncan lost a child?* Oh, Quinn, that poor man. That poor, dear man. Such a tragedy explains much."

Jane hugged Quinn, who rolled to his back the better to be hugged. This escalated to kissing, though Jane wasn't about to be distracted from their conversation—not yet.

"I gather these losses occurred when Duncan wasn't even as old as Stephen is now," Quinn said. "The past does not seem to trouble him."

Jane shoved at Quinn's shoulder. "Not trouble him? Not *trouble* him? Quinn, you snapped your fingers over a younger brother in distress and Duncan traveled two hundred miles without a qualm. He's barely left Stephen's side since, and no matter where Stephen sought to wander, Duncan wandered with him. That's biblical devotion to a very difficult young man, and you say Duncan isn't troubled. To lose a child, a wife and a child, *and* a livelihood all in such a short time. Our poor Duncan. Stop distracting me."

Quinn left off running his finger along Jane's décolletage and affected an innocent look that earned him another shove.

"I might be misreading my cousin, Jane. Duncan was necessarily concerned with his own situation when we were younger. I gather his uncle wasn't the compassionate sort, though the aunt left everything to Duncan upon her death."

"When I first met Duncan," Jane said, "I thought him cold, an academic longing for his secluded tower. Then I thought him merely reserved. Now you tell me he's known great loss, and I'm not sure what to think. What happened between Duncan and his pastor that would cause him to give up his vocation?"

"Maybe he hadn't a vocation. Tell me again why we're going out this evening."

"A pianist is performing at a musicale—a duke's son is debuting a new sonata. We must lend our cachet. Why would a young man who had no other professional training leave the church, Quinn? Why wouldn't he go back to the church, hat in hand, when he had a wife and child to support? Or did he leave because of the wife and child? Maybe she was a Dissenter?"

Quinn sat up. "You won't let this go, will you? Duncan is a surpassingly private man, and I've hesitated to probe old wounds."

Jane smoothed Quinn's hair and drew off the cravat she'd untied. "Until those old wounds are healed, we can obligate

Duncan to any number of properties, but he'll still find a way to wander. Might you unlace me?"

She scooted around, giving Quinn her back, and he started on her hooks. "Duncan likes wandering, just as Joshua likes running the bank."

Joshua Penrose, Quinn's financial partner, *loved* running the bank, thanks be to heaven. "We must pay a visit at Brightwell, Quinn. If Stephen needs a substantial sum delivered, then the money will be more safely sent with the ducal coach, outriders, grooms, and footmen."

Quinn kissed Jane's nape, which gave her a delicious, shivery feeling every time he did it—still.

"Tell me this, madam duchess: How is Duncan to accommodate and feed the army that you insist I take with me when I leave Town?"

Jane's dress fell open and Quinn switched to loosening her stays. "That's simple. Provisions can be sent as well. You say Brightwell is barely a day's journey from Town."

"In good weather, with good horses. Winter has begun, in case you'd forgotten."

When Quinn slipped his arms around Jane's waist and hugged her bare back to his chest, she was much too warm to notice mere winter.

"I'm a duchess and a Wentworth," she said, wiggling into his embrace. "A spot of weather shall not deter me."

"You'd leave the children?"

"Of course not."

Quinn's hold shifted. He had different sorts of kisses, silences, and smiles. He also had a vocabulary of embraces. The notion of traveling with the children had momentarily deterred him from a marital objective.

"I can't bolt for the shires, Jane. I have committee meetings this week and a directors' meeting at the bank."

"I must make preparations as well, but we'll not leave Duncan all on his own to endure whatever mischief Stephen is up to."

"Agreed," Quinn said, rising and extending a hand to Jane.

She stood, her dress falling halfway down her arms. "I know you love to hear the piano competently played, Quinn, but might we miss the first half of tonight's gathering?"

He stepped close enough that Jane could start on his shirt buttons.

"You're asking me to give up half an evening of cultural enrichment, mingling with good society, and furthering my political agendas merely so I can tarry with my duchess in the bedroom yonder?"

Quinn was still the best-smelling man Jane had ever met. She buried her nose against the join of his neck and shoulder. "I am asking you to make that great sacrifice yet again, Your Grace."

"Then my answer is,"—he scooped Jane into his arms and grinned like a plundering buccaneer—"of course."

* * *

In Matilda's opinion, most French men knew how to be naughty and gentlemanly with the same woman. They treated their mistresses with exquisite politeness in public despite the intimate nature of the relationship. They could also conduct a discreet, passionate affair with a well-born woman and still spend an evening partnering her at whist without considering the hours wasted.

Matilda had brought some experience to her marriage. If the duke had noticed, he'd been too polite—or too interested in his next invention—to mention it.

Prior to her marriage, when in Paris—and in Lyon, Nice,

and Marseilles—Matilda had done as the French women had done and enjoyed the company of those fellows who'd caught her interest. Only two had progressed past the point of flirtation, and those two had been sweet, considerate, and dear without capturing her heart.

Even those two, though, had offered overtures, leaving Matilda with the question of whether and how to respond. Duncan Wentworth gave her the entire field, invited her to take the white army, in other words, and decide *everything*.

Wrapped in his arms, she chose not to rush, but rather to savor what had to be a stolen moment.

She started by reveling in the pleasure of Duncan's embrace. He was lean and muscular, and when his arms came around her, Matilda relaxed in a way she hadn't relaxed for months. She was safe when he held her, sheltered from every peril except the very great danger of trusting him.

Before that injustice could poison all of her joy, she listened to his heartbeat, a slow, steady pulse beneath her cheek. Duncan wasn't a randy boy, giving in to a whim. He was all adult male, making a choice he'd justified with no less than three reasons.

And he wasn't ashamed to let Matilda know he desired her.

She anchored a hand at his nape and kissed him right on the mouth—no venerable, cautious Italian game, this. His lips were softer than she'd expected, and he tasted sweet and buttery, as if he'd pinched a few biscuits before their chess game.

When his hold on Matilda became more snug, she went a-plundering with lips and tongue. She felt the shock of that boldness go through him, a start perceivable only because she'd tightened her grip on him too.

"I'm sorry," she said, disappointment crowding her pleasure. "On the Continent…"

He resumed the kiss, this time tasting her as if she were a delicacy made up of complex spices. His kiss was a *thinking* kiss, one that gathered impressions and measured reactions.

Heaven help her, he could make a chess game of a kiss.

The emotions that swamped Matilda then came too fast to ignore. Rejoicing, to have found this man whose intelligence and compassion had formed a pact of mutual invisibility. Duncan was good-hearted, he was much smarter than he let on, and he was *aroused*.

Answering desire rose in Matilda along with a flood of yearning that revealed her previous encounters to have been mere dalliances. She wanted to consume Duncan Wentworth, to bolt him down like a starving wretch's first decent meal in ages.

And amid the clamorings of desire and joy ran a counter-current of despair. She could enjoy Duncan Wentworth as a respite, a boon, an unlooked-for pleasure, but she'd have to let him go. If she cared for him at all, she'd have to let him go.

He could make her weak and stupid, an easy capture for the colonel, and then where would Papa be? That question had her easing back, though not even thoughts of Papa's possible arrest could inspire her to move away.

"We would suit," Duncan said, his hand moving slowly on Matilda's back. "I am almost certain we would suit."

He could speak coherently, the blighter. His heartbeat was faster, some satisfaction, but he was entirely self-possessed, despite the arousal pressing against Matilda's belly. In bed, Duncan Wentworth would be formidable. His hand on her back said he'd be tender, too, and if she was starved for anything in this life, it was tenderness.

"This is not what I had planned," Matilda said.

"Nor I."

How bemused he sounded. Matilda tarried in his arms for another luscious half minute before she realized that he'd left up to her even the decision of when to abandon his embrace. He'd hold her until springtime, if that was what she wanted.

And it was.

"We must come to an agreement," he said, his lips near her ear.

"I cannot marry you."

"I was under the impression a courtship preceded that decision. Will you allow me to court you, Matilda?"

"Could I stop you?" He was still aroused and he could have this debate. What a singularly focused man.

He massaged her nape, slow circles that melted Matilda's knees.

"You could stop me with a word, my dear, and all that has passed between us since the end of our chess game would be forgotten."

She could not resist this studied, perfect intimacy. Not now. "Court me, then, but know that your efforts are doomed."

"Wentworths thrive on a challenge."

He whispered that warning in Matilda's ear, and she knew she'd be daydreaming of whispers shared with him in a darkened bedchamber.

"I referred, though, to a different agreement."

"I shall sit on the sofa now," she said, moving not one inch, "because as long as you're touching me, I'm witless and wanton."

"Then this will be a very tactile courtship, for your caresses have the same effect on me." He dropped his arms and took Matilda by the hand.

He might have been leading her to Cathay for all her

mind could function, and yet little time had passed since the end of their chess match—their first chess match and their first kiss. How appropriate, that the two occasions should occur in that order.

"What is this agreement you seek?" Matilda said. "This other agreement?"

"The agreement we must reach has to do with your past, the secrets you are keeping, and my obligation as a gentleman to safeguard your welfare."

Matilda settled on the sofa, across the room from the chess set. "Duncan Wentworth, are you preparing to turn up possessive now?" She could not allow that, not for all the kisses in England. For his sake, she could not allow *any* meddling possessiveness.

"Don't be ridiculous." Duncan took the wing chair and crossed an ankle over the opposite knee, the picture of masculine pulchritude at its handsome ease. "You have managed on your own for some time. You found your way to Brightwell, where, but for my unexpected appearance, you'd likely have spent a cozy winter subsisting on snared rabbits, fish, and overlooked potatoes and turnips with nobody the wiser. Any fool with pretensions to *possessing* you would soon find himself in the colonel's situation."

"What col—?" Oh, dear. *Of course*, Duncan would notice that slip. That slip *too*. "So what is this agreement you seek?"

"If you give me information, Matilda, I will use it to protect you. I will not share that information and I will not act without consulting you. In the instant example, however, if some colonel should come nosing about, I will consider him suspect on general principles. If a man claiming to be Thomas Wakefield corresponds with me, I will regard him as a threat unless you reassure me otherwise."

"You will interpret Stephen's theory to mean that what information I let slip, I let slip willingly."

"I shall."

This was . . . not good, that Duncan would involve himself in the capacity of bodyguard, without knowing why Matilda might need one. Not fair.

"What if you are protecting a traitor or a murderess?"

"You could, of course, have put a period to my existence the day we met, but your murderous impulses were apparently on hiatus that morning. If you are a felon of some sort, then I'm a fool, and I deserve the consequences that follow from believing you innocent."

Patently impossible, for Duncan Wentworth to be a fool. "I'm not a murderess." She might well be a traitor. Matilda herself wasn't sure.

Duncan's mouth remained a perfect uninflected pair of lips, while his eyes danced. "Ever so relieved to hear it."

Matilda should not be relieved. She should be packing for her often-delayed unannounced departure, burning her Book of Common Prayer—a grievous sin, surely—and leaving a note telling Lord Stephen to forward funds to her without a word to Duncan.

"I limit myself to one game of chess a day," Matilda said, "when I have a partner who can hold my interest." This was an admission, though Duncan likely couldn't appreciate it as such.

"Do I have the honor of holding your interest, Matilda?"

Matilda saw no advantage in dissembling. "You do. I wish it was not so, for all concerned, but, Duncan Wentworth, you do hold my interest." To make matters worse, she was beaming at him, like sunshine determined to melt away the final snow from early spring.

"Then I'll look forward to our next match." He rose and offered his hand, and Matilda let him assist her to her feet.

* * *

A week of careful study, bad roads, and awful tavern fare had not improved Parker's mood. Dukes were few and far between, a mere two and a half dozen in number give or take, but every damned one of them apparently owned a country estate to the west of London.

Some of these properties were hunting boxes, others minor holdings for warehousing dowagers or younger sons. Still others were lovely estates let out to climbing cits or ambitious horse trainers. To the extent Parker could inquire, he'd not found anybody of Matilda's description recently hired at any of them.

"The whole business wants more effort," Parker grumbled into his ale.

"Shall I fetch another pint, sir?" a serving maid asked. The Waddling Goose was a proper establishment, so her smile was merely polite. She was pretty, though, not one of the gap-toothed dumplings on offer in the humbler establishments.

"No more ale, thank you. When will my meal be served?"

"The private dining room is spoken for, sir. If you are willing to eat here in the common, the food is ready now."

"Are there many ducal properties hereabouts?" The locals knew more than Debrett's and would chatter at length on the least provocation.

She set her pitcher on the table. "Several, sir. There's His Grace of Grafton's stud farm, His Grace of Devonshire has a hunting box, and His Grace of Windham owns a significant parcel—"

Parker was coming to detest the words *His Grace*. "Have any of those dukes died in recent years?"

She looked at him the same way the old tollkeeper had, the same way many people had in the past week—as if Parker had left his wits back in London.

"I'm a military man," he said. "I've been gone from England for years. I haven't kept up with the doings of dukes."

"His Grace of Devonshire went to his reward the same year the Regent took the throne. So did the late Duke of Grafton. As far as I know, the Duke of Windham is in great good health, may God bless and keep him."

Oh, right. God bless and keep a man who likely owned five hundred times what he and his family needed to survive an English winter, while Parker, who'd risked his life repeatedly for the likes of their various graces, drank flat ale and grew saddle sore.

"Do any ducal holdings lie to the west of here?"

A trio of swells arrived at the front desk, bringing in a draft of cold air and the smell of wet wool. "Bring me a flagon of ale, wench!" one called. "I've always wanted to say that. Sounds jolly, don't you think?"

"Teddy's foxed," a second man said.

"Miss," Parker nearly snapped his fingers. "About the ducal holdings."

"I wouldn't know, sir. We're a market town, and I was born and raised here. I've never traveled to the west or even into London. You might ask the young gentlemen. Excuse me." She was off across the common, her smile shifting from polite to friendly.

Parker's coachman sidled past the newcomers, who were making loud noises about needing the private dining room ee-meed-jately.

"Have a seat," Parker said, having taken John Coachman into his confidence of necessity. "We won't be overheard as long as that farce is unfolding at the front desk. What did you learn?"

The coachman spared a pointed look at Parker's half-finished ale, which was what came from borrowing a marquess's equipage. Parker was a tolerated burden, rather than a respected employer. Because Parker had dealt with many a posturing general and pouting lieutenant, he pushed the tankard to the coachman's elbow.

"The stables are busy," the coachman replied, sampling the drink, "with half the local gentry heading north for some foxhunting, and the other half coming and going from London. This is good ale."

"It's tolerable, but then, this is a proper inn." A properly expensive inn, in other words. His lordship the marquess stayed at this establishment on the way to visit family in Bristol, which was why Parker had chosen to make camp here.

"No word of any young ladies fallen on hard times," the coachman said, downing the remaining ale. "The ducal properties are numerous."

"One gathered as much." Parker was haunted by the possibility that he'd already missed the ducal property he needed to find. Worse, Wakefield might have mis-remembered whose home had been memorialized in that landscape or mistaken a duke for an earl.

Or purposely sent Parker off in the wrong direction, except Parker had already combed most of Kent, Surrey, and Sussex looking for Matilda.

"Might I ask a question, sir?"

"You may."

"If we're looking for a female without means, one seeking

to avoid notice, why are we looking at only the best inns and raising questions with only the innkeepers or grooms? A woman in trouble would ask other ladies for aid and avoid drawing any attention from men."

The three dandies had taken over a table and were making rapid progress through a pitcher of beer.

A bolt of irritation shot through Parker to think of Matilda risking her safety among such as that lot. Those three probably considered themselves gentlemen, though by the time they'd swilled another pitcher, they'd pinch the bum of any woman foolish enough to come near them.

"You raise a valid point," Parker said. "What do you propose we, as a company of men, do about it?" Subordinates with any intelligence knew better than to bring up a problem without also having a solution in mind.

"Gentzel is a handsome lad, sir. He could chat up the ladies."

"He's one of our footmen?"

"A good man, though a Devonshire accent makes him hard to understand. Might I raise another thought, sir?"

No. No more thoughts, questions, or problems. Find Matilda or shut your gob. My career and possibly my life depend upon it. Except that Parker could ill afford to offend his brother's second coachman. In truth, this westward gambit was the most promising development Parker had pursued since Matilda had disappeared.

She was in more danger than she knew, if she was still alive. "Say on, man."

"We should be asking the local parsons about recent funerals of young women answering to the missing lady's description. Accidents happen, women despair, rogues abound."

The coachman was fairly young, but, like most of his

kind, his countenance was weathered. He offered his observations gently, for Parker was the young lady's heartbroken
fiancé, as far as anybody knew.

"As much as I'd like to, I cannot disagree with you,"
Parker said slowly. Matilda's death would be lamentable,
very lamentable. Parker still hoped to make her see reason
and go through with the marriage. He'd resume the duties of
a senior officer, leaving Thomas Wakefield to deal with the
consequences of his folly.

Parker would marry Matilda out of pity, because the
daughter of a traitor could not expect to find any better
source of protection than an unassailably loyal military
officer. She'd be grateful to Parker for honoring their betrothal, and contrite for having shown such infernally awful
judgment by running off.

And Parker's superior officers would commend him for
discreetly managing a very delicate business.

"I can have Fitzsimmons inquire of the clergy," the
coachman said, lifting the empty tankard a few inches in the
direction of the serving maid.

"Thank you," Parker said. "When we quit this establishment, we'll find humbler lodgings to the west and continue
our search."

The door to the private dining room opened, and a finely
dressed older couple emerged. The maid curtsied, and the
white-haired fellow passed her a coin.

"I believe my meal will soon be served," Parker said.
"Would you care to join me?" Loyalty should be rewarded,
as should initiative. Besides, Parker might need his brother's
coach and four again, and the coachman's good opinion
would be useful.

"I'd like that, sir. Nothing like fine English beef three
times a day, I always say."

Parker had risen and caught the eye of the serving maid when the three dandies shuffled past, bringing their tankards and pitcher. They made straight for the private dining room, the third one closing the door firmly behind them.

Chapter Ten

Duncan considered meeting Trostle in the study and rejected the notion. Matilda worked there, and the steward mustn't see her. The family parlor would send the wrong message altogether, and the formal parlor was for respected guests.

Duncan chose instead the frigid expanse of the portrait gallery, which the footmen and maids had thoroughly cleaned. Generations of Wentworths looked down upon spotless hearths, sparkling windows, and ornate plaster bearing not one speck of dust or a single cobweb.

Cold, lovely, and ostentatious. "No fires," Duncan said, when Manners would have ladled hot coals onto the grates. "Mr. Trostle won't be staying long."

"He's in the kitchen now, sir. Demanding his nooning and making talk."

"What sort of talk?"

Manners took down a lathe-turned wooden candlestick

from the mantel and re-fitted the beeswax taper so it stood straight in the socket.

"The usual sort with him." Manners drew himself up and gripped both of his lapels. "*A woman who doesn't know her place generally loses it.* He likes that one. Another is, *A fine thing, when the master of the household grasps upon whose hard work his wealth depends,* that sort of talk. Danvers says he's getting worse, but then, Danvers is pretty."

Duncan consulted his watch rather than observe Manners's ears turning red—again. "Do we know anything of Trostle's background?"

The footman moved on to the row of portraits, nudging this one straight, swiping a finger across that one's signature. "He's waiting for his father to die, a squire over in Hampshire. I gather he and his papa don't get along. Mr. Trostle isn't awful, sir. The fellow we had before him was worse."

The lot of factors and stewards Quinn had inherited from the previous Duke of Walden had been driving the estates deeply into debt. When the College of Arms had lit upon Quinn as the ducal heir after several years of searching, significant damage had already been done at the family seat near Yorkshire.

Brightwell hadn't fared much better.

"Your honesty is appreciated, Manners. You needn't defend a man you don't respect."

Manners came to a halt before the portrait of the late duke. His Grace was dressed for shooting, for tramping his acres with a pair of harriers panting at his heels, an unusual portrayal of an aristocrat. Brightwell was set in the distance on a tidy lawn, with beds of colorful tulips lining the lane and circular drive.

"I wasn't much older than Jinks when His Grace was alive. He was a dear old thing. Tried to teach me to play chess, of all the daft notions. Said a child could master the game, when I could barely keep my letters straight. Somewhere up in the attic, we have a painting of him at the chessboard, with the pieces arranged in some famous chess puzzle. He went a bit barmy toward the end, though he was always sweet. Didn't put on airs. Said what he thought. Didn't suffer fools—*or knaves*."

Manners aimed a pointed look at Duncan.

"Please have Mrs. Newbury send up a lavish tray," Duncan said. "Give me about ten minutes with Trostle before the tea arrives, and warn Miss Maddie that Trostle is underfoot."

Manners collected his bucket of hot coals. "Already done that, sir." He gave the gallery another inspection, then headed for the door. "Miss Maddie reminds me of somebody. Can't think who it is. The old duke used to have company by the score, but I were just a lad and mostly kept out of sight belowstairs. Still, it's on the edge of my mind, like a dream you can't recall if you try, but it steals closer in the middle of the vicar's sermon."

"I know exactly what you mean."

Though that tip-of-the-tongue, edge-of-a-dream feeling didn't pertain to Matilda in Duncan's case. She was an entirely new phenomenon, and she'd occasioned in Duncan something like spring fever. On the way home from visiting a tenant, he'd found himself humming old French folk tunes that fit with the rhythm of his horse's hooves slopping along the farm lane.

Humming. He never hummed.

He'd penned a report to Quinn that had nothing to do with pence and quid and everything to do with how nicely situated Brightwell Manor was for the setting it occupied. That epistle had gone into the dustbin, of course.

He'd considered sending to London for a new pair of

boots. Uncle had claimed one could tell a gentleman by his boots. Duncan's were old and comfortable, or perhaps tending toward disreputable. A suitor should not wear disreputable boots. *Colonel Alphonse* had doubtless courted Matilda in spotless boots.

"I am losing my mind," Duncan muttered to the ancestors on the walls.

Or perhaps he was becoming a Wentworth, capable of impetuous behavior, and even self-interested behavior. Capable of considering strategy and objectives beyond travel logistics or philosophical paradoxes.

"There you are, sir." Oscar Trostle strode through the doorway, hand extended. He was blond, blue-eyed, and moving toward middle age with the bluff good cheer of the Saxon yeoman. His boots looked new to Duncan and far too clean considering the weather.

Mrs. Newbury sent Duncan a fulminating look and drew the door closed.

Duncan turned to study the late duke. "Has the custom of knocking on a closed door gone out of fashion, Trostle?"

From the corner of his eye, Duncan saw Trostle weighing alternatives: Blame the innocent housekeeper for that rudeness or show contrition?

"I do apologize, Mr. Wentworth. With the roads in a state, I feared to be tardy."

Blame the weather, a safe option. Duncan ambled to the escritoire situated by a full-length window. The gallery had been designed such that portraits on the inside wall hung between the reach of the sunbeams pouring through windows on the outside wall, though the room at midday was flooded with light.

"I see you neglected to bring your reports." Duncan took a seat behind the desk.

"Beg pardon?"

No chair sat opposite the escritoire, by design. Trostle was left standing, like a menial in the presence of his supervisor. Silly posturing, but preferable to tossing the man through the window.

"You are Brightwell's steward. I assume you keep reports, ledgers, and wage books showing the exact state of the finances week by week. I am responsible for this property now, and that means you are answerable to me for your recordkeeping."

"Of course, sir. Of course." Trostle elected to wander the room rather than ask permission to be seated. "I hadn't considered you'd want to bother with all that detail. This fellow with the dogs is the old duke, the one who let this place get into such a muddle. I ought not to speak ill of my betters, but I'm told His Grace didn't have a head for numbers. Not his fault, of course."

No Oxford-educated chess enthusiast would lack a grasp of mathematics. Duncan took out a nacre-handled penknife and began trimming the quills in the standish one by one.

"The current duke believes his predecessor was victimized by scoundrels and scalawags," Duncan said, "people who betrayed the old man's trust at a time when he was most vulnerable." The shavings piled up on the blotter while Duncan pretended to ignore his steward.

"Never a good thing," Trostle said, "when a staff lacks leadership. I noticed that right off when I took over here. Everybody, from the tenants, to the neighbors, to the house staff, appreciates knowing who's in charge."

Duncan swept the leavings into the dustbin. "I agree, and as I am the person who now fits that description, I'd like your opinion regarding a number of matters."

He quizzed Trostle on everything from the number of

fresh heifers, to the repairs needed on the tenant cottages, to the state of the hedges—badly overgrown, which meant better sport for Trostle, who, as a squire's son, appropriated for himself the privilege of shooting Duncan's game.

"We'll always have a problem with poachers this close to London," Trostle said, gazing out at the snowy back garden. "If we were so inclined, sir, we could take steps to deter them beyond what our gamekeepers have been able to do thus far. The management of game has been left to us, and that can be a lucrative endeavor."

We, us, our... The words were intended to make Duncan feel complicit in the illegal and highly profitable business of supplying London establishments with fresh game. He'd heard those words before, suggesting an even more heinous complicity.

Women expect us to behave as God intended, Wentworth. Procreation is part of the divine plan.

Not like the females protest our attentions, Wentworth. Not for very long, anyway.

The memory of Vicar Jameson's casual excuses still sickened Duncan, and yet, Trostle was merely stealing rabbits, not destroying a young woman's virtue. All over England, trade in game went on despite grievous penalties for poaching and despite sore want of sustenance in many rural communities.

"Brightwell will not involve itself in illegal game sales," Duncan said, dusting his hands. "His Grace of Walden would be very displeased to learn of such practices, as would I."

Trostle leaned a shoulder against the edge of a bay window, his posture suggesting he felt no compunction to behave formally with his employer. "People need to eat, Mr. Wentworth. This estate needs income."

"I need my honor more, Trostle. You are doubtless

aware that the present titleholder comes from a distant and lowly branch of the Wentworth family. His Grace brooks no chicanery, no winking at the law, for he is held to a very high standard by his peers. My cousin must not only *appear* to be worthy of the responsibility he's been entrusted with, he must live up to the demands of his station in truth. I strive to do likewise in my own humble way."

Trostle glanced down the row of portraits. When his gaze lit on Duncan, amusement shown from blue eyes.

"You are my employer, more or less, sir. We manage Brightwell as you see fit."

No, we do not. A brisk rap on the door prevented Duncan from offering that correction. "Come in."

Mrs. Newbury entered with a gleaming silver tray in her hands. The tea service had to weigh two stone, but Duncan remained seated, as an arrogant prig would.

Neither did Trostle make any effort to help a fellow employee.

Duncan gestured to the blotter. "You may pour out."

She wrapped the handle of the teapot in her apron and poured a single cup, then stepped back.

"You are excused."

She curtsied, sparing Trostle not a glance.

Trostle watched her retreating form, and not respectfully. "You talk about living up to the demands of one's station. Brightwell's housekeeper would do well to recall her own station."

Duncan took a sip of tea hotter and stronger than he preferred. This was stage business, a display of superiority over an employee to whom he'd not offer so much as a tea cake.

"Explain yourself."

"I heard Mrs. Newbury was faking illness last week, and

just between us, sir, she's no better than she should be. You can put a lace cap on any female—that doesn't make her proper."

Duncan set down his teacup gently, lest the relief he felt become obvious. *Now I can hate you. Now you've eased my burden and made the way clear.*

"You imply that Mrs. Newbury lacks morals?"

Trostle grabbed a little French chair padded in red velvet and set it before the desk. He seated himself and leaned forward, as if imparting confidences.

"If your origins are humble, you might not know how a great house is run, sir. A housekeeper is allowed certain privileges, but she must not overstep. Mrs. Newbury oversteps. She goes through candles like a hostler consumes beer. I haven't wanted to say anything, because she'll not find another post as good as this one, but stealing is stealing."

Trostle's expression was that of a man from whom a confession had been dragged, but his gaze on Duncan was assessing: Had the performance been successful?

Well, yes, in a sense. "What you tell me is most disappointing, Trostle, though not exactly a revelation. The habit of graft is hard to break. I suspect many in the vicinity have come to view Brightwell less than respectfully as a result."

Trostle sat back, his features schooled to reluctant agreement. "I'm glad you see my point, sir. I've wondered about some of our tenants, too, and have been waiting for an opportunity to share my concerns with you."

Oh, waiting for an opportunity, *indeed*. Duncan finished his tea, knowing that sacking Trostle was not only the right thing to do, it was necessary for the good of Brightwell and all who relied on the estate for a livelihood.

"Trostle, you must not believe all the gossip that comes to you," Duncan said. "For example, I can tell you that

Mrs. Newbury was gravely ill and that the local physician refused to heed my summons. She was not faking sick. Not in the least."

Trostle rose. "Whose word are you taking for that, sir? That lot you have belowstairs has had years to guard each other's backs. They'll close ranks against you, whisper behind their hands about you. I've seen it before. No respect when respect is needed."

Leave. The single word begged to be spoken, to be shouted. "Respect must be earned, Trostle."

"I do my best, Mr. Wentworth, but you've a half dozen footmen, and not a one of them could be bothered to light this hearth. That's not respect."

That's economy, you dolt. "To light a pair of hearths nearly sixty feet apart in a room I intend to use for less than an hour is ridiculous, Trostle. Our interview is at an end."

You are sacked. Duncan said the words in his head, but as Trostle paused before the empty hearth, no words were spoken. That decision could not be unmade, no replacement for Trostle was on hand, and he was at least the devil the staff knew.

"I'm sorry to be the bearer of bad news, sir, but honesty is the best policy."

Turn the lying cheat off without a character. The voice in Duncan's head sounded very much like Quinn—a Yorkshire growl with more than a hint of menace.

"Here is how we shall proceed," Duncan said. "You will deliver to my butler all of the ledgers and books you've kept since becoming steward at Brightwell. Wage books, receipts, tithes, everything. I shall review those records and acquaint myself with Brightwell's financial history."

Trostle braced a hand on the mantel and studied the empty hearth. "That's a lot of history, sir."

A lot of theft? "I hope to see Brightwell set to rights for a good long while. That means developing a thorough grasp of every error made in the recent past. With winter setting in, such a task appeals."

"Very well, sir. I wasn't aware you'd hired a butler."

"I've promoted Manners." Duncan *would* promote Manners, as soon as Trostle had gone stealing and lying on his way. For present purposes, Duncan was advancing a knight whom Trostle had probably mistaken for a pawn. "He's hardworking, loves this house, and can be relied upon to put its welfare before his own."

Even in the face of that salvo, Trostle didn't flinch. "Commendable loyalty in a man so young, I suppose. I hope he proves worthy of your trust."

"As do I." *Let him go. Get rid of him. Turn him off.* Stephen's voice had joined Quinn's in Duncan's head.

"If you'll excuse me," Mr. Trostle said, "my missus will want a recounting of this interview. She sets great store by the goings-on here and shares my high hopes for Brightwell's future."

Trostle had a wife. Of course he had a wife. Most men his age had wives. "Have you children?"

"A pair of darling little girls, sir, and the missus and I spoil them shamelessly. They get their beauty from their mama, and my job is to buy the hair ribbons and keep the pony fed. My mother-in-law lives with us as well, and has made very pointed comments about my duty to provide her a grandson or two."

Even a scheming bounder could be a doting father, even a philandering rake could deliver a stirring sermon on the topic of self-denial.

"You may tell your missus that your duties will require you to travel in the immediate future," Duncan said. "I'm sending you to Bristol, where I want you to take a look at the circular saws used in the naval yards. We have a surfeit of lumber here, and I'm told those saws can cut wood at more than ten times the rate experienced sawyers can manage. Bring me an estimate of what it would take to set up a circular saw and sawpit here at Brightwell."

Trostle paused by the door. "You're sending me out to Bristol now, sir? In this weather?"

"The roads are passable, Yuletide is some weeks away, and the task requires a knowledgeable eye. If my request is beyond your abilities, then please say so. I'm sure the under-steward will cheerfully undertake the journey."

"Under-steward?"

Duncan rose. Even if Matilda joined the mental chorus clamoring for Trostle's dismissal, Duncan would not sack the man today, not until he knew the Trostle family's circumstances in greater detail.

"Brightwell is in trouble, Trostle. Despite your best efforts, the estate is not solvent, and more effort is needed to make it so. His Grace has broken the entail, and the property can thus be sold if I can't set it to rights. I'd rather not see Brightwell broken up or pass from the Wentworth family's ownership. Clearly, more resources are needed to address the situation here, and I have taken steps to hire an under-steward. Shall you make the journey to Bristol, or shall I send someone else?"

"I can do a bit of shopping for the missus in Bristol," Trostle said. "When would you like me to leave?"

"Immediately."

Trostle's annoyance was a fleeting glower at the door, then he recovered and approached Duncan with an out-stretched hand.

Duncan poured himself another cup of tea.

Trostle bowed and withdrew, while Duncan took his tea and stood before the late duke. "I should have sacked him."

His Grace remained memorialized with his loyal hounds, a gun propped over his shoulder.

"I should have sacked him without a character, but he has a family." Duncan took a sip of tea and nearly scalded his tongue. "I have family, too, and they would have sacked him."

"Talking to yourself," Stephen said from the doorway, "surely a sign of inchoate dementia. It's colder than the ninth circle of hell in here. Maybe you're in the early stages of hypothermia as well."

Stephen knew all about illnesses of both the body and the mind. What did he know about a troubled heart? "I sent Trostle to Bristol."

His lordship closed the distance to the tea tray. "Probably qualifies as a version of purgatory this time of year. Did he admit to stealing you blind?"

"More or less, and he attempted to sully the reputations of any loyal to this house. The tea is very hot."

"I like it hot. I'm the bearer of news."

Stephen was no longer a boy. Every time Duncan came to this realization, it made him a little sadder. The sun slanting through the windows illuminated the face of a young man rather than a youth. The manner in which Stephen grasped a delicate porcelain teacup—confident, graceful, unselfconscious—was a man's grasp, not a boy's.

"You aren't gloating, so the news can't be that awful."

"Quinn and Jane are paying you a call, and they're bringing the children."

Dear... *God.* "Meddling. Meddling when I can least afford their interference."

Stephen considered his teacup, the steam wafting up in a shaft of sunshine. "I'll do what I can, Duncan, but what will you tell them about our Matilda?"

* * *

"I learned after yesterday's interview with Trostle that I'm to host a visit from more family," Duncan said, settling a pair of spectacles on his nose. "This was inevitable, though no arrival date has been disclosed. The children will slow down the raiding party, but not stop its progress." He occupied the desk near the window, where the light was best for reading.

The current work in progress was his essay on the Vatican, which had fascinated Matilda, given his training in theology. She still had a pair of Duncan's eyeglasses—they helped a great deal when deciphering his handwriting—so he must be wearing a spare pair.

"You make a visit from family sound like Old Testament retribution." For Matilda, the news was sad, but hardly a surprise. She had promised Duncan only that her tenure at Brightwell would be temporary.

"Quinn and Jane are bringing the children, so I mustn't complain too loudly. Three females, the oldest of them about five years of age. One delights in seeing the great Quinn Wentworth on his hands and knees, trying to whinny like a pony but sounding like a bear in distress."

Matilda rose from her chair by the hearth and took the glasses from Duncan's nose. "You envy him that privilege."

Duncan appeared to thrive in solitude. His life was lived mostly through his intellect, and yet, he'd known Jinks was hungry. He'd pulled Lord Stephen back from the brink of adolescent despair any number of times. Among his correspondence had been a note to the Lady Elizabeth Wentworth on Birdsong Lane in London. If she was a ducal cousin, she was a child of tender years, and Duncan was doubtless her most devoted correspondent.

He was here, attempting a task he disliked, simply because another cousin—younger, with few trustworthy allies—had asked it of him.

Duncan Wentworth would make a ferociously loving father.

"This essay waxes too philosophical," he said, laying the pages on the blotter. "You must be ruthless with my prose, Matilda. Excise the churchly maunderings, leave the architectural descriptions."

"Never. You are the first writer I've come across who can connect the two—the theology and the builder's reality— and more than any other treatise, this one convinces me your work deserves publication."

He was pleased with her defense of his prose. She knew this by his scowl, by the impatient drumming of his fingers on the blotter. Already, she was learning to decode his mannerisms, learning to see what others would express with a smile.

She would be forced to leave him. His family was preparing to storm the premises—ducal family, no less. Matilda knew, with the same sinking sensation she'd felt when she'd realized what Papa had so carelessly left in his satchel, she would have to leave Brightwell and its owner.

An itinerant peddler had warned her that fugitives must always cut a fresh trail. Never double back, never return to a particular town or inn. Matilda removed her own spectacles and laid them beside Duncan's, then draped her shawl—one today—around his shoulders and settled herself in his lap.

"You must promise me something, Duncan."

His arms came around her slowly, securely. "There's little I could refuse you."

"You will publish these treatises. They are not the casual scribblings of a privileged younger son with no purpose in life. They are keen and respectful observations from a student of humanity. You look upon the world with a tolerant eye and a need to understand rather than judge."

His kindness, lurking beneath an enormous reserve and even greater intellect, had saved Matilda's life. Soon it would break her heart.

"You do me too much honor. I'd like to kiss you."

He would not so much as buss her cheek, not unless he was certain his kisses were welcome. Matilda loved that about him, loved the unbreakable self-restraint he wore like shining armor. He would no sooner raise his voice to a footman than he would castigate Stephen for the racket resulting from construction of a lift.

And yet, for a snared rabbit, Duncan Wentworth, unarmed, had taken on a felon wielding a knife.

Matilda closed her eyes. "I would adore for you to kiss me."

Duncan sailed past preliminary moves, cradled the back of Matilda's head in his palm, and settled his mouth over hers.

So warm. She sank her hands into his hair—how she loved to fuss and muss him—and kissed him back. A genteel brawl ensued, with tongues twining, bodies pressing close, and the occasional frustrated mutter when clothing became disobliging.

"I want you to teach me to curse," Matilda panted, her forehead pressed to Duncan's shoulder. "I want you to teach me the words nobody teaches a lady in English."

She ended up straddling Duncan's lap, his arousal pressing

between her legs. Too many layers of skirts, breeches, shawls, and petticoats came between them, and yet, she could feel his desire.

He drew the shawl up around her shoulders. "The usual expletives include damn, damnation, and hell, with the predictable variations. Bloody is considered inexcusably vulgar, and Stephen occasionally uses shite and bollocks to good advantage. If I can't get my hands under your bloody, bedamned, infernal skirts in the next ten seconds I will lose my damned mind and my bollocks will explode."

"Oh, that is lovely, Duncan."

"Also the perishing truth. Lean up."

Matilda hoisted herself a few inches by bracing herself on his shoulder, and he sorted out her skirts.

"I am courting you, you will recall," Duncan said. "If this variety of courting is not to your liking, you will please alert me to that fact."

"I like this variety of courting so much I want to unfasten your falls."

She'd made love in a moving coach (a hilarious undertaking), on a pile of straw (itchy), and once on a blanket beneath a venerable oak that had scattered acorns in all the wrong locations. Here, surrounded by years of Duncan's journals, the fire crackling, the house otherwise quiet, the setting finally seemed right even if the timing was all wrong.

"The sofa," Duncan said. "Let us at least afford ourselves the comfort of the sofa. Hold on to me."

As long as I can. Matilda wrapped her arms about his shoulders as Duncan rose with her and crossed the room, her legs scissored around his middle.

He carried her as if hauling full-grown females about was no effort, and when he settled with her on the sofa, Matilda held on for a moment longer. Leaving him would kill her, though she'd do it. Treason tainted all who came within its ambit, and Matilda brought treason with her everywhere.

"Your falls," she said, easing her grip. "Let me undo…"

He made no protest as she undid the buttons that held one side of his breeches closed. When she got her hands on him, his head fell back against the sofa, gaze hooded.

Duncan was not the classic English lord, with blond hair, blue eyes, and a gracious, flirtatious manner. He was serious, intelligent to a fault, and no longer young. Guilt stirred beneath the desire waking up every part of Matilda's body. He deserved a woman who'd stay by his side, love him for his many strengths, and never betray his trust.

She could not be that woman, and she could not deny herself the intimacy he offered her now. He'd forgive her for abandoning him—he was that honorable—but she might never forgive herself.

"I have not locked the door," Duncan said. "Stephen will barge in here thinking to protect my virtue, and I will have to kill him."

Matilda stared at him, then stared down at his exposed member. "Lock the door?" What was he going on about? Holy cherubim…Perhaps Frenchmen as a race were not particularly well endowed, or perhaps German dukes were only modestly—

Duncan kissed her nose. "I'll be back."

He set her aside on the sofa, crossed the room at an easy prowl, and flipped the lock. He shrugged out of his coat, tossed it onto the desk, and stood two yards away, his falls half undone, his hair tousled.

His expression was that of chess master contemplating the sacrifice of a major piece—even a queen, perhaps—in aid of serious strategy.

"You are sure, Matilda?"

Don't ask me that. "I know exactly what we're offering each other, and I know that I want to share this with you."

He ran his hand through his hair, stared out the window for a moment, and then rejoined Matilda on the sofa.

She had the sense that in those few instants, Duncan had weighed all the possibilities—from approaches to lovemaking, to her eventual departure, to the impending visit from the ducal relations—and he'd reached conclusions Matilda could only guess at.

She was too muddled to plan moves or deduce strategy.

"I'm out of practice," Duncan said, taking her hand and kissing her knuckles. "Years out of practice when it comes to intimate pleasures, but the longer I look at you, the more I touch you, the more ideas flood my mind, all of them lovely. Will you come with me?"

Chapter Eleven

"Your taste is refined, my lady," Wakefield said. "I will continue my search for the exact right piece to set upon your piano."

Lady Elspeth Cadwallader offered her hand. "Promise you will be tireless, Mr. Wakefield. My musicale is scheduled for the end of the month, and all must be perfect."

All had to be perfect, but at bargain prices and only after Wakefield had shown her half the French porcelain for sale in London and had sent to Paris for a few more pieces besides.

At his own expense, of course. "Both of your daughters are performing?"

"A duet," her ladyship said, beaming as if no pair of siblings had ever done likewise. "Written especially for them by a very talented fellow from a ducal family."

God rot all ducal families and their country holdings. "I'll look for a figure that represents harmony and dual forces, shall I? Psyche and Cupid?"

Her ladyship paused in the doorway to her parlor. "I mustn't be obvious, Mr. Wakefield. My daughters need husbands, but they need to be happy too. Cupid and Psyche had rather a difficult time on the way to lasting happiness, for all their union eventually prospered."

Her ladyship was so earnest in her regard for her children. Wakefield abruptly needed to be away from her and her maternal devotion.

"Not Cupid and Psyche then," he said. "Perhaps a shepherdess with her flocks." Such figures abounded, each one more insipid than the last.

Lady Elspeth was ever polite, and thus she accompanied Wakefield to her own front door.

"You must miss your dear Matilda terribly. Does she at least write to you?"

Her ladyship had clearly married young, if she had two daughters who were already out. Wakefield put her age at less than forty, and she was maturing gracefully. She had a way of making him feel as if nobody in all the world could locate the desperately needed painting, sculpture, or vase that would ensure her eternal happiness. She'd been widowed five years ago, and Wakefield hadn't heard so much as a snippet of gossip about her.

Standing in her foyer, parental commiseration beaming from her green eyes, Wakefield wanted to break something—the porcelain figure of Aphrodite on the sideboard, perhaps. He'd made not a farthing's worth of profit on that sale.

"Matilda is a conscientious correspondent, but a father worries." More and more, the longer she was missing, and still Wakefield's superiors urged him to leave matters alone. Weeks ago, he'd deduced that she was in London and trying to discreetly contact him. He'd deferred to the wishes of his superiors then, and regretted his decision ever since.

"The ocean is so dratted wide," Lady Elspeth said. "One of my worst fears is that my daughters will fall in love with Americans. I shall have to leave England if that happens, because what matters a Mayfair address if I can't hug my girls?"

She was tightening a noose of guilt with each well-meant word. "Your devotion to them does you credit, my lady. I will redouble my efforts to find you an exquisite piece for your musicale."

The butler had handed Wakefield's greatcoat to Lady Elspeth and then retreated into the bowels of the house. The day was beastly cold, and a bitter wind made a journey of even a few streets uninviting.

And Matilda is somewhere in the countryside, alone, without means.... Because the Crown and its various foreign counterparts must play their little games, in which Wakefield had always been a willing pawn, provided the compensation was generous.

"This garment is lovely," her ladyship said, holding up Wakefield's greatcoat. "I don't know as I've seen another like it."

"The workmanship is Russian. Matilda bought it for me when we spent a winter in St. Petersburg." He hadn't meant to say that, though it was the truth. "She has an eye for quality, in art, fashion, and the company she keeps."

"You're proud of her." Lady Elspeth smoothed her hand over Wakefield's shoulder. "I can hear that in your voice. I do hope you'll introduce us when she returns from her travels."

Not if she's wanted for treason, you don't. "The two of you would get along famously. She hasn't your ear for music, but she's passionate about chess and very well read." *Fat lot of good that would do her on an English winter night.*

"Tell her to come home. Broadening the mind is all well and good, and heaven knows once a woman marries, her time is not her own, but tell her to come home."

She passed Wakefield his scarf, a sumptuously soft purple cashmere Matilda had found in Edinburgh.

"What are we supposed to do with the empty hours, Thomas?" Lady Elspeth brushed her fingers along the curled brim of Wakefield's top hat. "Our spouses expire, and one can't be angry about that, though one is, and then our children grow up. Again, one knows the natural order calls for such eventualities, but what is one to *do* about them? You will think me pathetic."

Wakefield had made good coin gathering such confidences from unlikely sources. His role as a gentleman merchant made conversational intimacies natural, and he'd been well paid for his skills. He'd forgotten that confidences could be gifts, unasked for, freely bestowed.

Had he also forgotten how to be a father?

"We take comfort from our friendships, my lady, and should that fail, I'm told spoiling grandchildren is a fine pastime."

He offered his signature benevolent smile, she beamed back at him, and then he was out in the frigid air, cursing the Crown, foreign governments, musicales, and wayward daughters in particular. Pray God, Matilda eluded Lord Atticus Parker's clutches until Wakefield could find her, though better that Parker come upon her than some factor of a more ruthless bent.

"Her ladyship didn't like any of the angels," Carlu said, falling in step with Wakefield at the foot of the drive. "I told you she wouldn't."

Wakefield's porter had carried the figures, wrapped in thick wool and boxed with chopped straw, the distance from Wakefield's home to Lady Elspeth's.

"She likes *me*," Wakefield said. "I suspect that's the point of the exercise."

"My esteemed employer is only now realizing this? The English winter has curdled your brains, sir. My testicles, should I ever have occasion to see them again, are likely curdled, too, but the infernal cold has shriveled my manly abundance to—"

"Carlu, how many toddies did you enjoy in Lady Elspeth's kitchen?"

"Two. I believe rum was involved in the recipe. You know how I am about rum."

Wakefield walked quickly, the better to battle the penetrating cold. A top hat was damned idiocy in weather like this, but an English gentleman did not go abroad bareheaded.

"You're to return for the figures tomorrow," Wakefield said. "She wants a day to consider her decision."

"She wants you to come back tomorrow. Fortunately, the under-cook is friendly, and I flatter myself that—"

"Carlu, for God's sake, if you have something to say, say it."

Leather did not keep feet dry, but at least Wakefield had only a few streets to tramp in the slush and muck of London. Where was Matilda, and was she still wearing the single pair of half boots she'd taken with her months ago?

"Parker is making his way to Brightwell. His progress is slow—he's gone off on several goose chases—but within days, a fortnight at most, he'll find the place."

"We have some time, then." Not much, some. "Has Matilda been seen in the vicinity?"

"She has not, that we know of. The current owner of

Brightwell is some banker turned duke, an absentee land-lord. He's sent a cousin out to Berkshire to manage the place, though he's also broken the entail. Could be he's getting ready to sell. In any case, the house has only a small staff, and the cousin keeps mostly to himself."

"So we know where Parker is, but not where Matilda is." No different from a week ago, or four months ago.

"This is when you give me permission to travel to Berkshire, or you tell me we're to travel there with Tomas and Petras. We pay a discreet midnight call on this cousin, search his house from attics to cellars with no one the wiser, and when Parker arrives, we make sure the ditches are very slippery and deep."

"We don't even know if she's at Brightwell."

Carlu came to a halt at a street crossing. "Because we haven't been given the resources to establish that fact, but you've said she loved the old duke and she was never happier than when you spent a few weeks out there every summer. What sort of father leaves his daughter to face the likes of the colonel without reinforcements? And God forbid she's found by somebody other than the colonel before we can get to her."

The cold had driven all but a few souls indoors, and thus Carlu's insubordination hadn't been overheard.

"What if she stole those plans, Carlu? What if she was searching for them for her own purposes when Parker came upon her? Then my daughter might well be a traitor to the Crown, and any attempt on my part to rescue her only implicates me in her crime."

Another theory was bound to be popular with the military: Those plans implicated Matilda in Wakefield's crime. That notion had substantial factual support, viewed from a certain inconvenient perspective.

Eyes colder than a Moscow winter wind glared at Wakefield. "*She is your daughter.* If she's a sneak-thief traitor, she learned from your example or the example of others with whom you consorted. She has no other family, and yet you hesitate."

Condemnation dripped from every word, but then, Carlu was a man far from home, with a difficult past. He did not hold opinions, he championed eternal verities.

"She should have come to me, Carlu. Why didn't she come to me when she first found the plans?"

"Because you did not warn her of your little games; because you, like most Englishmen, lack a proper respect for the resourcefulness of women. Because the colonel could have had her taken up for questioning before you came down for breakfast. Warrants, writs, and summonses can be issued at all hours for a marquess's son turned loyal soldier, and Parker knows exactly how to obtain them. She can't come to you now because the damned colonel has been guarding your front door when you're not busy stuffing him with tea and biscuits in the family parlor."

All true. "Parker is no longer guarding my door, and Matilda is still in hiding."

"She's in hiding, *if* she's alive." Carlu stalked off.

Wakefield kicked the nearest pile of snow, sending slush flying up to strike him in his own face.

* * *

Duncan was not about to make love with his intended for the first time amid dusty old treatises, frigid air pouring off the window, no place to properly adore the lady except one lumpy sofa.

"Come with you?" Matilda frowned the same way she'd

frowned when Duncan had begun distracting her on the chessboard with his prancing bishops.

He stuffed his shirttails back into his waistband and did up the buttons of his falls. "The occasion wants comfort and privacy. Also warmth. I know where we can have all three." *And each other.*

She nodded, the barest gesture of assent, but Duncan rejoiced in the trust it signified. He led Matilda down the corridor and around one turn, then bowed her through a carved door.

"This is your sitting room," she said. "Your personal sitting room."

"Through there is my personal bedroom, where a blazing fire is kept burning, despite my orders to conserve fuel throughout the house."

She went to the mantel, upon which Duncan had displayed a collection of Stephen's sketches. "This is you, and that must be the duke. The resemblance is marked."

To behold her among his personal effects was a pleasure. What awaited them in the next room went beyond mere pleasure, and yet, Duncan let her explore. Every man had certain physical attributes that were mostly the same—a pair of hands, a nose, limbs, eyes, a mouth. What he chose to keep about him in his private quarters was unique to him.

"The duke is both taller and more muscular than I," Duncan said, "and he prefers numbers to letters. I would call him an altogether more robust specimen. The ladies call him gorgeous."

Matilda considered the drawing, her expression bringing to mind the early moves of her chess game.

"The duke is less refined than you are," she said. "More of a broadsword while you're a rapier. The look in your eyes is the same, though—assured enough to intimidate any who behold you. You have the same nose. His mouth is grim while yours is serious. I doubt he plays chess, but then, the ladies drawn to his appearance probably aren't interested in chess."

I am in love. I am in love with a woman who sees me as an improvement over my dear, wealthy, titled, handsome, younger cousin, with a woman who thrives on the intellectual exercise of a chess game.

"Who is this?" She ran a finger around the wooden frame of the only sketch Duncan had done himself.

"That is Jane with her oldest, Elizabeth, whom we call Bitty. The child is, in a manner of speaking, what brought Jane and Quinn together." Courting Matilda meant treating her as a member of the family. Quinn and Jane's unusual past was not a secret, but neither was it generally known.

"They anticipated their vows?" Matilda set the drawing back among the collection on the mantel and began rearranging their order.

"Jane was a widow in an interesting condition. Quinn had means and no patience for sentimental courtship rituals." While Duncan—for the first time in his life—wanted to escort a particular woman onto the ducal dance floor and waltz holding her in a scandalously daring embrace. At the conclusion of the set, he'd bow extravagantly over her gloved hand and gaze adoringly into her eyes, while Stephen, Quinn, and the rest of polite society goggled in awed silence.

Or laughed uproariously. Duncan didn't particularly care what they thought of him or his intended, and his indifference was not his usual studied detachment. They were family, of course their regard mattered.

Matilda mattered more.

So this was love. This daft, fierce, exaltation of emotions and sensations. "Will you come to bed with me, Matilda?"

She'd set the sketch of Jane and Bitty in the middle of the collection, an improvement over the previous arrangement.

"That's the best one of the lot. The others are competent, some of them interesting. They lack courage. The one of you and the duke, for example. See how unoriginal the composition is. Two men, side by side, looking directly at the artist. The background lacks a single symbol or contradiction, unless roman columns and latticed windows qualify. If not for your particular features, the sketch would have no texture, no topography."

More than her specific observations, the assurance with which Matilda spoke struck Duncan. She was confident of her artistic opinions and backed them up with technical assessments. Something less substantial than memory teased at the edge of Duncan's mind, an association, a snippet of text. He couldn't concentrate enough to bring the recollection into focus.

"And the sketch of Jane and Bitty?"

"The best art isn't perfect, and its imperfections are part of why it fascinates. The artist—I doubt it's the same hand as drew the others—took risks with the composition. The mother and child are not sitting idly in the middle of the page, but, rather, in motion and enthralled with one another."

Bitty was in Jane's lap, reaching up to encircle her mother's neck in a hug. Jane was bending toward the child, intent on arranging a blanket around Bitty's shoulders.

"We see barely a profile of the mother's expression," Matilda went on "and less than three-quarters of the child's, but the resemblance is caught in the features, and in the joy the mother and daughter take in one another's affection. They love each other, and the artist loved them, and had the bravery to put his tender regard on the page. This is *art*, and this is love. The artist's message could not be more boldly conveyed. These other pictures are so much sketching."

Stephen would wince to hear that opinion of his artistic efforts. Duncan nearly crowed.

He stood halfway across the room from Matilda and flailed about looking for words. *Thank you. Of course I love them. I'm not an artist. I'm not brave. I haven't been brave for years.*

He covered the distance and wrapped his arms around Matilda. "You see too much."

She tucked in close, quieting a panic inside Duncan. "I have seen too much. You drew that picture."

He would never, ever stop loving her. "I have others, from my travels. Stephen claims they have a unique charm. When Stephen is attempting to be kind, one worries."

"I want to see them, Duncan. I want to see every single one, and Stephen is jealous. He can make mechanical drawings and accurate elevations, but art has been denied him That is a sore affliction in anybody's life."

Duncan considered the idea that he might be an artist rather than a teacher, or possibly both. He couldn't hold the thought because Matilda was in his arms.

"I'll show you every sketch I've ever done, but right now, I'd like to show you my bedroom."

Matilda sighed, a happy sound accompanied by the fragrance of roses and the sensation of her relaxing in his embrace. Truly relaxing, giving him her weight, her trust, her everything. He knew, then, who and what he was: He was the man born to love and cherish Matilda Wakefield, for however long she allowed him those privileges.

* * *

"One must allow that the hostelry qualifies as lowly," John Coachman said.

"Humble," Parker replied, peering into the teapot. "Clean and respectable, but humble. Affordable to a woman with limited means, unremarkable to somebody trying to remain hidden."

No matter how long he let the leaves steep, the tea would never be strong—if it was even tea. At such an establishment, all manner of hedge sweepings ended up in the teapot, with nary a leaf of the real article to be found. John Coachman had ordered ale, though that option presented even more potential hazards.

This inn was quiet as more successful inns were not. Nobody made an entrance here, nobody shouted greetings to a jovial innkeeper or flirted with the pretty maids. The maids were too tired and skinny to be pretty; the innkeeper mumbled and shuffled in response to his wife's shouted commands.

To think of Matilda in such environs curdled Parker's belly, but better here than in prison. He had a plan for preventing that—a good plan—but that plan turned on finding Matilda and convincing her of a slight variation on the truth.

A variation she'd be eager to believe.

The inn stank of wet wool and damp leather, with the kitchen adding the aromas of cooked meat and leeks. Half of Wellington's campaign across Spain into France had borne these scents, and Parker would ever associate them with suffering and death.

He poured himself a cup from the teapot. The liquid was hot, and sugar and milk were on hand to disguise its true nature.

"Do we keep pushing westward?" the coachman asked. "The grooms expect to remove with the marquess to the ancestral seat at Yuletide. Most of them hail from Sussex and have family there."

The need to explore increasingly unprepossessing inns meant Parker had meandered for days in the wilds of Berkshire. To request more than a few weeks' leave for hunting would attract the notice of Parker's fellow officers, and that he was not permitted to do.

"We'll turn north soon," Parker said. "Matilda likes art and architecture. Oxford would appeal to her." As would the concentration of strutting lordlings who fancied a game of chess between their wenching and wagering. Matilda wouldn't play in public, of course, but she was incapable of walking past a game in progress, and the coffeehouses and taverns in Oxford had chess tables.

The idea comforted him—it was a good idea—and it annoyed: Why hadn't he thought of Matilda's little hobby sooner?

The door opened and two men entered, stomping snow from their boots and letting in a bitter draft.

The innkeeper's wife rose from her desk. "G'day, gents. Are you here for a meal?"

"A meal, your best spirits, and a room with a roaring fire," the smaller man said. He was slender, and his clothing had once been fine, probably several owners ago. His companion was taller and stockier, his fleshy jowls turned ruddy by the cold.

"We don't light the fires in the guest rooms until after supper," the woman replied. "And you have your choice of gin, whiskey, or brandy, all of it legal. Where you coming from?"

The brandy would be smuggled, watered down, and expensive, in other words. John Coachman took another sip of his ale, and Parker was abruptly glad to have a companion at his table. The two new arrivals were ruffians, probably members of the poaching gangs that plagued the English countryside in bold numbers.

The tea was every bit as bad as anticipated. Parker added a lump of crumbling sugar, a desperate measure indeed.

"Let a man know that he needn't do an honest day's work," Parker muttered, "and you've ruined his character for life." Parker's father, the late marquess, had offered that same sentiment, usually from the padded comfort of his elegant town coach.

"They work," the coachman replied. "They likely work very hard and have little to show for it, and they look as if they could use a friendly drink."

The notion was distasteful, also shrewd. Parker raised his hand. "Join us, gentlemen. The weather has stopped our westward progress and boredom threatens."

The two men exchanged a glance, smiled at each other and then at Parker.

"Don't mind if we do," the smaller fellow said. "Herman, pay the lady. You meet all the nicest people in the commons of our fine English inns."

"It's your turn to pay, Jeffy," the bigger man said. "I paid last time."

"For friendly company over a tankard of ale," Parker said, "I'm happy to pay, particularly if you fellows are familiar with the estates in these surrounds. We're looking for a ducal property that changed hands sometime in the past few years. Four stories, red brick, circular drive, set against a mature woods. The place might need some attention. It's a minor holding, and you know how the nobs can be about spending money that doesn't directly benefit them."

The travelers exchanged the barest whisper of a glance. *They knew.* They knew the exact property Parker had been searching for. They knew, and they would tell him everything he wanted to know if he and John Coachman had to drink them under the table to get the information from them.

* * *

Duncan's bedchamber was exactly what Matilda had expected—tidy, pleasant, uncluttered—and also a revelation. The art Duncan kept near him was personal and very fine: the duchess and her daughter seated at the piano, an oil of a flower girl with her wares. The colors were exquisite, the composition beguilingly simple. Papa would not rest until he'd discovered the painter's name.

Which Matilda could never tell him, of course.

On the windowsill sat a blue-and-white porcelain vase so delicate it seemed to hold the sunshine in addition to three purple chrysanthemum blooms. Saint-Cloud work, based on the creamy undertone of the white, or possibly—the finish wanted examination with a quizzing glass—Meniccy.

A patchwork quilt in purple, green, and cream squares was folded along the back of the sofa, the colors echoing in a floral rug and in the emerald bed hangings. The room smelled of beeswax and lemon spiced with lavender, and everything, from the oak parquet floor, to the wardrobe, to the desk by the window, glowed with evidence of good care.

"This was the old duke's room," Duncan said. "The connecting door in the dressing closet opens onto the duchess's dressing closet. Both spaces are paneled in cedar, which inclines one to linger over a choice between four white shirts."

And, someday, Duncan hoped Matilda would be at his side, guiding that choice. He didn't have to say that. Matilda could feel the hope filling the room even as she pretended to study a sketch.

"This must be Lord Stephen's brother. How old was he in this drawing?" Duncan's talent was evident in the realism of the portrait.

"Seventeen. Quinn sat for me dressed in his livery, but refused to let me draw him wearing it. Once upon a time, the current duke of Walden was a footman."

"That is doubtless a family secret." The footman version of the duke was an exquisitely masculine subject and subtly unhappy. Anxiety clouded his eyes, as did a pugnacity at odds with his long lashes and the slightly unkempt dark hair fringing his brow.

Duncan had perfectly caught the last rays of boyhood's sunset and the dawning power of the grown man.

"His Grace's past is not bruited about," Duncan said, shrugging out of his coat. "In two generations, his origins will be something Wentworths boast of. Shall I loosen your stays?"

"I wear jumps," Matilda said. "I grew accustomed to them in France, and with front lacing, one needn't trouble a maid for assistance."

Duncan positioned himself between Matilda and the window. "Shall I loosen your jumps?"

The sketches in the other room had derailed Matilda's desire, distracting her with a less fraught passion than what Duncan offered. Papa had claimed that Matilda's mother had a much better eye for art than he would ever have, and that he'd learned much from Mama.

Standing before Duncan, on the brink of making love in a proper bed with a proper man for the first time in ages, Matilda acknowledged an exhaustion that had little to do with food or sleep. She was tired of being self-sufficient, tired of being alone.

Would this interlude with Duncan sustain her when she

was forced back into unrelenting self-reliance, or weaken her? She was too soul-weary to care.

"If you would please unlace me," Matilda said, "I will oblige you with reciprocal courtesies."

He drew open the bow holding her bodice closed, then stepped near. "This is the last time I will ask you: Are you sure, Matilda? If we grant each other this intimacy, we can never un-grant it. I become yours in a way I have never belonged to anybody."

She kissed him to stop his words. Of course she wanted to claim him, to claim his body, his ferociously imposing mind, and his equally impressive decency, but she lacked the freedom to surrender herself in the same measure, and, thus, what he offered was impossible.

Frustration—physical and emotional—turned her kiss desperate. She lashed her arms around his neck and willed away all thoughts of treason and tomorrows.

"You should lock the door," she muttered, fingers going to the buttons of his falls. "We can't have a maid or foot man stopping by to build up the fire if we're—" He was in her hands again, as magnificently aroused as he'd been in the study.

"We will have fire enough and privacy enough. The staff knows to knock, and they know I occasionally tell them to go away. Hold still, please."

His fingers were deft, drawing the fabric of her bodice aside, button by button, to reveal the old-fashioned laces beneath. He untied her corsetry, then undid the bow on her chemise.

"Your move," he said, hands falling at his sides.

Oh, yes. Matilda considered options, strategies, and analogies. She slipped the pin from his cravat and untied the knot, leaving the ends trailing.

He drew the cravat off and laid it over the open door of the wardrobe. "Your slippers," he said, "and stockings."

Matilda sat and endured the warmth of Duncan's hands on her feet, ankles, and calves. He untied her garters, rolled down her plain wool stockings, and what should have been a mundane step in the process of disrobing became unbearable seduction.

He lingered at her ankle, shaping the bones with his fingers. His touch was warm, and so intimate Matilda couldn't bear to watch.

"I'm too skinny," she said, stroking his hair.

He rose and stood by her, such that she could press her cheek to his thigh. To rest against him was an exquisite pleasure, as was his hand caressing her neck.

"You have been through a trial," he said. "Flesh can be regained. Your move."

He took half a step back, and Matilda went for the buttons holding his shirt closed, then stopped, lest she give up every advantage in this game of arousal.

"To you, Mr. Wentworth."

He waved a hand. "The dress, if you please."

Matilda very much pleased. She drew the dress over her head and laid it on the sofa, then wiggled out of her jumps and set them on a chair. "The shirt."

Duncan pulled off his shirt and tossed it atop her dress, then sat and yanked off his boots. "I forfeit," he said, shoving his breeches down and stepping out of them. "I forfeit the whole match provided you'll join me in that bed."

He was naked in the winter sunlight, a mature god in lean, robust good health. His body hair shaded reddish, his proportions made Matilda ache. Duncan wasn't the idealized *David*, with head and hands too big, a torso too slender, posture contorted the better to convey artistic priorities. He was a flesh-and-blood man, and when he held out a hand, inviting Matilda onto the bed, she hesitated.

"You make me wish I had your ability to sketch," she said.

"You make me wish all manner of things. I intend to see many of those wishes come true in the next hour."

Matilda lifted the hem of her chemise, and before she could lose her courage, she pitched the garment to the floor. She'd lost much of her figure, her hands were no longer the soft hands of a lady, and her hair needed a serious encounter with a pair of shears.

None of which mattered when she beheld Duncan in his adult male glory.

He lifted her in his arms, laid her on the bed, and came down over her. "You've granted my first wish. What wish can I grant for you?"

Chapter Twelve

After Rachel's death, Duncan had wandered for four years in the Yorkshire countryside, eking out an existence teaching the children of farmers and squires. Guilt and anger had obscured any longing for intimacies with a female, and common sense had saved him from casual entanglements while at university.

He wasn't a virgin. Not by any means. As he'd recovered from his debacle with the church, the occasional willing widow had enlivened his young manhood considerably. Too many of those ladies had been inspecting him as a potential spouse, though, and he hadn't any interest in reprising that role.

Then he'd become responsible for Stephen's education, and opportunities for intimate congress with unattached women had become fewer just as his curiosity about the ladies had stirred back to life.

Women had a perspective that most man lacked. Women had courage most men overlooked. Women defeated most applications of simple logic, and they were surely interesting to look upon.

Women were not, in other words, boring.

Matilda was fascinating, all silky smooth skin, interesting angles and intriguing shadows. She was still slender—also warm and bold.

"From this day forward, I will have pleasant associations with damask roses," he said, nuzzling her ear. "The fragrance isn't the same on other women. On you, I can detect exotic spices. Perhaps that's the scent of mischief."

Her hand on his back stilled. "I smell of soap, you daft man. Kiss me."

Duncan obliged, starting with a joining of his mouth to hers. He *was* daft, for the big, soft bed allowed him the luxury of draping himself over Matilda, chest to breast, belly to belly, sex to sex. The intimacy was at once intoxicating and soothing.

"That tickles," Matilda whispered as Duncan nuzzled and tasted his way along her shoulder.

"Good." He pushed his arousal against her heat. "Retaliate however you please. I'm willing to sacrifice my stoutest pieces in the interests of capturing a queen."

"Not chess," she panted, running a toe up his calf. "I can't think if you speak to me in chess metaphors."

This was *lovely*. To feel Matilda unraveling beneath him, to come undone himself, one sigh, one caress, one wicked, teasing undulation of Matilda's hips at a time.

Duncan eased lower, taking a rosy, puckered nipple into his mouth. "You even taste of flowers."

She locked her legs around him. "That's the flavor of frustration, Duncan Wentworth. I want you—do that again."

He used a free hand to cup her other breast, applying pressure with his hand and mouth in unison.

Next time, no bed. If he were bracing Matilda against a wall, trying to balance on the narrow bench of a sofa, making love with her standing up, her back to his front— oh, the possibilities!—then logistics and sore muscles would give his self-restraint a sensory anchor. Devouring Matilda amid clean sheets and soft quilts was bliss, a feast before a warm hearth in the midst of deepest winter.

"Duncan..." She used leg strength to lift herself against him. "I adore your patience, but if you're waiting for me to send an engraved invitation—that is *delightful*."

He'd started the joining, shallowly, slowly, because this was more than becoming lovers. This was the beginning of a commitment he'd never thought to make again. Then too, if he sought a future with Matilda—and he did—then her pleasure was not only his obligation but also his ally.

Pleasure. Not logic, not keen observations, not pretty sketches.

He set up a languid rhythm, distracting himself by easing pins from Matilda's hair between kisses and caresses.

"What are you doing, Duncan?"

Advancing my knights. "Making love with my intended."

She buried her face against his shoulder.

He didn't know whether his admission pleased her, but she was certainly pleasing him. Matilda was a robust lover, meeting him thrust for thrust, and accelerating the tempo— or trying to. They wrestled for control, though in this arena Duncan had no intention of ceding the match.

"Duncan, why must you be so—oh, damn and blast you, you dratted, wonderful man."

She'd learned to swear. He tucked that victory aside and rode out her pleasure as she bucked and thrashed beneath him. She made not a sound, but her body spoke volumes. Matilda of the measured strategies and hoarded secrets surrendered in his arms, to intimacy and to satisfaction.

Mindful that she had not surrendered *to him*, Duncan let her have a few minutes of panting stillness before he withdrew.

"Hold me, Matilda. Please."

Her embrace was fierce as Duncan finished against her belly. The gratification was more in having exercised restraint than in sexual fulfillment, and the voice of conscience reminded Duncan that even withdrawing was not a guarantee against conception.

"Thank you," she said. "For all of it, but especially for denying yourself."

Duncan did not want her thanks, but perhaps on the Continent, the etiquette for such moments required it. He remained in her arms, bracing himself just enough to allow them room to breathe. Her scent was on him, roses and woman, and a tension he'd been carrying for years had fallen away. The urge to speak to her of that luscious feeling of freedom was bounded by caution.

Had Matilda made love with him because she wanted to stay with him, or because she planned to leave?

He eased away and took a handkerchief from the night table. "I won't be long." He passed her the handkerchief and took himself behind the privacy screen. A cold, wet cloth ruthlessly applied to intimate locations helped restore his mental functioning.

He climbed back under the covers, and Matilda bundled against his side. His breeding organs were all too ready for a re-match, which would be greedy and inconsiderate.

"Let me hold you," he said, wrestling Matilda atop him. "You do know that the measures I took are not sufficient to reliably prevent conception?"

She drew a finger along his brows, her touch exquisitely relaxing. "The women I've consulted said it's as good a precaution as any."

"My wife didn't find it adequate, but then, she was not a well-educated woman, and that precautionary measure was not consistently taken."

Matilda's finger traced down his nose to sketch his lips. "You were young. She was your wife. Why exercise restraint?"

"She was not my wife when she conceived the child, and I was not the father of her child."

Matilda looked both sad and unsurprised, as if she'd puzzled out the conclusion of a moralizing novel a hundred pages from the end.

"Tell me, Duncan. I suspect this story matters a great deal."

"The story didn't matter to anybody who might have given it a happier ending." The bitterness of that truth still haunted Duncan more than a decade later, but mostly as old grief, as disappointment in himself and in those he'd trusted.

Matilda folded down onto his chest and wrapped him close. "Tell me."

Even having become her lover, Duncan was hungry to know Matilda more intimately. He didn't know all of her secrets, he had not won all of her trust, but he'd made a start.

And she had made a start earning his. "Once upon a time," he began, "there lived a small boy who grew up in his uncle's vicarage. The small boy was taught right from wrong, and right from potentially wrong, until life presented him with not a single moral conundrum. He went into the church, and from there, the whole bloody business went straight to hell."

Matilda gathered him close. "I can keep a secret. Give me the rest of it."

She *was* keeping secrets. Now that desire had ebbed to a dull roar, her secrets bothered Duncan more than ever. He was keeping secrets too, though, and for what purpose except to pretend the past had happened to another man?

For the first time since taking off his collar, Duncan prepared to recite the whole, miserable, rotten tale. He stroked his hand over the woman whom he hoped to make his wife and vowed to give her and her alone the truth.

* * *

"If you'd told Mr. Parker about the woman, he mighta paid for more than a few pints," Herman groused.

Herm was practicing a card trick—a cheater's maneuver by any other name—though the dear lad would never be a card sharp. Herman lacked sincere friendliness, which Jeffrey knew to be the successful card sharp's most essential trait.

"If I'd told Parker about the woman," Jeffrey said, "I'd have been confessing to trespassing, you idjit. Do you fancy a trip to New South Wales?"

Herman attempted to shuffle the deck, the cards splattering all over the common's plank table. "You didn't have to mention that part. We mighta been passing by the home wood when we seen her, along the lane, like."

"Mr. Parker is a military man, Herm. Didn't you notice how he stood like he had a poker up his arse? His coach was crested, with the panels turned."

Herman gathered up the cards. "When did you see his coach?"

Herman, Herman, Herman. Ma's last words had been to look out for Herman, but a brother grew weary of such a thankless task.

"Man's gotta step around to the jakes, don't he?"

"So what's being military got to do wiff it? Half the men in England have taken the king's shilling a time or two."

"He's military and he's related to a title, close enough to borrow that fine coach. He's got younger son written all over him. What's he doing, skulking about with the crests turned, biding at a lowly place like this, except trying to avoid notice while he hunts down a wife what's run off."

Herman began arranging the cards in a manner that would disadvantage any who sat down for a friendly game.

"Damned female knew which end of a pistol was what," he said. "Following the drum does that to women. Makes 'em bold. Our *Mr. Parker* likely dragged her all over the battlefields."

Mr. Parker, indeed. "Exactly, but a woman like that won't want to be found. She ran off for reasons. The lord of Brightwell manor could be harboring a fugitive wife and might not even know it."

Herman pushed the deck across the table. "And where there's a fugitive wife, there's often a reward."

Jeffrey cut the cards. "Or there's a gesture of appreciation from the lady's current protector, for not revealing her whereabouts to her heartbroke husband. We can't lose, Herm."

Herman dealt for a game of piquet. "But we were poaching at Brightwell, and trespassing, and we put hands on the landowner, Jeffrey."

A serving maid scrubbing tables looked up at that bit of foolishness. Jeffrey winked at her. She went back to her drudging.

"He coulda had us up before the king's man, Herm. That was a serious pistol, he had a witness in the lady, and we were taken unawares."

Herman studied his hand. "But he didn't bother with us. He were too interested in the lady."

"Exactly. So now we'll be interested in the lady too."

* * *

"You went into the church." Matilda rejoiced to have a piece of Duncan's past entrusted to her keeping, even as her own dissembling bothered her more.

"Like a coach horse to his oats," Duncan said, drawing lazy patterns on her bare arm, "and with nearly as unsophisticated a grasp of the potential hazards."

She could fall in love with his touch, if his sheer decency weren't even more alluring. "And then what happened?"

"I was given a post as curate to a vicar in rural Yorkshire. What family I had was in York, and a Yorkshireman's speech was the sound of home to me. Better still, my vicar was a well-loved clergyman. His sermons were tolerant and even humorous. He chided gently if at all, and his demeanor was jovial."

A perfect mentor for an earnest young man, in other words. "This paradise must have a serpent."

"The usual complement of the seven deadly sins, though I didn't expect to find them in my vicar. I came upon him trifling with a maid. The verb does not do justice to the potential harm inflicted."

That sort of trifling. "He had her skirts up?"

"He'd pinned her against a sideboard with his weight, and her skirts were in his hand. She was trying not to touch him, turning her head to avoid his kisses. *Please stop, Vicar. I'm a good girl, Vicar. Vicar, you mustn't.*"

Matilda scooted closer beneath the covers. "You intervened."

"I asked him what on earth he was about, for the girl—she was barely sixteen—was clearly unwilling and not his wife." Duncan's hands went still. "He laughed. He did not let her go."

No wonder Duncan understood a snared creature's plight. "And you did not desist with your remonstrations."

"I hauled him off of her and physically threatened the most beloved man in the parish. He stopped laughing and proceeded to lecture me. Women protest for form's sake, which I might have known had I been more than a pious boy. Women enjoy it, they've been enticing men since Eve plucked the apple, and if they conceive, that is clearly God's will. If they die in childbed, that's the price they must all pay eternally for plucking that one apple. Scripture tells us all of this, though not in any passage I could find."

"Scripture written and propounded by men," Matilda said.

Duncan regarded her in the gloom of the bed hangings. "A valid point. Not one I considered at the time."

"So you left the church. A sound decision."

He drew the covers up over Matilda's shoulders. "I did not leave, I was drummed out of the regiment. The second time I caught the vicar at his pleasures, I went to his wife. She informed me that I was jealous of my superior, and if I breathed another word of what I'd mistaken for familial affection, she'd see me defrocked. I had mistaken *nothing*."

The tale would grow worse, which felt perilously like being exiled from home in winter with no means of support. Matilda was particularly grateful for the warmth and privacy of the bed, given the bitter tale Duncan told.

"What did you do?"

"I confronted the girl, offered her my pittance of a savings and an exquisitely written character in the event she wanted to flee. She was from a foundling home in York and

knew nobody in the parish to whom she might have turned.
I was not confident that she even understood the connection
between copulation and conception."

"You explained it to her."

"Vicar had assured her that nobody conceived from a few
little interludes of harmless sport. Vicar was a man of God,
he would not lie. He would fornicate, exploit, and cite scripture for his own purposes, but she assured me emphatically
that he would not lie about *that*."

Duncan's distaste for mendacity had been learned early
and well.

"He got her with child," Matilda said, "and you offered
to marry her."

Duncan rolled, so he was on his side, and Matilda lay
facing him. "First, I went to the bishop, thinking that surely,
surely the spiritual authority in a position to right this wrong
would insist on intervening. If nothing else, the vicar's
eternal salvation was imperiled. The bishop laughed as well.
At me. If anybody ever addresses me as 'my boy' again, I
will not answer for the consequences."

"I don't understand. You reported a vicar committing
adultery, a man breaking his marital vows and preying on an
unwilling woman. What was there to laugh about?"

Duncan brushed a lock of hair back from Matilda's brow.
"Adultery is conjugal relations with another man's wife.
Rachel was unmarried, therefore, adultery did not occur. The
bishop recited from the same primer the vicar had: Women
tempt men on purpose, they entice us, they offer weak
protests to heighten the pleasure of the chase, they hope
to get with child so we're bound to support them. Besides,
the vicar was happy to manage a rural congregation in the
godforsaken West Riding, and he excelled at coaxing funds
from the local squires, barons, and wealthy yeomen."

"That is vile." Matilda was angry for the poor maid, but she was equally incensed for the young curate.

"That is the way of the world, I was told. David, whom God loved most dearly, had two hundred concubines and was a scheming murderer. Who was I to judge a good man for a few harmless pleasures?"

Another curate, one *without* a true vocation, might have withstood this collision of piety and evil, but not Duncan Wentworth. "Such a church did not deserve you."

"The bishop agreed. I was instructed that if I failed to acquire a greater sense of tolerance for human failings, if I was unable to grasp that no man is perfect, then clearly, I lacked a true calling. The girl would be given a few coins if she conceived, and the appropriate charities would see to *the rest.*"

He spoke calmly, as if reciting the course of a battle fought long ago on foreign soil, though Matilda sensed that the conflict yet raged inside him.

"Which means," she said, bringing Duncan's knuckles to her lips, "the bishop had been confronted with the same situation previously, had a solution in place, and was complicit in the vicar's knavery."

"The bishop, the vicar's wife, the church elders...a great joke was in progress, and nobody had warned the maid or the new curate. He was not the butt of the humor, though. By the time I returned from consulting my bishop, Rachel had conceived. She was past the stage where the herbwoman's tisanes could be safely attempted."

Those tisanes could kill a woman if used carelessly. "Was she given a few coins?"

"She was berated for enticing the vicar into sin. I came upon the lady of the house delivering this tongue-lashing, which proceeded unabated as I stood witness. I collected my things, left without a reference, and escorted Rachel to Leeds. A schoolteacher's salary was inadequate to arrange regular meals, much less regular medical care. The child came early and preceded her mother into death by a handful of days."

He fell silent, and Matilda waited for yet more sadness.

"I seriously considered joining them." Spoken softly, wearily.

"You did not, because suicide is a sin."

He drew his finger along Matilda's lips. "I did not, because I am a Wentworth. We are cursed with tenacity. I failed Rachel, I failed her child, I failed my calling. She put her trust in me, and I failed her. At first, I reasoned that continued life was to be my penance. I did not deserve the comfort of death."

"Which is youthful, melodramatic balderdash. You did everything in your power to right a grievous wrong."

He caressed her lips again, sweetly, gently. "So fierce, Matilda. I took years to come to that conclusion. The guilt has ebbed, though it will plague me all my days. My strengths and abilities as a curate were not equal to the challenge before me. I learned bitterness and rage, but I also learned that I love to teach. In the company of children, I took a small revenge against those who had betrayed Rachel. I taught the children well. I made sure they knew their letters and ciphering, that they could go out into the world with more than the ability to empty a chamber pot or recite rote prayers."

Suffer the little children to come unto me.... "As revenge goes, that's commendably farsighted. I hope the bishop died of dysentery."

"He remains in his office. The vicar and his wife retired five years ago to a peaceful old age."

"That must be galling."

"I suspect this is why man turns to God, as a final arbiter of life's unfairness. I dream of publicly denouncing the bishop, but what good would that do Rachel or her daughter? I am also still technically ordained—I was not defrocked—and vengeance is unbecoming of the clergy."

"You tried to bring the matter to justice, Duncan. You offered the truth to those in a position to make amends. Few would have been as honest."

He sat up just as Matilda reached for him. "And my honesty arguably resulted in two avoidable deaths." He climbed from the bed naked and went to the fire, adding coal and poking the flames to life. "Truth always comes at a price. If you never explain how you came to be wandering in my woods, I will accept your discretion as the wiser course. Sometimes, the past should remain buried."

Duncan stared into the flames, a perfect lance of a man in three-quarter nude profile. He clearly did not believe that philosophy of silence. He'd been forced into it by circumstance.

As Matilda had.

"Come back to bed," she said, patting the quilt. "I'm sorry the church betrayed your trust. You deserved better."

He did not deserve for Matilda to betray his trust, either, and yet she must, and soon.

* * *

Having told the story of his disappointed youth, Duncan hoped for some great insight into what he should have done instead or how he might have more effectively couched his accusations. Curled around a sleeping Matilda, no such revelations befell him.

Nothing had changed for having entrusted that tale to another, nothing except that Matilda had put her finger on the harm done. Rachel and her baby had been victims of injustice, and Duncan's faith in his spiritual superiors had been betrayed.

If faith in those authorities was misplaced, then all faith was without grounds. Duncan's innocence had been laid to rest as surely as Rachel and the child had. What did that leave but determination to avoid such entanglements in the future, and to move forward with an expectation of disillusionment?

Duncan kissed Matilda on the temple and rose, then drew the covers over her. He hoped she would join him in this bed from now on, but he would not voice that request. She must come of her own free will, as she had the first time.

He dressed and made his way to the family parlor, intent on creating a household budget. Matilda longed for a home of her own, and Brightwell needed a consistent hand on the reins.

Trostle's successor—for he would have one—would be held to account, just as Mrs. Newbury and Manners expected to be. A budget wanted thought, and remaining at Matilda's side was not conducive to anything but yearnings and conjectures. Then too, if Duncan remained with her, he'd awaken her, and she needed her rest.

The family parlor was warm, and Duncan's knee was grumbling at him. To his disappointment, he was not to have solitude.

"Why aren't you hammering and sawing away on your lift?" he asked.

Stephen had spread diagrams all over the reading table, a ruler, carpenter's compass, and abacus among the documents. He was in his Bath chair poring over the drawings, and did not look up when Duncan posed his question.

"You really should set up a sawpit," he said. "As much mature lumber as you have, as much coin as it would fetch on the market, you should make the investment."

I had planned to be in Rome this time next year.

Duncan had not planned on falling in love with Matilda. "Draw me up a proposal, complete with budget, site plan, and estimated operating costs. Better still, buy this property from me and turn your talents to making it profitable." He took the reading chair Matilda favored, closest to the fire, rather than examine Stephen's sketches.

"What has turned your reliably dull disposition so rotten?" Stephen asked, tucking a pencil behind his ear. "You've barely made a start on this place and already, you're ceding the match."

Duncan rubbed his knee, a futile undertaking once the damned thing decided to ache. "Have you ever tried to hold authority accountable for wrongdoing?"

Stephen capped a bottle of ink and set it on the standish. "Yes, and that folly inspired my dear papa to break my leg. He said he'd done me a favor. If I was so intent on begging for food, I might as well have a twisted limb to evoke the sympathy of passersby."

That was more than Stephen had ever said about the origins of his injury. "He broke your leg *on purpose*?"

"As much purpose as Jack Wentworth had about anything when he was three sheets to the wind. I expected him to share with me the first food he'd brought to the house in three days. This time of year . . ." Stephen's gaze went to the window. "I hate this time of year. I don't hate England, but I hate the darkness."

He also hated pity—probably more than darkness, cold, snow, or his late father—so Duncan temporarily ignored the disclosure of Jack Wentworth's evil.

"I've asked Matilda for permission to embark on a courtship."

Stephen stared at him for a good five ticks of the mantel clock. "You are begging for heartbreak. Damned near demanding it at sword point. I expect you alone of all people to behave rationally, and yet, you offer your name to a woman who is likely wanted for hanging felonies."

Hence the uneasy roiling in Duncan's gut. "I'll take her to the Continent where the king's men cannot pursue her." Though what Matilda wanted more than anything was a home and family of her own, not life as a fugitive.

"And what if her troubles follow you there? Will you change your name, cut off all ties to family, expect her to do likewise?"

This conversation was extraordinary, not for the content— one Wentworth making a futile attempt to talk sense into another—but for the fact that Stephen was the party counseling prudence.

"Most criminals are safe enough if they can elude justice for any length of time," Duncan said. The runners and patrollers preferred to go after game laying a fresh trail, when the motivation to pay a reward was still high.

"Matilda has been running for months, Duncan."

"You don't know that. You reach that conclusion based on her slenderness and her secretiveness."

"She might never tell you what mischief follows her, until it has become your mischief too. Abetting a felon, becoming an accessory after the fact, will see you hanged, and that scandal is no way to repay the loyalty of your cousins."

Duncan rose and closed the curtains, for only cold and darkness lay beyond the window. "Tell me, Stephen, did my many attempts to persuade you to moderate your behavior ever succeed because I'd made you feel guilty?"

"Of course not, but why Matilda, Duncan? Why a woman about whom you know virtually nothing? You can have your pick of heiresses, bluestockings, well-read widows.... I could line women up from here to London who'd accept a proposal from a ducal Wentworth, regardless of his age or mental condition. You instead choose a woman who might be led away in chains tomorrow. Why?"

The question had no logical answer, and Duncan had come to this parlor for solitude. He'd wanted to savor the intimacies he'd shared with Matilda, not fall into a brown study over a past he could not change—another past he could not change.

"Matilda is intelligent," he said, "learned, well traveled, and favorably disposed toward me, despite my dull character and ancient years. She is unmarried and her heart is not elsewhere engaged. Should I turn my back on her because of events that don't concern me?"

Stephen wheeled away from the table and shifted to the chair near the fire. Duncan knew better than to offer assistance.

"You speak as if you have only two choices," Stephen said, propping his leg on a hassock. "We are Wentworths, and we don't meekly endure what life hands us. I account myself responsible for Jack Wentworth's death, for example."

Duncan stopped three steps short of the door. "Drink killed him."

"In the philosophical sense, perhaps. He was already quite drunk and intent on becoming drunker. He reached for the bottle on the windowsill, which contained rat poison. I had placed the bottle there myself. Not very bright of me— or perhaps it was brilliant, in a diabolically evil sort of way. Papa always kept his blue ruin on the windowsill."

"You did not kill him, Stephen. You were a child, a small

boy no more capable of plotting murder than I am capable of witty flirtation aimed at women half my age."

Stephen withdrew the pencil from behind his ear and flicked it over, under, and through his fingers.

"Believe that if you must, Duncan, but when Papa was choking his last, he bid me to run for the surgeon. I hadn't run for four years at that point, courtesy of my father's loving discipline. I could lurch, hobble, struggle, and crawl, but not run. So I ignored the dictates of honored authority and didn't even try to make haste. By the time I had fetched Nan Pritchard from the pub, Jack Wentworth was wonderfully, absolutely dead."

Duncan knew a confession when he heard one, and a plea for absolution. "If Jack Wentworth was too drunk to know rat poison from gin, then his death was an accident, Stephen. Had you tried to intervene, he'd be just as dead, and you might have a useless arm to go with your poorly knit leg. Forgive yourself, though in my estimation, you have nothing to forgive yourself for."

Stephen brushed a glance over him. "Jack was making plans for my older sisters that no decent man contemplates for any woman, much less for mere girls who call him father. My point is that I was eight years old, crippled, unlettered, and none too bright, and yet, I might have put that rat poison into Jack's blue ruin rather than wait for an accident to solve my problems. I had an option, but I would not admit that to myself."

More than anything, Duncan wanted to put his arms around Stephen and comfort that guilty, battered eight-year-old boy. Stephen would gut him with his sword cane and serve the pieces to the house cats if Duncan so much as hinted of sympathy.

"No eight-year-old should have to contemplate patricide."

"No eight-year-old," Stephen replied, "should have had Jack Wentworth for a father. The fact remains that you need not meekly accept that the only solution to Matilda's problems is to run from her past."

I can stand and fight her enemies—if she wants me to. But then, how had fighting for Rachel turned out? "My thanks for your counsel. Does Quinn know about the rat poison?"

Stephen shook his head. "He'd blame himself. Bad gin fit the situation well enough. You can take my secret with you when you and Matilda disappear to Cathay."

That smarted, as it was intended to. "Design me a sawpit, please."

"What's the point? You'll be in Cathay."

"Perhaps I'll be right here, raising a family with my devoted wife." Duncan quit the room rather than listen to Stephen deride such fanciful twaddle.

Chapter Thirteen

Matilda would have considered this meal a feast just a few short weeks ago, though her appetite was nowhere to be found. The dining parlor was cozy, the fowl and ham well prepared, and the apple torte delicately spiced. Lord Stephen regaled her with tales of his exploits in Copenhagen, where he knew neither the language nor the customs.

"I thus came to the battle of wits unarmed," Lord Stephen said, topping up Matilda's glass of Sauternes.

"Shakespeare," Duncan muttered, from the head of the table. "Though relying on the Bard to supply your humor rather underscores your point. Excuse me, please. It's time I sought my bed."

He rose and bowed to Matilda, then left her alone with Lord Stephen and an abundance of food.

"Duncan becomes even more polite than usual when he's upset," Stephen said. "He saw you nick the roll."

I have lost my touch. "I'm merely taking a snack to my room for later."

Lord Stephen cut another serving of apple torte, set it on a plate, added a few slices of cheddar, and passed it to her.

"That's a snack for later. The roll in your pocket is stolen goods, to sustain you when you leave here in about"—he glanced at the mantel clock—"five hours."

Matilda had not decided to leave. She had decided that she needed to leave *soon.* Duncan's tale of disappointment and betrayal at the hands of the church only made the decision more imperative. He did not deserve to be entangled with a woman who'd quite possibly lead him to the gallows. Then too, his family was planning a visit.

Better for all concerned if Matilda decamped before they arrived. "I won't leave tonight."

Stephen peered at his wine. "Duncan could divine the reason for that assurance, and he could do so without even thinking about it."

Daunting thought. "Today is Tuesday," Matilda said. "The laundry was done yesterday, and the dress I wore when I arrived will not be dry until tomorrow at least. I would not leave in a damp dress."

He lifted a glass a few inches in Matilda's direction. "I take your point. Nor will you leave in a borrowed dress— because if the rag you arrived in is found here, that's evidence you were on the premises—but you will leave. Why?"

Matilda toyed with her torte. Cook had used the honey liberally, though Duncan's piece sat untouched on his plate.

"I am not safe here."

Stephen snorted. "He'd die for you. I'd die for you because he'd expect it of me and I haven't anything more pressing to attend to at the moment."

Matilda put aside her fork. "Then you and he are not safe

because of me. When I leave, I will not take my Book of Common Prayer. You will burn it for me, please."

"If you like, though that has to be a mortal sin. I haven't committed one of those in quite some time."

"So glad I could provide you a bit of diversion." She rose and curtsied, ignored the apple torte and cheese on the table, and left Lord Stephen to enjoy his dessert.

A prudent woman would go straight to her room, count up her coins for the fifth time that day, and ensure her meager belongings were neatly stowed in the wardrobe, ready to be tossed into a spare shawl and bundled together for travel. Matilda had been prudent, before fear and confusion had sent her down cow paths and game trails, into overgrown woods, and into Duncan Wentworth's arms.

She tapped on his door, then let herself in. He sat before the fire in a dressing gown and silk trousers, his feet bare. His hair was damp and he remained seated when she closed the door.

"Madam "

"I was Matilda to you yesterday in that bedroom."

He held out his hand, and she took a seat on the hassock before his reading chair. "I was courting you yesterday. Why allow me that fiction, Matilda?"

Had he determined her motives from one stolen dinner roll? "I told you nothing can come of your ambitions where I'm concerned." She folded her fingers over his and pressed the back of his hand to her heart. "I do not have a choice, Duncan. I have studied the board from every perspective, and very few moves are left to me."

He kissed her fingers. "You have committed treason."

Four words Matilda barely allowed herself to think, and he offered them calmly. "On what do you base your conjecture?" Matilda took heart from their joined hands.

Duncan had reached a conclusion; he did not sit in judgment of her.

"You admit that you have involved yourself in trouble of the highest order. You are fleeing the authorities, but not the magistrates and their parlor sessions. Your crime is thus an embarrassment to the Crown, *if* you have committed a crime. I think it more likely that you are protecting your father, or possibly your erstwhile fiancé.

"I flatter myself," he went on, "that you also seek to protect me. From one perspective, I am a nobody. A failed clergyman who has racketed about the Continent in the guise of a tutor, when in fact I am a duke's poor relation. The poor relation, the tutor without students, might need some protection. From another perspective, my family is titled, we have wealth beyond imagining, I hold land in my own name and have assets many would envy. And yet, you believe that your misdeeds could bring me low. What wrong has as much power to ruin as treason?"

He rose, and Matilda was certain he intended to summon the footmen to lock her in the butler's pantry.

He twisted the latch on the lock. "You have the privacy of the confessional. If I can help you, I will. I hope that is a statement of the obvious."

The suitor had departed, in other words. In his place was the decent gentleman who'd first captured Matilda's trust.

Did he still have it?

Yes, and he always would. "I have committed treason—I'm nearly certain of that—and I have been terribly, unforgivably stupid. My father's life hangs in the balance, and I have no good options."

Duncan went into the bedroom and came back with a quilt. He draped that around Matilda's shoulders and resumed his seat.

"Tell me what happened and leave nothing out. Do not flatter anybody, do not protect anybody, most especially, do not protect *me*. The truth and the truth alone will serve, or you will depart from my household and never return."

* * *

Duncan abetted a traitor, and by demanding the whole story from Matilda, he became an accessory to her crime after the fact—unless he turned her over to the authorities.

That was the sensible choice, and Duncan had learned to his sorrow the price of ignoring common sense. Apparently, the lesson needed some review, because for no inducement, not even to preserve his life, would he betray Matilda's trust.

"Papa is an art dealer," Matilda said, gathering the quilt close. "A gentleman art dealer. He's also a sometime spy, from what I can gather. When I traveled with him, that possibility was only a passing notion, but part of the reason I married was to make certain that my path and Papa's diverged, lest he be caught in the pay of the wrong party."

"Your father was a free lance," Duncan said, as the fire crackled softly and the winter wind soughed beyond the window. "A mercenary."

"I don't know what he was. On the Continent, the line between diplomacy, trade, and espionage blurs. Those who dabble in statecraft like it that way, while I could not abide the court intrigues and the conversations that abruptly changed topic when I joined them. Papa was always going out late at night or whispering with the servants in the pantries. I ignored the lot of it."

This recitation apparently annoyed Matilda, which was fortunate, for it made Duncan furious. "You were part of his *camouflage*, to use the French word. His deception. He *did* trade in art, he *was* a doting papa showing his daughter the Continental sights. He also traded in secrets."

She held her hands out toward the fire. "I came to that conclusion only recently. I missed the evidence: Papa never worried about money. He never mentioned needing to save for his old age, never talked about setting aside a sum for my settlements. I'm well fixed, as it happens, though I can't touch my widow's portion at present."

"Your father had no financial worries, but he'd sold his soul." Duncan had met such men, some of them wearing a priest's collar, and he could not respect them.

"If Papa sold his soul, I know not to whom. We always had more servants than any two people required, and they were a canny and polyglot collection. Many of them came with us to London, even though Papa is done with his travels."

Matilda shifted, so she sat in profile, expression pensive. She was pretty—many women were—but what distracted Duncan was the marvel of her mind. She was laying out a story for him with the precision of a chess match recited from memory. She *had* studied this board, at length, and she had avoided putting her father in check.

Barely.

"We moved every few months," she said, "and we never stayed in the same lodgings twice. Now I know that fugitives take that precaution. Papa held dinner parties with people I could never recall meeting, and many of his art clients were amazingly uninformed regarding the pieces he had sold them. My late husband noticed that, and he was a man much preoccupied with his mechanical inventions. In hindsight, I was blind."

As Duncan had been blind when he'd taken his curate's post. "You were kept in the dark. Hindsight was doubtless the second-to-last imp to escape from Pandora's box. It yet flies about the world, creating all manner of havoc."

Matilda sent him a fleeting smile, *Mona Lisa*–sweet, a little wry. "I love you. I wish I didn't. I wish you'd chased me from your home wood on the end of a pitchfork. But you didn't."

Duncan wanted to leap from the chair and bellow her admission to the rafters—*Matilda loved him*—instead, he twitched the quilt up around her shoulders. Those three words were a parting gift, unless he could convince her to stay and fight for their future.

"Thank you for that declaration," he said. "The sentiment is entirely reciprocated, but at present, I'm attempting to focus on the unfortunate situation in which you find yourself. What caused you to flee your father's household?"

Her smile faded like the last rays of sun from the evening sky. "I had attracted the notice of Colonel Lord Atticus Parker, a marquess's younger son making a career in the military."

"The war hero," Duncan said, hating the fellow on general principles.

"Atticus is not a bad sort."

Duncan hated him a little less. "He sought to win your hand, and all you can say about him is that he's *not a bad sort*?"

"He was levelheaded under fire, fought alongside his men, and held some impossible hillside when holding it was needed. He's dogged like that. His courting had the same quality. Flowers twice a week, chocolates from Paris on Sunday. A walk in the park on Friday morning, a waltz on Wednesday night."

"Sounds dull rather than dogged. I expect his chess was uninspired."

She closed her eyes. "Terribly. I lost on purpose with Atticus at least often enough to protect his pride. That should have told me something, but all the while, he was advancing his pawns, and eventually I gave him permission to pay me his addresses. I thought my father would be relieved that I was considering remarriage."

"I met men like your father in my travels with Stephen. They fawned all over the lad, flattering him shamelessly."

"Why flatter a youth on a grand tour?"

"Because those who deal in intrigue are always attempting to recruit from the ranks of aristocracy's younger sons. Spares especially have nothing better to do than resent their lot and feel ignored, and Stephen was and is the ducal heir. A spot of lucrative espionage would have appealed to his vanity. Spying then becomes a means of blackmailing further services from the unsuspecting dupe. Stephen loathes idleness, though boredom never had a more expensive cure than crime."

The fire popped, and Matilda started. Duncan went back to hating Atticus Parker unreservedly.

"Parker is searching for you?"

"Atticus caught me with the evidence. I was in Papa's study because we never let that hearth go cold. I went there to fetch a carrying candle to light the sconces in the family parlor, where Atticus and I spent Tuesday evenings together. I needed to trim the wick on the carrying candle, so I rummaged in Papa's desk for a pair of scissors."

Duncan longed to take Matilda in his arms while she revisited this memory, but touching her would distract him unbearably.

"What time of the evening was this?"

"A little past eight. Parker would come by at nine for tea, dessert, and conversation. I am a widow, I need not be chaperoned for such a call, and thus Papa usually absented himself on Tuesday nights."

"Your father was from home this particular night?"

"He was. I think Papa's life was easier when I was stashed in a castle by the North Sea. My life was easier, too, though I was bored witless."

Your husband owned a damned castle? "Parker came upon you in your father's study?"

She bowed her head, hunching in on herself. "Worse than that. I did not find the scissors in the desk drawer, so I searched Papa's satchel. This satchel should have confirmed his spying, if nothing else did. It has hidden pockets and secret panels all obscured by the design tooled into the leather. I was searching them one by one when I came across a document written in a combination of German, French, and Spanish."

"Code?" Though those were hardly obscure languages to a Continental traveler.

"I sat at the desk, pulled out pencil and paper, and began translating. A lively curiosity has ever been a failing of mine."

I am in love with your lively curiosity. Matilda would have had a half to three-quarters of an hour to work, if Parker were punctual. "What did you find?"

"Plans to invade France, I think. No specific dates, but ports of entry, potential billets, Dutch involvement, none of it quite coherent, but then, I was not the intended recipient of the information and my command of Spanish is lacking."

"We are at peace with the French." *For now.* Napoleon's rampages had lasted most of twenty years, and warfare had become a way of life for many. Still, invading France struck Duncan as an unlikely initiative, or perhaps a contingent scenario, just as certain government offices were always prepared for the death of the monarch.

"I know what was on that page, Duncan, and I did not bring the information to the attention of any proper authority."

"Because you did not know on whose behalf your father had possession of it."

Matilda scooted around so she faced Duncan rather than the fire. "I suspect Atticus courted me to gain access to the house, to have an excuse to watch Papa. I had the sense Papa would rather I'd refused the colonel's suit, but who refuses a war hero from a titled family?"

Matilda had not only refused Parker, she'd run from him. "Parker would have given evidence against your father?"

"He's a war hero. He of all men would not abet a traitor. For all I know, he bid me good night, made straightaway for the authorities, and obtained permission to question me or even arrest me. If I had been taken into custody, Papa's arrest would have undoubtedly followed. I dared not waste hours waiting for Papa to come home from his late-night entertainments."

"You fled before you could incriminate your father." Her reasoning was damnably sound. Better that Wakefield be suspected of treason than condemned to die for it. "Parker came upon you in the study?"

Even as Duncan reconstructed the chain of events with Matilda, he was plagued by questions.

What suitor could have bothered with treason and secret plans when faced with Matilda by firelight? She was no longer as underweight, no longer pale and exhausted. Duncan yearned to sketch her, to lose himself in a game of chess with her, to carry her to his bed and indulge in wild pleasures until spring.

Those longings twined around each other, forming a tangle of desire, yearning, and frustration—which Duncan ignored. Treason was the worst of the hanging felonies, and

Matilda's decision to flee the scene, while it protected her father in the short term, all but put a noose around her own neck.

"Lord Atticus came upon me in the study," she said. "How long he'd stood in the doorway watching me, I do not know. The clock said I'd been working for less than a quarter hour. That dreadful translation held my attention. I looked up and he was there before the desk, framed by the shadows in the corridor. I folded the paper from Papa's satchel and my notes and slid them into a drawer I could lock, then rose and greeted my guest."

Her father's nemesis. Duncan added Thomas Wakefield to the list of those deserving undying enmity.

"Atticus was his usual cordial self," Matilda went on. "He turned the conversation to what sort of house I'd like, and which of London's better neighborhoods appealed to me. I doubt I made sense, but he didn't seem to notice my discomfiture."

"Was the translation gone after he left?"

"The papers were right where I'd put them, but Atticus had excused himself after I'd served the tea. I was alone in the family parlor for a good ten minutes while he heeded the call of nature. He had time to pick the lock on the drawer and study what I'd written. I took the papers with me when I left."

No seasoned soldier took ten minutes to piss. "You never had an opportunity to discuss this with your father?"

She swiped at her cheek with the edge of the quilt. "I quit the house as quickly as I could lest Atticus come back and arrest me. I also did not want Papa to admit his crimes to me. He cannot be convicted on even a war hero's mere hearsay."

"You have considered both turning him in and ignoring

what you've learned." The moral conundrum was impossible: to betray a beloved parent or one's country?

Matilda spread her hands before her, bringing to Duncan's mind quotes about all of great Neptune's ocean being inadequate to wash away guilt.

"Tell me, Duncan, did you consider remaining silent about your vicar's behavior?"

He took her hand in his and kissed her fingers. "Yes, and I have often wondered if Rachel and her daughter would be alive if I'd held my peace. Tagging along after an underpaid teacher through a bitter Yorkshire winter ruined her health."

"I suspect despair ruined her health."

Despair was threatening to spoil Duncan's current plans as well. He kept hold of Matilda's chilly hand, cradling it in both of his. "You are in a truly difficult position, and I have made it more complicated."

Matilda sat straighter and freed her hand from his grasp. "Not if I leave, you haven't."

"Please don't leave," Duncan said. "I'm asking you not to leave, Matilda. I want a chance, at least, to consider your situation. You are arguably no longer an Englishwoman, for example, if you were married to a German fellow. Can a foreigner commit treason?"

That earned him one instant's knitted brow. "Perhaps not, but she can be arrested for conspiring against the Crown, and Papa is still a British subject."

"With whom did you conspire when you bolted from Town, alone, in the middle of the night? With whom did you conspire when you cut off all contact with your father?"

The puzzle called to Duncan, the odd details and ragged edges of Matilda's story. Why had the great war hero not married previously? Where was Matilda's father now, and who was watching him? Why would such dangerous and incriminating information have been left in the keeping of an art dealer?

Though Duncan knew why. Wakefield was a seasoned spy, a reliable courier, bought and paid for. He shipped all manner of goods to and from the Continent, and could easily hide documents among his paintings, manuscripts, musical instruments, and fancy porcelain.

Entrusting documents to him was akin to hiding them in plain sight, a generally sound strategy.

"You are tired," Duncan said. "I apologize for questioning you at such an hour, but thank you for confiding in me."

He ought not to thank her. By sharing this tale with him, she'd all but announced an intention to flee Brightwell rather than implicate him in her difficulties. That strategy—bolting into the night—had kept her father alive and at liberty so far.

Matilda rose, the quilt wrapped about her like one of her shawls. "I'd like to share your bed tonight. To sleep with you, if that's not asking too much. I will understand if you'd rather not have a traitor—"

Duncan lifted her into his arms, quilt and all. "You are always welcome in my bed, and I do not see that you have committed treason. I see that your own father has embroiled you in schemes not of your making, and a man purporting to be a suitor has courted your affections under false pretenses."

He carried her into the bedroom and set her on the bed.

"Your perspective has a certain appeal," Matilda said, scooting back onto the mattress, "but I doubt the authorities will agree. I purloined evidence of possible treason, shielded my father from the truth, and avoided being questioned by those who could get to the bottom of the situation."

Duncan knelt to remove her house slippers. "You destroyed all of the evidence?" Smart woman.

"I burned those papers within a day of leaving Papa's house. That feels good."

He was shaping her feet against his palms, learning the contours of her arches, and losing all interest in talk of treason and schemes.

"If you join me in this bed, Matilda, I cannot promise that sleeping is all we'll do." Her garters had been tied in simple bows, which Duncan released without raising her skirts. He rested his forehead against her knee, trying to collect his wits, to check the headlong rise of desire.

Desire—the third-to-last imp to leave Pandora's box?

Matilda brushed her hand over his hair. "I can assure you, Duncan Wentworth, we will share more than slumber tonight, but first you have to help me out of this dress."

* * *

The roads in rural Berkshire were a horror worthy of Dante's purgatory, though Parker had no choice but to put up with them. The coach had broken a wheel in a frozen rut, and now—a few scant miles from his quarry—Parker was in a bitterly cold saddle, John Coachman riding beside him. A quarter moon on the snow made traveling on to the nearest inn possible, which was fortunate for Parker's frozen backside.

The grooms, wheelers, and coach had been left in the last village, which, God be praised, boasted a wheelwright among its denizens. No lodging was to be had, though, and Parker wasn't about to go into enemy territory after dark without a subordinate.

"I should send word to his lordship of our mishap," John

Coachman said, his breath clouding in the night air. "The marquess likes to know his vehicles are well maintained."

Oh, right. Tattle to his lordship over a minor mishap. "What is your name?" Parker asked.

"Angus Nairn, sir."

The name had been given after a slight hesitation. Coachmen were proud of their office, second coachmen doubtless prouder still.

"You're a Scot? You don't have an accent."

"The burr was beaten out of me. I'm a coachman, and I wear his lordship's livery. That's all anybody need know of me."

A fine answer that subtly emphasized Parker's lack of authority. The marquess held Nairn's loyalty, and not simply because he provided Nairn's livelihood. In the military, Parker had enviable rank, but he was nonetheless a mere *employee*. One whose life was forfeit in the interest of a king who'd never done an honest day's work in his exorbitantly expensive, indolent, royal life.

"Do you ever resent that livery, Nairn?"

"No, sir. I have honorable work, good teams, and generous pay."

The breeze was picking up, and at this time of year, all breezes were bitter. Parker was bitter, unlike the coachman, who was grateful simply to stay out of the wet. Parker's pay was not generous—not in peacetime—his shaving water was rarely as hot as he liked it, his tea never strong enough.

While his lordship the marquess, who'd never charged into enemy bayonets, had all the luxury and comfort a man could waste.

Matilda held the key to improving Parker's fortunes, and he honestly hoped to spare her any criminal repercussions. She was sensible for the most part, and she'd bring some wealth to the marriage—always a fine thing in a bride.

"The White Pony is on the right," Nairn said, as a huddle of buildings came into view at the bottom of a gentle declivity. "Humble, but it's as close to Brightwell as we'll get, if those two swindlers can be believed."

"They played an honest game, Nairn. I simply wanted to curry their favor with some easy coin. Their directions have proven accurate so far." Herman and Jeffrey had been left with the coach in the last village, the better to afford Parker time to gather intelligence unobserved. "We'll scout the terrain tomorrow while the coach is being repaired. Miss Wakefield has been wandering this long, she won't leave a comfortable nest when she doesn't have to."

"And if she chooses to remain in that comfortable nest?"

The village huddled in the bleak winter moonlight, a feeble glow spilling from a few windows.

"I'll arrest her if she proves difficult. I care for my intended very much, but I know my duty."

Nairn remained silent, though Parker had spoken nothing but the simple truth. Either way—arresting Matilda or marrying her—Parker's fortunes would improve, and no superior officer would fault him for that objective.

Chapter Fourteen

"I would like to hear Stephen's version of your stay in Prague," Matilda said. "Yours was enraptured, agog at the beauty and history of the city."

Duncan had given her the first turn behind the privacy screen, and yet, she needed to hear his voice as she took down her hair, needed to know he wasn't summoning the footmen. The fear was ridiculous. Duncan Wentworth had given his word to help her, and he was spending the night with her.

Nonetheless, she was uneasy, once again thinking like a fugitive.

"Prague is unlike any other city we visited," Duncan said. "I gather you've never been?"

"I have not. Moscow, three times, but never Prague." The woman in the mirror was familiar and strange. She resembled the Matilda who'd seen much of the Continent with Papa, and yet, she was older, wiser, no longer innocent.

No longer simply Thomas Wakefield's chess-playing oddity of a daughter, a woman without a country, or an eccentric nobleman's British wife.

"I cannot believe the average Englishman will go much farther afield than Paris and Rome." Duncan spoke over the sound of covers being turned back and batted smooth. "A pity, when great treasures lie farther afield. You could run, Matilda. Take up residence overseas."

You could run. "Would you run with me?"

"Yes. We can leave in the morning."

She braced herself against the washstand, unprepared for that swift, affirmative reply. "Duncan, if you come with me, you are...never mind." They'd had that argument, and Duncan was nothing if not astute.

She unpinned her hair and applied the brush. "You should send your essay on Prague to the London publishers. Everybody raves about or complains about Paris or Rome. Your material is fresh, and your style original. People pay money for good writing, I'm told."

Wearing nothing but his silk trousers, Duncan appeared behind her in the mirror. "If we leave England, we will live a precarious existence, always anticipating the Crown's reach. Our children will be raised to the same life you abhorred, never staying in one place for long, never forming lasting friendships. Always wondering why Mama and Papa change the subject when their quiet conversations are interrupted by a child. Is that what you want, Matilda?"

That was exactly what she did not want. "I want to live. I want my father to live to a ripe old age surrounded by good art." She also wanted a family with Duncan.

And a home of their own. *Ah, well.*

Duncan took the brush from her and used it in long, soothing strokes. "We will consider your situation at greater length in the morning. Their Graces are due for a visit any day, and Quinn is adept at survival under difficult circumstances. He has resources I lack, and he will put them at our disposal if I ask him to."

"He's that loyal?"

"He is, and Jane's loyalty approaches the ferocity of a blood oath. May I have a lock of your hair?"

He asked, even about such a small gesture. "Of course."

A soft snick followed, then Duncan was braiding Matilda's hair. Where had he learned that skill? "What was your dream, Duncan? When you put that sad business in York behind you, what did you aspire to?"

"I aspired to be a schoolteacher. To guide the minds of the yeomen's and tradesmen's children. The wealthy have their universities, their public schools, and tutors. I sought to contribute where learning was a more precious commodity."

A worthy, honorable dream. "You took on Lord Stephen's education, and then you were saddled with Brightwell."

"One of Jane's more inspired notions." He brushed Matilda's braid aside and kissed her nape. "Her best, as it turns out. Shall we to bed?"

Matilda bundled against him, grateful beyond words for his steadfast calm. "I'm frightened, Duncan. I was afraid before, afraid to die on the end of the rope, disgraced and condemned. Now I am afraid for you too. You really should have that dream."

His arms came around her, secure and sheltering. "Most challenges benefit from measured consideration, and virtually every problem can wait until morning. Brightwell is of no interest to anybody, a neglected estate in the hands of a duke's obscure relation. You are safe here with me."

Six of the most precious words in the language, though *the sentiment is entirely reciprocated* ranked even above them. Matilda kissed him for that gift, kissed him for all of his many gifts, laid at her feet for no reason she could fathom.

"Take me to bed, Duncan."

He obliged with *lovemaking*, when Matilda would have gloried in a mindless tumble that drove her worries aside for a few minutes and yielded a dreamless sleep. Duncan instead began with slow caresses, a tactile exploration of Matilda's curves and hollows, her responses and sighs.

His kisses were tender, then plundering, then consuming as he backed her toward the bed and followed her down to the quilts.

"I want—" She yanked on his trousers.

He braced himself on one arm without breaking the kiss and kicked free of his clothing.

"Your chemise," he muttered, skimming his mouth down to where her neck and shoulder joined.

Tossing aside her last garment took Matilda about three seconds, then she and Duncan were naked and panting. He settled over her and she twined her arms and legs around him.

"I want forever with you," she said. "I want chess matches and travelogues and—" *Children. God willing.*

He kissed her before she could admit to that folly. "We'll visit Prague on our honeymoon. In spring."

"Please, yes."

He began the joining with maddening self-restraint. Matilda marshalled the tattered remnants of her patience and set about to outlast him. He was relentless and determined. She was more determined still.

They played to another draw, both of them ceding the game at the same moment amid a conflagration of pleasure that stole every thought and worry from Matilda's grasp.

"I'm done for," she whispered, fingers trailing through Duncan's hair. "Ruined for all time."

He kissed her nose and levered up enough so that cool air eddied between them. "Ruin was never this satisfying before."

Nothing in Matilda's experience had been as satisfying as making love with Duncan. The gratification went beyond mere sensation to an intimacy of the heart and mind she'd never shared with another.

I cannot leave him. The thought coalesced as Duncan padded behind the privacy screen, his naked flanks gilded by firelight. *I cannot abandon a man who has made my problems his own and promised me Prague in springtime.* This was not a decision so much as an acceptance of the inevitable. Matilda's path and his were one, no matter where that path took them. He was her home and her heart, and she, his.

He returned to the bed, a flannel in his hand. "For my lady."

While Matilda tended to herself, Duncan banked the fire. He was comfortable in his own skin, a surprise given his reserved nature, and Matilda loved looking at him.

"How can you be dignified even when you have no clothes on?"

He set the poker on the hearth stand and pushed the screen against the stones. "Wentworths set little store by dignity, but we very much value our self-respect." He climbed back under the covers and drew Matilda against his side. "You are tempted to resume worrying."

"Worry has become a habit."

"While solving puzzles is my habit." He kissed her temple. "Go to sleep, and dream of our next game of chess."

She fell asleep, dreaming of Duncan, and not of chess.

* * *

"Parker continues to sniff at each bush and hitching post," Carlu said, "and his coach was last seen not five miles from Brightwell and making straight for the estate village."

Thomas Wakefield pretended to study the letter on his blotter, though he already knew damned well what it said. "If you intend to bruit family secrets about, at least close the door."

Carlu folded his arms. "Everybody in this household knows you've left Miss Matilda to the wolves. What we don't know is why."

Wakefield was having some difficulty with that question himself. "Because larger issues come to bear on her situation. Matilda should never have bolted the way she did." Much less taken an epistle not intended for her eyes.

Carlu prowled the study like a hungry cat. "Parker has all but found her, and you wait here in London, sipping your tea and reading your mail. That is not the behavior of a loving father."

That was the behavior of a desperate man. "Parker has not found her, more's the pity. He's a gentleman, he'll deal with her carefully. She can tell him she simply lost interest in his suit and left London rather than give him his congé." Please, ye saints and angels, let that be Matilda's strategy.

Carlu advanced and slapped both palms on the desk. "She trounces Russian princelings at chess. She married a German duke and likely spent the wedding breakfast telling him how to run his duchy. Sending one presuming Englishman packing would not have challenged her but for your damned schemes."

A promise of slow death burned in Carlu's dark eyes.

Perhaps he, like half the Continental nobility, had fallen in love with Matilda.

"Carlu, you forget yourself. I suspect you're growing homesick."

Carlu leaned nearer, bringing with him the scents of wool and leather. "I do not *forget myself*, Thomas Wakefield. The coach will be out front in a quarter hour. You and I, Petras and Tomas, are traveling to Berkshire."

Wakefield rose, though his height would be no defense against the reflexes of a younger, angrier man.

"I have sent missive after missive to the general since Parker took a notion to go searching for Matilda. I have heard nothing in response. Now I learn damned Battersleigh was called to Gibraltar on some emergency or other, and I have no idea to whom I could take this matter in his absence."

Carlu straightened. "Then you should have marched yourself down to Horse Guards and asked a few discreet questions. You excel at discreet questions. This whole scheme was General Battersleigh's idea."

A quiet little favor, Battersleigh had called it. A matter of military housekeeping.

"In Battersleigh's absence, I will do as any experienced operative does when the lines of communication have gone silent. I'll remain at my post and wait for further orders."

Carlu's mouth quirked in a smile rife with deadly charm. "Oh no, no, no, Mr. Wakefield. That might be the protocol for the military mules, bound in harness to their chain of command. Those of us entrusted with more delicate matters know that when we are without guidance from our superiors, we use our own judgment and make shift as best we can. Pack a bag, sir. We're off to rescue a fair maiden."

Leaving nobody to rescue her father. "Without Battersleigh

to take a hand in matters, Matilda can see me hanged, Carlu.
Parker would love that. Catch me out, now that I've retired,
and Battersleigh nowhere to be found. That's not how this
game was supposed to end."

Carlu headed for the door. "Parker all but has your
daughter. This is no longer a game, and for as long as you
took the coin of any willing to pay your price, you probably
deserve to hang."

"Then you hang with me."

"We must, indeed, all hang together," Carlu retorted, "or
most assuredly we shall all hang separately."

He was quoting some dastardly American, traitors the
lot of them.

Which was fitting, given the situation.

* * *

"What do we know for certain?" Stephen asked, settling
onto the wooden bench at the edge of the parterre.

Duncan knew absolutely that he was in love with Matilda
Wakefield, and that—oddly and inconveniently—made ana-
lytical thought difficult. He tossed Stephen his coat and
picked up the scythe.

"We know that one Colonel Lord Atticus Parker might
consider himself her suitor, that Thomas Wakefield bides
in London looking like a harmless art dealer, that Matilda
is terrified. If her father was carrying secrets for foreign
powers or stealing military plans to pass along to Britain's
foes, then her fear is justified."

Stephen poked at the melting snow with his cane, making
a pattern of holes in a perfect semi-circle.

"We have precious few facts, Duncan."

Duncan took a swipe at the overgrown hedge. "We know

Parker came upon Matilda translating a message that dealt with England invading France through the Low Countries."

"Why invade France?" Stephen asked, resting his cane across his knees. "England is in a poor position to resume hostilities. The bulk of our seasoned troops are cashiered out or serving in far-flung locations, and the national exchequer is sorely depleted. Then too, the French pose no threat to anybody."

Stephen was right, of course. Napoleon's frolics had left France bankrupt, all but devoid of healthy men below the age of fifty, and plundered by its own army. The next crop of cannon fodder had yet to reach its majority, and, more pertinently, France had no functioning cannon left to speak of.

"In my essays," Duncan said, swinging his scythe, "I mention the sad state of the French countryside, the devastation, the legacy of ruin left by the emperor." Not because an Englishman was tempted to gloat, but because until the very end of the war, Napoleon's fighting hadn't taken place on French soil.

France had been looted by her own leadership and would be decades recovering.

"You mention the devastation," Stephen said, pushing to his feet, "in the essays you've done nothing to see published. Matilda says you're a literary genius." He took up a rake, and in a halting, careful fashion, swept up the trimmings Duncan had cut from the hedge.

"When Matilda is under threat of death at the hands of the Crown, my scribblings are of no moment." *Be careful*, Duncan wanted to add, because Stephen was none too steady on his legs, and the most difficult tasks for him were those that challenged his balance.

"I am puzzled as to why the Crown hasn't found her," Stephen said. "Every village has a militia, every turnpike a platoon of tollkeepers. A handbill posted in the commons of the coaching inns, a reward, a few dedicated runners...For as long as she's been in hiding, for as close as she is to London, somebody should have picked up her trail. The English delight in hanging traitors, no matter their rank or gender."

Stephen *was* being cautious, raking gently while he plucked Duncan's last nerve. "You will please not remind Matilda of that last fact." Though Stephen's observation was also bothersome: a lone young woman at large with plans in her keeping that could cause international embarrassment, put troops at risk, alter the course of history...

Why no hue and cry? Why no newspaper articles or broadsheets? Why no sketches of Matilda littering every drovers' inn in the realm?

Duncan made another pass at the hedge, pruning a few inches at a time when he wanted to hack the plants down to the roots.

"I am puzzled by other aspects of her situation," he said. "Parker was a deadly dull suitor with a predictable and uninspired rotation of gestures that passed for his version of courting. He's a military man accustomed to strict schedules and protocols. Why did he arrive more than thirty minutes early to that one appointment with Matilda?"

"Because he was in love with her?" Stephen suggested. "I nearly am."

I am, most assuredly. "When the condition troubles you in earnest, you will please keep the affliction to yourself, for the sake of your own pride and my dignity."

The rake slipped and Stephen nearly went down. Duncan ignored the stumble as he'd ignored a thousand others.

"I'm in love with her mind," Stephen said. "This is a novel brand of infatuation for me. I rather like it. One can be besotted and enjoy spectacular chess without risking having his brains blown out. What else bothers you about her situation?"

Duncan found a rhythm, swinging the blade with enough momentum that the scythe did the work with the least effort from him.

"Matilda said her father always had too many servants. Where were those servants when she tolerated Parker's company on Tuesday evenings?" Duncan asked.

"Matilda and Parker were a courting couple. I'm told leaving the parties alone for short periods is part of the process. Why plant hedges if they require pruning year after year?"

The pile of trimmings was growing and would make a nice bonfire some evening.

"For privacy's sake," Duncan said.

"The entire garden is visible from the upper floors."

"For damned beauty's sake. Why did Matilda have to light the candles in the family parlor when a regular caller was expected? Lighting candles is the duty of a servant, and according to Matilda, her father's house is awash in domestics. Leaving a widow and her suitor some privacy is one thing, avoiding regular tasks is another."

Stephen paused in his raking. "I can't see what lazy footmen have to do with treason."

"Nor can I, but establishing a pattern means examining all the anomalous facts." Duncan took a particularly vigorous swing at the hedge, sending twigs flying.

"We should be having this discussion with Matilda," Stephen said. "She has facts in her possession she doesn't know she has. I wish Quinn and Jane were here."

Duncan wiped his brow with his sleeve. "I do as well, which is unsettling. One hates to impose, but in this case, the family duke has some valuable perspective to add. Quinn can think like a criminal, while I think like a philosopher."

Stephen hobbled back to his bench using the rake as his cane. "The family duchess will have something to say. Women notice things."

And Stephen noticed women, which was normal at his age. "Matilda suspects Parker courted her so he'd have access to the Wakefield premises."

"Parker was spying on the spy?" Stephen sat on the bench to wrestle out of his coat, something he would not have managed while standing and trying to balance using the rake.

"Parker is a war hero. For him, it wouldn't be spying. It would be…"—Duncan's next swing took off a good foot of hedge—"patriotic duty."

"He does his duty by lying to an innocent woman. Not my kind of hero."

That rankled as well. If catching Wakefield at his espionage was the objective, why not follow Wakefield? Why not infiltrate his army of servants? Why not take Matilda aside and explain to her the situation her father had placed her in?

Too many questions, not enough answers.

"Who is Colonel Lord Atticus Parker?" Duncan asked, starting on the next section of hedge. "What do we know about him and his people? Does he have ties to the Continent? Where did he meet Matilda and who introduced them?"

"You will whack down this whole garden and be no closer to those answers. Why don't I have any bloody wind, Duncan? I work with weights, I make myself walk, I avoid the near occasions of gluttony and inebriation—mostly— and still, I have no stamina."

This lament was unprecedented in more than ten years of keeping close company with Stephen. He rarely acknowledged his limitations, unless it was to make a jest of them.

"The problem is your balance," Duncan said, starting on the next hedge. "You must limit all of your activities to avoid falling. If you could put yourself in a situation where falling was not possible, then you could build up to steady exertion."

Stephen pushed to his feet, coatless, the rake in his hand. "You mean like rowing? I can't fall if I'm sitting in a punt."

"Rowing, swimming, riding…you can build up your wind as long as you're not on your feet while you do it."

I will miss you. The thought came between one swing and the next, a bittersweet pang of sentiment that was also the lot of every teacher. Students moved on to greater challenges, to life and adulthood. Matilda would understand why having a single pupil for the past ten years had been enough for Duncan, why Stephen's courage and tenacity meant so much to him.

"I have ever admired your ingenuity," Duncan said, wielding his scythe. "You never give up, you never give in to despair. Your resilience is boundless, your imagination nimble. You will find a means of increasing your stamina, just as I will find a way to put Matilda's situation to rights."

The rake scraped quietly against the snow-crusted ground. "The only witness to her alleged treason is this Parker person. Eliminate him and you eliminate the problem."

That solution had occurred to Duncan before he'd risen from his bed and kissed a sleeping Matilda's shoulder. "Logical, but lamentably illegal. Parker has superiors, people counting on him to deal with Wakefield once for all."

"Then eliminate Wakefield."

"Another logical suggestion and delightfully simple,

though Matilda's whole aim has been to prevent her father's downfall. By protecting him, she has created problems of her own." This hedge was older than the last and more thickly overgrown. Duncan swung hard.

"Then eliminate Matilda Wakefield," Stephen said. "Turn her into Mary Ellen Wentworth, and take up residence in Vienna or Georgia."

"Run, you mean." If the problem was that Matilda was wanted for high crimes, then leaving Britain was a possible solution. Duncan wasn't convinced Matilda's supposed guilt was the fundamental issue, however. More was afoot than a spy's version of chess gone wrong.

Stephen, who would never run again, leaned on his rake. "She gained possession of treasonous correspondence. She did not report that to anybody in authority. She absconded with the evidence, she is apparently the daughter of a known spy and the widow of some wealthy German. I'd run like hell, though of course that will make her look even more guilty than she already does, and put your neck in a noose as well."

"I've told her I'm willing to take that risk, but first I owe Quinn and Jane an explanation." And then—possibly within the week—Duncan could quit England's shores for all time. Why, when he professed to enjoy travel above all things, did that prospect now hold no appeal whatsoever?

* * *

Matilda had awakened alone, and for the first time in ages, she'd been content to drowse beneath the covers. Duncan's warmth and scent lingered with her, as did an odd sense of well-being. She'd made a choice—she'd chosen *him*—and the rest of the game would sort itself out for better or for worse.

Duncan had left a tea tray by the hearth, so Matilda was thus wrapped in his robe, enjoying a hot cup of gunpowder and a buttered currant bun when Danvers came in carrying a bucket of coal.

"Gracious me, I do beg your pardon, Miss Matilda." Danvers set the bucket down. "Might as well build up the fire whilst I'm here, unless you'd rather I didn't." Danvers wasn't blushing. The maid was, in fact, smiling.

So was Matilda. "Please do build up the fire. Would you happen to know where Mr. Wentworth is?"

Danvers set aside the hearth screen. "In the garden, along with Lord Stephen. They're battling the hedges, which is thankless work for a gardener. Less to do in the spring if they tend to it now, I suppose. We're all a-twitter to soon be entertaining the duke and duchess here at Brightwell. Cook is poring over her recipes, and Mrs. Newbury and Mr. Manners have us cleaning up a storm."

"Duchesses are people, Danvers, the same as anybody else. Give the woman clean sheets and hot tea, she'll probably be easy enough to get along with." In Matilda's experience, even princesses and queens valued those amenities.

"Yesterday we scrubbed the whole nursery. We haven't had children on the premises since the old duke entertained, years ago. Had house parties, shooting parties, card parties...Brightwell were grand once." She swatted a rag along the mantel, then ran her cloth around the base of the brass candlesticks.

"Will you decorate for Yuletide?"

Danvers paused in her dusting. "We haven't, not usually, but with company coming, we really ought to. I'll say something to Mrs. Newbury. She might be waiting for Mr. Wentworth to give his permission. Enjoy your tea, Miss Matilda." Danvers hurried out, leaving the bucket behind.

Matilda considered calling the maid back and warning her to keep Mr. Wentworth's private business to herself, but the admonition would be pointless. Servants had few enough joys in life, and gossiping about their employers figured near the top of the list.

They would gossip among themselves, but apparently not with others outside the household.

Matilda dressed, some of her pleasure in the day ebbing. By Christmas, she and Duncan might be on a ship for America, where the Crown had no authority. Perhaps they'd establish a home in Stockholm, though pitch-dark winters and relentless summer daylight did not appeal to her.

Very likely, they'd move frequently, uproot their children and any servants, and change their names from location to location.

While Papa lived out his dotage in Mayfair, surrounded by servants and beautiful art. That thought should please Matilda. Instead, it struck her as grossly unfair.

Unjust, even. She made her way to the study, intent on immersing herself in Duncan's beautiful prose. He did not deserve a life of obscurity in foreign climes, but then, neither did Matilda. She'd made an error in judgment, fled when she should have remained near enough to consider the chessboard at greater length.

"Water over the dam," she muttered, taking up her edited version of the essay on Prague.

Sometime later—she lost track of the hours when she read Duncan's travelogues—Jinks interrupted with fresh oil for the lamps. He had to stand on a chair to trim the wicks of the candles on the mantel, though he was a nimble little fellow.

"Will you get outside to enjoy the sunshine?" Matilda asked.

"'Deed I will, Miss Matilda. I fetch the post, you see. I take Mr. Wentworth's letters to the inn, and I bring back any mail for Brightwell. I mustn't drop anything in the snow, and I mustn't tarry at the inn to gossip. Mr. Wentworth says fetching the post is a very important job. Sometimes, we get letters from our duke Birdsong Lane, Mayfair, London—and those are franked because he's a nob."

The day was as pretty as a winter day could be. Brilliantly sunny, no wind, the sky as bright blue as Duncan Wentworth's eyes.

I am hopelessly in love. "I have a packet to mail myself, Jinks. Can you wait a bit for me to join you?"

Jinks clambered off his chair. "You want to go into the village with me?"

Matilda could not entrust this correspondence to anyone else. "We'll go straight to the posting inn and come straight back. I've been sitting long enough."

The boy wrinkled his nose. "Should we tell Mr. Wentworth that you're leaving the property?"

Matilda had left her father's household on the spur of the moment, though even hindsight supported that decision. She could not afford to be reckless merely because the day was sunny and her heart was lighter.

"I'll wait for you on the path in the woods and you can take my package into the inn with the other letters. I won't leave Brightwell, but I'll keep you company on the way to the inn."

Still, his gaze was dubious. "You aren't bringing a satchel or bundle with you? Mr. Wentworth won't like it if you run off."

What staunch loyalty for such a small boy. "I will bring nothing except my letter. If I wanted to run off, would I take you with me as far as the village, then leave you to tattle on me? Would I leave from the woods, where my footprints in the snow would reveal exactly which direction I fled?"

Jinks's brow furrowed. "You'd pike off after dark, nobody the wiser. That's what Manners says. Danvers says won't nobody be piking anywhere, and Mrs. Newbury says idle talk never beat a carpet."

"Give me ten minutes." Matilda rummaged in the desk drawer for clean paper on which to jot a note.

Jinks pelted out the door, then banged it closed behind him. The entire house was livelier this morning in anticipation of the ducal visit, though Matilda wasn't looking forward to meeting Duncan's cousins.

She finished her note and sealed it, then met Jinks in the scullery, where he slung an oilskin pouch over his shoulder.

"In case I slip in the mud. Anybody can slip. Lord Stephen said so."

"We'll be careful." Matilda pulled her hood up around her face. "There and back before anybody knows we're gone."

Chapter Fifteen

The gardens looked less unkempt, and a great pile of brush and bracken had accumulated in the lowest parterre. Duncan's back ached, his arms burned, and his thighs were in a righteous fury, but the work was satisfying.

"Are we about damned done for the day?" Stephen settled on the edge of a large urn sporting the snow-encrusted remains of a dead chrysanthemum.

"Done for the morning. I will pay for this exertion, though I did not want Jane making one of her infernal housekeeping lists. Overgrown gardens are fine in fairy tales. In real life, they are evidence of sloth and eccentricity."

Stephen's cheeks bore a slight flush, and he, too, had shed his coat. "You've been at Brightwell a few weeks, and you're already an expert on country life. Such a quick study. Perhaps an overgrown garden is evidence of ambitions beyond one's abilities. A fellow plants a hedge, thinking to provide shade for a few rabbits, some geometry for his parterres. The English climate comes along and turns one hedge into an annual Herculean labor."

Duncan set down the scythe in a dry fountain. "Plans go awry. True enough." He fished a whetstone from the pocket of the coat he'd draped over the bench.

"Shame to have to leave all this," Stephen said. "Brightwell has possibilities."

"You are leaving us?"

"I'll wander on, or I'll look after the place for you if you like. You and Matilda will have to travel soon. Winter makes a journey harder, which is good when your pursuers don't know where to find you, but bad when you're trying not to be found."

Duncan drew the blade along the stone. "I ask myself: Why should Matilda spend the rest of her life in hiding when her great sin was that she simply came upon an upsetting situation and did not want to have to explain it to the authorities? Wakefield created this mess, perhaps he can resolve it."

"And what of the fiancé? Matilda is convinced he's onto Wakefield's game, and Parker is military. His interest in a career spy is unlikely to be casual."

Duncan flipped the scythe, applying the second side of the blade to the stone. "The military hero stands to burnish his halo, however quietly. If he captures a spy, verifies the fate of stolen plans, and exposes a treasonous plot, his promotion to general officer is likely assured."

Stephen pushed away from the urn and retrieved his coat from the shoulders of a statue of the *Venus de' Medici*.

"I hadn't considered that Parker would be tracking Matilda down for his own glory. Not a very suitor-ly thing to do."

"You have bracken in your hair."

"So do you."

A moment of swatting at hair ensued. Between one brush of his fingers through his locks and the next, Duncan's mind seized on a thought.

"If Matilda marries Parker, he cannot testify against her."

Stephen finished dusting twigs from his hair and gave Venus's breast a pat. "What are you going on about now?"

"Spousal privilege. Just as a priest cannot be compelled to give testimony regarding what he's heard in the confessional, spouses cannot be compelled to testify against each other." This legal detail was profoundly unsettling, also a well-established aspect of English law.

"Matilda wasn't Parker's wife when she stole the plans," Stephen said. "Does that matter?"

"If she's his wife when she's put on trial, no." Was the war hero clever and selfless enough to offer Matilda this protection? "And she didn't steal anything. Her father was in possession of those plans, and he hasn't accused her of theft."

"Cases such as these require brandy," Stephen said. "And victuals. I'm starving."

Duncan began walking toward the house. "How can you think of food when—damn."

"You swore," Stephen said, hitching along beside him. "Why on earth would you—? Damn."

The ducal coach rattled up the drive and continued around to the front of the manor, another large conveyance following closely behind it.

"The invading forces have arrived," Stephen said. "Prepare to man the turrets and defend your lemon drops."

Jane and Matilda would get on famously. They were both serious, brilliant, determined ladies with a sense of mischief.

"This is not an invasion." Duncan resumed walking, his pace more deliberate. "These are our reinforcements."

"Which is why you'll warn Matilda privately before you let Quinn and Jane have at her."

"The children will take her captive." A lovely thought, Matilda spirited away to the nursery, where she'd be forced to read stories and marvel at Bitty's lone card trick by the hour.

"I'm surprised Matilda wasn't out here supervising us," Stephen said. "You cut a fine figure when you shed your jacket and coat."

"Doubtless she was admiring me from the windows."

"I was watching for her, and I didn't see her."

Duncan longed to give Stephen a shove—affection and annoyance, in one casual gesture—but one didn't physically shove Stephen.

"Find your own true love," Duncan said, "and leave mine alone."

"I'll intercept your reinforcements," Stephen said, turning for the back terrace. "You find your true love and explain to her about how the Duke of Walden nearly died with his neck in a noose."

"No talk of nooses and death, please. I'll bring Matilda down to meet the cousins in the family parlor. Say nothing about her, no matter how severely you're questioned."

"Bring her down straightaway. Mortal man is helpless to resist Jane's interrogations."

"Give me five minutes, and don't eat all the tea cakes before Matilda and I have a chance at them."

* * *

Matilda's instincts were stirring back to life. Not only the instincts of a fugitive, but also the instincts of a chess player. In the middle of a good game, she lost track of time, lost

track of her surroundings. She became a mind absorbed
in an intellectual challenge. What options had she left her
opponent? What would a person of her opponent's character
and experience do with those options?

Did she and Duncan have to leave England? Could she
find a way to resolve her difficulties without risking death as
a traitor? What had Papa been doing with those plans?

Had he stolen them *for* the Crown or *from* the Crown?

She stopped several yards short of where the path through
the trees opened out onto the inn's side yard.

"If you're questioned regarding this package, you don't
know anything about it," she said, passing the missive
to Jinks.

"Which I don't." Jinks shifted from foot to foot on the
muddy path. "Would you mind if I stepped around back for
a moment after I've picked up the mail?"

Twenty yards away, a groom was leading a coach-and-
four up from the stables. No crests showed on the doors,
though the conveyance was fine. One wheel lacked the red
trim of the other three, suggesting a recent repair.

Matilda backed up a few steps so a thick oak stood between her and the innyard. To be out in fresh air on a sunny
morning was wonderful, but she refused to take unnecessary
chances.

"Step around to the jakes if you must, Jinks, but don't
be long."

He grinned and dashed off, as Matilda pulled her hood
up and rested her back against the rough bark of the tree.
She'd met Duncan in these woods just a few short weeks
ago. What a difference, between that woman—frightened,
alone, nearly starving—and the woman who'd awoken with
a new dream, no longer alone. She was still wary—she
might always be wary—but no longer panicked.

She peeked around the tree to see the coach halt and a footman set down the steps. The coachman wore livery, though Matilda couldn't make out more than a fancy embroidered hem beneath his greatcoat.

Jinks skipped down the inn's steps and dodged around the corner of the building. He'd not tarried inside, bless the boy.

A hand clamped around Matilda's shoulder. "Now who have we here?"

She whirled, but the snow robbed her boots of purchase, and she could not break her captor's grasp.

"I do believe we and the lady are acquainted, Herm." A small, weasely man in much-mended garb held a knife, while his larger companion gave Matilda a shake.

"Be still, you. Jeffrey and me have a score to settle, and we don't much care how we settle it."

More than their appearance, their voices struck a chord in Matilda's memory. These were Duncan's poachers, the men who'd set snares for helpless rabbits on land they didn't own.

"What can you possibly want with me?" she spat. "These woods are the last place you two should be plying your criminal trade."

"We're not plying anything," the smaller man said. "We're gallantly aiding a lady fallen on trying times. Colonel Parker said so. He's ever so worried about you."

Colonel Parker. Matilda had the space of two heartbeats to consider options and outcomes. She could demand to be taken to Duncan, and promise these louts payment for delivering her. That choice would irrevocably entangle Duncan and his family in her troubles.

She could go meekly into Parker's arms. She might well end up dead, she might also end up married to Parker, but Duncan—blameless, decent Duncan—would be safe.

"You come from Colonel Lord Parker?" she asked.

"That's his coach over yonder," Herman replied. "Poor sod's been lookin' for you everywhere."

A cold wind blew through the bare trees, and Matilda said a prayer for fortitude. *Duncan, I'm sorry.*

"Then take me to the colonel at once. This instant, and unhand me or it will go the worse for you when the colonel finds out how I've been treated."

She'd learned to use that tone on her castle servants, a lazy bunch who'd taken advantage of her husband's chronic distraction. Herman turned loose of her, and his companion's knife disappeared beneath a winter coat.

"Come along, then," the shorter man said, "and be quick about it."

Matilda marched smartly from the woods, praying that Jinks either stayed out of sight or knew enough not to interfere.

"Miss?" The coachman from the big vehicle called down to her. He was a trim man not much older than Matilda, with the weathered features common to his profession.

"Good day," Matilda said, drawing herself up. "These men tell me this coach belongs to Colonel Lord Atticus Parker. Can you confirm that assertion?"

The coachman wrapped the reins and climbed down. "Miss Wakefield, is that you? We've been so worried. So very, very worried. The colonel has been beside himself, and he will be overjoyed to find you hale and whole."

"This is the colonel's coach, then? He's here? I'm looking for Colonel Lord Atticus Parker and no other." Please let the dread in her voice sound like reluctant hope. A movement at the corner of the innyard caught her eye, but she dared not look for fear she'd see Jinks preparing to intervene.

A tread on the inn's front steps sent foreboding skittering up her spine.

"I would know my intended anywhere," Parker said. "Matilda, I have prayed for your safety nightly, and now the prodigal has been found."

Matilda turned slowly, all choices and options falling away. She wanted to live. She wanted Duncan to live and to have the freedom to wander as he pleased, secure in the love of his family. She wanted Papa to enjoy a peaceful old age, and she wanted very much to cry.

"Atticus," she said, stepping toward him. "I'm so glad you've found me."

She wrapped her arms around him, and he enveloped her in a gentle embrace. "Have no fear, Matilda. I'll ensure that your little queer start has no lasting repercussions, provided you tell me everything."

She quelled the urge to wallop him and instead nodded. "I will tell you every bit of it, but not in the middle of an innyard, where anyone might overhear. Take me home, Atticus. I want to go home."

She had no home of her own, and accepting Atticus's protection meant she never would. She would have what Atticus allowed her and nothing more, though Papa and Duncan would be safe.

"My intended will return with us to London," Atticus said.

Please, Jinks, become distracted by some birdcall, by the reflection of the sunlight on a mud puddle, by the gossip offered by a passing potboy.

Matilda climbed into the coach unassisted and left the door open for Atticus.

"Eager to be on your way?" he asked, taking a place beside her on the forward-facing bench.

"I've learned not to linger in the open," Matilda said,

though her precautions had been inadequate. "I have nothing left of great value to carry with me. We can be on our way immediately."

"What else have you learned?" Atticus rapped on the roof with his fist.

The opening moves were a delicate and interesting aspect of any chess game. Matilda chose the simplicity of truth, though the feeling of the coach rocking into motion, of being torn from the only haven she'd known, made her chest ache.

"I've learned that I am not equal to the challenges faced by women of the lower orders. I've learned that I was a fool, and that a head for chess does not imbue me with any ability to fend for myself—just the opposite. I've learned to appreciate basic comforts." *And I've learned what the love of a good man feels like.*

"Why did you disappear, Matilda? Did Wakefield threaten you?"

How concerned Atticus sounded, how ready to be outraged on her behalf. "I know not whose livery the coachman and grooms wear, my lord, and another lesson I've learned is that privacy should never be assumed. We can discuss the rest of my situation in London."

The coach horses set a spanking pace onto the main thoroughfare, despite the muddy condition of the road. Every turn of the wheels made the ache in Matilda's heart sharper.

What have I done? What will Duncan think?

"We can be in London by nightfall," Atticus said, "and I took the liberty of getting us a special license. By tomorrow evening we can be married, and Wakefield can't say anything to it."

Oh, God.

Oh, *Duncan*.

"I'd like that." The lump in Matilda's throat was the size of Brightwell's home wood. "I want an end to this situation, Atticus, and if you can guarantee me that Papa and I will be safe, then I am happy to marry you."

"I can make that promise," the colonel replied, taking her hand. "Let me handle everything, and your troubles will be over."

Matilda gazed out the window as Duncan's woods were lost around a bend in the road. *My troubles have in truth just begun.*

* * *

Odd emotions stirred as Duncan made his way up Brightwell's back stairs. Stephen's half-finished construction project meant the railing between the ground and first floors was missing, and the smell of sawdust permeated the air.

Change had come to Brightwell. The staff had been in a cleaning frenzy, the footmen had scrubbed the library from shelves to grates, and the garden was being retrieved from ruin. This house could have become the home Matilda had longed for, but that wasn't meant to be.

"Have you seen Miss Matilda?" Duncan asked a maid scurrying past.

"Not since I came upon her—" The maid blushed as only a redhead could blush. "Not since she broke her fast, sir."

Came upon her in your bed. Duncan should have been mortified rather than amused.

"If you see her, please let her know that company awaits in the family parlor." Because Matilda was family now and should meet her prospective in-laws in as comfortable a setting as possible.

"She's usually in the study at midday," the maid replied. "Poring over them manuscripts. Likes to open all the draperies and sit by the fire."

"Right, the study. My thanks." Duncan spun on his heel and made for the study, where he should have thought to look first.

Matilda wasn't in the study, she wasn't in her bedroom—though her personal effects were still hanging in the wardrobe, a shamefully vast relief—and she wasn't in Duncan's apartment.

Hiding? Rummaging in the attics? Napping in some quiet corner because Duncan had twice interrupted her slumbers to make love with her?

"Cousin Duncan!" A high voice bellowed. "We came to see you!" Booted feet beat a rapid tattoo as a small female barreled toward Duncan.

He caught her up in his arms. "Elizabeth, a pleasure to see you." And to hug her, and to enjoy again the little-girl reality of her.

"Am I almost grown up yet?"

"No, thank the celestial powers. You are still your delightfully five-year-old self."

"I want to be grown up," she said, squeezing him about the neck. "Then I can have a fine coach, and waltz, and never, never, never have to sit still in church. Cousin Stephen said I was to fetch you, or you'd be forever trying to put your old self to rights. Is this your new self?"

"What do you think?"

"You are not the same," she said, wiggling to get down, then seizing Duncan by the hand. "You smell happier. You smell of climbing trees and making dams in the stream, not books and coal smoke, and boring old lessons. Cousin Stephen says you have a new friend."

Bitty stopped at the top of the steps and speared Duncan with a glower. "Friends aren't cousins. You are *my* cousin."

She held up her arms and Duncan sat her on the bannister. Down she went, skirts flying, right past a startled Manners.

"Cousin Duncan, come along!" Bitty yelled from the bottom of the stairs.

"That one has a fine set of lungs," Manners said.

"If she directs you to saddle her dragon, you will deposit her on the nearest bannister and bid her good hunting."

"Yes, Mr. Wentworth."

Duncan took the stairs at his usual decorous pace, but where on earth could Matilda have got off to? The niggling fear that she'd bolted had no basis in fact. She'd left her effects in her room, she'd had no reason to leave, she'd—

"Mama, I found him!" Bitty bellowed, taking hold of Duncan's hand when he reached the bottom stair. "I told him we have come to pay a visit."

The family parlor door opened to reveal Jane, Duchess of Walden, looking as serene and benign as a Renaissance madonna. Jane was dark-haired, on the tall side, and a mother three times over. If anything, years of marriage had gilded her beauty with humor and a certain wily tenacity that often masqueraded as graciousness.

"Jane, a pleasure." Duncan kissed her cheek and endured a hug, Bitty still kiting around on his hand. "I hope the journey was uneventful."

"With three children? Surely you jest. Fortunately, Elizabeth was up on the box or in the saddle with her father from time to time. She was vastly disappointed that no highwaymen presented themselves for target practice. You look well."

Duncan felt well, but for his worry regarding Matilda. The morning's exertions in the garden agreed with him, putting Brightwell to rights agreed with him. Spending the night with Matilda agreed with him very much.

"Thank you. I hope somebody thought to order a tea tray."

Bitty towed him into the parlor. "I told Uncle Stephen not to be a hog with the tea cakes or you would be very disappointed in him. I am never a hog, but sometimes I am an adorable little piglet, right, Papa?"

Quinn turned, a sandwich halfway to his mouth. Still no gray in his hair—he and Duncan had something of an unspoken contest in that regard. With his free arm, he cradled an infant, who surveyed the room with the equanimity any ducal child ought to claim from birth.

"Duncan."

"Quinn."

They did not embrace. They had never embraced. They'd lived under the same roof for years without even speaking much. Duncan's job had been to keep Stephen out of trouble, and he'd done that to the best of his ability. Quinn's job had been to not make Duncan's task more difficult. Then Jane had come along, and Quinn's responsibilities had taken on new and besotted dimensions.

"I'll take that baby," Duncan said, plucking the child from her father's arms. "You'll get crumbs in her hair."

The infant waved a fist and smacked Duncan on the shoulder.

"She's pleased to see me." Duncan was more than pleased to see that the baby was in the pink of health.

Quinn regarded Duncan with the blue-eyed acumen that had made many a bank customer squirm. "You've no pin in your cravat."

"Quinn," Jane said. "Duncan hasn't been in the room five minutes and you're interrogating him."

"He always wears a cravat pin."

Stephen, who'd been steadily ingesting tea cakes, paused. "So lovely, to be discussed in the third person by one's nearest and dearest, isn't it? These cakes are wonderful."

"Don't be a hog, Uncle Stephen." Bitty bounded from Duncan's side. "You should save one for Hester. Nurse had to take her upstairs to finish her nap because Hester is *little*."

Hester was Bitty's younger sister, and as quiet as Bitty was exuberant. Hester had picked her first lock at the age of two and a half. Jane worried that the child had inherited her uncle Stephen's mind for mechanical devices.

Duncan looked forward to teaching Hester to play chess.

Though if he and Matilda emigrated to some far-flung clime, he'd likely never see Hester, Bitty, or Artemis again. That thought disagreed with him almost as much as not knowing where Matilda was.

"I will leave defense of the tea tray to mine host," Jane said. "Bitty, you may take three tea cakes, one for you, one for Hester, and one for Nurse, then you will join me in locating the nursery."

Bitty snatched up three cakes. "I don't have to take a nap, do I?"

"No," Duncan said, nuzzling the baby's head before passing the infant to Jane, "but you will have to choose your bed, re-organize the toys, and decide where to stable your dragon."

"Come along, Mama. George is a very particular dragon. He must have the best cave in the house and the best story-books to read."

Peace settled over the room when Jane and the children departed.

"So where is Matilda?" Stephen asked, his mouth full of tea cake.

"She should be joining us shortly." Duncan hadn't thought to look for her in the nursery. Perhaps she'd crossed paths with little Hester and her nurse, and been charmed into joining them abovestairs.

"His Grumpy Grace scared her away," Stephen said, gesturing at Quinn with his teacup. "She heard the dread Duke of Walden had come to call with his Vandal horde. She'll hide in a closet until you're gone."

"Don't joke about a missing child," Quinn said. "Bitty would still be locked in that cupboard unless we'd kept searching for her."

Stephen and Quinn bickered when other brothers merely shook hands and exchanged pleasantries.

"Duncan kept searching for her," Stephen said, hobbling to the sofa. "You were still muttering about 'the child must learn' and 'she can't be frightening her mother like this.' "

Bitty had gone missing one fine morning last spring, and her parents had decided she was making a bid for attention in anticipation of the baby's arrival. Duncan had not agreed with that hypothesis, and he'd begun a systematic search of the ducal residence. His diligence had been rewarded an hour later when a tearful Bitty had been found in a cupboard in the linen closet, where the housekeeper had inadvertently locked her.

His search had not been the result of a logical conclusion, but rather, of a nagging question: What if Quinn and Jane were wrong about their own daughter?

"So tell me about the woman who has moved Stephen to raptures," Quinn said, taking the reading chair near the sofa. "And don't pretty it up. Jane is certain you have trouble afoot here at Brightwell."

Stephen had doubtless dropped epistolary hints for Their Graces' delectation. Duncan decided to start with facts.

"Matilda is the daughter of a well-to-do art dealer named Thomas Wakefield. He might well be a traitor to the Crown, and Matilda has been inadvertently caught up in his schemes."

Quinn turned on Duncan an expression the duke usually reserved for his younger brother. "When you set out to create a muddle, you create a spectacular muddle."

"I've also proposed to the woman," Duncan said, "or asked leave to pay her my addresses."

"Beyond spectacular," Quinn said, sounding impressed. "For the first time, I must admonish Stephen not to follow your example. What do you need from me? Shall I play the duke, threaten a few Cabinet ministers, have a word with King George?"

"All in a day's duking," Stephen said. "Duncan will doubtless consult Matilda before he gives you your marching orders. Matters have progressed to a serious state."

Quinn yanked off one boot, then the other. "Treason is always serious."

"I meant matters of the heart. Tell him the whole of it, Duncan."

Duncan did not tell Quinn the whole of it—a couple was entitled to some privacy—but he sketched in the major points: a message possibly in code, invasion of France, a suitor who was probably himself scheming to thwart Wakefield's espionage, question upon question, and the likelihood of leaving Britain in the near future.

"I don't like that part," Quinn said. "Jane will never stand for it."

"I am not courting Jane," Duncan said, though the idea of fleeing, while logical and necessary, also brought with it significant heartache. All Matilda wanted was a place to call home, a patch of ground on which to live out her days.

All Duncan wanted, much to his own surprise, was to give that to her.

"Matilda promised me that you and Jane would be taken into our confidence before we made any final decisions."

"Where is Matilda?" Stephen asked again. "I've left her a good half dozen tea cakes, but they'll grow stale before she deigns to join us."

Duncan for once could not muster any interest in the sweets. "Perhaps Jane has waylaid her."

"Jane will soon be napping," Quinn said, propping his feet on a hassock, "if she knows what's good for her."

"I don't know where Matilda might be, but I'll ask Mrs. Newbury—"

The door swung open to reveal Manners in the company of a red-cheeked, winded Jinks.

"The boy is demanding to speak with you, sir," Manners began. "Told him it weren't his place, but he's powerful agitated, and—"

"Miss Matilda left," Jinks cried. "She said she wouldn't, and then she did, and them two rotters I seen at the inn afore are swilling gin like their nag just won the Derby. She said she wouldn't leave us, said she wouldn't leave Brightwell, but she was in that coach, and now she's gone."

Chapter Sixteen

"This is the marquess's own team," the coachman said. "He values his horseflesh, and it is not worth my job to drive one of them from merely off to seriously lame. I doubt his lordship would lend you a conveyance again if he learned I'd abused his cattle at your direction, sir."

Angus Nairn was that plague of senior officers the world over, the conscientious subordinate. Not loyal to his master, but loyal to duty, inasmuch as duty involved thwarting the ambitions of his betters by citing rules, conventions, and other excuses.

In the military, such punctilious fellows seldom rose above a lieutenancy.

Matilda remained on the forward-facing seat beside Parker and said nothing. Gone was the gracious, worldly, blue-stocking Parker had met at a Paris soiree. Parker's intended had grown skinny and silent, spending most of the past hour staring out the window and ignoring him.

Time to get some answers from the lady. "We will stop for a change of horses and for sustenance," Parker said. "Go easy on the team until we reach a decent inn."

Though the blighted man *had* been going easy on the team, which dithering he claimed was necessitated by the muddy roads.

"Right, sir. The Speckled Hen isn't but three miles farther on. We should be there in less than an hour."

Because the road in winter was banked with snow, and traffic heading west was busy, Parker's coach was frequently forced to pull off to wait for vehicles passing in the opposite direction. Matilda seemed indifferent to the delays, to the chill in the coach, to everything. Military wives were supposed to be uncomplaining, but the best of them were *cheerfully* uncomplaining.

"I will need a moment's privacy," Matilda said, when at last the coach swayed into the Speckled Hen's innyard.

"I'll get you a room where you may refresh yourself while the food is being prepared." And he'd commandeer the private dining room if he had to declare martial law to do it.

Matilda nodded, as if she were too busy watching a drama visible only to her to bother replying. Perhaps her recent experiences had set off a touch of melancholia or hysteria. Women were delicate, and fleeing in the middle of the night to wander the countryside alone was not the behavior of a lady in possession of all of her wits.

The inn, fortunately, boasted only an old couple in the common. The place was clean, cozy, and worthy of a titled family's custom. Parker ordered a meal for two in the private dining room.

A maid bustled in, setting down plates laden with beefsteak and mashed potatoes, boiled turnips, and bread.

A gentleman's pint and lady's pint came next, though Parker waved the lady's pint away and ordered a tea tray instead.

Matilda was to be the wife of a colonel—a general if all went well—in His Majesty's armed forces. She was owed hot tea and the inn's good china, as was Parker. When she joined him at the table, the remote quality that had enveloped her in the coach remained, though she took the chair he held for her.

"We have privacy, my dear," Parker said. "You will answer a few questions while we eat."

Matilda bowed her head, her hands folded in her lap. She moved her lips silently, clearly offering a grace for the meal.

Fair enough. She'd likely not had regular sustenance, and gratitude was fitting in her circumstances.

"I will tell you whatever you wish to know," she said, spreading the table napkin on her lap, "but there isn't much to tell. Might I have the butter?"

Parker passed the butter. "Why did you run?"

She dipped her knife into the butter and put a generous portion on her bread. "Papa is in grave danger, Atticus. I have thought and thought about a document I came upon in his satchel, and I am convinced that somebody on his staff is guilty of serious wrongdoing. Have you ever noticed his servants?"

This was interesting. "One generally doesn't, if the staff is well trained."

"One generally does, if the staff is underfoot at all hours of the day and night, traveling with one everywhere. I didn't see the difference until I went to live with my husband. At the castle, the servants were nearly invisible. In Papa's house, they hover. I suspect Papa is all but a prisoner, and he hasn't dared speak up about his circumstances because he's been desperate to keep me safe."

What flight was this? Parker cut into his steak—slightly overdone, not tragically so—and prepared to patiently attend to a lot of nonsense. Thomas Wakefield was not held hostage by his servants, though, upon reflection, they were a motley bunch.

"Please do elaborate, my dear. Your father has ever struck me as a man competent to look after his own self-interest, but women notice things men overlook. I am eager to hear any and all theories you care to put forth."

While you avoid explaining to me why you ran from our engagement.

Matilda set down her fork and knife and chewed her meat slowly. Playing chess with her was exactly like this. Bloody slow and without visible evidence of a strategy. When she decided to focus on the game, her sheer unpredictability could result in victory. In the usual course, she moved pieces at random, experimenting her way to defeat nearly as often as she stumbled to victory.

She leaned closer. "Did you know that Papa's porter is a *Corsican*? I cannot credit that Carlu would involve himself in dangerous schemes when he has honorable work and a good roof over his head, but Atticus, I saw information I should never have seen. The handwriting was Carlu's—he uses a distinctive script—and the only possible explanation is that Papa has become the unwitting victim of desperate villains. He is in very great danger, and I still don't know what to do."

She cut off another bite of meat, but put her fork and knife down without tasting the food. "I am afraid, Atticus. I am afraid that if you are not very careful, much harm will result to people I care about dearly. You must tread cautiously or that harm could befall you too."

How very intriguing. Parker had not known the dark-
eyed fellow minding Wakefield's door was a *Corsican*. An
accomplice, doubtless, a fellow sneak thief of state secrets
and private scandals.

"What of the rest of the staff?" Parker asked. "Have you
suspicions regarding them?"

She stared at her plate, and he had the odd thought that
she was trying not to cry. Matilda wasn't the crying type,
thank heavens, but at the sight of her, pale, gaunt, struggling
so to find words...Parker's gentlemanly upbringing did not
allow him to ignore her upset.

"Take your time," he said. "Unburden yourself of all
your fears and nightmares, and I will see that everything is
resolved as quietly as possible."

"I can make you a list of his staff," she said. "Papa's
servants are notably un-British. Papa would never betray his
king and country, but even a well-meaning man can be taken
advantage of by ruthless schemers."

True enough, alas.

She sketched a portrait with possibilities. Parker poured
her a cup of tea and set the cup and saucer by her plate.

"We will make a list and consider the evidence," he
said. "Strategy is a skill every senior officer commands in
quantity. Trust me, my dear, and all will come right. Tell me
exactly what sent you alone into the night."

Parker had hit upon the notion of exposing a single
spy out of expedience. Career advancement in peacetime
was difficult, and then the opportunity to ensnare Wakefield
had fallen into his lap. A comment overheard here, a quiet
suggestion there, a pointed remark from a grumbling general, and he'd been given the means to use Wakefield to his
own advantage.

But if instead Parker uncovered a whole nest of spies,

quietly, and on terms that would reflect well upon his superior officers? Even the marquess would have to applaud such an accomplishment. A baronetcy wasn't out of the question.

"You promise you won't laugh?" Matilda asked, cradling her teacup in her hands. "I need you to take my situation seriously, Atticus. I did not leave my home on a whim."

"You fled because you were afraid."

"And shocked, also horrified. I don't know what exactly I found—my foreign languages have grown rusty with disuse—but what I was able to deduce frightened me."

She *had* been pathetically relieved to see him, embracing him right in the innyard and before the servants.

"What did you find?" And where was that evidence now? Parker had made a copy, but she'd said the original was in the servant's—*the Corsican's*—handwriting. That development was just too lovely to ignore.

"Atticus, I am not certain, but I have reason to believe that Spain is planning to invade England. The defeat of the Armada was Spain's greatest humiliation, Papa always said, and England's resources are spread thin now. We are vulnerable to attack, and Spain has never forgotten the drubbing they were given. The French are happy to aid in England's downfall, and I might have seen evidence of French collusion with Spain."

Good heavens, she'd garbled everything. "Why not bring this evidence to me straightaway, Matilda?"

"I am not clever like you, Atticus. I must think and consider everything before I come to a decision. I was shocked, upset, bewildered, and thought only to remove the evidence from Papa's household. Without the document that I found, nobody could move that dastardly plot forward, could they?"

An old saying popped into Parker's head: Even a broken clock is right twice a day.

"You set out alone, with little coin, and nowhere to go, because *you were trying to save England*?"

"Of course. Why else would I abscond with the villain's plans? Why else would I travel in secret at great risk to myself? For all England's enemies knew, I *did* give those plans to you, because we most assuredly have not been invaded, have we?"

The logic, or lack thereof, was stunning. Parker nearly burst out laughing. "We have not been invaded, but Matilda, while I applaud your patriotism, I must inform you that another perspective might pertain to the facts."

"You think Papa is a traitor? When that satchel was carried by Carlu more often than anybody else?"

"Your father has much to answer for, which we can discuss at greater length at another time. I am more concerned, madam, that *you* will be accused of treason, which is a serious crime indeed."

Matilda stared at him, her expression blank, then filling with ire. "I *risked my life* for months, I thwarted King George's foes, I solved a very delicate problem without involving anybody else, and I'm to be *tried for treason*? If that's how you foresee this situation unraveling, then I'll thank you to set me down at the next crossroads. You offered me safety, Atticus, not the threat of a noose. You're a war hero and you have strategy coming out your fingertips. You will set the generals and ministers straight, or there will be no wedding."

There had to be a wedding. *Had to be*, for the sake of all Parker held dear. Then too, Matilda had been well dowered before her short-lived marriage to the German. She had a widow's portion now, as well as most of the original settlement funds under her control.

"Calm yourself, Matilda. I said I'd resolve the situation, and I will."

"For months, I've hidden myself away, expecting Carlu or one of his cohorts to leap out of the bushes and cut my throat. Now I find my heroism will be rewarded with mutton-headed histrionics on the part of the very people whose realm I've saved. Why is there no word to describe a woman's brave deeds? Heroinic? There should be such a word. Pass the salt."

Parker passed the salt and let her grumble, while he marveled that Matilda had an imagination after all. The quiet, pretty lady who'd always kept to the harmless side of art world gossip and never worn too many jewels was, in fact, fanciful in her way.

Parker told himself this was a good quality. He began to consider the possibilities her fairy-tale version of events offered for a war hero who'd uncovered a nest of spies *and* rescued a valiant subject of the Crown from possible assassination at the hands of traitors.

That version of the facts could work. It could work very nicely, indeed.

* * *

"Jinks says Matilda never attempted a struggle." Quinn offered that observation casually, though Duncan longed to reply by knocking the duke from his horse and pounding on His Grace's handsome face.

"How could she struggle?" Stephen retorted. "She was accompanied on either side by the Treacher brothers, then confronted with Lord Atticus and his liveried minions."

Jinks had lurked in the inn's stables, watching the drama unfold, while Duncan had been greeting his family and dreaming impossible dreams. The boy had lingered long enough to ask questions in the manner of nosy children the world over, though one result was that Parker had a good ninety minutes' head start.

The other result was that Herman and Jeffrey were enjoying the hospitality of Squire Peabody's saddle room, awaiting the magistrate's next parlor session. On Monday both brothers would be bound over for trespassing, poaching in a forest, and assault with a weapon.

To bring them to justice had been profoundly satisfying, though Duncan had asked for a sentence of transportation rather than the most severe penalty.

"We will dispatch minions of our own to trail Parker's coach," Duncan said. "Quinn, who among your current coterie do you recommend for that task?"

"Ned," the duke said, naming a boy who'd graduated from tiger to groom. "He knows how to stay out of sight, and he's not in livery. You refuse to acknowledge that Matilda went willingly. Nobody reported any resistance on her part, not even when we questioned your poachers separately."

"And who shall accompany Ned?" Duncan asked, for somebody needed to watch Parker at all times, and somebody else needed to carry intelligence back to Duncan.

Quinn brought his horse to a halt at the foot of Brightwell's slushy drive, for a return to the house was necessary before anybody set out for London. "You might well be sending these fellows off on a fool's errand, Duncan. Matilda never promised you anything but heartbreak. Now she's delivered on her promise, and yet you persist. If she's made her choice, why can't you respect that?"

Stephen made a sound of exasperation and kneed his horse into a canter, while Duncan remained at the foot of the drive, wrestling with...what? Not his conscience, but rather, his heart.

And Quinn's protectiveness. "You are preaching logic to a man who thought himself wedded to rational thought, Quinn, and yet, I know Matilda. She offered me more than a promise of heartbreak."

The hoofbeats of Stephen's horse faded, leaving only a chilly wind soughing through the bare trees. In a few hours the light would fade, and traveling would become more difficult as the temperatures dropped.

"Matilda offered you a traitor's noose," Quinn retorted, "and even I cannot protect you if you entangle yourself in high crimes. You are nothing if not sensible, and I rely on you to set a good example for my siblings. To chase off after a woman who has reconciled with a titled fiancé, to flirt with a traitor's death...why do that? You of all people know where foolish gallantry can lead."

Duncan no longer possessed a reasoning mind. His cognitive powers had been replaced with a morass of emotions, hunches, and questions, but he could reply to Quinn with certainty in two regards.

"First, your siblings are adults. They no longer need a good example, having matured into fine and formidable individuals, worthy of the ducal branch of the Wentworth family. We have to let them go, Quinn, and be there for them when they need us, as Stephen is here for me now."

Quinn's brows twitched down. He gazed up the drive, he fussed with his horse's mane. "Go on."

Meaning, Quinn would discuss Duncan's observation with Jane, which was sufficient concession for the nonce.

"Second, I am no longer that good example you allude to. I am no longer the man who came down from York ten years ago, full of learning and determined to outrun a bleak past. My family has given me the time and resources to deal with what troubled that fellow, and I realize now he wasn't wrong. I am not now, nor have I ever been, guilty of foolish gallantry. I did the right thing when I involved myself in Rachel's situation. Those around me acted shamefully, but I would make the same choices again, given the chance, and they would be the correct choices."

These concepts weren't complicated, but they were painful. Honor was not a promise of good outcomes and worldly rewards, it was simply a promise to the world of integrity in all circumstances.

A promise Duncan had kept. He'd promised Matilda safety at Brightwell, and that promise had *not* been kept.

He urged his horse forward, because time was of the essence. Quinn's mount came along, though Duncan didn't particularly care if the duke was paying attention.

"You're older," Quinn said. "I know that, but I fail to see how embroiling yourself with spies, liars, and an ambitious younger son makes any sense."

"Nonetheless, I am honor bound to pursue this matter, Quinn. You can either support me in that end or take your ducal consequence and run back to London like a good boy."

The silence that followed was interesting. Nobody told Quinn Wentworth to run along, probably not even his duchess, but the safe course where Matilda was concerned was also the cowardly course.

And I am not a coward.

That thought was a gift, and the one that came after it dealt the last blow to Duncan's doubts:

Matilda is not a coward either, else she'd never have been able to love a man such as me.

"Duncan, you aren't making sense." That was a plea, not

an accusation. Quinn was begging Duncan to return to the rational, taciturn posture of a man who'd rather translate Virgil than wade through Byron's messy subtleties.

Alas, that careful, hurting man was no more. "Quinn, shut your mouth. You are trying to be helpful, but you've failed to mention the one hypothesis that explains all the facts."

Not a hypothesis, a great, blooming, sunny certainty.

"You've lost your mind?" Quinn was warming up for a ducal tirade, which amounted to a series of pithy verbal slices that left a subordinate's confidence in ribbons. These displays were less and less frequent, but Duncan could not afford to indulge his cousin's moods.

And he was not Quinn's subordinate.

"The signal reality of my dealings with Matilda is that she is an honorable woman. She left London to protect her father. She made shift without resorting to outright crime even when that left her nearly starving. She told me her circumstances as soon as she realized she could safely do so. She has worked harder for her wages than anybody I know born to service, and she has not once complained about the burdens thrust upon her."

"What has this to do with anything?" Quinn began. "Of course, she'd present herself as the pattern card of feminine—"

"*Matilda is protecting me*, you lackwit. She's protecting me, you, the Wentworth name, her father, likely her father's entire household. If she's intent on preserving others from harm, then of course she would sail into Parker's arms impersonating a muddled and weary bride."

The horses slopped into the stable yard, where Stephen waited on the steps of the ladies' mounting block. Grooms took both mounts, though Duncan gave orders that the duke's horse should be walked rather than unsaddled.

"You're going after her," Quinn said. "You're sending me ahead to scout the terrain—lackwit that I am—and then you'll come charging to her rescue."

"Thank the celestial intercessors somebody can make Quinn see reason," Stephen said, heaving to his feet. "I thought we'd have to get Jane involved."

"We'll get Jane involved," Duncan said, striding for the house. "We'll get the entire staff, King George, and the Archbishop of Canterbury involved if needs must, won't we, Quinn?"

Stephen came up on Quinn's other side. "Won't we, Quinn?" He elbowed his brother in the side, hard. Quinn shoved him back, but Stephen had apparently been ready for that, because he caught himself on his canes and flashed a wicked grin. "*Won't we*, Quinn?"

"If you get Jane involved," Quinn said, "then…"

Duncan marched onward, mentally preparing for a solitary ride to London by moonlight.

"Then," Quinn said, "I suppose the Duke of Walden must interest himself in this little drama as well."

"Right answer," Stephen said. "You spared yourself a thrashing, and my money would have been on Duncan."

He slugged Duncan on the arm as they reached the side entrance. Duncan bellowed for Manners and Jinks as Jane came swanning down the steps, the baby in her arms.

* * *

No game of chess, no house-party tournament, no high-stakes play had ever taxed Matilda's mental powers as this game with Lord Atticus Parker taxed her. She must appear overcome with relief to be in his company, though fear rendered her nearly speechless.

She must seem befuddled and full of fanciful misconceptions, while in fact being more clear minded than she'd ever been.

She must be creative, spinning theories on a gossamer web of facts, lies, and suppositions, while she was increasingly certain that Papa was a traitor, else why would the Crown be so persistent in tracking down Thomas Wakefield's daughter?

Atticus would not still be offering to marry her if he weren't convinced she was truly at risk of prosecution.

Amid all of this storytelling and strategizing, she must in no way betray the horror she felt at abandoning Duncan without a word. He would be furious, but worse, he would be hurt. She should be glad he'd have good cause to turn his back on her and relieved he'd not become entangled in her problems after all.

She was instead enraged and bereaved, though she could show Atticus none of that.

"You have given me some interesting ideas to consider," he said, refilling his coffee cup.

They were taking supper in the private dining room. Matilda had spent her afternoon "napping," which meant no helpful maid had come by who might have been trusted to get a note back to Brightwell. Correspondence was going somewhere, though. While pacing past her window, Matilda had seen a liveried groom canter from the innyard in the direction of London.

Be careful, Papa. Be very careful.

"I have had weeks to think matters over," Matilda said. "My imagination has run riot with worry, and I will be only too happy to put the whole business behind me."

Untrue, of course. She wanted Duncan beside her, not this supercilious suitor turned interrogator.

"That will take some time, I'm afraid. Military intelligence likes to make a thorough job of its investigations, and they will have many questions for you."

Matilda set down her fork. The time had come to advance a few pawns. "I have questions as well, Atticus. You seem to be in possession of many facts pertaining to my situation, but I must ask how you came by them? Papa would never have confided the whole of the problem to you when he was seldom allowed to go anywhere without footmen, a porter, or grooms at his side."

Some of the smugness left the colonel's gaze. He was doubtless realizing that every discussion he'd had with Papa had been overheard. Every confidence passed along, every boast or veiled threat had been made before witnesses loyal to Thomas Wakefield.

"I am also curious to know what you were doing in rural Berkshire," she went on. "You have no relatives in the area that I know of."

He patted her wrist. "Your ordeal has resulted in a nervous disposition. No matter. I can be patient, and I will answer all of your questions in time. I do have relatives in Bristol and was on my way to visit them."

"That's not what your coachman said."

A good chess player could move a piece while watching her opponent for a reaction to that move. Matilda watched Parker, and his reaction was fleeting but obvious to a practiced eye. He was annoyed and preparing to lie.

"Of course we were looking for you. Every time I walked down a London street I looked for you. When I paid calls on neighbors in Kent, I looked for you. When I endured an interminable house party in Brighton, I looked for you.

I listened for word of you in all the club gossip. I waited daily for a note, I importuned your father to leave no stone unturned in his own search. You caused a great deal of up-heaval when you disdained the aid of wiser heads, Matilda. I hope you realize that."

Matilda *realized* Atticus was trying to make her feel ashamed. His little sermon had the opposite effect, for she was growing angrier with each bite of overly salted ham and each sip of unimpressive wine.

Why hadn't Papa thought to look for her at Brightwell? He knew she loved the place, knew she'd once dreamed of buying it for herself. Why hadn't Papa sent one of his legion of servants to leave a note for her at the Brightwell posting inn? When she'd lived in Germany, he'd occa-sionally written to her using her mother's maiden name, though Matilda had never thought that quirk more than a family game.

Why hadn't Papa put a notice in the London newspapers? He'd told her long ago that if she ever feared for his safety, she should watch the positions-sought advertisements. He would advertise as a porter who spoke Corsu and German, willing to work overnight hours.

Papa should have spotted such an advertisement. Matilda had placed three and received no response from her father.

Why did Papa take to spying in the first place, and would Matilda have kicked her heels at boarding school for another ten years had Papa not wanted a young daughter to burnish his image as an art dealer enjoying the cultural riches of the Continent?

"You hold your tongue," Parker said, blotting his lips with a table napkin. "Good. I care for you sincerely, but you are in a great deal of trouble, Matilda. Your father and I put it about that you were traveling in America, and that taradiddle was growing difficult to support. When it becomes known that you simply wandered the countryside, unchaperoned and alone, your reputation will suffer.

"Between that," he went on, "and your father's unfortunate possession of suspicious documents—documents which you admit you purloined—I will have all I can do to placate my superiors, keep your neck out of a noose, and shield your father from the worst consequence of his folly. The sooner you marry me, the better."

Why was Atticus so eager to marry a potential traitor?

"I am a widow of means," Matilda said, setting her plate aside, "connected to a titled family. For me to travel without an escort is hardly objectionable. Traveling in your company, however, will raise a few eyebrows."

And make the trail easy for Duncan to follow. That thought hurt. Duncan was not looking for her trail, nor did she want him to.

She also did not want to marry Atticus Parker, though she would if she had to.

"Has your appetite deserted you?" Atticus asked.

Half of Matilda's dinner remained on her plate. "It has. Would you like to play a game of chess?"

He gave a mock shudder. "The most tedious game ever devised for the amusement of gouty old men. Thank you, no. I'll escort you to your room."

Matilda did not need an escort to travel up one flight of stairs and down a short hallway. Parker was making some sort of point—that he was a gentleman, perhaps. He held her chair, he held the door, he politely followed her up the steps, then took the wrong direction on the second floor.

"My room is the third door on the left in that direction," Matilda said.

"I had your things moved to a more commodious chamber," Parker said. "You are to be my wife, after all."

That again. Matilda let him lead her to another room, this one facing the stable yard. The chamber was about the same size as her previous quarters, with the same appointments. She had no *things* of her own, but the brush, hand mirror, shawl, and nightgown the innkeeper's wife had lent her were laid out on the vanity.

"I'll send the maid along," Parker said. "We'll be in London by this time tomorrow."

Matilda had doubts about that. "I am anxious to see my father. He will be very grateful that you made it possible for me to return home."

Atticus remained in the doorway, his hand on the latch. "You'll have a new home very soon, Matilda. Let that thought comfort you as you dream, but answer one more question for me. What did you do with this curious missive you claimed to find among your father's belongings? Can you direct me to it now?"

He'd waited until they were alone to ask that question, but Matilda had already decided upon her answer.

"Do you think me stupid enough to carry plans that could jeopardize England's safety when my own existence grew more precarious by the week? I burned that letter at the first opportunity."

The relief in his eyes was genuine. "Well done, my dear. Very, very well done."

He drew the door closed on that odd comment, and Matilda went to the window.

This was why he'd put her in a different room. The first chamber had looked out over the front of the inn, and Matilda's window had been a few scant feet higher than the awning above the front door. With some luck and care, she could have climbed out the window and down a trellis. This room offered a twenty-foot drop to the muddy innyard.

Colonel Lord Atticus Parker, her concerned, trustworthy, war-hero, self-appointed fiancé, was a gentleman, and Matilda was his prisoner, or the next thing to it.

Chapter Seventeen

"Who is Lieutenant Colonel Lord Atticus Parker?" Duncan asked as the coach swayed around yet another turn.

More to the point, *what* was Atticus Parker? A younger son, war hero, and gentleman, or an ambitious officer who'd exploit any opportunity to better his situation? Both? A suitor moved by genuine concern for his intended?

"Lord Atticus was the Marquess of Creswell's spare," Jane said, "until the heir assumed the title. The current marquess has three sons and a daughter, and he and his marchioness were reportedly a love match."

The baby started to fuss, poor little mite. Jane and Quinn had been at Brightwell for mere hours before Duncan had ordered a fresh team put to. He'd sent a grumbling Quinn ahead to London on horseback, while the nurses were in the next coach back with the older girls. Stephen was serving as an outrider, and Jinks was up on the box, peppering the coachman with questions.

"So like many spares, Lord Atticus is making his career in the military," Duncan said, "and doing a splendid job of it. What else do we know of him?"

"I've danced with him," Jane said, putting the baby to her shoulder and rubbing her back. "He made waltzing with a duchess not a privilege, but a duty. He cuts a fine figure in regimentals, had an adequate store of small talk, and hasn't ever married."

"Why not?"

The baby was in a fractious mood. She escalated from fussing to making I-am-about-to-start-bellowing-my-discontent-for-all-to-hear noises.

"I beg your pardon?" Jane asked, patting the baby's back more quickly.

"Why hasn't a colonel in His Majesty's military married? An officer's wife can do much to advance his career, and army life without a spouse is lonely." Countless women had followed the drum with Wellington's army, countless others had traveled with it as cooks, laundresses, and seamstresses. The general opinion on the matter was that men fought more fiercely when they were reminded about who and what they were fighting for.

"Maybe Lord Atticus hasn't met the right woman," Jane said. "Did you know your Matilda is a duchess?"

The unhappy infant was making enough racket that Duncan wasn't sure he'd heard Jane clearly. He took Artemis upon his knee and gently bounced the child in rhythm with the coach's movement.

"Did you say that Matilda is a *duchess*?" She'd failed to note the details of her marriage in her Book of Common Prayer, which volume Duncan had had packed with his own effects for this journey.

Though perhaps to Matilda, a man's titled status didn't signify.

"She married a duke," Jane said, "either Danish or German, I forget which. The poor fellow didn't last long, but Matilda is the Dowager Duchess of Bosendorf."

Of course she was a duchess. The castle, the house full of servants she'd managed, the husband with the leisure time to make automatons...

"This fact weighs against the notion that Parker was smitten with her," Duncan said. "Dowager duchesses tend to be financially secure and very well connected."

"As is the younger brother of a marquess."

The baby was cooing now, while Duncan's knee had begun to ache. Another vague connection teased at his awareness, something about younger sons of the aristocracy.

"Why do the children always behave for you?" Jane asked. "Even Quinn hasn't your ability to charm that baby."

"Quinn is a duke. I am a mere teacher. He has authority by virtue of his status, while I must enchant with knowledge and the promise of eventually imparting some skills. I do believe Lady Artemis has your smile, Jane."

"What will you do about Parker?"

"I'd like to put out his lights, but then, he doubtless believes he's rescuing Matilda from a dire fate." And his belief might be accurate.

"You aren't convinced of that?"

Duncan passed the now-smiling infant to her mama. "I doubt Parker will keep his peace regarding the fact that Thomas Wakefield was in possession of compromising information, though I'm troubled by one aspect of the situation in particular."

In fact, Duncan was troubled by every aspect of the situation.

"What would that be?"

The coach slowed, suggesting a change of teams was

in the offing, or that Stephen was inquiring at another inn regarding a certain colonel.

"Parker had to have read the translated notes Matilda made regarding the intercepted message," Duncan said. "She put them in a desk drawer, but those locks are laughably easy to pick. Why is Wakefield still at large?"

The lights of an innyard came into view, illuminating Stephen still in the saddle, in conversation with a hostler.

"You're trying to make some point of logic," Jane said. "I left my logic back at Brightwell, along with my ambitions for a good night's rest."

"Colonel Parker is a loyal soldier. He stumbled across sensitive information in the wrong place, if Matilda's conjectures are to be believed. That information, at the least, put Thomas Wakefield's loyalties in doubt. Parker has had months to incriminate Wakefield without any mention of Matilda's role, and has apparently refrained from doing so."

The coach came to a halt and the usual shouting for a fresh team, hot bricks, and a quick pint for the lads ensued.

"Are you suggesting Parker has an agenda other than staunch loyalty to the Crown?" Jane asked.

"Perhaps Parker's sole priority is protecting Matilda's good name, but if so, he's joined the growing legions who've either abetted treason or become accessories after the fact."

The innyard was lit with torches, which reflected on the muddy snow. Stephen passed his flask to the hostler, then bent low in the saddle when the hostler spoke to him.

"Have you another theory?" Jane asked.

Duncan had dozens, some leading to misery, some to tragedy. "Another theory is that Parker has notified his superiors regarding the whole mess, and they have

directed him to curry favor with Wakefield and pretend
to be the concerned suitor. When Parker can promise his
generals that not only should Wakefield be arrested, but
also Wakefield's daughter and his staff, then the trap will
be sprung."

"Is Matilda to be the bait that inspires Wakefield's
confession?"

"Possibly."

Stephen was tasked with making inquiries at each inn
along the way. So far, the grand coach with an odd wheel
had kept up a good clip in the direction of London. Thank
the heavenly powers that Jinks had spotted that odd wheel
on Parker's conveyance, for that detail had made tracking
the vehicle much simpler.

Stephen directed his horse across the muddy yard and
came to a halt beside the coach window. "Parker is here,"
he said, quietly. "I let on that I was trying to reach London
ahead of my friend, a colonel traveling with his wife,
likely using a crested coach with the panels turned and one
replacement wheel. The colonel and his wife have retired
to separate rooms, though his colonelship is demanding
brandy, a writing desk, and the inn's best paper."

Duncan surveyed the innyard, the edifice facing it, and
the stables flanking the far side of the yard. Light shone
from one window about twenty feet up on the side of the inn
across from the stables.

"Matilda will be in that room," he said, nodding. "That's
the busy side of the innyard, also a virtual tower for anybody
intent on escape. A sheer drop, no handy tree to climb down,
no balcony to secure the sheets to. With one man watching
from the stables and another posted outside her door, she'll
be a virtual prisoner."

"That's two men," Stephen said, gaze on the only upper

window giving any light. "We have four times that number. We can simply demand to speak with her—"

Duncan shook his head. "We have something better than a duke's loyal minions."

"We have a man in love?" Jane asked.

"That too. Jane, you will please invade yonder inn demanding that you and your offspring be treated in the fashion to which any duchess is accustomed. Stephen, you will be the petulant knight lordling. John Coachman, like the stalwart rook, will be a tower of indignation over the inadequacies of every team that's led out from the stables."

"While you do what?" Stephen asked. "Pray for us like a bishop?"

"To blazes with the bishops. I will advance a pawn who is almost as loyal to my queen as I am."

* * *

The inn's staff had apparently been told that Matilda was not to be disturbed. She paced the confines of her room, unable to sleep, unable to organize her thoughts. Traffic in the innyard had slowed, but the mail coaches and other conveyances continued to straggle through despite the darkness.

Wild schemes flitted around in her imagination: Wait for a coach to pass beneath the window and leap onto its roof...except, no coaches came that close to the building, and if she missed her target, she'd end up seriously injured. If she did manage to land squarely on the roof of a moving vehicle, she'd doubtless be returned to Parker as an hysterical female in want of the loving protection of her fiancé—or husband, as Parker had styled himself.

What if she protested the marriage ceremony? Would

Parker have her arrested while a priest looked on? Would Parker have Papa arrested?

A commotion in the innyard drew her attention to the window. A coachman and a hostler were having a disagreement, the coachman contending that the team led out would never do for Her Grace.

Was another duchess on the premises? Parker had pointedly refrained from referring to Matilda by either her name or her title.

The hostler gestured to the horses and to a large coach sitting amid the slush and mud of the innyard. The conveyance was majestic, a crest emblazoned on the door.

"The *Duchess of Walden* does not tolerate puny wheelers or lame leaders!" the coachman bellowed. "Either present me with adequate cattle, or you'll hear from *His Grace of Walden* in no uncertain terms."

A shiver prickled over Matilda's skin. Had she been meant to hear this altercation? Duncan's family held the Walden title, and that man with two canes making an awkward progress across the yard had to be Lord Stephen. Anxiety and despair buffeted her, for surely Duncan was pursuing her, and surely that would not end well.

She studied the innyard, which had stirred to life with the arrival of a second crested coach. A woman got out holding hands with a small girl, a second woman climbed down with a child in her arms. A youth scrambled off the box and went to hold the reins of the on-side leader.

Instinct prodded Matilda to look elsewhere, to resist the curiosity stirred by arrivals and altercations.

Duncan stood in the shadows of the stable's eaves, his stillness alone calling attention to him. He'd had the same stillness at the chessboard, which convinced Matilda that his appearance at the inn was not a coincidence.

Nor did it bode well.

A raised voice came from the corridor, the words indistinct. A moment later, Matilda's door opened and a small boy in a knit cap bustled in carrying a bucket of coal.

"What sort of inn would this be if we let a lady's hearth go cold?" the lad groused. "For shame if this fine establishment should be disgraced, and all because some nob hasn't got the sense God gave a senile hound. The guest will have her coal or my name isn't Duncan Stephens."

The boy's name was Hiram Jingle, and he was doing a fine impersonation of a sulky under-footman.

"The room is chilly," Matilda said, for the benefit of Parker's footman, who was lurking in the doorway and looking annoyed. "Please thank the innkeeper for his consideration."

Jinks made a racket, dumping coal, poking it about on the hearth, sweeping ashes from the bricks.

"Some folk don't know how to treat a lady," Jinks muttered. "Other folk would rather die than see a woman distressed unnecessarily."

Oh, Duncan.

"I much prefer that sort of fellow," Matilda said, "the sort who has a consideration for a woman's well-being. Rough louts who leave a lady's fire to go out, so she shivers all alone by the hour, should be made to pay for their inconsideration."

The footman had the grace to tromp back to his post in the corridor.

"Perhaps you'd like a tea tray, ma'am?" Jinks asked. "Nothing like a nice hot cuppa tea to end the day. The kitchen's all in a lather over some duchess and her brats, but I'm sure we could send you up a tray."

That was for the benefit of the footman, who'd doubtless be curious about a duchess in the house.

"A nice hot cup of tea would be agreeable. Hughes," Matilda called to the footman, "a tea tray, if you please."

"Finish up, boy," Hughes said. "You can tell the kitchen to send the lady a tray."

"I don't take orders from you, guv," Jinks said, "and you're letting out all the warm air."

Hughes withdrew, but left the door ajar, as a proper guard would.

"You heading to London?" Jinks asked, making another pass with the hearth broom.

"With all possible speed," Matilda replied. "We'd be there by now but for a lame horse."

"The muddy going is hard on the beasts, but never fear. If that pair of ducal barges can navigate the king's highway by moonlight, you'll reach your destination tomorrow."

Duncan was going ahead into London. Why?

"I've never enjoyed Town in winter," Matilda said. "The coal smoke turns everything gray and hopeless."

Jinks dumped the ashes into the dustbin. "Spring comes, ma'am. Spring always comes. Don't lose hope. Sunny days will come around again."

Matilda approached the hearth and held her hands out to the rejuvenated fire. "He means to marry me tomorrow, Jinks," she said very softly. "The colonel says he seeks to protect me." Though such protection would also break her heart, if protection it was.

"What should I tell the others?"

"I can't marry Atticus Parker, and I can't let him arrest my father."

"Mr. Wentworth won't let him arrest *you*."

"He more or less already has."

The door scraped open. "Begone, boy." Hughes jerked his thumb toward the stairs. "The lady needs her rest."

"A body won't find any rest in a freezing cold room," Jinks retorted. "You ever tried to fall asleep when you're shiverin'? Can't be done." He gathered up his empty bucket and gave the hearth a visual inspection. "Some people would thank me for tending to my duties, might even pass me a copper or two for being so conscientious. Other people is idiots what disgrace their livery."

"Thank you for the coal," Matilda said. "You give me hope that chivalry is not dead."

"'T'weren't nothin'." Jinks touched the brim of his cap, bowed, and strutted from the room.

Hughes drew the door closed after him without sparing Matilda so much as a glance.

She went to the window, where a fresh set of hot bricks was being loaded into the floors of the ducal conveyances. Hostlers backed prancing teams into the traces of both coaches, and some moments later, the nursemaids, one for each child, trooped from the inn into the second coach. A woman escorted by Lord Stephen emerged from the inn, a baby in her arms.

Fussing and shouting ensued, a footman trotted across the yard with a hamper in each hand and passed one into each coach. How many times had Matilda enacted this scene with Papa all over the Continent?

And had all that racketing about from capital to capital been to further the agenda of a spy?

Duncan emerged from the shadows of the stable, and closed the door of the coach housing the two children and their maids. A boy in a cap scrambled onto the bench of the lead coach as Lord Stephen handed his companion inside.

Don't leave me. Matilda wanted to fling open the window and shout that plea, even though it would bring Parker running.

Duncan took one last look around the innyard, pulled on his gloves, and climbed into the first coach. He utterly ignored Matilda standing by her window, and she reciprocated by refusing to raise so much as a hand in parting. With a snap of the whip and a shout to the leaders, the coaches lurched forward, and disappeared into the darkness of the winter night.

* * *

"Matilda is not at Thomas Wakefield's home and neither is her father," Jane said. "If anybody should have been able to get answers from Wakefield's staff, it's a duchess making a social call and claiming to be interested in acquiring expensive art. The knocker was off the door, the butler's livery was less than tidy. Jinks found an empty bay in the carriage house, and no traveling coach."

Duncan wanted to smash the porcelain figurines on the mantel of the duchess's family parlor, his impulse partly a result of sheer fatigue.

He and Jane had reached London after midnight, and neither of the servants dispatched to trail Parker's coach had reported to the ducal town house despite morning being all but gone. Quinn was nosing about his clubs, listening for any gossip pertaining to Colonel Lord Atticus Parker, while Stephen...

"Has Stephen come down yet?" Duncan asked.

"I don't believe he has." Jane took a seat on the parlor's red velvet sofa, her manner maddeningly serene. "He claims to love travel by horseback, but I suspect it taxes him."

A blond Viking of a footman brought in a tray laden with sandwiches and biscuits.

"Thank you, Ivor," Jane said. "Duncan, eat something. You slept through breakfast, or kept to your room to brood rather than partake. You can't rescue Matilda on an empty stomach."

Duncan was beginning to wonder if he could rescue Matilda under any circumstances. He took a wing chair and let Jane set a plate before him rather than provoke the duchess to further scolds.

Matilda was a duchess. Her Grace of Bosendorf, an imposing title, and fitting for a woman who'd held a gun on armed thieves and survived on her own in the English countryside for months.

Too good a woman for Atticus Parker, regardless of the colonel's noble motives.

"Kristoff is below," Ivor said, referring to one of the footmen who'd been tracking Parker's coach. "If Your Grace wishes to speak with him—"

"Send him up," Duncan said, "and we don't care if he's sporting a day's growth of beard and has horse manure on both boots."

"Spoken like a Wentworth," Jane murmured. "Do as Mr. Wentworth says, Ivor."

The footman bowed and withdrew, nearly running into Quinn at the door.

"You have news," Duncan said, otherwise the duke would not have returned home.

"I have news," Quinn said, kissing Jane's cheek and taking the place beside her. "I'm not sure it's good news." He reached for a sandwich.

Duncan swatted his hand aside. "Report first, eat later."

Quinn's glare was frigid, also the same posturing Duncan

had seen him turn on arrogant lordlings and other heedless puppies. Duncan's return glower was a promise of lingering death for any man who put sustenance above Matilda's welfare.

"Welcome to the family," Quinn said, exchanging some sort of glance with Jane. "I had my doubts, but my duchess—as usual—had the right of it. I ran into Elsmore at the club."

"The Duke of Elsmore," Jane said. "Bachelor, on the sensible side of thirty. Said to be wealthy, Quinn considers him trustworthy."

"He went to school with Lord Atticus," Quinn went on. "Elsmore does not care for the man."

How Quinn had wrested that confidence from His Grace was a mystery known only among dukes, and Duncan frankly did not care if thumbscrews had been involved.

"Does Elsmore envy the war hero a soldier's glory?"

"His Grace has no patience with bullies, with courtesy lords who terrorize the younger lads, who charge usurious interest on schoolyard loans, who forge a letter that nearly got another boy from a lesser family expelled."

And this wolf in war hero's clothing had Matilda. "His Grace of Elsmore was a font of interesting information."

"Elsmore is usually the soul of discretion," Quinn said. "We've had to deal with each other regarding the occasional delicate financial matter, and I would trust Elsmore before I'd extend that honor to any other peer."

"Elsmore was the first to call upon us when Quinn gained the title." Jane opened the halves of a sandwich, then put it back together and passed it to Quinn.

"Jane is the Duchess of Mustard," Quinn said. "Woe to any new kitchen maid who forgets to put mustard on my sandwiches."

Even as one part of Duncan's mind whirled with speculation regarding Parker's motives, another part of his mind—or maybe his heart—watched the smiles Quinn and Jane exchanged, the way they sat so comfortably right next to each other. All of life for them had acquired a certain joyous intimacy from which others were excluded, and yet, the glow of that intimacy reflected onto any in their ambit, as a blazing hearth warms an entire room.

I want that. I want that with Matilda. "Did Elsmore have anything else to add?" Duncan asked.

"Eat your sandwich," Jane said, lifting Duncan's plate in his direction.

"The only other fact Elsmore added," Quinn said, "was that the Marquess of Creswell and his younger brother do not get on well. No details. Younger sons in titled families can be discontent, and despite the lofty commission purchased for him, Parker fits that description."

The tickle in the back of Duncan's mind regarding younger sons grew to an itch. What *was* it . . . ?

"As usual," Stephen said, wheeling into the room in his Bath chair, "nobody sought to summon me when food was on hand."

"You do not join us fresh from your slumbers, Stephen," Duncan said. "Where have you been?"

Stephen drew up to the low table. "How can you tell?"

"You are in riding attire, and the mud on your boots would have been cleaned off by the boot boy last night. You've therefore already been abroad today and you went on horseback."

Stephen helped himself to a sandwich. "Where did I go?"

Someplace that a man on horseback would be received more respectfully than a man in a fancy crested town coach. Someplace useful, where information could be gathered relevant to the current dilemma. Someplace where Stephen had connections of his own, connections not accessible to anybody else in the family.

"Horse Guards," Duncan said. "Your military friends share your interest in modern weaponry, and soldiers love to gossip. What did you learn?"

Quinn had paused mid-reach toward the sandwich tray. "Never, in an eternity of trying, could I have come up with that guess."

Was that *respect* in the duke's eyes? *Pride?*

"A moment's consideration of the facts," Duncan said, "and you would have landed on the most plausible choice. Stephen likes to test me, but his little riddles are usually obvious in hindsight."

Stephen also liked—craved—to be of use, hence his raid on a citadel neither Duncan nor the duke would have been able to breach.

"I delivered a few of my sketches to the artificers," Stephen said, "and dropped a hint or two that one Colonel Lord Atticus Parker was trying to curry favor with Quinn. The rest was a matter of looking interested and dismayed."

Duncan let Stephen draw out the moment, because Stephen's excursion had been a brilliant inspiration. Of course the war hero would be the subject of talk among his fellow officers.

"In an eternity of trying," Duncan said, "I could not have prompted the lowliest corporal to discuss Parker with me. I gather the news was bad."

Stephen took a bite of his sandwich, and again, Duncan allowed him his theatrics.

"Parker is no bloody war hero to his fellow officers," Stephen said, "excuse my language. He got his men trapped on a hillside and threatened them with flogging when they prevented him from bolting into enemy fire. The junior officers and enlisted men held the position while Parker screamed at them to charge into certain death. Next thing they knew, the battle had been won thanks to their efforts, and Parker was getting commended in the dispatches."

"Bad news indeed," Duncan said, getting to his feet. "Parker is a bully and a cheat, and he has my duchess."

Kristoff, another Viking on the duke's staff, rapped on the doorjamb and waited, cap in hand. He wore a workingman's garb, and looked much the worse for his travels.

"Come in," Duncan said. "Have you found my duchess?"

"She's at the Creswell town house, sir. Ned is standing watch, though the boy is nearly dead on his feet. The marquess is away at the family seat, and the staff was surprised to be hosting Lord Atticus. He is not a favorite with them, and he's brought along a woman who seems less than thrilled to be in the colonel's company."

"So we know where Matilda is," Quinn said, around a mouthful of sandwich, "we know the manner of man holding her captive. Why can't I just play the duke and demand her release?"

The king could move in any direction on the chessboard, but he could travel only one square at time. When he was out of moves, the game ended.

"Because Parker will simply refuse to surrender her," Duncan said. "He'll claim she's not home to callers until this wedding she warned Jinks of has transpired, if Parker even admits she's on the premises. You will be checkmated at the door."

"What if I—?" Jane started, but Stephen interrupted.

"What does that leave, Duncan? You've gathered all the information we can lay our hands on, time is running out, and marriage is forever."

Marriage, which meant Parker could not be made to testify against his wife. Marriage, which would preclude forever any union between Duncan and his duchess. Thomas Wakefield's life hung in the balance, as did Matilda's happiness.

At least.

Jane and Quinn exchanged another look, this one worried. Quinn patted Jane's wrist, and she shifted subtly closer to him. Husband and wife, wife and husband, the two as one flesh...Insight struck like a thunderclap, stunning in its impact, the effect reverberating through Duncan's body and mind.

And his heart.

"That leaves the bishops," Duncan said. "We need a set of eyes watching every entrance to the Creswell abode, and we need them there *now*."

* * *

"We can be married the moment the priest arrives," Parker said. "The sooner we speak our vows, the sooner I can honorably decline to share what I saw you doing in your father's study all those months ago."

They had arrived in London at midmorning, and Matilda had promptly demanded a nap. She'd pretended sleep, her mind refusing to quiet. As soon as she'd risen to heed the call of nature, a maid had come bustling in to make the bed.

Parker had sauntered in not five minutes later.

Matilda was in another borrowed nightgown and dressing gown, and she'd been given a bedroom that once again had no means of escape.

"For you to be in this room with me now is hardly proper, Atticus."

He wrinkled his nose. "Suppose not, but then, by tonight we will be man and wife. A little familiarity in the interests of apprising you of your good fortune shouldn't bother you. You're a widow, after all."

He peered at his reflection in the cheval mirror and twitched at the lapel of his uniform. In every way, Parker looked the part of the loyal officer, but would even a loyal officer see his father-in-law hung for treason?

"Why such haste regarding the vows, my lord? Do you expect me to marry in the rag you found me in?"

He turned his right side to the mirror, adopting the contrapposto stance of heroic statues from time immemorial.

"That is a worthy point. One cannot marry a duchess in rags without causing at least the priest to raise an eyebrow. Something ready-made will have to do. I'll find you a modiste who can alter a completed article to fit you and we will still sit down to supper as man and wife."

Such urgency—to protect her? And yet, Parker did not offer to send for the London modiste whom Matilda favored.

He shifted, putting the other foot forward.

"I'd like my father to be present at the ceremony," she said. "Papa is doubtless worried about me, and he'll be endlessly grateful to you for bringing me to safety." *If safety this was.*

Parker paused in his preening. "My dear, I sense that you do not grasp how truly precarious your position is. If Wakefield should be arrested, you are the very first party the Crown will suspect of conspiring with him. Distance from your dear father is the wisest course for you. Unless we are well and truly wed, I will have no choice but to reveal that you were translating highly sensitive stolen correspondence, and that you dodged off for parts unknown rather than entrust me with the information you found."

Assuming Parker had read the same information, what had *he* done with it? How did he know that the document had been stolen rather than entrusted to the Crown's courier?

"What will happen to your career when it becomes known that you have married the daughter of an accused spy—assuming Papa wasn't in possession of that missive for lawful reasons?"

And who would accuse Papa if Parker did not? The question chilled her, bringing her whirling thoughts to a stop. Parker and Parker alone apparently knew the details of this situation—Parker, Matilda, and Papa.

"I will have married an innocent, as far as the world knows. I will shelter her from any hint of suspicion."

"I am innocent," Matilda said. Something Parker should have been desperate to believe about his intended. "I was looking for a damned pair of scissors when I found that letter, and I'm still not entirely sure what it said. Neither do I know whether that missive was in Papa's possession or secreted among his personal effects by another intended to incriminate him."

Another who now sought to marry her?

"Temper, my dear." Parker strode for the door. "I'll see that a suitable dress is delivered within the hour and send a maid to do something with your hair. If we are to allay inconvenient suspicions, the clergyman must be greeted by a radiant bride, and your travels have taken an unfortunate toll in that regard. We shall contrive, nonetheless, and you will soon be safely established as my lawfully wedded wife."

No, I will not. The Archbishop of Canterbury could not force her to speak her vows with Parker, not until she knew what game he played.

"Find me a dress, Atticus, and send me a maid. Radiance will require some effort."

He bowed and withdrew, clearly pleased with himself, while Matilda was increasingly certain the colonel was not a loyal soldier and not at all interested in safeguarding Thomas Wakefield's future—or her own.

Chapter Eighteen

"I got no farther than you did," Carlu said, studying the winter ale served by the Brightwell village inn. "The manor house staff is either loyal or telling the truth: They know nothing of a woman fitting your daughter's description. Had it from the butler himself, and his version of events was repeated by the stable lads and farmer Jingle."

Carlu had become a dark angel of conscience, never referring to Matilda as anything save "your daughter." Thomas Wakefield hoped she'd still claim him as her father, if this mess ever sorted itself out.

"So she's not here, never was here," Wakefield said, "and we have no idea where the colonel might be either."

Petras pulled up a chair. To him, a Muscovite born and bred, England had no winter worth the name.

"Some ale, sir?" a serving maid asked.

"Please." He smiled as only a young man convinced of his own charm can smile. The maid blushed—all the maids blushed for Petras, and Carlu kicked him under the table.

"Do I take it Tomas is enjoying a constitutional?" Wakefield asked when the maid had scurried away.

"Tomas has indulged his fascination for wildlife," Petras replied. "He found many trails in the Brightwell home wood, some of them made by a woman, others by a child. The majority, though, were created by men. A day old, no more."

"A party searching for game?" Carlu asked, frowning at his tankard.

"Gamekeepers wouldn't stick to the well-worn trails," Wakefield said, "nor would poachers in search of game. A man intent on poaching game would move deliberately and quietly, not march around making a racket. Any dog tracks?"

Petras waited until the maid had set his ale on the table and then moved away before he replied.

"No dogs. The woman's boots were made by Hoby."

Hoby, the most successful bootmaker in London, said to have several hundred cobblers and cordwainers in his employ.

Matilda had worn Hoby boots. "She wasn't here," Wakefield said, though that fact was no cause for rejoicing. He'd been certain Matilda had at least come this way if not bided in the area.

"Parker was here at this very inn," Petras said, in the same tones he might have used to observe that rain was on the way. "He made a pest of himself with the maids."

"A ditch," Carlu muttered. "A cold, muddy ditch beside a lonely, dark road. Why do you never listen to me, sir?"

"We're here, aren't we?" Wakefield replied. "Empty handed, as usual. If Parker passed through here a week ago, then what does that matter to us?"

A pressing need to shake some answers from the fools at Horse Guards had Wakefield nearly bolting from the room. That would cause talk, though, and at all costs, he must move about in as unremarkable a fashion as possible.

"Parker was here *last night*," Petras said. "We missed him by hours."

Carlu's glower should have left a circle of flames around Wakefield's chair.

Tomas strutted in—Tomas had perfected the strut, and the dark-eyed stare that made a lady's knees go weak, to hear him tell it. He took the fourth seat at the table and appropriated a sip of Petras's drink.

"The ducal driveway tells a tale," Tomas said in the most unremarkable tones. "Two large coaches, traveling at the same time. The tracks go up, the tracks go to the carriage house, the tracks go right back down the drive, all within the space of—I'd say—several hours, no more than a day or two ago, based on the melting and the mud. Fresh teams put to, footmen, grooms, or stable lads hopping about. Big horses in both directions, not puny nags from the last coaching inn. An outrider on another big horse."

"Private teams," Carlu observed. "Parker's titled brother travels out to Bristol frequently. The marquess might have private teams in the area."

"Parker did not pay a call on Brightwell," Wakefield retorted, "much less abscond with Matilda, and depart without causing gossip."

The serving maid came by again. "Ale for you, sir?" she asked Tomas.

"Please, fair maiden. And one of your smiles would illuminate the rest of my day."

The maid did smile, and blush, and curtsy before she backed away from the table.

Both Petras and Carlu kicked Tomas under the table. "Now is no time for one of your performances," Carlu hissed.

Tomas shrugged. "If a man as well favored as I did not attempt harmless flirtation, the maid would remark it and be needlessly offended. I owe it to her and to our attempts at discretion to make her smile."

"The Portuguese are a peculiar race," Petras observed philosophically. "All that hot sun."

"And the wine they consume," Carlu suggested. "Inferior vintages in great quantities. Curdles small brains faster than those with greater endowments."

"No talk of endowments," Wakefield said, because this lot could turn crude innuendo into an art form. "Where did Parker go?"

"London. He left no vales, he was traveling with liveried servants, and the crests on his vehicle were turned, which only proves he's an idiot. What good is it to turn the crests if you have half a dozen self-important buffoons swarming about in livery? He left yesterday about midday."

Carlu, Petras, and Tomas did humble work, mucking stalls, fetching the post, minding the front door. They were also professionals at a game more complicated than chess could ever be, and they were watching Wakefield with a casual regard that suggested his life was in danger.

As Matilda's life had been in danger for months. The queasiness Wakefield had lived with since her disappearance escalated to dread, if not terror. For her, and for himself.

"I never meant for this scheme to get so out of hand," he said.

Nobody spoke. The maid set down a fourth serving of ale and withdrew.

"I missed my wife," Wakefield went on softly. "I was

drifting from one city to another, and I was offered a chance to do more than peddle inferior portraits and incomplete tea services."

Carlu flicked a glance at Tomas and Petras. All hands were in evidence—Carlu's casually wrapped around his tankard, Petras's resting on the table, Tomas's linked behind his head. In the time it took the maid to curtsy, all three men could be holding knives.

"You were offered easy coin," Carlu said. "You had enough, you simply wanted more."

"Greed is so unbecoming," Petras observed. "So common."

"A sin," Tomas added. "A deadly sin. Of the seven deadly sins, I prefer lust myself, though gluttony and sloth have much to recommend them as well."

"Pride is more your forte," Petras suggested. "Envy besets me."

"Leaving wrath to me," Carlu said. "What are your orders, Mr. Wakefield? Do we return to London in search of Colonel Parker, or will you continue on to Oxford without us?"

Wakefield would never make it to Oxford. His fate would be a cold, muddy ditch on a lonely road, and not because he'd taken coin for advancing the affairs of this or that party, but rather, because Matilda had been caught up in his schemes and left to shift for herself. Those engaged in espionage did so according to rules as well defined and unrelenting as the *Code Duello*, and even more rigid.

Silence stretched while the maid came by again and used her rag to wipe down the table. Tomas turned a soulful gaze on her.

"Fair lady of the dazzling smiles, might you know where a handsome, lonely stranger such as myself could find employment in the area?"

She looked him up and down. She could apparently be

charmed, but she could not be made a fool of. "Mayhap they need a new footman up at Brightwell."

"Brightwell?" Carlu asked, all innocence.

"That's our ducal estate," she said. "Not far through the woods, though the lanes take a bit longer. Mr. Duncan Wentworth is putting it to rights for His Grace of Walden. They might need a new footman or groom."

Petras passed her his empty tankard. "They're short of help?"

"The Jingle boy usually comes for the mail. He's not here and the morning is long gone. Relying on a boy is never a good idea when the task is important. My sister works at Brightwell as the upstairs maid, and she says…"

The maid fell silent, glancing around the common. Wakefield had taken a corner table, as always, and the rest of the room was deserted.

"Sisters have the best gossip," he said. "My own could fill your ear with more nonsense and tattle than any London newspaper."

He had no sister.

"Molly is like that," the maid replied, bending closer to scrub at the table. "She doesn't listen at keyholes, but she hears things. That lady who was biding up at Brightwell must have come with Jinks yesterday to pick up the mail, you see, and then she got into the coach with that regimental pest, and now Jinks is neglecting his job. Something's afoot, though you didn't hear it from me."

Carlu laid a coin on the table. "We have enjoyed the ale and service here exceedingly. I don't suppose you know where our friend Colonel Parker got off to? Proud fellow, not overly burdened with patience?"

The maid pocketed the coin. "If that lout is your friend, you have my sympathies. Never heard such a lot of giving orders and sending back trays. Missus says his brother the marquess isn't like that, but the Quality can be a trial."

"Would you happen to know if this particular trial traveled on to Oxford or back to London?" Carlu asked.

Always verify intelligence when possible, Wakefield thought. What had his servants verified about him?

"London. His coachman were determined to return to Town whether his colonelship was willing or not. They took the woman with them, though she had no baggage. Danny what works in the stables said she hugged that obnoxious colonel like he were her long-lost husband."

He nearly is.

Petras laid another coin on the table. "We're for Oxford, and we appreciate your fine service."

Tomas rose and bowed over the maid's hand. "I will remember you in my dreams, fair lady."

She swatted him with her rag, and even Carlu smiled.

Wakefield was not smiling, though he was determined to reach London before the day ended. Petras, Tomas, and Carlu were minions, pawns in the game of intrigues and counter-maneuvers Wakefield had dabbled in for years. They were doing more to safeguard Matilda's well-being than her own father had, just as the pawns usually did more to join battle on the chessboard than the noble pieces.

"Come, gentlemen," Wakefield said. "I've a notion to get back on the road."

They walked with him to the door, exactly as if Wakefield were a prisoner under armed escort. Was Matilda feeling imprisoned by Parker's protection? Why had the staff at Brightwell refused to mention her, and who had been in those two carriages pulled by the big, fine horses?

Wakefield climbed into the coach, certain of two things:

First, he knew he was done with the spying and intrigues, done with the generals and their little housekeeping matters, this time for good. Second, if Matilda survived this quagmire, she ought to disown her only surviving parent. Wakefield had considered himself a competent spy until now, but no sort of father for quite some time.

* * *

Inaction was killing Duncan, hour by hour, and yet, the sun had set without a priest having been summoned to Parker's abode, and no coaches bearing Matilda had departed. A fashionable modiste had arrived, footmen and seamstresses in tow, and though darkness had long since fallen, they had yet to leave the premises.

"We should storm the gates," Stephen said, making a slow circuit around Quinn's billiards table, "not that storming is my forte."

"Duncan is right," Quinn replied, wasting his shot on a maneuver involving three bumpers. "We'll be turned away at the drawbridge if we attempt to storm the portals of a marquess's home. Perhaps a little creative housebreaking is in order."

Amid the worry tearing at Duncan's insides, an odd comfort glowed. "That the situation has inspired Stephen to pacing and the family duke to criminal schemes warms my heart, but we won't know Parker's motives unless and until a priest arrives. I'm also curious regarding the whereabouts of Mr. Wakefield."

"Aren't we all?" Stephen muttered, bracing a hand on the back of the sofa. "I don't see how you can sit here, calm as a dowager with her cats, when Matilda is in Parker's hands."

"I am far from calm." Duncan considered the possibilities

on the billiards table, much as he'd analyze a game of chess. "We are operating at a critical disadvantage in terms of information upon which to base our attack. What if we storm the castle, have Parker arrested for kidnapping, and Matilda is then arrested for treason? What if we find a way to steal into her bedroom in the middle of the night, and she refuses the opportunity to flee again?"

She would be that brave, that stubborn. She'd only told Jinks that Parker intended a distasteful marriage. She hadn't shared her own strategy.

Duncan took his shot, a conservative choice that nonetheless advanced his lead.

"So I break in," Quinn said, "and I'm discovered where I haven't been invited. I'll be tried in the Lords, and they don't convict their own." His tone was dubious, because Quinn was not one of *their own*. He was an upstart guttersnipe who'd come into a title through merest chance.

Also a man who could be felled by a bullet, the same as any other.

"I never thought of having Parker arrested," Stephen said, sinking into a chair. "That could work."

Duncan marshaled his patience, a task of Herculean proportions. "Or it could get Matilda sent to Newgate."

"She wants rescuing or she never would have told Jinks that marriage is in the offing," Quinn said. "You were right about that. She knew that information would inspire you to heroics, though I'm damned if I can approve of any scheme that brands you a traitor."

Some heroics, playing billiards while losing my mind. "Heroics," Duncan said, returning his cue stick to the wall rack, "come at a cost. Heroics force a confrontation and can result in heavy casualties and lost ground, none of which can be undone once the hero has charged forth. Heroics can result in innocent deaths, and I'll have no more of those on my conscience."

Quinn and Stephen exchanged a look, though neither spoke.

"You have nothing to say to that logic," Duncan muttered, heading for the door. "I'm going for a walk."

"At midnight you're captivated by the notion of wandering the streets?" Stephen asked.

"In the middle of London?" Quinn added. "Not without me."

"And not without me," Stephen added. "I'll slow the pace lamentably, but I will be damned if I'll let you stumble about in the dark without at least my sword cane for protection."

They were serious, and Duncan was demented. Also touched.

"I have a theory," he said. "A theory based more on fancy than fact, and if my theory is correct, Matilda is in more danger married to Parker than she will be wandering the English countryside at the mercy of brigands and poachers."

"So why are we hesitating?" Stephen asked, gently. "Why aren't we taking Parker into custody, and shaking him until his teeth rattle?" He hefted his leg onto a hassock with a sigh that spoke of fatigue and pain.

"Because Parker will be the outraged swain, the loyal soldier who knows nothing of any purloined correspondence. He will be the tireless gentleman and officer, mad with worry for his missing lady. If Matilda contradicts that story with some tale of encoded missives and spies in Mayfair, she will be writing her father's death warrant, if not her own."

"Jane wants to call on Parker," Quinn said, "though I don't trust even her to handle him."

"This is complicated." Stephen stared into the flames of

the hearth. "I normally enjoy complications and do all in my power to create them. I hate this."

I love Matilda.

Duncan had lifted the latch, intent on leaving this cage of speculation and worry, when the door opened from the other side. Ivor stood in the corridor in plain clothes, a young woman at his side.

"Mr. Ventvorth, the lady is asking to speak with you."

The young woman wore a cloak with a collar of meticulously tatted lace. Her gloves were plain kid and clean, though far from new. She likely didn't wear them much, suggesting she worked with those hands. She was on the thin side, a possible indication of low wages, and pale, which could result from long hours indoors. Her eyes were reddish about the rims—too much close work by candlelight?—and shadowed with fatigue.

Duncan ran through that sequence of observations and conjectures in the time it took Ivor to bow the lady through the doorway.

"You are a seamstress," Duncan said. "Duncan Wentworth at your service. What have you to tell me?"

"Perhaps she'd like to have a seat," Stephen suggested, struggling to his feet. "Ivor, get the woman some sustenance, and have a guest room made up."

"That won't be necessary," the lady said. "You're right, sir. I am a seamstress. Madam Foucault's head girl, and I won't be staying. If somebody could walk me home once I've said my piece, I'd appreciate it. I'm to return to the marquess's house at first light, so the bride's dress will be perfect for the ceremony."

"Bloody hell," Quinn growled, and the seamstress took a step back.

Ivor scowled thunderously. Stephen smiled.

"Please do have a seat." Duncan gestured to the sofa. "The hour is late and His Grace's manners have gone begging. I take it the bride sent you to us. Might you tell us your name?"

The woman passed Ivor her cloak and sank into a chair. Her dress could not have been plainer and hung loosely on a gaunt frame, and yet, there was embroidery on her cuffs as well.

Red and white roses, delicately wreathed in greenery.

"I'm Mary Bisset, and yes, I am here because the bride—the duchess—sent me. Even that popinjay of a groom could not intrude for the fittings. Madam doesn't allow that nonsense when we've work to do, and we always have work to do." She chafed her hands and held them out to the fire.

Duncan's heart beat faster, with both hope and dread. "You have a message for us?"

Mary nodded, scooting on the chair to get closer to the fire. "She said to find the Duke of Walden's house on Birdsong Lane and ask for Mr. Duncan Wentworth. I'm to tell you that the ceremony is scheduled for eight in the morning. She doesn't want to marry him, sir. The dress fit well enough, and she pitched a tantrum worthy of Mrs. Arbuckle's twins, ripping the lace from the décolletage and cuffs. Said she had to have embroidery, and no duchess was ever married in a shoddy dress. Even the groom didn't attempt to argue with her."

Lace could be stitched onto a dress from whatever stock was in store. Embroidery was a more tedious undertaking. Matilda was thinking clearly, which helped Duncan think clearly.

"I know the Arbuckle twins," Stephen said. "Sweetest pair of cooing doves you ever did meet."

Mary gave him an incredulous look. "Not when their

dresses are too snug or their underskirts are the same shade as some other lady's. Wellington himself wouldn't take on that pair."

"Did the bride say anything else?" Duncan asked. *The* bride, not *Parker's* bride.

Mary's brow knit. "She didn't say much at all, sir. She let us do our fittings, let us do all that work the livelong afternoon and into the evening, and then cut up something awful right before supper. His groomship told Madam we have the night to finish the dress, and poor Maisy and Helen are still there stitching themselves blind. I got stuck working overnight before Lady Lucy DeWinter's come-out, so Madam said I could grab a few hours' sleep and do the final adjustments in the morning."

Ivor returned with a tray of buttered bread, pared apples, sliced cheese, and cold ham. He set it before Mary and poured her a cup of tea. The look she gave him was beyond grateful, and he withdrew only as far as the door.

Duncan took a seat on the sofa, guarded relief gradually penetrating his fatigue and worry.

"So the bride had a spectacular tantrum just as the dress was completed," he said, "and the groom has given you orders to finish your work in time for a ceremony at eight in the morning. How did Her Grace convey to you that you were to contact us?"

"She ordered everybody out of the room but me—she's some sort of pumpernickel duchess, you know—but even a duchess can't undo her own laces. We were behind the privacy screen, nobody else in the room, and she told me that she did not want to marry the strutting buffoon—and I ask you, who would?—but she might not have a choice. I was to find you lot, and make sure you knew when the ceremony was scheduled."

"We have less than eight hours to intervene in this farce," Stephen said. "I, for one, will spend some of those hours sleeping. I am confident that well before dawn, a clearer head than mine will have concocted a solution to this puzzle, for none occurs to me."

Mary was making good progress with the tray Ivor had brought, putting Duncan in mind of a hungry Matilda.

Stephen limped from the room, leaving Duncan with Quinn, Mary, and Ivor.

"We should all get some rest," Duncan said, though what he sought was solitude to think. "Ivor, you will please see the lady made comfortable for the night, and ensure she's back at her post at dawn. Miss Bisset, if you can relay to the duchess one message, privately of course, it would be this: Her knights will charge before the ceremony begins, and she is to do nothing to put herself at risk of further harm."

"That's all?" Mary asked, a buttered slice of bread in her hand. "Her knights will charge before the ceremony begins, and she's not to put herself at risk of further harm?"

Thank heavens for a sensible young woman with good recall. "That's not quite all. You have done me and the duchess a significant service at great inconvenience to yourself. You are tired and hungry, and need not have bothered with this drama. What can I do to show my appreciation?"

She gestured with the bread. "This is appreciation. Haven't had a decent cup of tea since my grandmother's funeral."

"A tea tray is a mere courtesy," Duncan said. "You deserve more than that for aiding a stranger."

Quinn came up on Duncan's side. "I am a duke, Miss Bisset, though I've never regarded that as a particular benefit to anybody. If you want a cottage in Chelsea, I'll see it done. If you want your own millinery shop, that's the work of a moment. I am in Mr. Wentworth's debt to a greater extent than any duke has ever owed anybody, and my wealth is at his disposal to see you compensated for your trouble."

Mary set down the half-eaten bread and sent Ivor a questioning glance. "I wouldn't know what to do with my own shop."

"You'd make money with it," Quinn said. "Keep a decent roof over your head. In addition to Mr. Wentworth's gratitude you have my own. My duchess is in a position to see that you will have substantial custom and nobody wants to go blind sewing for a pittance if they don't have to."

Mary studied the tea tray, which was French porcelain because Quinn liked for his duchess to have pretty things. "May I think about it?"

"Of course," Duncan said.

Steam wafted up from the cup she cradled in her hands. "Will *he* walk with me in the morning?" Mary asked, nodding at Ivor.

"It will be my pleasure," Ivor said, bowing.

"That's all right, then," Mary said, taking another bite of bread.

Duncan had no sooner bowed his good night to the lady when Quinn took him by the arm and steered him into the corridor.

"I meant what I said." Quinn's grip was as fierce as his tone.

"I do not typically ascribe a penchant for dissembling to you."

"Nor would Jane tolerate a lying duke." Quinn turned loose of Duncan's arm. "I honestly meant that my debt to you cannot be repaid in this lifetime."

What in the name of the seven wonders of the ancient world was this about? "It's late." Duncan moved toward the steps, desperate for solitude in which to consider the information Mary had provided. "We're tired, and we can continue this discussion at first light." Or never. Quinn Wentworth in a forthright mood was a disquieting prospect.

"We will have this discussion now and not visit the topic again, because your sensibilities are delicate. Jane says you think we regard you as a poor relation."

Her again. "I am a poor relation, by ducal standards."

Quinn stopped at the foot of the staircase. "You saved *Stephen's life*. He was an impossible boy, plotting his own demise, *planning* for it, and I had no idea what to do. You came down from York by post, no questions, and you *saved his life* one foreign language, one theorem, one learned tome at a time.

"When I didn't know what a bunch of letters on a page meant," Quinn went on, "you spent every Sunday teaching me to read, though you had to travel for hours each way to make that happen. Every accomplishment I've achieved has rested on that foundation. You were good in a world where I had no examples of goodness, and I will be *damned* if I'll let Atticus Parker hand you misery or put you in Newgate in return for that goodness."

Quinn Wentworth did not make speeches, but that was... a speech.

Duncan cast about for anything to say in reply and could offer only the truth: "Stephen saved my life too. You all did. I was in the grip of unrelenting despair and failing rapidly."

"To hell with despair. You're a Wentworth." Quinn yanked Duncan into a hug and thumped him once on the back. "Tomorrow, we save your duchess, or my duchess will take matters into her own dainty hands."

The duke ascended the steps as if such affection was normally exchanged among the Wentworth family members. He didn't look back, didn't stop at the top of the stairs. He proceeded in the direction of the apartment he shared with Jane until he was lost around the turn in the corridor.

While Duncan stood alone in the shadows at the foot of the stairs, trying to put a name on the emotions rioting through him. Surprise, certainly. Teaching Quinn to read had been easy—the duke was as bright as his younger brother, and equally determined. A handful of Sundays explaining phonetics, reading the Book of Common Prayer with Quinn, and he'd puzzled out the rest for himself.

Becoming Stephen's tutor had set a wonderful puzzle before Duncan: How to occupy an overactive mind when that mind was housed in an underactive body? How to foster emotional maturity in a youth who was treated as a perpetual toddler?

Those tasks had given Duncan's life meaning, and had also brought him joy. He'd had no idea Quinn felt a sense of indebtedness, though if Quinn did, Stephen likely did as well.

"Perhaps," Duncan muttered, taking the steps slowly, "this is what it means to be a family—to be a Wentworth." A sense of belonging, acceptance... a knowing of one's place and cherishing that place.

And some fine day, Matilda might be a Wentworth, too, provided Duncan could checkmate Atticus Parker at daybreak. Duncan ascended the stairs, his heart full of hope—the lone comfort against all the ills to escape from Pandora's box.

Chapter Nineteen

Matilda passed her night in useless speculation. Why should an exhausted seamstress who'd been given nothing for her trouble take the time to rouse a ducal household long after dark? Would Parker go through with the ceremony? Would the ceremony be real or a sham?

Where was Papa? If he'd left the country, then Matilda need no longer be as concerned for him, and could focus all her worry on herself and Duncan. Parker could have Duncan arrested, and Duncan—untitled, without significant wealth, too honest for his own good—would face the very fate Matilda had tried to spare him.

And yet, she could not defeat Parker on her own, and if any truth had emerged from all of her pondering and fretting, it was that Parker was her enemy, and likely the Crown's as well. She had no evidence, no logical syllogism upon which to base that conclusion, other than the fact that a doting swain did not lock his intended in her chambers each night.

"Is Your Grace awake?" a maid called from beyond the bedroom door.

"I am now," Matilda muttered. "Come in."

The next sound was metal on metal—the lock being opened—and then the maid came in bearing a tray.

"Good morning, Your Grace." She set the tray beside the bed. "Would you like to sit by the fire, or will you have your tea in bed?"

The clock on the mantel said the hour was just past seven. Outside, daylight had barely begun its advance against darkness.

"I'd prefer chocolate," Matilda said. "You may return this tray to the kitchen." Anything to push the morning's schedule back by even five minutes.

The maid was well trained—or accustomed to the whims of aristocrats—and showed not a trace of irritation. "My apologies, ma'am. Is there anything else you'd like me to bring up from the kitchen?"

What took significant preparation? What would not be on hand, ready for the breakfast meal?

"A compote of sliced oranges, pears, and apples, with a dash of cinnamon and a sprinkling of chopped walnuts."

The maid curtsied at the door, the tray on her hip. "Very good, ma'am."

Her departure was followed by another soft snick of metal on metal.

When the food arrived, Matilda ate slowly. She sipped her chocolate slowly, finding the brew too rich and too bitter. She demanded a final adjustment to the bodice of her dress, though that was in hopes of seeing the seamstress—Mary was her name—who'd been the only possible ally on hand the previous night.

Mary was straightening a hem that had never been crooked on a gown that was too lovely to be worn by a reluctant bride, when Parker's voice rang out from beyond the sitting room door.

"Her Grace is to be in the family parlor in ten minutes. I'll send the footmen to haul her down bodily if her nerves should overtake her good sense."

He sounded far too pleased with himself, probably because the ceremony would go off exactly as scheduled.

The modiste was boxing up the last of the embroidery supplies and refusing to meet Matilda's gaze. Madam Foucault was a spare, gray-haired woman, and though she dressed with understated grace, her mannerisms were those of a general commanding an army on short rations.

"I do not want to marry that man," Matilda said. "You are my witnesses that he's coercing me to the ceremony."

Madam turned a tired, pitying expression on her. "Nerves, Your Grace. All brides have nerves. You donned that dress willingly enough."

And as slowly as I could. "I am the widow of a duke. I do not have bridal nerves. I need to leave this house without being forced to marry that man." Mary had given no indication that she'd been able to find the Wentworth town house, much less speak with Duncan.

Madam closed the lid of a quilted box. "Then you should not have accepted his lordship's suit if you did not want to marry him. Men are entitled to rely on the encouragement we give them. And if you changed your mind, why did you permit yourself to be fitted for that dress, hour after hour? His lordship is the son of a marquess, a colonel, a war hero. I could name you a dozen young women who'd marry him and be grateful."

"I am not among them. Should I be grateful to be kept

prisoner? Grateful that the only choice a woman can claim—the power to refuse a suitor—has been denied me?"

Madam stacked three boxes on the sofa, one atop the other. "Mary, cease fussing. Our work is done, and if we want to be paid, we'll ignore Her Grace's little bout of indecision. Take the boxes down to the kitchen."

Mary sent Matilda one glance—apologetic?—and rose. "It's a lovely dress, ma'am. A queen would be happy to wear that dress when reviewing her knights on parade."

"I am not a—"

Mary regarded her far more directly than a seamstress should regard a duchess.

"I'm told the queen is the most powerful piece on the chessboard," Mary said. "Not that I've ever played."

Madam glanced at the clock. "Mary, cease nattering and take these boxes downstairs."

"Somebody left a pin near my right shoulder blade," Matilda said. "I cannot speak vows while I'm being stabbed in the back. Mary, you will remove the pin for me." She infused her order—it was not a request—with all the dignity a duchess could command.

Madam looked torn, then she swept a curtsy. "Best wishes, Your Grace. Mary, see that the duchess is made comfortable, then gather up the boxes." Madam tapped twice on the door, which was opened from the far side, then departed.

"Come," Matilda said, marching into the bedroom and moving behind the privacy screen.

"Two footmen wait right outside your sitting room door," Mary said quietly when she and Matilda were alone. "You wouldn't get ten paces down the corridor if you fled. I have a message for you."

"From Mr. Wentworth?"

"Aye, Your Grace. After I left here last night, I'd barely

reached the street corner when a strapping blond fellow came up beside me and told me I shouldn't be abroad so late on my own. Had an accent, and he wasn't threatening me in the least."

Duncan was a fine strapping fellow, but he had no accent and wasn't blond. "The fine fellow was watching this house, I take it?" *Thank you, Duncan, for not losing me or losing heart.*

"The fellow was a footman to the Duke of Walden, and he took me to Mr. Wentworth straightaway. Mr. Wentworth said that your knights will charge before the ceremony, and you weren't to do anything to put yourself in harm's way."

The ceremony was scheduled to start in *six minutes*.

And yet, Duncan would not fail her. Was incapable of failing those he cared for, regardless of their station or the danger to himself.

"Then I'd best take myself down to the family parlor. Thank you, Mary. You might well have saved my life."

Mary's features were too finely drawn to be pretty, her figure lacked the curves bestowed by regular, ample nutrition, but she had a lovely smile.

"Seamstresses hear everything," she said. "We see everything, and I knew you weren't a happy bride. His Grace said I might have my own shop."

"You'd rather have the handsome footman?"

"To be honest, I might like both, Your Grace."

"Then I hope you get them." Because for a woman to have both the man she loved and something meaningful besides—a home, a shop, a calling—ought not to be an impossible dream. "Thank you again for your aid. It's time for you to leave, and for me to cry off at the altar."

Mary gathered up the boxes and accompanied Matilda

into the corridor. One footman went with the maid, the other stayed right at Matilda's elbow as she descended the stairs. Somewhere in the house, a clock chimed eight times as she reached the bottom of the stairs.

"This way, Your Grace," the footman murmured, turning to the left.

Matilda disdained to take his arm. "No need to direct me. I can hear the colonel shouting plainly enough."

* * *

The war hero expected to be obeyed, and Duncan delighted—*delighted*—in the fact that nobody was obeying him.

"But, my lord," a footman sputtered, "the gentleman said he'd brought the ring, and every wedding requires a ring. You said we was to be certain that nothing interfered—"

"He's not a bloody jeweler," Parker bellowed. "Those two aren't a jeweler's bullyboys."

Quinn and Stephen were the pair in question, the duke looking ferocious despite his Bond Street tailoring, while Stephen examined the heavy gold handle on his sword cane.

Over in the corner, the priest paged through his prayer book and pretended to ignore the verbal altercation.

"In fact," Duncan said, "you are correct, my lord colonel. I am Mr. Duncan Wentworth. I have with me Lord Stephen Wentworth, and Quinton, His Grace of Walden, whom I am honored to call my cousins. We are under the impression you intend to hold a wedding."

"And what bloody bedamned business is it of yours if I do?" Parker was resplendent in his regimentals, and they nicely matched his choleric complexion.

"Why?" Duncan asked. "Why marry a woman who does not seek to marry you?"

The priest looked up.

"You know nothing of the situation," Parker said. "Her Grace welcomed my suit and welcomes the protection marriage to me will afford her."

Matilda entered the room, a footman trailing. She was magnificently attired in a dress of pale green that had purple, red, and blue flowers embroidered on the hem, cuffs, and cream underskirt. Her hair had been done simply—a braid coiled into a chignon, and she wore no jewelry.

To Duncan she had never looked lovelier, or more furious.

"Your Grace." Duncan bowed, Stephen and Quinn doing likewise, while the priest murmured a greeting.

"*My Grace*," Matilda said through gritted teeth, "has been a prisoner in Colonel Parker's keeping since he took me from a Berkshire coaching inn two days ago."

"You came with me willingly," Parker retorted. "I have a special license, and I say we must be married."

The priest cleared his throat. "Perhaps we should give the couple privacy."

"A fine idea," Parker began. "Her Grace has been through an ordeal, and a few minutes to discuss—"

Duncan snatched the prayer book from the priest and tossed it to Stephen, who caught it one-handed.

"I beg to differ, *Reverend*. You just heard Her Grace state that this man all but kidnapped her and kept her a prisoner. Now you suggest that the duchess be left alone with him. How thoroughly did the colonel bribe you to inspire such a lapse in your calling?"

A flush crept up past the priest's collar. "How dare you speak to a man of the cloth so disrespectfully?"

"He dares," Quinn said, "because he is a man of the cloth himself, and if you don't listen to him, I'll see you and your bishop defrocked by nightfall."

"Best run along," Stephen said, waving the prayer book. "Fast as you can. His Grace has a temper."

"The lady is not willing," Duncan said. "Ask her for yourself."

The priest's Adam's apple bobbed. "Madam?"

"Your Grace." Duncan, Stephen, and Quinn all spoke at once.

"I beg your pardon. Your Grace, are you inclined to marry Lord Atticus?"

"I most assuredly am not."

The priest looked to Parker. "I'll be going. Your special license will be valid for another—"

"Out," Duncan said, motioning toward the door. "And don't come back. The rest of you fellows, leave us."

The footmen all but scampered for the door.

"You gain entry to my house under false pretenses," Parker said. "You disturb nuptials in which you can have no interest, and you order my staff about. Who the hell are you, and why shouldn't I have you thrown in jail?"

Matilda was pale and outwardly composed. Her eyes were shadowed and a vein throbbed at her throat. Temper, perhaps, along with fatigue and worry.

Damn Parker for all of that, and for betraying England.

"You are the only person here who deserves to go to jail," Duncan said, "and in point of fact this is your brother's house. I doubt very much that he'd object to my calling under these circumstances, and his lordship would thank the Almighty that the nuptials were not yet in progress."

"The lady will marry me if she values her freedom."

"*Your* freedom is at issue," Duncan said. "Marital privilege means you could not testify against Her Grace. Could not testify that you found her translating a message that purported to deal with troop movements or military maneuvers. Marital privilege also means *she could not testify against you*."

Matilda stared at Duncan for a moment. "Of course."

Parker pointed a gloved finger at Matilda. "She's a traitor. She learned of a plot to invade France, and said nothing about it to anybody. She instead absconded with the evidence, refused to confide in me, and I well know she was protecting her father. She made her choice—family over honor—and I seek only to protect her from the consequences of that choice."

Parker was nigh shaking with righteous conviction, or possibly with fear.

"My lord," Duncan said, "do have a seat. The game is up. You have been found out, and you must face the consequences."

"I never mentioned a plot to invade France," Matilda murmured, turning a puzzled gaze on Duncan.

Parker had gone silent, and as pale as new snow under winter moonlight.

"Think back, Your Grace," Duncan said. "When Parker came courting, a house full of valuable art and usually bustling with too many servants was all but deserted. Why else would that be, except by design? He arrived early for a regular call, you say, but, again, why? He was wandering where he shouldn't have been, sneaking about the premises. You said you don't know how long he lurked in the corridor, observing you."

"This is preposterous," Parker muttered. "Wild accusations intended to protect a traitor."

Duncan had left the parlor door open, and he hoped the entire staff was eavesdropping.

"You are a younger son, my lord," Duncan said. "Your brother bought your commission and expected you to make your way in the military. Perhaps during your stint in Paris, perhaps in Amsterdam, somebody approached you offering coin for a few tidbits of gossip. Gossip is harmless. Coin is necessary. You decided you could take that coin without compromising your honor."

"Be quiet," Parker said, sinking onto a tufted sofa. "For the love of God, shut your mouth."

For the love of Matilda, Duncan wasn't nearly finished.

"Taking the money was easy, leaving that little game proved impossible. Perhaps a woman was involved, or possibly even a child. You did take the money, and then your new friends made it plain that they owned you. You disobeyed them at the cost of your life. They would not do you the courtesy of a knife in a dark alley. They'd instead turn you over to your superior officers."

Parker looked up. "Where could you possibly come by such wild, ridiculous notions?" He was blustering, and badly

"You don't deny these ridiculous notions," Duncan retorted.

Stephen pulled the trigger on his sword cane, so the bayonet snapped into view. "Sorry," he said, smiling. "The mechanism wants maintenance." He fiddled with the cane's handle and folded the knife out of sight.

Parker's shoulders slumped while Duncan waited as patiently as he'd ever waited for the slowest of his scholars. Quinn remained standing near the door, as motionless as a cat waiting for a pigeon to wander just two steps closer. Matilda, too, held her silence.

"I never told them anything that mattered," Parker said. "Never told them more than talk overheard in the officers' mess or the gentlemen's retiring rooms. Nothing important."

"But you took their money," Matilda said. "Why, Atticus?"

He dropped his head into his hands, the picture of adult male misery. "They made it so easy. Passed me a bit of coin, *for my trouble*. Their objective was to prevent war—surely that was in England's best interests?—and they reminded me that my king didn't care one whit what became of me or any other soldier in uniform. Kings don't care, emperors don't care, generals don't care. We're pawns to them. That's simply the truth."

"And sometimes," Duncan said quietly, "family doesn't care either? What did you do with the plans you found on Wakefield's desk?"

"Passed them on, though I had only hasty recollections of Matilda's translation to go by."

Duncan squashed a frisson of pity for this inept spy in uniform. "Did it never occur to you to question the people telling you where to look?"

Parker sat up. "These are not men who'd take kindly to questioning. They'd never given me bad information before, and they were right: Wakefield was in possession of very sensitive plans."

"And you," Stephen drawled, "were doubtless scheming to beat them at their own game. Clever fellow that you are, you intended to expose Wakefield as a spy—as a leader of spies—and do your war hero part for England while putting yourself unassailably above suspicion. Instead of pocketing paltry sums for passing on gossip, you doubtless sought a promotion to general officer—the fellows at Horse Guards have remarked your objective well. You simply underestimated the lady and those loyal to her." He swept Parker a bow. "Forgive me if you have failed to rouse any emotion in my bosom save contempt."

Stephen was entitled to his dramatics, and he'd spared

Duncan a recitation of the charges. What Parker lacked in honor and brains he made up for in ambition.

Matilda came to stand immediately before the colonel. "Atticus, did you never wonder why such important plans were left in such an unprotected location? I found that document while I was searching for a *pair of scissors*. A valet, a footman, anybody might have found it. You were all but told where to look, weren't you?"

He stared up at her. "What are you saying?"

"My father is not a traitor. I am not a traitor, but you, my lord, have been a very, very great imbecile."

"A pawn," Duncan said, "to use your term, and they are easily sacrificed, as you have been sacrificed. Lord Stephen, Your Grace, if you'd escort his lordship abovestairs, he'll want to change out of uniform. The marquess has been summoned, and he will be consulted before other authorities are involved. At the very least, you will resign your commission, my lord. The criminal charges will be complicated, though they'll be nothing compared to the scandal."

Parker made a sound worthy of a dyspeptic cat.

"Come along, Colonel," Quinn said. "I can tell you all about how to barter your linen for privileges in Newgate. I can even tell you the exact protocol observed before a hanging. Being a military type, you will be vastly comforted to know there's etiquette involved. All quite civilized, though not exactly a dignified way to die."

Quinn assisted Parker to his feet by virtue of a hefty shove under the colonel's elbow, then he and Stephen left, keeping Parker between them.

"All those months," Matilda said, staring at the empty doorway. "All those nights shivering in hopes I'd not freeze to death before dawn. The days without eating...I was helping to catch a traitor while being made to feel like one.

Where is my father, Duncan? I still don't entirely grasp who was spying upon whom, or for what purpose, and I want very much to hear what Papa has to say."

While Duncan wanted only to hold his duchess and never let her go. "Thomas Wakefield returned to London yesterday. I can take you to him now, if you like."

She kissed Duncan's cheek. "Please, and when I've heard Papa out, I have a few things I'd like to say to you. I am...I am glad to see you."

That was encouraging, though Duncan dared not return her kiss until the whole drama had played itself out. "I have some sentiments to convey to you as well, but they can keep a while longer."

Five minutes later, he handed Matilda into the ducal carriage and took the place on the backward-facing bench, the better to behold his beloved and the better to keep his damned hands to himself.

Chapter Twenty

Duncan had never looked handsomer to Matilda, or more remote.

"You were very confident in your conclusions with Atticus," she said as the coach lurched forward. "When did you put the pieces together?"

He took off his hat and ran a hand through his hair. "I'm not sure I have all the pieces, but I was certain that Parker would offer you marriage as a means of avoiding the duty to testify against you. Then I realized that's a drastic remedy.

"Why not simply hold his tongue?" Duncan stared out the window as he went on. "Why not accuse Wakefield and remain silent about your role? One of the first lessons a boy learns on the path to becoming a gentleman is to remain silent rather than jeopardize a lady's good name. Your description of Parker's tepid courtship confounded me, and then his continued pursuit of you in the absence of any passionate display of affection…"

"You concluded the marriage would benefit him, rather than benefit me." Why had Matilda been unable to consider that possibility?

"I examined that perspective. You are also a duchess with connections all over the Continent. Those connections would benefit an ambitious officer. They would benefit a spy even more."

Sometimes, Duncan's logic was a little too infallible. "You think Parker was told to court me?"

Duncan considered her, his expression unreadable. "I think the idea was planted somewhere between his ambition and his arrogance, and in that abundant and fertile soil, the concept took root. How are you, Your Grace?"

Your Grace, not *my dear*. "I could hardly tell you I was a duchess, Duncan. You probably would not have believed me."

"You forget, I count a duchess among my cousins. I might well have believed you. Jane is looking forward to making your acquaintance."

To perdition with Jane. "Duncan, are you angry?"

The carriage slowed to take a corner, and Matilda felt as if the few inches between her knees and Duncan's might as well have been the English Channel.

"I have not the gift of dissembling," he said. "Not even for you. I am consumed with fury, ready to lay about with my fists, to shout vile oaths, and draw blood with my bare hands. I am not angry with you, I am not even very angry at Parker, who likely would have made some attempt to be a decent husband to you. I was ready to kill that damned priest."

"The priest?"

"He would have married you to Parker, despite your protests, despite your refusal to speak the proper vows. For money, he would have obliterated your legal personhood by signing the appropriate lines. If I ever had any doubts about my decision to leave the church, they have been laid to rest."

Matilda switched seats, so both she and Duncan were facing backward. "Duncan, you sent him packing. You snapped your fingers and he scurried away, clutching his prayer book and hoping you wouldn't say anything to his bishop."

"What I want to say to his bishop isn't fit for a lady's ears."

A knot of worry in Matilda's belly began to ease. "If you feel that strongly, then you ought to speak up. A certain Continental duchess will happily join you when you call upon the bishop."

The coach came to a stop.

Duncan donned his hat. "Good to know. Would that same duchess like for me to join her when she confronts her father?"

Was the question as neutral as it seemed? Matilda was angry too, ready to curse and pitch fine art in all directions.

She stared at her gloves, which had been sewn with pearls in honor of the wedding that had not—thank God and Duncan Wentworth—taken place. "Please come with me, Duncan. I can't do this alone."

Something soft and warm grazed her cheek. "If you are as upset as I believe you to be, then you must speak up, Matilda. I am also furious on your behalf, but he is your father."

Matilda straightened. "Meaning I'm supposed to honor him, that my days might be long upon the earth?"

"Meaning that if you want me to thrash Thomas Wakefield within an inch of his cowardly, conniving life, I will cheerfully do so. Quinn will take up when I leave off, Jane will want a turn, and Stephen will finish the old schemer off, but we do so only if we have your permission."

Matilda was still anxious, still angry, but she had a reason to smile too. "Thank you for that. When we're through with Papa, I want an interview with you."

Duncan opened the coach door and kicked down the steps. "You shall have it."

* * *

Carlu opened the door before Matilda had knocked upon it.

"Your Grace." He swept a bow with a Continental flourish. "On behalf of the entire staff, welcome home. Shall I announce you? Mr. Wakefield is taking breakfast before a planned call on Colonel Lord Atticus Parker."

Throughout that little speech, Carlu had alternately beamed at Matilda and cast Duncan curious glances. Duncan pointedly ignored him, except to pass over his hat, gloves, and walking stick.

"No need to announce us," Matilda said, tucking her gloves into the pocket of her cape. The words *It's good to be home* refused to pass her lips. "It's good to see you, Carlu. I have missed the staff." She had not missed her father.

Had Papa missed her? Worried for her?

Now, when the moment of reunion with Papa was upon her, Matilda was particularly glad for Duncan's steadfast presence. He seemed utterly composed, possibly even bored, as she led him past a fortune in tastefully displayed art.

"Don't let me say anything I'll regret," she muttered, pausing outside the door of the breakfast parlor.

"In this life, I think it a greater regret to have left words unspoken than to have aimed them at those who've earned our ire. The more pertinent question is, will you accept his apology?"

"You are certain he'll offer one?"

Duncan's gaze flicked over Renaissance saints in gilded

frames, antique porcelain, and an original King James Bible displayed at the end of the corridor.

"Your father will apologize, or I'll make him wish he had."

Matilda leaned in, resting her forehead against Duncan's chest. She did not want to open the door, did not want to confront the author of her troubles.

"You are my duchess," Duncan said, taking her in his arms. "You have been wronged by the one man who was honor bound to value your well-being above his own. You are entitled to justice, and I would dearly like to see that you have it."

She nodded, sheltering in his embrace and gathering her resolve before she stepped back.

Duncan opened the door for her, as if he were her footman, then followed her into the parlor and closed the door behind her.

"Papa," Matilda said. "You're looking well."

She'd caught him with a silver forkful of eggs halfway to his mouth. He set the fork down, and to his credit, he half rose, smiling hugely.

Her mood must have communicated itself to him, because he finished getting to his feet more slowly.

"Matilda, good morning. Welcome home. I am very pleased to see you in good health, and to see that Colonel Lord Parker has not accompanied you."

Papa sent an inquiring glance in Duncan's direction, but Matilda was not inclined to offer introductions.

"I do not care that"—she snapped her fingers—"for what pleases you. I was very nearly married to Colonel Lord Parker this morning, or should we call him Colonel Lord Traitor? He chased me from the wilds of Berkshire, where I might have frozen to death or starved, and told me that I was two steps from a noose myself. My crime, of course, was attempting to protect you. This has apparently become a hanging felony."

Papa's faltering smile disappeared altogether. "You seem none the worse for your ordeal, daughter."

"You will address the duchess as Your Grace until she has given you leave to address her otherwise." Duncan spoke patiently, as if Papa were a servant new to his livery.

"And who are you, to be instructing me on the—?"

Duncan held up a hand. "Her Grace was not finished."

Not nearly. "I sent you three messages, Papa, and you never replied. I waited, I hoped, I prayed. I had no idea for whom you were spying, or if one of your abundant staff was the party responsible for landing me in such trouble. You made no effort to find me, no effort to bring me to safety. I was bait in another one of your little games, and I need to hear what mattered to you more than my life."

Matilda's voice was shaking, and her knees were shaking, but it was Papa who subsided into a chair.

"Your life was never in danger, Matild—Your Grace."

Duncan held a chair for her. "I beg to differ, Wakefield. When I first met Her Grace, a ferocious snowstorm was bearing down on the shire. The duchess was alone, had obviously not eaten well for weeks, had no decent shelter. Those challenges she'd have met, but two armed felons were roaming my woods in search of game. They would have delighted in trifling with a woman weakened by deprivation and hardship. A woman far from home whose plight was ignored by the very man responsible for it."

To hear Duncan recount her own situation, his voice calm to the point of dispassion, affected Matilda as living through the experiences had not. She sank to her seat, lest she advance on her father and do him a grievous injury.

"Papa, how could you do that to me? How could you do that to anyone?" Matilda might have descended into shrieking, except that Duncan stood silent and steady behind her chair.

Papa sat not at the head of the table, but in the seat to the left. He looked to have aged, now that Matilda studied him, and yet, he had not missed meals, had not shivered his way through nights spent in haylofts and sheep byres, had not fended off the advances of knaves and blackguards.

"I could not find you," he said, "and by the time you sent those messages, Parker was all but sleeping on my porch steps. We knew Parker was involved with the wrong people. He lives quite well on his officer's pay, never seems to be short of blunt, and kept mistresses who reserved their favors for wealthy men. When we realized he was in the pay of foreign powers, we alerted the marquess. Parker's brother did not believe us. His lordship demanded proof."

"So you manufactured it," Matilda said, "dropped the bait in his lap, and then I got in the way. There was no plot against France, and there certainly wasn't any affection on Parker's part for me."

Papa tried for a smile. "I wouldn't go that far. You are a duchess. Parker doubtless esteemed you on that basis alone."

Matilda closed her eyes and fisted her hands in her lap. "To covet the benefits of my worldly station is not the same as to feel affection for me."

She was enraged at her father, enraged at foolish games played on a chessboard she'd never sought to understand, but amid all of that anger she also realized that Duncan Wentworth had *not* been enamored of her station. Duncan had not known he courted a duchess, had not cared that her problems might cost him his life.

"Tell her the rest of it," Duncan said. "Her Grace's time is precious and you have wasted more than your share."

What *rest of it*?

"You ask why I could be prevailed upon to engage in these stratagems," Papa said. "I told myself that I wanted you to be secure when I went to my reward, and that was a fine argument, until it became apparent you'd have no trouble finding a proper match." His gaze fell upon a porcelain vase on the mantel, a vividly detailed blue dragon swirling across a glaze of white. "That's Ming Dynasty, you know. Worth a fortune."

"Wakefield, get to the point."

"I like... I cannot resist beautiful art. Being a keen observer and careful listener allowed me to have beautiful art while serving my country. When certain people asked me to ensnare the marquess's brother, I was not in a position to refuse them. I knew Parker had not engaged your emotions. I did not know you'd find the evidence that was meant for him and disappear with it."

"And?" Duncan prompted.

"And I am sorry, Matilda. I am very, very sorry. I never meant for this to involve you, other than requiring you to endure long evenings listening to Parker's opinions on military affairs while he made up excuses to absent himself from our guest parlor. I never foresaw that you could be so clever and determined. I never realized Parker would be so desperate."

Matilda had expected a great drama, not this sad, quiet conversation, surrounded by pretty art, tea, and toast.

Duncan's hand rested between her shoulder blades, a slight warmth radiating from his touch.

"Your mistake, Wakefield, is not that you left a trap for Parker where Her Grace could stumble into it, it's that you and your generals did not call the game off once you knew she was in danger. You failed her and left her to the elements. How do you propose to make reparation?"

Matilda hadn't thought this far, but Duncan was right: She wanted more than an apology. Words were easy, too easy for a man of Papa's glib charm.

"I could not call the game off," Papa retorted. "A marquess has significant consequence, and then a general became involved, and who was I—?"

Duncan leaned over the table. "You were Her Grace's only source of protection, though I hesitate to refer to you as a father of any kind. The two brigands threatening me in my own woods were criminals, in the process of committing hanging felonies, and both armed. The duchess, though exhausted and nigh starving, bested them both, or I'd likely be dead. There is *nothing* I would not do for this woman, including see you ruined or worse."

Duncan made a very convincing knight. Very convincing.

Papa stared at his vase. "Matilda, what can I do to show my remorse?"

"All I ever wanted was a home," she said. "A place to call my own, to raise a family or simply grow old tatting lace and petting my cat. I never asked to be the bait you dangled before an ambitious younger son for your generals and lords. Even Parker offered to provide me a home of my own."

But what did she want now? She'd been a duchess in a huge stone castle by the North Sea, and even that formidable edifice had not felt like a home to her.

Duncan paced to the mantel. "Perhaps you'd like this home or some of its contents? The place is certainly well situated, and I'm sure if your dear father is sincere in his guilt, he won't begrudge you the one thing you've always wanted and never really had."

Papa watched Duncan with a brooding curiosity, as if Duncan were familiar but Papa could not recall where they'd met.

"You remind me of somebody," Papa said.

"Duncan Wentworth, at your service." He did not bow but instead studied the dragon.

The house was more of a showplace than a home. Matilda did not particularly care for its appointments, though the location was enviably refined, and the building itself well constructed. Papa, though, treasured this place.

More than he'd treasured his only daughter?

"I'll take the house," Matilda said, "and all of its contents. You may have a week, Papa, and then you will depart on an extended tour of the Continent. Take a few items of sentimental value, but don't think to loot the whole inventory. I want none of the current staff underfoot, and I expect you to pension them all generously. Bide with friends, if any you have, or set up a household in Paris. I care what becomes of you, but for now, having a substantial body of water between us would be well advised."

Papa looked like he wanted to argue.

Duncan held the dragon vase up to the morning sunlight, held it high enough that if he dropped it, the dragon would shatter.

"You want the house," Papa said slowly, "and its contents."

"Little enough compensation for putting a woman at risk of death, bodily harm, and worse," Duncan said, returning the dragon to its perch. "Did you know you're an accessory to kidnapping? I'm sure your generals will flock to your defense when those charges are laid, though, of course, they were complicit in the crime too. Matilda might have gone with Parker willingly at first to spare harm to the innocent, but she did not agree to be locked in her chamber and forced to wed him."

Matilda liked that Duncan had thought three moves ahead of Papa's strategy. She liked the utter lack of a facile retort from Papa as well.

"I neglected to introduce Mr. Wentworth to you properly," she said. "He's cousin to the Duke of Walden, and on particularly good terms with Lord Stephen Wentworth."

Papa rubbed his forehead as if weary. "I will sign the house over to you legally, with all of its contents, as is. When I have established a household on the Continent, I'll write to you here."

Matilda rose. "I won't be here, and neither will all of this expensive, beautiful art. Safe journey, Papa. You may write to me care of the Duke and Duchess of Walden on Birdsong Lane. Mr. Wentworth, if you'd see me back to the carriage?"

Duncan sketched a bow in Papa's direction, then held the door for Matilda. He assisted her with her cloak at the door rather than allow Carlu to perform that courtesy, and ushered her out the front door and into the waiting carriage.

This time he took the place beside her on the forward-facing bench. "Well done, Your Grace. You served him a very tidy checkmate."

Matilda took Duncan's arm and arranged it around her shoulders. "I never have felt like a duchess nor cared to be addressed as such." The coach moved off, and a simmering relief gathered momentum in Matilda's heart.

"How shall I address you?" Duncan asked.

My dear. She'd loved it when he'd called her that, but today was a day for besting foes, confronting traitors, and putting the past to rest.

"I'd like it very much if you'd call me Mrs. Wentworth."

"I'd like it very much if the whole world called you Mrs. Wentworth, but first, we have a few matters to discuss."

The last, lingering shadow on Matilda's mood dissipated. She knew exactly what to do with all of Papa's precious clutter, she'd never have to deal with Atticus Parker again, and she'd soon become Mrs. Duncan Wentworth. She fell asleep in Duncan's embrace and dreamed of baby bunnies.

* * *

Jane had taken one look at Matilda and enveloped Duncan's beloved in a silent hug. The ladies had disappeared abovestairs, arm in arm, heads close together.

"Parker will resign his commission," Quinn said, prowling around the Walden estate office. "Though the generals might mutter about treason and making an example of him, he'll likely subsist in foreign parts on a remittance from his brother, possibly for the rest of his life."

"Please see to it that the colonel's fate remains uncertain for at least a short time," Duncan said. "Matilda wandered in the wilderness for weeks when her only crime was trying to protect her idiot father. Let the great war hero face the thought of ignominious death, let it wrap around his awareness until all of his arrogance is effectively strangled and some humility has room to grow."

"Are you handing out penances now?" Stephen asked, taking the couch along the estate office's inside wall.

"Not penance," Duncan said. "Detention for a student with more pride than brains. The colonel was a greedy fool. But then, a system that confers vast wealth on one brother and leaves the other with little isn't exactly brilliant."

"Our Duncan is a flaming radical," Stephen marveled, polishing the gold handle of his walking stick on his coat sleeve. "My staid, reliable cousin now spouts revolutionary notions. Years in low company on the Continent have clearly had an effect."

Duncan took the seat behind the desk, his knees suffering a curious weakness after the interview with Wakefield. Wakefield had let his generals continue their dangerous game rather than risk their displeasure. Duncan had held out hope that Thomas Wakefield had been *unable* to help his daughter, not merely unwilling.

Wakefield had simply chosen thirty pieces of silver over his own honor. Perhaps Matilda's father should have studied for the church.

"You sent Wakefield packing?" Quinn asked.

"Matilda gave her papa a week to pension the staff, choose a few mementos, and quit the realm. He betrayed her trust, exploited her, failed her when she needed him.... She's being more lenient than I would be."

"No she isn't," Stephen said. "You are the forgiving sort, else you'd have tossed me from the deck of a few ships. I've never thanked you for your forbearance."

Quinn pretended to dab at a smudge on the silver wax jack gleaming in the midday sunshine.

"Don't be maudlin," Duncan retorted. "You are an antidote to boredom, and those are ever in short supply onboard a ship."

Where was Matilda? Would she sleep the day away? What were her plans for Wakefield's house, and when could Duncan be alone with her again? He had told the truth earlier in the day when he'd informed the marquess's butler that he was in possession of a ring for the duchess.

"I'm also dead on my feet, as the saying goes." Stephen scooted to the edge of the sofa and hoisted himself into his Bath chair. "All of this drama has left me in need of a nap. Somebody should write to the household at Brightwell and let them know your duchess is safe."

"I'll tell them myself when I return there shortly," Duncan said. "I was hoping you'd come for another visit after the first of the year."

Stephen had wheeled himself halfway to the door. "I didn't quite finish my modifications to your back stairway, did I?"

Quinn set down the wax jack. "You let Stephen start hammering and sawing when you know what his little projects end up costing?"

"I know I will be without a steward come the new year," Duncan said, rising. "I'll write to Trostle today informing him of my decision and send the letter by express. Trostle has family, and they have means. Let them deal with his venery. I suspect Jinks's uncle would make a very trustworthy steward, but I'd like to put that request to him in person. Right now, Stephen has projects in progress that will enhance the value of my home, and I find his company *delightful*."

Stephen smiled at his knees. "Now, you're telling falsehoods, old boy. True love has addled even your impressive—"

The door opened and Matilda slipped into the room, Jane on her heels. Duncan's duchess looked rested, and she was wearing a high-waisted dress of green velvet—a simple, elegant frock, not that expensive concoction sewn for her wedding with Parker. Her hair was in a braided coronet, like a tiara, but prettier.

"Quinn and Stephen," Jane said, "you will join me for luncheon now."

"Yes, love," Quinn said, marching for the door. "You heard her, Stephen."

Stephen wheeled himself into the corridor, Quinn following. Jane paused at the door, looking both pleased and worried.

"We'll be down shortly," Matilda said.

"No hurry," Jane replied. "None at all. Take your time." She smiled, and Duncan had the certain thought that if he failed to arrive at table as an engaged man, Jane would order him right back upstairs to see the business done properly.

As well she should.

"She's very dear," Matilda said, when they were alone behind a closed door. "They all are. You are fortunate in your family."

Duncan held open his arms and Matilda came to him. "*You* are very dear," he said. How precious she was in his embrace. She wasn't the wraith she'd been weeks ago, though she was still petite.

With the heart of a lioness.

Matilda seemed content to hold him and be held by him, but the Wentworths waited below, and Duncan could be patient no longer. He stepped back, though only far enough to sink to one knee.

"I was stumbling about in a woods of my own making," he said, "and you rescued me. Had you not taken me in hand, I'd be bewildered still, increasingly given to conversation with long-dead philosophers, my wealth plundered by crooked hirelings, my family despairing of me. Without you, I cannot be the person I hope to be, Matilda. Please make your home with me at Brightwell, or anywhere, and be my wife."

He took the simple gold band from his pocket and tucked it into her grasp, folding her fingers around a token too plain for the sentiments sparkling in his heart.

"Duncan Wentworth, you took my part when I had no allies, you protected me, and would not let me come to harm. You played me to a draw. Of course I will be your wife."

He sprang to his feet, not a twinge of protest from either knee. "Do you mean that? You'll put up with my silences and my ducal relatives? You'll show me how to turn Brightwell into a home? Help me sort through my journals and possibly even publish them? Stephen will visit frequently—the man's lonely, does he but know it—and I suppose we'll have to entertain. I hate entertaining. The lady cousins will come down from the north, and we will be expected to offer hospitality. I have no notion—"

Matilda kissed him mid-babble. "I am a duchess. Hospitality is easy. We offer food, warmth, safety from the elements, and good company. You excel at hospitality, but Duncan, about your journals?"

He had to kiss her back, at length. He was considering locking the door when his mind seized on a detail. "What journals?"

"Those brilliant works of scholarly charm that will fetch a very handsome sum from any number of publishers."

"Scholarly charm is a contradiction in terms. I like the part about the handsome sum. To make Brightwell worthy of a duchess will require a very handsome sum." Which he would somehow come up with, if he had to offer Latin classes to the squire's sons to do it.

Matilda locked the door and then returned to his embrace. "Papa's art collection will fund all the renovations we'd ever care to make at Brightwell. My dower portion will take care of any remaining—"

"Your dower portion is for you, and for your children."

"*Our* children. I sent your treatise on Sicily to my man of business, Duncan. He's probably even now having copies made to send to every reputable travel publisher in London and Paris. We'll take bids and negotiate."

Children. Matilda had mentioned children, and . . . Duncan left off nuzzling the spot below her ear. "What *are* you going on about?"

"Parker found me near the posting inn not only because the day was too pretty for me to hide indoors, but also because I was determined to mail a sample of your writing to my English solicitors. I will see your travelogues published, and your genius will be admired and compensated as it deserves to be admired *and compensated*. I wanted to do at least that much for the man who saved my life."

She patted his lapel and Duncan knew why cats purred. "All I did was offer you a meal, my dear. You saved my life." Duncan was talking about more than her ability to fend off poachers, and she seemed to know that.

"We did not play to a draw," she said.

She tucked in close, and Duncan sent up a prayer of gratitude for locked doors and honest duchesses. "Neither of us lost." Though he was quickly losing any interest in joining the family for luncheon.

Matilda stroked his chest this time, then slid her hand lower. "We both won."

Lovely, lovely woman, and Duncan aspired to be her lovely, lovely man. "Jane said we need not hurry downstairs. Let's both win again, shall we?"

"A fine notion, Mr. Wentworth."

They were very late for lunch, and not exactly on time for dinner, or breakfast, but they did both win—every time.

Keep reading for a peek at the next book
in the Rogues to Riches series,

FOREVER AND A DUKE

Coming in Fall 2019

Chapter One

Wrexham, Duke of Elsmore, kicked his heels in the Wentworth and Penrose conference room until the Duke of Walden himself held the door for a smallish female. Mrs. Eleanora Hatfield preceded her employer into the room as if he were her footman rather than a wealthy peer.

Rex liked women—almost all women, which was a source of constant delight and even more constant difficulty. He would have risen to his feet had any female joined the meeting, because manners were the least courtesy the ladies were due.

With this woman, a man would sit about on his lazy backside at his peril. Walden's bank auditor did not walk, she marched, plain gray skirts swishing like finest silk. Her posture would have done credit to Wellington reviewing the troops before a battle. She wore her dark hair in a ruthlessly tidy bun; a pair of spotless spectacles perched halfway down a slightly aquiline nose.

She had the figure of an opera dancer and the bearing of a thoroughly vexed mother superior.

Rex took in these details—and interesting details they were—as the lady crossed the room and snapped off a shallow curtsy. She declined to offer her hand, as was a woman's prerogative.

He bowed, and for once refrained from smiling at a female. He had an arsenal of smiles. Friendly flirtatious, bored, condescending, menacing—that one was not for use with the ladies—but this woman would likely slap him silly for such posturing.

Walden dealt with the introductions, and all the while Mrs. Hatfield studied Rex as if deciding where to take the first bite of him.

"Madam, a pleasure. Elsmore at your service."

She aimed a glower down that not exactly dainty nose. "Likewise, Your Grace."

"I'll leave you two some privacy," Walden said. "Would not do for Wentworth and Penrose to be privy to the concerns of a rival institution's director. I'm down the corridor if I'm needed." He sent Rex an unreadable look, then left, closing the door.

"Which of us do you suppose would be calling upon Walden for aid?" Rex asked. "I don't quite count His Grace a friend, but I have asked this favor of him, haven't I?"

Mrs. Hatfield opened a drawer secreted at the head of the table and withdrew several sheets of paper and a pencil.

"The favor you seek is from me, Your Grace. Applying to my employers was mere courtesy, but it's my expertise that will see your accounts set to rights. I'll need to know exactly what evidence you have of errors in your bookkeeping, and the sooner we embark on that discussion the sooner you can get back to"—her gaze flicked over him—"whatever it is you do."

"I'm sure your time is quite valuable," Rex said, pulling out a chair for her. "I appreciate that you're willing to take on this project."

He more than appreciated it. If his books were problematic, whether due to errors, bad accounting procedures, or something else, even his own solicitors would learn of it only after Rex had solved the problem.

Mrs. Hatfield looked at the chair, then at him, her air of annoyance fading into puzzlement. "You need not act the dandy with me, sir. I am entirely capable of managing both my skirts and a chair. One can, if one dresses sensibly."

Mrs. Eleanora Hatfield did everything sensibly. Rex knew this from the tiny dash of lace at her collar, from the small, plain watch pinned to her cuff—an odd but practical location—and from the inkstain on her right thumb.

She was painfully sensible, while he was . . . painfully worried about his wretched, blasted, bedamned bookkeeping.

"Holding a chair for a lady is not acting the dandy, madam, but, rather, being a gentleman. If the fellows at this institution have inured you to discourtesy, shame upon them, for I am unwilling to commit the same transgression."

This skirmish over a chair mattered. Rex needed her help, but he would not be treated like a pestilence when he'd committed no wrong.

Her brows drew down, and fine dark brows they were too. Nicely arched, a little heavier than was fashionable. As she rustled closer, he considered that she wasn't so much annoyed with him as she was flustered.

"Does nobody hold your chair, Mrs. Hatfield?" He'd seated her at the head of the table, so he took the place at her left. "Mr. Hatfield has much to answer for."

She tidied the blank papers into a stack and took up the pencil. "Mr. Hatfield is none of your concern, Your Grace. Tell me about your situation, and spare no detail for any reason. My discretion is absolute and I gather the situation is becoming urgent."

Rex began a recitation of the family's history, which, as far as titleholders were concerned, went back for three dreary centuries. The previous Elsmore peers had had a knack for coming down on the right side of political dramas, which had started them off with an earldom, then seen them elevated to ducal honors. When the national turmoil grew especially fraught, a younger son would be dispatched to profess loyalty to the opposing side, such that the family fortunes remained secure no matter who ended up in power.

"The accounting problem is doubtless minor," Rex concluded, "but over time, small amounts can add up. The Dukes of Elmore have always had a sterling reputation, and I will uphold my responsibility to continue that tradition."

"How did you first become aware you had discrepancies?"

An auditor ought not to have such pretty eyes. She peered over her spectacles, looking like a solemn little owl, except that an owl's eyes didn't slant like a cat's or shade toward bluish gray. Nor did an owl have the capacity to appear concerned over a few missing quid.

"One of my aunts noticed a few discrepancies."

"Were there other incidents that gave you concerns?"

So many, Rex had been unable to ignore them. "A few here and there. Must we trouble ourselves over those details now?"

She put down her pencil. She checked her watch and compared its time with that told by a great monstrosity ticking away on the mantel. Rex had the sense she was choosing her words, or perhaps counting to ten.

"The word 'auditor' comes from the Latin *audire*," she said, "meaning 'to hear.' An auditor listens, Your Grace. We used to listen to the accounts read out while we kept tallies in our heads. Now we not only pay attention to the books, we attend to what happens around those books. Anybody can make an error in calculations or transcription. You can see a seven where I see a one. But if what's occurring is more than random errors, then there's a pattern to be discerned, and that means I need all the information you have."

She spoke so earnestly, as if instructing a slow scholar who very, very much needed passing marks.

Rex rose, inactivity being foreign to his nature. "You want to know how much I lost at the club last night? What I spent at the haberdasher's? What baubles I purchased for my current *chère amie*?"

"Yes, though I doubt you have a current mistress."

A frisson of unease had Rex pretending to examine a sketch of a small boy with a large dog. "You can tell that merely by looking at me?"

"By reading the paper," she said, using a penknife to sharpen her pencil point. "You are escorting only the most eligible of the blueblooded young ladies these days. It's considered good form to approach marriage without other entanglements, and you are of an age to marry. You have no direct heir, no younger brother even. Hence, my conclusion. Now, might we resume our discussion of your books?"

Rex's social life apparently did not interest her beyond what was reported in the tattlers, but, then, his social life seldom interested him. He wandered back to the table and sent the lady a questioning glance.

"Mind if I sit?"

"Your Grace, if you insist on silly social rituals we will accomplish little. You must treat me as if I were a chambermaid or a footman, an employee, though one who labors with her mind rather than her hands. No more of your chair-holding, bobbing about, or pretending you need my permission to sit."

Her handwriting was painfully neat, her attire painfully plain, and yet simple manners flustered her.

Rex remained by the chair to her left. "As a boy, I slurped up proper deportment with my morning porridge, and as a peer, I hold myself out as an example of British manhood at its most refined, at least when there's a lady present. With you, I must tend to the silly rituals or I will lose my good standing in the Decorous Dukes club."

That salvo earned him not even the hint of a smile. "You may sit." She set her knife aside. "Sir."

"Don't pout," he said, patting her wrist. "A man who insists on showing you common courtesies is not the worst fate that could befall you. Once you've concluded your little inquisition, our paths will hardly cross." A pity, that.

She held the pencil, now dagger sharp, poised over the paper. "Yes, they will," she said ominously. "Until I have solved the problems besetting your accounts, our paths will cross frequently."

About the Author

Grace Burrowes grew up in central Pennsylvania and is the sixth out of seven children. She discovered romance novels when in junior high (back when there was such a thing), and has been reading them voraciously ever since. Grace has a bachelor's degree in political science and a bachelor of music in music history (both from Pennsylvania State University), a master's degree in conflict transformation from Eastern Mennonite University, and a juris doctor from the National Law Center at the George Washington University.

Grace writes Georgian, Regency, Scottish Victorian, and contemporary romances in both novella and novel lengths. She's a member of Romance Writers of America, and enjoys giving workshops and speaking at writers' conferences. She also loves to hear from her readers, and can be reached through her website, graceburrowes.com.

Looking for more historical romance?
Forever brings the heat with these sexy rogues.

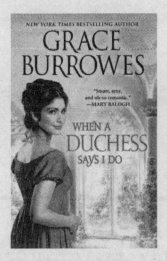

WHEN A DUCHESS SAYS I DO
By Grace Burrowes

When Duncan Wentworth comes across a woman alone in the woods of his estate, decency compels him to offer aid. Matilda Wakefield can't entrust her secrets to Duncan without embroiling him in the problems that sent her fleeing from London, but neither can she ignore a man who's honorable, a brilliant chess player, and maddeningly kissable.

WHEN A ROGUE MEETS HIS MATCH
By Elizabeth Hoyt

After a decade of doing the Duke of Windemere's dirty work, Gideon Hawthorne is ready to be his own boss. But the duke isn't going to make leaving easy—he wants Gideon to complete one last task. And as payment, he offers the one thing that could seriously tempt Gideon: Messalina Greycourt's hand in marriage. Includes a bonus story by Kelly Bowen!

THE HIGHLAND EARL
By Amy Jarecki

Mr. & Mrs. Smith meets *Outlander* in this action-packed Scottish romance in which a marriage of convenience leads to secrets that could be deadly. Lady Evelyn has no desire to wed the rugged Scottish earl her father has chosen, but at least she'll be able to continue her work as a spy—as long as her husband never finds out. Yet the more time Evelyn spends with John and his boys, the fonder she grows of their little family, and the last thing she wants to do is put them in danger.

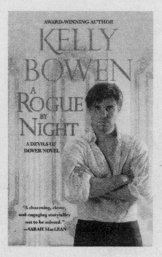